What readers have said about previous Collins & Clark books

'This was a very good enjoyable read. The banter between colleagues is very funny and fits well into this book between the serious parts.'
Neil Mullins
★ ★ ★ ★ ★

'What a joy this novel is to read. There is non-stop action and intrigue to keep you turning the pages and two very likeable protagonists with some good repartee to keep you warm and amused.'
Elaine Tomasso
★ ★ ★ ★ ★

'Clive, Michael, and Agnes make a great team in this British procedural. It's sometimes easy to forget what it was like for police in the days before CSI, DNA, and surveillance cameras everywhere but McGrath has written a cracking good mystery story that reminds you of the basics.'
Kathleen Grey

★ ★ ★ ★ ★

A Death in Spring: 1968
A Collins & Clark Story

Jim McGrath

ISBN-10: 1-91-260552-X
ISBN-13: 978-1-912605-52-1 (j-views Publishing)

Published by j-views Publishing, 2018

Body set in 11pt Brioso Pro, chapter titles and headings in Motorway

www.j-views.biz

publish@j-views.biz

j-views Publishing, 26 Lombard Street, Lichfield, UK, WS13 6DR

A DEATH IN SPRING: 1968

A note on the time and geography of the story

Attitudes to homosexuality in 1968

This book is set in 1968, one year after homosexuality was decriminalised in England and Wales. At the time many people, perhaps the majority, had very negative views about homosexuals and were happy to express them publicly in very strong terms.

In 1968, the term "gay" was not used to describe a homosexual and the idea of a homosexual community was unheard of. I certainly can't remember hearing either phrase during the 1960s and nor could any of my gay friends. At the time, gays described themselves as homosexuals, homos, queers or poofters. Like the "N word" when used by a black person, such terms were not considered derogatory when used by other homosexuals. However, when used by heterosexuals, they were often intended as an insult or slur. The homophobia was all in the tone used and context. Other, even more insulting terms were used, a few of which appear in this book.

The attitudes, prejudices and norms of the time, and how they start to change between the 1960s and the mid-1970s are reflected in the Collins and Clark Series.

Terminology

The term "serial killer" was coined by Robert Rissler, FBI Behavioral Science Unit, around 1972. However, it took the film The Silence of the Lambs to make it a familiar term among the public in the UK. The official definition of a serial killer is someone who commits "three or more separate events (murders) in three or more separate locations with an emotional cooling-off period between homicides".

Police Equipment in 1968

Many reference sources state that police radios were introduced nationwide in 1969. However, police officers I have spoken to say that they were in use in Birmingham in 1968. Although, as one retired officer put it, 'They were about as useful as a chocolate teapot.' The two main problems were that the batteries often ran out, because they had not been properly charged, and coverage was poor with perfect reception at Point A but no reception –thirty yards away.

Personally, I thought that police sirens had replaced bells on all vehicles by 1968, but I've been assured by David Brown, who was a serving officer at the time, that this was not the case.

The Black Country

Birmingham lies to the south of the Black Country and although neighbours, the differences in attitude, accents and customs were significantly different prior to the 1980s. Simply put, if you wanted to insult someone from the Black Country, you called them a "Brummie".

The Black Country has no clearly defined borders, but it is usually defined as "the area where the coal seam comes to the surface". This includes Brierley Hill, West Bromwich, Oldbury, Blackheath, Cradley Heath, Old Hill, Bilston, Dudley, Tipton and Walsall, but not Wolverhampton. However, using other criteria, it is accepted by many in the region that Wolverhampton is part of the Black Country.

Each town has its own version of the Black Country dialect and none of them share any resemblance to the typical "Brummie" accent. The following few words are used by Clark and other characters throughout the book to give an impression of how a person from West Bromwich might sound.

Ain't	will not
Bostin	good/great
Dain't	did not
Kidda	friend
Sommut	something
Tarrar or tarrar a bit	goodbye
Wem	we are
Wi	we
Wiek	week
Yam Yam	person from the Black Country
Yow	you
Yowm	you are

Acknowledgments

Once more I must acknowledge a huge debt of gratitude to David Brown. David served in the West Bromwich and Lichfield City Police Forces for several years during the 1960s and early 1970s before becoming a social worker. He has acted as technical advisor on the book, grammarian and critical friend. As a painter of considerable talent, Dave understands the creative process and has been a constant source of encouragement and support throughout the writing of the book.

I'm very grateful that David has given me permission to adapt his short story In the Trees for this book. I also happily acknowledge that I used information contained in his story The Little Blue Teddy to describe the devastating effect that a train has on hitting a human body.

Finally, I must once again thank Dave for painting the cover of this book. His previous covers have received rave reviews and I think this one is a cracker.

I would also like to thank Stephen McGrath, who served in the Staffordshire Police for nearly thirty years. I have adapted one story he told me for inclusion in this book. In addition, a passing remark he made led to the idea for a major character and storyline in this book. Thanks, Steve.

For Finbar and Tallulah – dream big. Also in memory of Clive Clark, the best number 11 I have ever seen in an Albion shirt and the scorer of 29 goals in the 1966/67 season.

Contents

A DEATH IN SPRING: 1968

JIM McGRATH

A COLLINS & CLARK STORY

J-VIEWS PUBLISHING, LICHFIELD, ENGLAND

Prologue

Phillip Mabbit was a loser. He lost at everything he did. Jobs, friendships and especially betting. Sitting in the car, he remembered his first bet. It had been in 1956 and he'd put his entire week's wages of £9 10s. on Devon Loch to win the Grand National.

With just three jumps remaining, the Queen Mother's horse had taken the lead and cleared the last fence half a length ahead of E.S.B., and took a commanding lead on the final stretch. Then, in front of the Royal Box, with only 40 yards to the winning post and five lengths ahead, he inexplicably jumped into the air and landed on his stomach, allowing E.S.B. to overtake and win. Afterwards, the Queen Mother said: 'Oh, that's racing.'

However, for Phillip it was walking to work for a week, going without any lunch in the canteen and having to stay in and listen to his father moan at the news twice a night for a week. On the last day of the week he'd met Liz, and they'd been married two years later in 1958, by which time he was betting daily on the horses and the dogs. Always chasing the big win which would set him and his family up for life.

Instead of living the good life, he was now sitting in a car, near Warley Park, waiting for a man he didn't know to leave the Bear's Head. A man he was going to run over and kill, in order to settle a gambling debt of nearly three grand he owed.

He checked his watch. It was 10.45pm and the pub was starting to empty. He'd sat in the same place for three nights over the last ten days and the man he was to kill was always last out. This wasn't because he was a drunk, but because he was the leader of the local gang in Smethwick which ran gambling, protection and prostitution on the dark streets of this small town just three miles from Birmingham, and people were too afraid to ask him to leave.

At 11.05 the man left the pub and walked to the traffic lights on the corner. He waited patiently until the lights turned green and then stepped into the road. As he neared the far side of the road Phillip Mabbit crashed into him at forty miles per hour and sent him tumbling down the road. Mabbit saw him lying in the road ten feet away and pushed his foot to the floor and ran over him a second time. Clear of the body, he put his foot down and sped away towards Birmingham and the scrapyard where he was to deliver the car.

As he drove he felt a mixture of emotions – relief that he'd been able to do it, fear that someone may have seen him, and a desperate desire never to get involved in anything like this again. 'I'm never going to have another bet again,' he said, and meant it, for he knew that he'd just played the biggest hand in his life.

As he drove to the scrapyard, the same question he'd asked Johnny kept returning, 'Who wants him dead?'

Saturday 20th April 1968, 21.00hrs

Birmingham

The killer looked stunning. At 5 foot 10, he had a trim muscular body, bright blue eyes and full sensuous lips. His blond hair was parted on the left and combed towards the right, where it touched his eyebrow. His dark blue, two-piece suit and open-neck white shirt offset his light suntan to perfection.

He knew that the queens would swoon and gabble, the pitch of their voices rising as soon as they saw him. But he wasn't interested in them. He had very specific tastes. He was searching for fresh young meat. He went looking regularly now, but only occasionally did he find what he wanted. Maybe he'd be lucky. Maybe tonight his hunt would end in success.

He paused for a moment before he got out of the car. Consciously, he allowed his face and jaw to relax. As he looked in the mirror, a half smile appeared on his lips, softening his face further. It was show time, and he was ready.

Crossing the road, he stepped through the Toreador's swing doors and found himself standing in Birmingham's only pub for homosexuals. It was nine o'clock and the bar was crowded with the usual array of young and old queens, each trying to outdo the other in how camp they could be. There were also a few bodybuilder types who desperately wanted to be Tom of Finland, but the vast majority were young and middle-aged men, dressed in respectable two- or three-piece suits, or slacks and jackets. Their homosexuality was a secret kept from family, work colleagues and straight friends.

Most incongruous of all were a couple of old female prostitutes standing at the bar with their pimp. They were wearing matching black leather skirts, jackets, stockings and high heels. A full half-inch of slap had been applied to their faces to cover the crevices that lay beneath. Maybe their trade is naughty boys who want to be chastised for being queer, he thought as he walked to the bar.

The overall atmosphere was strangely subdued, as if all those present were trying very hard not to attract the attention of the police, or Birmingham's moral majority, who would welcome any excuse to close the bar down. Parliament might have just agreed that consensual sex between two men was legal, but they all knew that attitudes took longer to change than the law.

He decided he would only stay half an hour. He had to be disciplined. If he followed the routine and never deviated from it he'd be safe. If he found nothing in the next thirty minutes, he'd leave. He ordered a half of mild and walked slowly around the pub, sipping his drink. He was conscious of the barman watching his every move. The barman's eyes never strayed from his arse and groin. He felt a flash of pleasure course though his body at being so openly wanted, but knowing he was unobtainable. He wasn't like these filthy creatures.

The bar had four gathering points, each demarcated as clearly as Berlin was between the American, British, French and Russian sectors. At the back of the pub, beyond the bar, were two groups that never mixed. One consisted of the older white men, who chatted and watched. The other was comprised of a small group of Asian men. Neither was of any interest to the killer.

Opposite the bar, a petition split the remaining space in two. The section nearest the downstairs toilets was for the queens and their friends. It was from here that most of the noise, laughter and mock shock originated as detailed descriptions were shared about latest conquests and disasters. He wasn't interested in the occupants of this hysterical world.

The section nearest the door was occupied by the less flamboyant drinkers, who stood or sat in small groups, talking quietly. This was his hunting ground. The well-dressed young and not so young men looking to meet someone like themselves, who wouldn't attract any second looks on the street. The ones that looked normal.

As he walked about, he nodded at one or two people who were obviously interested in him but didn't return their smiles or say anything. His first circuit of the bar was unsuccessful. Nothing of interest here, he thought. Then, he felt the familiar thrill as the swing doors opened and a young man entered. He was twenty, twenty-two at most. Six foot, slim with long brown hair and wearing blue slacks, a pink button-down shirt and a navy blue windcheater. His movements were athletic, effortless and natural. Now, if only he sounded as good as he looked.

The newcomer approached the bar but before he could order, the killer moved next to him and asked, 'Can I buy you a drink?'

The young man hesitated, looked at the man, liked what he saw and said, 'Thank you. That would be nice.'

'My name's John, what's yours?

'Joseph.' The young man paused, then made up his mind, 'but you can call me Joe. Pleased to meet you.'

Thirty minutes later, they drove off in John's car towards Summer Lane. At this time on a Saturday night, John knew the area would be deserted with the factories and wholesalers closed and locked. He had no difficulty finding the deserted alleyway and abandoned building he'd scouted earlier. Pulling into a narrow alleyway, he parked up, the passenger door just inches away from a crumbling factory wall.

Joe was eager to start and leaning across, kissed the beautiful stranger he'd just met. At the same time, he undid his zip, pulled out his semi-erect penis and placed John's hand on it.

But instead of holding him, John pulled away as if he'd been burnt by a hot plate.

'What's the matter? Don't you fancy me?'

'Oh, I do. I most certainly do. That's the problem.'

'I don't understand?'

'I know you don't. But you will.'

Joe realised something was wrong half a second before the point of John's elbow slammed into his left temple. Stunned, the young man fell back in his seat and tried to reach for the door latch. Grabbing a short iron bar from beneath his seat, John smashed it down on the back of Joe's head. The young man slumped against the side window, unconscious. Unfortunately for him, that state wouldn't last long. Soon he would be awake and then the real pain, the real terror, would begin.

Saturday 27th April 1968, 09.00hrs

Handsworth

Detective Constable Michael Collins had been awake for ten minutes, but lay motionless; warm, content and looking forward to the day. Agnes stirred beside him and he gently kissed her on the lips. Opening her eyes, she smiled and asked, 'What's the time?'

'Just gone nine, on this grand spring day. How did you sleep?'

'Wonderfully,' she said, remembering their lovemaking of the night before. 'How about you?'

'Terrible. I was awake all night.'

'And what, pray, kept you awake.'

'Well, I'm madly in love with this beautiful older woman and she uses me for her carnal delights, but refuses to make an honest man of me.'

'Oh, you poor dear. That must be awful. Have you told her how you feel?'

'Dozens of times. But she always rejects me.'

'Well, what can I say, except that it's your turn to make breakfast.'

'There you go again. Changing the subject.'

'I am not. I have a meeting at Bull Street Meeting House at 11.30 and you have to take Sheba for a walk before you go to your football match with Clark.'

'You're a hard woman, Agnes Winter – and for your information, I'm not going to my football match with Clark. I'm on duty, covering for Clarkee.'

'And why would you do that on your rest day?'

'Because Clarkee is me friend. Besides, I'm desperate to earn enough to buy my beautiful, but haughty, mistress a present worthy of her beauty.'

'Do you know how ridiculous you sound?' said Agnes, with a smile. 'Mind you, I do like the idea of being haughty. Now move,' she said and, using her feet, she pushed Collins towards the edge of the bed.

He rolled out, slipped on the blue silk dressing gown that Agnes had bought him for Christmas and headed for a shower and shave.

As arranged, Collins met Clark at the Endwood Court Island at 12.30. It was FA Cup semi-final day and Albion were playing Birmingham City of Division Two at Villa Park for a place in the Final. Collins had volunteered to work crowd control, which had freed Clark to attend the match as a spectator.

'Yow know, Mickey, I reckon it's written in the stars. Ruth's going to have her babbie and wem going to win the Cup.'

'How is she?'

'Big, huge in fact, but fine. Yow know, kidda, I spent two grand of Victor's money on that Harley Street specialist, but it will have been worth every penny when I hold me kid for the first time.'

'I bet it will,' said Collins. As always, when Victor's name was mentioned, Collins' mind went back to the bitterly cold night in 1963 when he had been nearly beaten to death by a gang of paedophiles. They had left him with a permanent bump in his nose and several crowns, which had been required to repair the chipped and broken teeth he'd suffered. Worst of all, though, were the memories of the savage beating he'd taken. More than once, he'd screamed in his sleep as he dreamed of his fingernails being pulled out by unseen men.

As they neared Perry Barr, they saw Berny Whitehouse.

He was on crowd control with his horse, Silver Star, and it looked like he'd already found some early custom.

'What's up?' asked Clark.

'Not much, Clarkee. One of these little shits whinnied at Silver as we trotted by. I'm waiting for the culprit to own up.'

Collins looked at the kids. There were five of them, all about fifteen, hemmed in by the horse and a four-foot stone wall, over which a privet hedge grew. As the horse moved ever closer, its hooves stamping on the pavement, the youths were pale with fear. Up close, the horse was bloody enormous. 'Where yow going?' Clark asked.

A tall, lanky, gobby kid, standing at the back of the group, said, 'The match.'

'The match, eh. Who do yow support?' asked Clark. 'Now, think careful before yow answer or Silver here will stamp on someone's toes.'

'We're Baggies fans.'

'In that case, who's your favourite player?' asked Collins.

Various answers rang out, 'Clive Clark', 'Astle', 'Tony Brown'. The gobby one had to be different, and said 'Osbourne.'

'OK,' said Clark, 'them's the right answers. Now, apologise to the nice policeman and his horse and get off to the game.'

A chorus of apologies followed and the lads hurried off down the road.

'What would you have done if they'd said they were Blues fans?' asked Berny.

'Let yow trample on 'em a bit.'

Berny grinned and, checking for traffic, manoeuvred his mount back onto the road.

When he returned home that night, Clark was nearly delirious with joy. Despite a great display by Birmingham's centre forward, Fred Pickering, Albion had won 2-0 with goals from Jeff Astle and Tony "Bomber" Brown. Now all he had to worry about was getting a ticket for the Final on the 18th of May. Unlocking the front door, he was all ready to launch into a passionate blow-by-blow description of the match, but something in Ruth's face stopped him.

'What's wrong, love?'

'There's someone to see you. He says his name is Tom Laurence and that he knew you in the War.'

Clark's face broke into a wide smile when he heard the name, but Ruth held up her hand to cut him off and whispered, 'He's been crying. I think he's in trouble.'

Clark kissed Ruth on the forehead and brushed his hand across her swollen belly before walking into the lounge. Tom was sitting in the armchair near the bay window. His eyes were red and the tears on his cheeks were fresh. He rose as Clark entered and held out his hand. 'Long time no see, Clarkee.'

'That it is, Tom. That it is. Ruth tells me yow need to talk to me about sommut. I'm guessing it's a police matter.'

'You'd be right, but I don't think the police are too interested in it.'

'Let's get a brew on, or would yow prefer sommut stronger and wi can have a natter?'

'Tea will be fine.'

Minutes later, Ruth appeared with a tea tray. She laid it on the coffee table and, without speaking, left, closing the lounge door as she went.

'OK, Tom, what's the problem that brings yow here?'

Tom hesitated and looked at the floor.

Clark waited, but it was obvious that his old friend found it impossible to start. As gently as he could, he asked, 'Is this to do with yow being queer? Have the police picked yow up for sommut?'

Tom's head snapped up, 'You knew?'

'We all bloody knew.'

'But no one said anything.'

'Why should wi? Nowt to do with us. Yow were a bloody good commando and that were all we cared about. None of us were too bothered about what yow and the Captain got up to.'

'God, twenty years, and here's me thinking none of you knew.'

'So, what's wrong?'

'I met a young man, Joseph, Joseph Webb, about three years ago. We've been together ever since. I'm obviously older than him and I know he has to sow some wild oats, so I turn a blind eye to what he gets up to when I'm away on business. Last weekend, I was in West Germany. When I got back Monday, he wasn't home. I was worried but I thought he might be staying with one of his friends, so I left it. On Tuesday evening, I went to the police at Steelhouse Lane and reported that my lodger had gone missing.

'The desk sergeant took a description and disappeared into the back room for a few minutes. When he returned, there was a Detective Inspector with him. A right heartless bastard. He said a body, matching Joseph's description, had been found that afternoon in Newtown and he wanted to know if I would be willing to go to the morgue.' Tom paused, trying to compose himself. 'Well, to cut a long story short, it was Joseph and some bastard had given him a right going-over.'

'I'm sorry for yowr loss, Tom. To lose anyone to murder is a terrible shock, but I don't see how I can help yow. It sounds like CID Central have it in hand.'

'No, they fucking don't,' shouted Tom, no longer able to control his pent-up frustration. 'They're doing fuck all about it. Just as they did fuck all about the other three.'

'Other three?'

'Yes, one in Stratford-upon-Avon, one in Wolverhampton and the first one in Birmingham about a year ago. Someone is killing young homosexuals and the police are doing fucking nothing about it.'

'How the bloody hell do you know these murders are connected?'

'I don't. Not really. But I don't believe in coincidences and neither did you back in the War. What was it you said when you shot that French bastard who was setting his mates up? "Once is bad luck, twice is suspicious and three times is a bullet in the head"?'

'Yeah, sommut like that, but I were a prat back then.'

'Yeah, you were,' said Tom and smiled for the first time. 'But you were right about that Vichy bastard and I'm right about this.'

'OK, I believe yow. Yow always had good instincts, but yow can't tell me that the police haven't linked the cases.'

'Well, if they have, why are they still carrying out separate investigations?' Tom stopped to wipe his eyes. 'They think that the four murders are unrelated.'

'Maybe they have linked the murders but don't want word to get out that there's a multiple killer on the loose?'

'No, that's not it. They've definitely rejected the idea that the killings are linked.'

'How can you be so sure?'

'The morgue attendant in Birmingham is one of us. He's seen the police reports on the Birmingham killings.'

For a moment there was silence, then Tom said, 'Can you help me, Clarkee? I've got no one else to turn to.' His voice was low, broken and desperate. Tears once more began to flow freely down his cheeks.

'Yeah, I can help,' said Clark, 'but I need to speak to me mate in CID. I'll tell yow what, give me yowr number and address, and me and Mickey will call around and see yow on Tuesday evening. That will give him a chance to mooch around and see what's what, OK? While yow're at it, get the morgue attendant there and anyone else yow can think of that might be able to help.'

Tom couldn't answer. His tears dripped onto his heaving chest and all he could do was nod silently.

Monday 29th April 1968, 08.45hrs

Handsworth

Collins was enjoying a cup of tea and a piece of toast before he went on duty, when Clark slid into the empty seat opposite. The police canteen was more than half full and there was the usual sound of swearing and laughter as events from the weekend were discussed and embellished. Upright Freddie – or, as he was now known, the Rev. Freddie Bartholomew – seemed to be the main topic of conversation.

'What's Freddie been up to now?' asked Collins.

'Yow know that row of houses near the doctor's on Holly Road where the prozzies work?'

'You mean the ones with the balconies?'

'That's them. Well, Sunday night, Freddie and his disciples decided to picket the houses and turn away any punters that might be looking for a shag on the Sabbath. Well, none of the English lads would go in. They just kept walking. But four Chinese geezers turned up and were none-too-pleased to find a bunch of Bible bashers blocking their way.'

Hang on a minute, isn't that where Gloria and her mates operate from?'

Clark nodded in confirmation and a smile spread across his lips. 'When they opened up there, Gloria said they picked them houses 'cause it were near the doctors and saved them travelling to the clinic for their jabs.'

'That sounds like Gloria, always practical. I suppose all hell broke loose.'

'You got it in one. Seems the lads had been looking forward all week to a bit of rumpty pumpty and weren't going to be denied. They were no bigger than me but what they lacked in size, they made up for in inventiveness. They used fists, elbows, feet, a broken fence and the empty bottles from a crate of Corona pop to try and get past Freddie and Co. Heads were split open, noses broke, teeth punched out and that were before Gloria and her mates piled in. By the end of it, wi had about twenty people screaming, punching and clawing – and that were just the coppers. It took twelve of the lads and two Black Marias to sort it out.'

'Sounds fun.'

'It were better than that.'

'Is Gloria OK?'

'Yeah. If there's ever an atomic war, I'm going to hide under her. She's bloody indestructible.'

'So what did you book them on?'

'Nowt. Freddie's mob refused to press charges, said it would be unchristian, and besides wi couldn't understand a word the Chinamen were saying.'

'They only spoke Chinese?'

'Na, it were their Wolverhampton accents.'

Collins grinned. 'So you just let them go?'

'Yeah, wi warned the lot of them, then held them until after the last bus had gone. I'm sure they enjoyed their walk back to Wolverhampton in the rain. Anyway, what yow got on yowr plate at the moment?'

Collins knew his friend too well not to miss the implication behind his apparently casual inquiry. 'What do you want this time?'

'Funny yow should ask,' said Clark and proceeded to summarise his conversation with Tom Laurence on Saturday night.

Collins listened and when Clark had finished, asked, 'What do you want me to do?'

'I was thinking yow could visit your girlfriend in Central CID and find out what she knows about the lad's murder.'

'She's not me girlfriend.'

'No, but she'd like to be. I've seen the way she looks at yow. Like a fox salivating over a chicken. Give her any encouragement and she'd have yow, upside down, backwards or side saddle.'

'You've got a filthy mind, Mr Clark. Katie is just being friendly to a fellow Dubliner.'

'If yow say so, but I reckon if Agnes don't snap yow up soon, Katie will. Yow'll speak to her, yeah?'

'Yes, I'll speak to her. Just to shut you up, you daft Yam Yam.'

'When?'

'This afternoon. I have a meeting with Keating in town. He says he's got some info for me. I'll drop in on Katie afterwards.'

'Good lad. Because I forgot to mention wi have an appointment with Tom at his place tomorrow.'

'Well, in that case we'd better go have a dekko at the scene of crime before then. You said it was off Summer Lane?'

'Yeah.'

'OK, I'll meet you there at 4.'

'Hang on, it's the United match tonight.'

'So? Kick-off's not 'til 7.30.'

'After Saturday, it will be packed.'

'Well, it's not as if they won't let you in, thanks to your trusty warrant card.'

'OK. Are yow still coming tonight?'

'Yes,' said Collins, not admitting that even after five years of encouragement from Clark, Collins was still not a football fan. He attended the odd game, just to keep Clark quiet. He could appreciate the skill involved, but found it impossible to share the same passion and tribal loyalty that Clark and the other Baggie fans had. His childhood heroes had been hurling players and his loyalty was to the Kevin's Hurling Club and to County Dublin – especially when they were playing Cork.

Birmingham, 14.10hrs

Richard Keating was sitting at the back of the Gunmakers Arms nursing a pint when Collins arrived. Most of the lunchhour custom had disappeared and there was only a smattering of drinkers finishing up before closing time at two thirty. Collins looked at Keating and raised his hand to his mouth and mimed the drinking of a pint. Keating shook his head. Crouching low to avoid hitting his head on the smoke-blackened beams, Collins crossed to the bar and ordered a half of shandy.

Taking his drink, he wandered over to the table and sat down beside Keating. As always, the car dealer was immaculately turned out. Wearing a tailored dark grey suit, white shirt and plain gold cufflinks, he looked more like a prosperous stockbroker than a second-hand car dealer from Handsworth. He also smelt better than most women. His aftershave was strong and expensive. However, hidden beneath his stylishly cut, long hair was a 4 inch scar that ran diagonally from the bottom of his ear into the hair and down to the nape of his neck. It was a present from a botched robbery circa 1958 when a jeweller had slashed him with an antique cheese knife that was still sharp after sixty years' service. Keating had spent two days in hospital and eighteen months in Winson Green Prison. He'd left swearing that he'd never spend another day behind bars.

Both men sat with their backs to the wall, so that they could see everyone in the bar and anyone who entered. 'How's it going, Richard?'

'Not bad, Mr Collins, not bad.'

'So, what did you want to see me for that you couldn't tell me at the showroom?'

'It's Tony.'

'Your brother? What's the prat done this time?'

'It's not what he's done. It's what he's planning to do.'

Collins leaned forward. He could see the doubt in Keating's face as he struggled to balance his loyalty to his brother and his almost pathological desire to stay on the right side of the law. Finally, he seemed to make up his mind and said, 'He and his mates are planning to hijack a lorry load of fags next Thursday. I told him not to get involved. That bunch couldn't organise an orgy in a brothel, but he's young and stupid. I'm worried that they'll hurt the driver and go down for some serious time.'

'OK. When and where is this taking place?'

'In his own bloody backyard, that's where. Would you believe they're going to grab the lorry from the Boundary Café car park after it closes and the driver settles down for a kip? I mean, if the guy shouts or screams he'll wake up about thirty other drivers and they'll give Tony and his mates a right good kicking before you lot arrive.'

'I see. And when is it planned to crack off?'

'Sorry. Ever since I told him it was stupid idea, he hasn't spoken to me.'

'So no earlier than ten thirty and probably around midnight – to allow the driver to drift off?'

'That sounds about right.'

Collins reached into his jacket pocket and started to withdraw his wallet when Keating stopped him. 'That won't be necessary, Mr Collins, I can't take money for shopping me own brother. It would be like taking thirty pieces of silver.'

'OK, I owe you one.'

'You could do me a favour and we can call it quits.'

'What's that?'

'Grab them before they pull the driver out of the van. That way, no one gets hurt and Tony is looking at attempted robbery or robbery at most, and not robbery with violence.'

'Fair enough. I'll see what I can do.'

'Thanks, Mr Collins.'

Collins pushed his untouched half of shandy across the table and stood up. 'I'll see you around,' he said and left.

Outside, a light drizzle was falling. Looking to the skies, he saw a patchwork of dark rain bearing clouds against a clear blue sky. Occasionally the sun shone through but it did little to mask the chill carried by the spring wind. Turning his collar up, Collins set off past St Chad's Cathedral and headed for Steelhouse Lane Police Station and Katie.

While he would never admit it, Clark was right. He knew Katie had a thing for him and in odd moments he'd found himself thinking about her red Irish hair, porcelain white skin and a laugh that made him smile whenever he heard it. But he also knew that nothing would ever come of it. Still, there was no harm in thinking about what might be.

Steelhouse Lane Police Station, Birmingham 15.00hrs

Katie McGuire was at her desk eating a sandwich when Collins knocked on the open door and walked into her overcrowded office. Files lay everywhere and were piled two feet high in places. Seeing Collins, she stood up and brushed the crumbs from her uniform. She was what the Irish called "a fine big girl". Not fat, but tall and solidly built. With her long red hair tied back and held in place by a large silver hairpin of Celtic design, wild green eyes and a pretty face, she was more than just a fine big girl. Dressed for a dance, she would be stunning in all her Rubenesque glory. But despite her looks, Collins had no doubt that she could hold her own in a fight against most men.

'Well, if it's not Detective Constable Collins. When are they going to make you a sergeant?'

Her welcoming smile was infectious and Collins grinned as he moved some files off a chair and sat down. 'When they're good and ready.'

'Ah sure, you should give them a push. You do know you got the top marks in the Sergeant's Exam, don't you?'

'No, I can't say I did. How the hell do you know that?'

'The sign on the door says Intelligence Unit. They won't let me do any real police work so I like to do a bit of spying on the side. I've always seen meself as Dublin's answer to Modesty Blaise. Digging up bits of vital information and stealing it away from gangsters and international criminal masterminds.'

'I could see you as a femme fatale honey trap.'

'Really. That's the nicest thing you've ever said to me, Mr Collins, but I'd need a code name,' she paused, examining the far wall for inspiration. 'How about the Scarlet Medusa?'

'Sexy and dangerous. Suits you.'

'Enough! You're being too nice. You're after something and I know it's not me body, unfortunately.'

'Sure, you can read me like a book. I need some information.'

'Then I'm your girl – or I would be, if you gave me a bit of encouragement.'

Collins was never sure if Katie was teasing him or if she meant it when she made such suggestions. Ignoring the invitation, he said, 'Last week, your lot found the body of Joseph Webb, a twenty-two-year-old homosexual, who'd been murdered. I'm wondering what you can tell me about the case?'

'And why do you want to know about the queer fella. A friend of yours?'

'His friend contacted Clark. Seems he's concerned that someone's been killing young homosexuals for the last year and we're doing nothin' to catch him.'

'So Clarkee set you up for this?'

Collins nodded.

'Well, you can tell him that there is no mass murderer doing the rounds, bumping off queers.'

'How can you be so sure?'

'Because in each case we have a description of the murderer and none of them match. They're all completely different – even the heights are different.'

'But what about the victims' injuries?

'Well, it's true they were all beaten up before they were killed. But the first was strangled, the second stabbed, the third smothered and the lad Saturday week last was beaten to death with a tyre lever.'

'So you're saying they're not connected?'

'Not just me, but Inspector West. He might be a fat, lecherous slob but he's been out to the pubs where those fellas were picked up. Spoke to the staff, clientele and the local coppers.

He's certain that the murders are unconnected. There's just too much variation in the description of the killer and the cause of death to think that one man did all four.'

'So we've got four different men out there bumping off homos. Is that it?'

'You know as well as I do that hardly a week passes without a couple of queers getting beaten up. The law of averages says that one or two of them are going to end up dead eventually.'

'OK. This won't please Clark or his friend. Just to prove that I've done a good job, is there any chance you could copy West's file and send it over to me tomorrow and anything you've got from the post-mortems?'

'All right, but I'm only doing it because you're Irish and one day I might need you to take me to a dance at St. Francis.' Is there anything else you require, O great one?' She fluttered her eyes ostentatiously.

'Well, now that you mention it.'

'Yes?' Katie said, leaning forward.

'Can you give me the address of where the last body was found? I have to meet Clark there and I didn't jot it down.'

Katie threw the pencil she was holding at Collins before she found the file and gave him the address.

Collins smiled and leaning forward, kissed Katie on the cheek. 'You're a darling,' he said and was out of the door before she had time to react.

Newtown, 16.00hrs

The rain had become heavy. Blue-black thunder clouds moved in a stately procession across the late April sky and carried with them the promise of even heavier rain to come.

Collins turned off Summer Lane and flicked his windscreen wipers up a notch. Within a couple of minutes, he was lost in a warren of side streets and lanes that had been turned into mini canals by the downpour. He remembered something Clark had told him when he was educating him about all things Brum. Birmingham has more miles of canals than Venice. Well that's certainly true today, he thought as he drove past the numerous small workshops and larger factories that sat cheek by jowl with each other.

Gone was the smoke of the 1950s, thanks to the Clean Air Act of 1956. However, the familiar smell of hot swarf remained, as turning machines pared millimetres of metal off machine parts destined for every corner of Britain and the world. For many of the businesses, their largest customers were the car industry giants situated nearby in Longbridge and Coventry, Dagenham in Essex, and Ellesmere Port in the Wirral.

As he neared the factory where the body of Joseph Webb had been found, Collins noticed that increasingly premises were empty and the signs of recent demolition more obvious. Adan Lane was right at the end of this downward spiral. There was only one building left standing in the small cul-de-sac: Arthur Wright and Sons, which faced the derelict back wall of another forgotten company. Above the open rolling steel shutters, a bedraggled sign in white paint read "Goods Inwards".

All that was left of a once vibrant manufacturing community were uneven patches of waste ground, with grass and wild flowers trying their best to push their way past broken bricks, pieces of concrete, smashed chairs, sheets of asbestos, plasterboard and shards of broken slates. Out of place in this industrial wasteland, a small clump of daffodils clung to life near the front of the factory.

Thieves had stolen the lead from the roof of the old factory and nature had very quickly got to work destroying the building. Rotted timbers, rusted pipes and a collapsed wooden stairs could be seen through the open roller door. In the gloom of the building, Collins saw Clark standing in the old loading bay. He was examining a hoist that had once been used to lift heavy loads onto horse-drawn wagons and later trucks.

'Found anything?' asked Collins, as he shook the rain from his mac.

'A bit. It looks like the poor sod was tied to this hoist by his hands and then pulled into the air using that wheel over there. From what Laurence told me about Joe's injuries and the area of concrete stained with blood, my guess is that he would have been standing on tiptoe during the beating or else suspended an inch or two off the floor. Any higher up and the blood spread would be wider.

'It's also odds-on that the killer scouted this place in advance. I mean, unless yow work nearby yow'd never know it were here. And I don't think this guy is daft enough to kill on his own doorstep. No, our killer definitely checked the site out before the kill.'

'There's also some paint on the wall across the lane, dark blue. It looks like car paint,' Clark said and grinned.

Collins immediately recognised that his old mentor was testing him. 'OK, let's have a look at it.'

Both men jogged across the road and stood as close to the wall as they could to avoid a soaking. Clark pointed to a thin line of paint that ran vertically down the wall in a broken line for about 20 inches. Collins examined it closely, then stood up smiling. 'The passenger tried to get out but couldn't because the car was parked too close to the wall. He had no escape.'

'Very good. Give the little boy with the Mickey Mouse ears a goldfish. He dain't want a fight with the kid or to risk the lad running off. So he parked up in the lane, then he probably punched or hit Joe. The kid tried to open the door, but was knocked out and then taken to the open factory, strung up, tortured and killed.'

'That confirms your idea that he scouted the place in advance and if this paint is from the killer's car, then the edge of his passenger door is going to be missing its paint.'

'Yep. When yow get the files from your girlfriend, check to

see if that berk West did a canvas of the area for a man in a blue car acting suspiciously.'

'Will do.'

'Yow see. I ain't just a pretty face.'

'I don't think anyone has ever accused you of being a pretty face. '

The Hawthorns, 21.03hrs

Collins stood halfway down the Brummie Road End. Like a kid's rubber ball on the sea, he was being pushed backwards, sideways and forwards by a massive tide of humanity that he was powerless to resist. If he fell, he'd never be able to get up. The Hawthorns had an official capacity of 45,000, but that night there were at least 55,000 people in the ground and the noise they were making would have moved the needle on any Richter Scale in the world. Collins had never felt, heard or seen anything like it in his life.

The cause of this unprecedented outpouring of joy, noise and local pride was that just two days after reaching the FA Cup Final, Albion were playing the reigning League Champions, Manchester United – and winning 6-1.

Beside him was a small forty-seven-year-old man who was delirious with joy. He couldn't believe what he was seeing. Denis Law had missed from a yard out. After he'd stamped on the ball, it had spun backwards up his leg and chest and over the bar. George Best, from eight yards out, had missed his kick entirely and blushed when the crowd gave him the bird. Astle had scored a hat-trick while Ronnie Rees, Tony Brown and Asa Hartford netted one apiece. .

Collins realised that somewhere in this vast swaying mass of humanity were the five lads whom Berny had treated to a very close inspection of Silver Star on Saturday. God I hope no one gets crushed, he thought.

The noise suddenly reached a new crescendo when all four sides of the ground rose to salute Jeff Astle's hat-trick by singing, 'Astle is our King! Astle is our King! The Brummie

Road will sing this song! Astle is our King!' Only when it died down did Collins hear the announcer repeat his earlier message, 'Would Detective Constable Michael Collins please report immediately to the main office in Halfords Lane, where an urgent telephone message awaits him.'

Clark shrugged his shoulder in commiseration as his friend started to push his way to the front. At pitchside, a barrel-chested police constable barred his way but stepped aside when Collins flashed his warrant card. At the players' tunnel, Collins was shown the way to manager's office where a young woman, her face flushed with excitement, pushed the phone message into his hand and dived out of the door to catch the closing moments of the match. Collins read the short message and called the station.

Sergeant O'Driscoll was his usual laconic self when he answered the phone, but his instructions were clear. 'Uniform need you, Mickey. They're at Hill Top, near the old ack-ack site.'

Handsworth, 21.45hrs

Collins had no problem spotting the two patrol cars. Both had their headlights on and were about halfway up the hill. He was impressed that they had managed to get so near the summit. To drive any further, you'd need a 4x4 or, better still, a tank.

As he parked up on Ashcroft Avenue, Collins remembered what Mrs Wilcox had said about the ack-ack guns bringing down a German bomber in 1942. She'd moved out two years ago when her husband died, but Collins had liked the cheerful old woman and hoped she was well and enjoying her retirement at some seaside retreat. Her husband, on the other hand, had been a miserable old git.

Opening the boot, he pulled out his wellies and started to

think about how opposites seemed to attract. There was the cheerful, vivacious Mrs Wilcox and her stern, dower husband. Clark, with his sharp mind, compassion for the underdog and killer instincts hidden behind a "simple Black Country lad, me" persona, and Clark's wife, Ruth, quiet, friendly, caring and loyal, who'd seen more horrors by the age of thirteen than most would see in a lifetime, but who never allowed it to poison her view of the essential goodness of mankind.

As he started up the track, his thinking turned to Agnes and himself. They were as different as salt and sugar. She was 22 years older than him, and twice as smart. A true English rose, from a well-connected middle-class family with plenty of old money, and a Quaker to boot. What did she have in common with a twenty-eight-year-old copper from Dublin, who, until a grateful newspaper owner had left him £7,000, had been living week to week on his police pay and saving up to buy a bloody dressing gown? Love was nuts, he decided.

Arriving at the parked cars, the latest probationer at Thornhill Road, PC Alex Fletcher, greeted him. Not sure how to address a Detective Constable, Fletcher settled for what he'd heard around the station. 'Evening, Mickey.'

'What have ya got?' asked Collins.

'You'd best come and have a butcher's yourself. Harris and I were just heading back to the station when he spotted the lights in the trees. Twenty minutes earlier and it would still have been light and we would have missed it.'

'Somebody actually drove to the top?'

'Yep.'

'Bloody hell.'

The copse of trees was a mere 20 yards from the top of the hill. Collins could see the torches of the three police officers who were standing near the vague outline of a Ford Cortina, which was partially sticking out from the woodland.

'Glad you're here, Mickey,' said Dave Harris, a twenty-year veteran of the force, who'd thought he'd seen everything until tonight. 'There's a woman in the car. Every time we try to get near her, she starts screaming. Looks like she's been beaten, maybe raped. Her clothes are all over the shop. Worst of all, she got a six-inch screwdriver. She keeps gabbling on about how if she gets out, he'll kill her.'

'Not much chance of that,' said Fletcher.

Collins ignored the remark and slipped his mac off. 'Maybe it's the uniforms that are scaring her. I'll see what I can do. Did you call Scenes of Crime?'

Yeah,' said Harris, 'they're on their way.'

Collins took Fletcher's torch and slowly approached the car from the passenger side, keeping the beam focused on the ground so as not to startle the woman. 'Who are you?' she shouted when he got within ten yards of the car.

'I'm a police officer. You're not in any trouble. I just want to help. Can I come in and sit with you? I promise I won't try and force you to leave the car.'

'Promise?'

'On me mother's grave.'

'All right, you can come in.'

Collins walked round the car, turned off the torch and climbed into the driver's seat. He guessed that the woman was maybe five or six years older than him. She was naked except for an old tartan travelling rug draped around her shoulders, which barely covered her lap. Even in the pale moonlight, it was obvious that she had been viciously beaten. Both of her eyes were black and blue. The left one was half closed and her right cheek badly swollen, where an elbow had probably caused a fracture. By the way she was breathing and grimacing with every slight movement, Collins guessed that she also had a couple of broken ribs beneath the blanket. The bastard had done a real good job on her.

Instinct told Collins to say nothing. He just sat there quietly, allowing the woman to get used to his presence. After maybe four minutes, she finally said, 'Thank God you're here.'

'Are you OK?'

'No, but I'll live.' She spoke slowly, as if in a daze. Her eyes stared into the middle distance.

'My name's Michael, what's yours?'

'Jean Rogers.'

'Well, Jean, can you tell me what happened?'

'The car wouldn't move. John said it had got bogged down in the soft ground and he needed to get a tow. He told me to lock myself in and not leave the car – or else he'd finish what he'd started. I think he just went off and left me. The bastard. He knows I can't drive.'

'Who's John?'

'My husband.'

'Your husband?'

'Yes.'

'Isn't it a bit strange to be up here with your husband? I mean, it's usually courting couples who come up here.'

'I know,' she whispered. Looking at the floor, she continued, 'I've been seeing someone and John found out. He wanted to see where we... you know.'

'I understand; go on.'

'I thought he'd forgiven me. We made love. He was a bit rougher than usual but it was good. After we'd finished, he went mad. Calling me a whore and a cunt. And started to hit me and rip the rest of my clothes off. The more I screamed and begged him to stop, the more he seemed to enjoy it.'

She stopped talking and gazed into the night, exhausted. After a few minutes, she gathered herself.

'What happened next?' asked Collins.

'He started to cry. That was the worst part of it. I tried to put my arms around him, but he just pushed me away and jumped out of the car, as if touching me made him feel dirty or something. He grabbed my clothes and threw them all over the field. I don't know where he went. The tow should have been here ages ago.'

Two sets of headlights illuminated the hillside as a pair of Land Rovers bounced over the rough hillside. 'I think we need to go now. That might be the tow and we need to get you some clothes,' lied Collins. 'OK?'

'OK.'

'Good girl. Now you stay there and I'll grab my mac for you.'

'Can't you just get my skirt and blouse?'

'Sorry, Jean. Scenes of Crime will need them.'

Jean nodded and watched as Collins walked over to the three police officers who were watching the car. As Collins picked up his mac, Harris asked, 'How is she?'

'Bad, but she'll be all right.'

Returning to the car, Collins handed Jean his mac and turned his back as she struggled into the coat. When she was finished, she slid out of the car still gripping the travel rug. Collins took the blanket and draped it around her shoulders.

'Steady now,' he said. 'The ground's rough, so keep looking down and don't look back or you'll trip over.'

At that moment, the first Land Rover turned off the track and its headlights illuminated the stranded car and trees that surrounded it. The temptation was too great for Jean. She had to take one last look at the spot where she had been humiliated and her marriage ended. And there in the glare of the headlights, she saw her husband's body hanging from a tree, gently turning in the light wind. His right shoe was now scraping against the roof of the car, courtesy of his stretched neck. It was then that she started to scream. She only stopped when she sank to the ground, unconscious.

Tuesday 30th April 1968, 03.00hrs

Birmingham

It was nearly 3am when Collins left the Accident Hospital in Birmingham. Jean had four broken ribs, a fractured cheek bone, multiple bruising and contusions, concussion and a very bad case of shock. The doctors had given her a sedative to help her sleep. He'd have to return the next day to take a full statement.

Putting the Mini Cooper in gear, he pulled away from the curb and soon turned left onto the Bristol Road. There was no traffic about and the streets were deserted. The heavy showers of earlier had given way to a fine misty rain and the tarmac shone black, slick and dangerous in his headlights. He rotated his head to ease the stiffness in his neck and wondered what the final score had been at the Albion. Whatever it was, he'd be listening to descriptions of the match from Clark for the next month. *Wonderful*, he thought.

Ahead, two men crossed the road at a slow trot. Both had their heads down, but he immediately recognised the man nearest to him. Toby Drew, one of the most dangerous criminals in Birmingham. Behind his expensive manners was a man who was very happy to put people in hospital – or worse, if they got in his way. Collins only caught a glimpse of the other man's back, the collar of his well-cut navy overcoat turned up against the drizzle.

What's a toerag like Drew doing out in the middle of the night? wondered Collins. He filed the sighting away until he could record it in his notebook.

Handsworth, 09.00hrs

Collins arrived at the station with less than five hours of sleep under his belt and headed straight for the CID

Room. DCI Hicks was at his desk, the familiar stink of his Gauloise cigarettes already filling the room. After all the recent scares about cigarettes causing lung cancer, Hicks had tried to quit. But for the entire six weeks he'd stayed off the coffin nails, he'd been bad-tempered, argumentative and a right royal pain in the backside. Collins and DS York had been relieved when he'd finally cracked and went back on them, especially as he now only smoked about half what he used to.

Collins flopped into his chair and rubbed his eyes.

'Late night?' asked Hicks.

'Yeah. I didn't get back from the hospital until nearly four. I have to go back there today to take Mrs Rogers' statement.'

'Nasty business. I assume they sedated her.'

'Yeah.'

'Well, I'd leave it 'til late afternoon before you see her. No good talking to her if she's still doped up to the eyeballs. What else did you get up to yesterday?'

'I saw Richard Keating. His brother and some of his mates are planning to knock off a lorry load of fags at the Boundary Café next Thursday.'

'Bloody hell, he shopped his own brother!'

'He reckons they're a bunch of amateurs and are sure to be nicked. He's worried that if it goes ahead and the driver gets clobbered, Keating junior could get a long stretch for robbery with violence.'

'What are you going to do?'

'The café's just over the border so technically it's the West Broms' problem but...'

'He's your grass and you'd like to see it through?'

'Yeah.'

'OK, I'll phone the DCI at West Brom. He's a good man. I'm sure there'll be no problem. But he'll want one of his own in on the job. Any preferences?'

Without hesitation, Collins said, 'Sergeant Andrews.'

'Fair enough. Leave it with me. What are you going to do?'

'With York on secondment at Sheldon, I'll organise the lads. I was thinking we'd have about ten, if you come along.'

'Yeah, count me in. It'll get me out the office. Anything else?'

'Nope.'

'What about your visit to buxom Katie? Slip your mind, did it?'

'How the hell did you know about that?'

'That's for me to know and you to find out. Come on, what are you and Clark up to now?'

Collins quickly explained Clark's request. Hicks listened without interruption and waited until the end before he asked, 'Is there anything in this Laurence character's story?'

'I doubt it, from what Katie said. Besides, West might be an arrogant slob, but he's not so incompetent as to miss anything obvious. I'll have a better idea when I've had a dekko at the file from Steelhouse Lane. It should be here with the ten o'clock post.'

'OK, you do that. I'll ring West and explain that all you're doing is trying to reassure an old friend of Clark's. He'll understand. But if you find anything, let me know first before you and Clark go stamping all over another officer's inquiry. OK?'

'Yes, Sir.'

'Now, go on and get us both a coffee and a round of toast.'

As he'd anticipated, a copy of West's file on the killings arrived with the early internal post and Collins settled down to read it with a second cup of tea. Inspector West had liaised with his counterparts in Wolverhampton and Stratford-upon-Avon, and had visited the Toreador in Birmingham, the Manhattan Club in Wolverhampton and The Other Queen's Head in Stratford. West's report was long on words but short on details. There was no mention of any blue paint at the scene of Joe's murder, which meant that either it was put there after the murder or West's team hadn't properly examined the crime scene. Despite the apparent lack of rigour on West's part, he had at least summarised all the main points, including cause of death, weapons used and a description of the killers. Based on these facts, Collins found himself reluctantly agreeing with the Inspector's conclusion that the deaths looked like the work of four separate killers.

Knowing that he would need to convince Laurence that there wasn't a single killer, he decided to summarise the information West had collected. Taking a foolscap sheet of paper from his desk drawer, he turned it sideways and drew four columns. After working solidly for 20 minutes, he had summarised all of the relevant information.

Victim's Name	Description of killer	Cause of death/ injuries inflicted	Pick-up/ dump location/ Date found
Daniel Stokes	Tall, over 6'. Early 20s. Long black hair, jeans and T-shirt. Small scar on right cheek. Handsome, described by barman as "A lovely, well-built bit of rough." No name heard.	Strangled/ beaten.	Toreador, B'ham. Found on bombsite in Sparkhill. 4/6/67.

Victim's Name	Description of killer	Cause of death/ injuries inflicted	Pick-up/ dump location/ Date found
Alan Green	5'8". Over 30. Brown hair cut short. Greenish eyes? Good-looking but starting to run to fat around the waist. Charcoal grey suit, blue shirt and red tie. Paid for his drinks from a wad of pound notes held together with a $ money clip. No name heard.	Stabbed/ beaten.	The Manhattan Club, W'hampton. Found in disused warehouse, 2 miles from club.
Peter Marshall	Tall, 6'. Slim. No more than 30 but with prematurely grey hair brushed back from his face. Thin, sharp features and a deep tan. One of the punters who spoke to him briefly said he may have been American or Australian.	Smothered /beaten. The Other Queen's head, Stratford. Found in disused warehouse in Sheldon near Elmdon airport. 2/1/68.	Found in disused warehouse in Sheldon near Elmdon Airport. 2/1/68

Victim's Name	Description of killer	Cause of death/ injuries inflicted	Pick-up/ dump location/ Date found
Joseph Webb	5'10". Very handsome. Blond hair parted on the left with a fringe covering forehead. Blue eyes, like Paul Newman. Lightly tanned. Dressed in a dark blue, two-piece suit, with open-neck white shirt. According to a punter, he looked very fit and walked like a sailor.	Beaten to death with tyre lever.	Toreador, B'ham. Found in disused factory off Summer Lane, Aston. 22/4/68.

Birmingham Accident Hospital, 15.00hrs

Jean Rogers was sitting by her bed, examining her hands as if she'd never seen them before, when Collins arrived. The bruising had blossomed overnight and the extent of her injuries were now plain to see. She pulled together the lapels of her hospital dressing gown to hide the rainbow of bruises that covered her chest, but soon gave up. It really didn't matter any more.

Collins took the visitor's chair from the next bed and sat

down. 'I won't ask how you're feeling. Today must be awful for you.'

'The worst I've ever known.'

'I'm sure it is but—'

'I know you have to ask me a few questions. I've seen Z Cars and Softly Softly. You go ahead and ask. But first, do you think we could get out of here? Maybe sit outside?'

'I don't see why not. You stay there and I'll find a wheelchair.'

Minutes later, Collins returned with an old wooden chair that had probably seen service during the First World War. 'It's all I could find,' he explained as he helped Jean to slide into the chair.

They discovered a glass-covered veranda on the ground floor, which led down to a small walled garden with a lawn designed for the inhabitants of Lilliput. At its centre was a carved statute of Pan. In the corner, a few white flowers edged with pink clung on for dear life to the magnolia tree. New buds were just starting to appear on the two rose bushes that stood watch at the bottom of the garden – even here, in the middle of Birmingham, the smell of spring and new life was all around.

Collins knew that, sometimes, taking a statement was like pulling a particularly stubborn tooth. Every little bit had to be dug out. On other occasions, witnesses just wanted to unburden themselves and they vomited out information with no coaxing whatever. Collins guessed that Jean wanted to tell him her story, in her way, so he remained silent and waited. After maybe three or four minutes, she started.

'John and me were all right at first. We'd been married about four years, but there was no sign of any children. So we went to the doctor and he arranged for us to see a specialist. I don't know why, but both of us just assumed that the problem was with me. John was wonderful about it. I don't think I ever loved him as much as I did during the four months we spent waiting to see Mr Lockwood. Anyway, on our second visit, Mr Lockwood confirmed that there was no chance of us starting a family as John was infertile. He thought it had probably been caused by the mumps John had when he was twelve.

'Well, John went to pieces. He stopped making love to me and went mad if he saw me walking about the house in my underwear. He even moved out of our bedroom. I tried everything, Mr Collins, but nothing worked. He seemed to think that he was no longer a man because of— which was stupid. He's never had any trouble, you know,' Jean hesitated, 'in the— bedroom. I was so unhappy and so alone. I still loved him. I wanted him to hold me, to love me like he used to, but he wouldn't. Well, there was this man at work, Richard. He just seemed to know that there was something wrong and he took an interest in me.'

I bet he did, thought Collins.

'A shoulder to cry on and, well, one thing led to another.' Jean paused, 'God, I must have been bloody stupid. He wasn't interested in me or my problems; he just wanted to get inside my knickers and he was patient enough to do just that.'

'I'm sorry.'

'Don't be. I got what I deserved. And now, do you know what? I'm pregnant with that bastard's child and my husband is dead because of me.'

'When did you—?'

'Not until this morning. They did a pregnancy test. They do one whenever a woman has serious stomach injuries. Just to be sure.'

This wasn't about police work anymore, but Collins didn't mind. The poor woman was wracked with pain and guilt. She needed to talk to someone. Another woman, who would listen and not judge. Collins quickly made up his mind. Jean wasn't the typical beaten woman that Agnes cared for, but she had been beaten and she needed help. Leaning forward, he placed his hand on hers. 'Listen, I have a friend called Agnes. She'll be able to help you.'

'No one can help me.'

'You've not met Agnes Winter. I'll arrange for her to come and see you tomorrow.'

'No. Not tomorrow. They're discharging me. I'm going home. Give me your number and I'll call you when I'm up to seeing her.'

'OK, but you have to promise that you'll call.'

Jean whispered, 'Yes.' Collins jotted his number down and handed her the slip of paper. With great care, she folded the note into four and placed it in the pocket of her dressing gown. Patting her pocket, she said, 'There you are, safe as houses.'

For the next hour, Collins gently led Jean through the events of Monday night. She'd obviously been thinking about it. But while her latest account contained many new minor details, the essential story was no different from what she'd told him in the car. Satisfied that he had an accurate record of what had happened, he passed the statement across for her to sign.

As she signed, he asked, 'Are you going to be all right?'

Returning the pen and paper, Jean smiled. 'Don't worry about me. You've been smashing. I know what I need to do to get over this. I need to get away. Start afresh, and that's what I'm going to do. I'll be fine.'

Sutton Coldfield, 19.30hrs

Clark pulled up outside Tom Laurence's house. Situated off the main road, the house had been built at the turn of the century and was what estate agents liked to describe as "a large family residence in a prime location, surrounded by mature trees and wild holly bushes." To Collins, it seemed far too large for just two men.

Clark rang the bell and, moments later, Tom Laurence appeared. With introductions made and handshakes exchanged, Tom led Clark and Collins to the back of the house. The room they entered was easily 40 foot by 25. Immaculately furnished, it was dominated by two brown leather Chesterfield settees facing each other, with a long oak coffee table between them. Two matching armchairs had been moved close to the settees, giving the impression of a figure U. Already present, drinks in hand, were five men.

'This is my friend, Clive Clark, and his colleague, Michael Collins. Don't call Clarkee Clive, or he might feel the need to break your arm.' There was a smattering of subdued laughter from the men. 'But other than that, I trust him more than any man on earth, so you can speak freely. Clark and Michael are here to talk to us about Joseph's death and to see if there are any links with the other three murders in the last year. I'm not going to introduce everyone at once. We can do that as the evening progresses, but I do need to point out Patrick. He was Daniel's friend.'

Collins knew that Daniel Stokes had been the first victim, found on a bomb peck in Sparkhill in June 1967. As he looked at Patrick, he realised that the dark haired, strongly built man of thirty was still in mourning. He carried his pain about him like a smothering cloak. The grief surprised Collins. He'd never really thought that a man could love another man in that way. He'd always assumed it was just about sex. Collins went over and, holding out his hand, said, 'I'm sorry for your loss.'

'Thank you,' said Patrick, his voice low and soft.

As Clark moved to offer his condolences, Tom asked, 'Can I get you gentlemen a drink before we start?'

'Why not?' said Clark. 'Wim not on duty. I'll have a beer and this excuse for an Irishman will have a tea, or have yow gone all posh on us and gone over to coffee?'

'Tea will be fine,' said Collins.

As Tom went to make tea, a tall, slim, twenty-something man with shoulder-length black hair and plucked eyebrows stood up. 'Make yourselves comfy while I get your beer,

Clarkee. Tom's saved the armchairs for you.' His voice was high and he walked with a sway that would have made any skirt swish beautifully from side to side. Returning with a glass of beer, he handed it to Clark but his eyes remained focused on Collins. Holding out his hand to the young detective, he said, 'I'm Richard. My drag name is Lady Peach, given to me by an appreciative lover who thought my arse was as luscious as a peach.'

'And which school were you at when he said that, darling?' asked a small, thin, middle-aged man with a goatee beard. Everyone laughed, including Peaches, who, pointing, said, 'That's James. He's bitter and twisted because he's never had the pleasure of me in his bed.'

'Which makes me unique in the greater Birmingham area.' This time, the laughter was full and unforced and both Collins and Clark joined in.

Ten minutes later, with his teacup nearly empty, Collins took the summary notes he'd prepared earlier out of his pocket. Leaning forward, he said, 'OK, I've done a bit of digging and there doesn't appear to be a link between the first three murders.' The faces of the assembled men registered a mixture of disappointment and anger.

'What about Joseph's murder?' asked Tom.

'It's too early to say for sure one way or the other, so I'd like to deal with his case separately if I can. First, let's look at the three earlier victims. They do share certain similarities with each other. They are of a type. The youngest was 18, the oldest 25. All were between 5' 11" and 6' 2" and of slim build. The heaviest was under twelve stone. All were abducted from a pub or club that homosexuals are known to frequent. They all appear to have left voluntarily and then driven to a location where they were beaten and murdered using a variety of methods. None of them were sexually assaulted or mutilated, although the killer, or killers, in each case did kick them repeatedly in the genitals – but that's fairly normal in assaults on homosexuals.'

'You mean queer bashing,' said a blond haired man in his forties, with a regulation short back and sides and a chest full of fine yellow hair breaking out from his open-neck shirt. 'You should call it what it is.'

Collins looked at the man for the first time. 'I'm sorry, but do I know you?' asked Collins.

'I'm Peter Morecombe. I work at the morgue in Birmingham. I've seen you around. You too, Constable Clark. I think you're wrong. I've only seen two of the bodies and read the reports from the other two attacks, but I think the bastard doing this gets off on the beatings. It's the beatings that are the common feature of the killings, not how he murders them.'

Collins knew enough morgue assistants to know that they were worth listening too. 'Go on,' he said, shuffling forward on his chair.

'My guess is that he wanks off as he knocks seven bells out of the poor lads. After he's come, he's no longer interested in them and kills them as quickly as he can. By then, they're probably unconscious anyway. Have you seen the autopsy reports from Wolverhampton and Stratford?'

'No, I didn't have time to get them,' said Collins. 'I've only seen the reports on Daniel and Joseph. For the other killing, I'm relying on Inspector West's notes.'

'That wanker. Given half a chance, he'd hold the killer's coat while the bastard kicked the shit out of the poor lads.' Peter paused as he tried to regain his composure. Taking a deep breath, he said, 'I'll send you a copy of the other autopsies by express post tomorrow.'

'Thanks. That would be helpful.' Collins didn't ask how Peter had got hold of another force's autopsy reports. 'You're obviously not a fan of the Inspector?'

'Let's put it this way. What that bigot lacks in intelligence, he more than makes up for in ego.'

'Did they all have the same eye colours?' asked an immaculately dressed man of about thirty, who was sitting at the end of one of the Chesterfields. His demeanour was as languid as the smoke that was slowly rising from his king-sized Dunhill cigarette.

'I don't have that information,' said Collins and cursed himself for turning up so badly prepared.

'Sorry, Mark,' said Peter. 'Two had blue eyes, one had brown and Joe, as we know, had hazel eyes.'

'No similarity there then,' said Mark. 'Did they share any characteristics other than their age, size and general body shape?'

'No,' said Collins, 'and we have four very different descriptions of the killers. Even their heights differ.'

'How tall were the killers?' asked Mark.

'Witnesses say that the man who picked Daniel up was over 6 foot, but the suspect in Alan Green's case was only 5 foot 8. In Peter Marshall's case, the killer was 6 foot, but in Joe's case he was about 5 foot 10,' said Collins, reading from his notes.

'It's very easy to change how a person looks, even their height,' said Mark.

Collins looked closely at Mark for the first time. His voice was soft and mellifluous, yet it flowed effortlessly into every corner of the room. There was something very familiar about him, but Collins was unable to place him. 'I'm sorry,' he said, 'I didn't catch your name.'

'I'm Mark Cavendish.' Immediately, Collins realised it was the Mark Cavendish, star of stage and TV, and leading man in many a medical drama or who-done-it. If anything, he looked more handsome in the flesh than he did on TV.

Collins stopped himself blurting out, 'You're that actor on TV!' and instead said, 'How do you mean?'

'In the right hands, a bit of make-up, a few wigs and prosthetic noses and ears can entirely change how a person looks in less than an hour.'

'What about changing height? That ain't so easy,' said Clark.

'You'd be surprised. A good pair of lifts can add two, maybe three inches to a person's height. And how they carry themselves can give the impression of a tall or a short man.'

'Are yow saying it could be an actor wem after?' asked Clark.

'Possibly. But it could just as easily be a make-up artist or anyone with experience of the profession. Even a good amateur could probably pull it off – if they took care.'

Collins sat back in his chair, looked at Clark and moved his eyes towards the door.

Clark picked up on the signal and said, 'Tom, do yow think yow could do Collins another cuppa and top me up while wi have a quick natter outside?'

'Of course. Anyone else like another drink?'

Tom was still taking orders when Collins and Clark stepped into the cool spring night.

'What do yow make of it, Mickey lad?'

'I don't know. I don't know if there's one killer or four killers. What I do know is that there are a damn sight more questions than answers and so far we've done a piss-poor job of examining all the options.'

'I agree. So what are wi going to do about it?'

'Investigate it, what else?'

'Yow know we'll never get official clearance for a cross-force investigation, don't yow?'

'Yep, but since when has that ever stopped us?' said Collins, smiling.

'So where do yow want to start?'

'We need to re-interview the staff and punters at each venue and speak to those who knew the victims. I also need to read the Wolverhampton and Stratford autopsy reports.'

'Ok then. Wi have a plan. Anyway, best get back in or they might think wi've eloped.'

On their return, the room fell quiet and six pairs of expectant eyes focused on them. Clark gave a brief nod and Collins stepped forward. 'Clarkee and I have had a chat and we think there is something that needs investigating here.' Before Collins could continue, the small group broke into a round of applause. Richard and Mark both called out 'Yes!' while Tom, with tears in his eyes, turned and hugged Patrick.

Collins held up his hand for silence. 'It's only fair to warn you that this won't be an official enquiry. We need firm evidence before we can get a cross-force investigation going and we need to stay below the radar or else we'll get our ears boxed. It might take a bit of time.'

'That's not a problem. At least someone is doing something. That's all that matters,' said Tom.

'Where will you start?' asked Mark.

'We'll start by going to the venues and talking to the staff and customers,' said Clark.

'Sorry, Clarkee love,' said Richard, 'but that's not going to work. People are scared of coppers – usually you lot are locking us up. You'll stand no chance if you go in on an official basis.'

'Well, maybe wi could go in undercover, like,' said Clark.

'Sorry again, darling,' said Richard. 'You'd be spotted quicker than a dose of VD at the clinic.'

'So what do yow suggest?'

'Well, handsome there might pass as queer,' he said, nodding in Collins' direction. 'Mind, he'd have to relax a bit and learn the lingo. I'd be willing to teach him.'

'I bet you would,' said James. 'He'd be safer with a bunch of lifers than with you.'

When the laughter had subsided and Richard had protested his innocence far too much, Mark said, 'Richard's right. Clark would be recognised for what he is within a couple of minutes. However, Michael could pass as queer – or, at least, someone who might be queer, if he had someone to hold his hand and vouch for him with the locals.' Mark paused. 'Look, all I'm doing at the moment is preparing for a new play. Why don't I show Michael the sights and introduce him around? I can say that he's a friend of mine who is an insurance investigator and I've asked him to look into the murders. What do you think?'

'Do yow think it would work, Tom?' asked Clark.

'I don't see why not, especially if Mark lets it drop that Michael isn't sure if he's queer or not,' said Tom.

'Hang on a minute. Don't I get a say in this?' asked Collins.

'Na. I think it's a bostin idea,' said Clark, grinning wildly.

'I'm friendly with the guy who owns the Manhattan. Why don't I give him a call and ask him to put the word out about our private investigation?' said Mark.

'That's a great idea,' said Laurence. 'The rest of us can get the ball rolling by contacting everyone we know.'

Before departing, Collins agreed to meet Mark at the actor's flat on Wednesday afternoon to discuss what they would do. Clark cried off, claiming that he had a union meeting to attend.

As they drove home, Collins asked, 'What's this about a Federation meeting? On a point of principle, you never attend any.'

'Yeah I know, but I thought yow and Mark should have some time alone to cement yowr new relationship,' said Clark, eyelids fluttering. 'Mind yow, don't let Katie know or it'll break her heart.'

'Well, while I'm with Mark, why don't you get your lazy arse down to the Toreador and have a chat with the staff? Go early evening; it will be quiet and I doubt your uniform will scare them off.'

'OK, but if anyone asks what I were doing there, I'm going to say I was only following orders.'

'When was the last time you followed orders?'

'Let me think. Oh yeah, June 1943. I remember 'cos it were the last time I made a mistake.'

Wednesday 1st May 1968, 09.00hrs

Handsworth

Collins kicked the CID door closed with his heel, laid a cup of steaming hot tea on his desk and handed the other to Hicks. 'Any news on York?' Collins asked. 'We're starting to miss him around here.'

'Well, now that you mention it,' said Hicks. 'While you were at the hospital yesterday I got a call from his gaffer in Sheldon. Seems they want to change his rank from Acting Inspector to Inspector. They wanted to know what I thought of the idea.'

'Bloody hell, he only went there on secondment. What did you say?'

'I told them they'd made a good choice.'

'So that's that. We need a new Sergeant. Any ideas, Sir?'

'Just one,' Hicks paused for effect, 'You.' Hicks laughed as Collins' mouth momentarily fell open.

'Bloody hell, Boss. Are you sure?' I mean I've only been in the job for five minutes. Plenty of blokes have got more wool on their backs than me.'

'I spoke to the Super yesterday. He's going to talk to the Chief Constable at some shindig they're attending this afternoon, but he reckons that the Chief will rubber stamp it. Until it's finalised, you're Acting Sergeant. Congratulations,' said Hicks, holding his hand out.

Collins grasped the offered hand, dumbfounded by what he'd heard. His joy and excitement made it impossible to think straight. All he wanted to do was call Agnes and tell her the news. He couldn't think of anything to say and settled for, 'Thanks, Boss.'

'Do I need to ask who you'd like as your replacement?'

'No, Sir. There's only one man for the job,' he said, smiling.

'He's turned down CID several times. What makes you think he'll take it this time?'

'The baby, Sir. He doesn't want to work regular shifts any more. He's worried he'll miss his kid growing up. Play on that and I think you've got him.'

'Fair enough, you know him better than anyone. OK, get out of here and ask Clark to come and see me.' As Collins reached the door, Hicks asked, 'When are you going to brief us on the hijack?'

'This afternoon, before the shift goes out on patrol. Sergeant Andrews will be there.'

'Fair enough.'

Collins found Clark in the canteen and slid into the seat opposite. Looking concerned, he said, 'What the hell have you been up to this time, Clarkee? Hicks is raging. He wants your balls for earrings. You'd better get in there and sort it out.'

'What's got his goat? I ain't done nowt.'

'I don't know. He just said, "Find the little sod".'

'OK. I'll go and sort the barmy git out. Don't drink me tea, and leave me bacon butty alone. I've only just started it. I'll be back in a tick.'

'What do you think I am? I can afford to buy me own sandwich.' Somehow, Collins kept his face straight as Clark strode across the canteen. As soon as he was out the door, Collins grabbed Clark's tea and the uneaten half of his bacon sandwich and headed for the Station House. He wanted to phone Agnes and he needed to start planning for the afternoon's presentation.

Collins left the Station House at ten to one. His plans for Thursday night tucked securely under his arm, he was already rehearsing in his mind the briefing he'd deliver in a little over an hour. He was halfway across the courtyard when he was hit with a wet chamois leather from behind. The slimy rag curled around his face and neck, and dirty water dripped down inside his collar. An instant later, Clark jumped on his back and wrapped his legs around his waist. 'Yow thieving, conniving little bastard. I'll learn yow to eat me bloody bacon sandwich.'

Faces quickly appeared at windows surrounding the courtyard. For the last hour, everyone in the station had known that Clark was looking for Collins and now the show was on they weren't going to miss it.

Hampered by the loose sheets under his arm, Collins grabbed Clark's legs and stared to run up and down like a bucking bronco trying to throw the smaller man off. Shouts of 'Ride him cowboy', 'Yee haa!' and even a fairly good rendition of Rawhide echoed around the yard. But whatever he did, the smaller man hung on. Digging his knees into Collins' side, Clark slapped him about the head and ears with the slimy rag, pulling his hair and slapping the younger man's backside.

Collins tried desperately to think what he could do to dislodge his unwanted jockey when he spotted the air pump. Unlatching it from the wall, he stuck the nozzle up Clark's left trouser leg and pushed the red button. A stream of cold air shot up Clark's leg and a force of 35 pounds per square inch rattled his underpants. Laughter cascaded down from the windows as Clark hung on, screaming obscenities and wringing the wet dirty rag out over Collins' head.

Collins had just completed three circuits of the yard when Superintendent Wallace appeared. Heads were quickly withdrawn and windows closed at the sight of him. Collins, head down, only just stopped short of ramming into the Super. Shamefaced, Clark slid off Collins' back.

'What the hell are you two playing at? This is a police station. Not a kids' playground.'

'Sorry, Sir,' said Clark. 'I was just showing Collins a new self-defence move.'

'Self-defence, my arse,' said Wallace, before his face broke into a broad grin. Holding out his hand, he said, 'Congratulations to you, Detective Sergeant Collins, and you, Detective Constable Clark. Both well-deserved appointments. I'll be seeing the Chief Constable this afternoon and I'll clear it with him. There'll be no problems.'

As he walked to his car, Superintendent Wallace was still smiling. There was nothing wrong with staff morale in his nick. That was for sure.

Turning to Collins, Clark held out his hand, 'Congratulations, yow Irish bog-dwelling git,' said Clark.

'And the same to you, you Black Country shite.'

A t five to two, Collins walked into the parade room and pinned a map of the Boundary Café Car Park and surrounding buildings to the noticeboard. There were six PCs present, including Alex Fletcher and Dave Harris, and one WPC, Marie Bolding. Clark took up his usual place at the back of the room, leaning against the door, where he was joined by Sergeant Andrews from West Bromwich. At two sharp, DCI Hicks walked into the room. Immediately, there was a scraping of chairs as all present stood to attention.

Taking his place beside Collins, he said, 'Take your seats, lads. Before I hand over to Collins to brief you, I have a bit of news. Sergeant York won't be returning to us. He's been snatched away by Sheldon's finest.' There was a good-natured round of booing from the assembly against Sheldon, who were the station's archrivals in the Police Football League and now they'd pinched York, the best goalie in the force. Hicks held up his hand for silence. 'I've asked Constable Collins to fill in as Acting Detective Sergeant.' A round of table thumping approved the news in traditional fashion. 'Constable Clark has also agreed to act as Detective Constable.' Before he could finish, the room erupted as hands were smashed down onto desks and cries of 'About bloody time' rang out around the room.

'Shut the fuck up, yow yampy sods,' said Clark. 'Anyone would think yow've got rid of me.'

As order was restored, Hicks said, 'OK, Sergeant Collins, over to you.'

For the next fifteen minutes, Collins outlined his plan for Thursday night and took questions from the floor. He made two amendments to the plan following suggestions from Clark and Andrews, and by 2.25 was back in the CID office.

Edgbaston, 15.30hrs

Cavendish lived in a four-storey block of private flats, set back from the main Hagley Road and surrounded by trees and well-tended flowerbeds. The main diamond-shaped flowerbed was crammed with a multitude of different daffodils. They danced in the light May breeze with abandon, as if they knew that their short celebration of colour would soon end. Collins' mind went back to Synge Street School in Dublin and Brother Anthony's attempt to share Wordsworth's delight upon coming across a swathe of golden daffodils tossing their heads beside the banks of Ullswater with a bunch of hormone-ravaged teenage boys.

Collins read the neatly typed names beside each flat number and rang number 24. A buzzer sounded and he pushed the door open. The hall had a parquet floor with a lift on the left and a stone and iron staircase at the far end of the hall.

Collins headed for the staircase. He counted eight flats on the ground floor, each separated by a small alcove in which either a vase of fresh flowers or a small statue rested. None of the flowers were withered. *I wonder how much they slap on the service charge for that,* he thought as he headed up the stairs.

Cavendish was waiting for him, leaning against the door post. He was wearing a white shirt, black slacks and matching leather slippers, a Dunhill cigarette hanging from the corner of his mouth. He looks like an older version of James Dean, thought Collins as the men shook hands.

'Come in, Michael. Can I call you that?'

'Of course. I think it might give our cover away if you called me Constable Collins.'

Cavendish smiled at the joke and led the way into a large lounge that overlooked the rear gardens. The room was decorated in muted greys and soft whites that contained a hint of blue. An expensive Grundig stereogram rested against one wall and was surrounded by purpose-built shelves housing maybe 500 LPs and an equal number of books, mostly plays.

Cavendish switched the gramophone off just as Finlandia was about to reach its great nationalistic outpouring of love and pride for the land of a thousand lakes. 'Can I get you a drink?' he asked.

'Tea or coffee would be fine,' said Collins and sat down in one of the Queen Anne armchairs placed each side of a fine cherry wood coffee table.

Moments later, Cavendish laid a tea tray on the coffee table. It contained a cup of tea, a plateful of chocolate biscuits and a large scotch. 'Just so I don't make a fool of myself, and now that we're alone, I need to confirm that you are straight, aren't you?'

'Yes,' laughed Collins. 'I've been with the same woman now for five years.'

'That doesn't prove anything, my love. I've known men who've been married thirty years and their wives have no idea what they mean when they say they are going out for a night with the boys.'

'Well, I'm not one of those.'

'OK. So what do you know about queers?'

– 51 –

'My landlady unofficially adopted a young lad five years ago who'd been thrown out of the house because he was a homosexual. I've got to know him pretty well, although he never discusses what he gets up to in detail. He's at university at the moment. And, of course, I've arrested a few for—'

'Lewd behaviour in a public place or gross indecency?'

'Yes. Other than that, I don't know many.'

'I wouldn't be so sure about that. There are bound to be a couple of queers in your life that you know nothing about. Probably in your station.' Cavendish paused briefly as he thought about what he was going to say next. 'What you need to understand is that the homosexual world is made up of a very mixed bunch. There are the raging queens like Richard, who don't give a flying fuck what people think of them, right down to some very unhappy men that find it impossible to accept they are queer. So you'll have no problem fitting in if you play the part of a youngish man who is new to the game and isn't really sure if he's queer or not. The only problem with that cover is that a lot of guys will see your uncertainty as both attractive and a challenge. Therefore, if you're happy with it, I suggest that we give the impression that you and I are an item.'

'And what would that entail?' asked Collins.

'Relax, my handsome prince. I promise not to grab your cock. Nothing more than a peck on the cheek, a lingering glance and occasionally holding my hand will be required. Do you think you can manage that without pulling away?'

'As long as you don't stick your tongue down me throat, I should be all right,' said Collins, with a smile.

Laughing, Cavendish said, 'I think I can resist your charms. Now, I assume you know a bit of the lingo, but there's some stuff you probably don't know.'

'When you're ready,' said Collins, taking out his notebook.

'Let's see. At a minimum, queen, basket, bitch, butch, camp, chicken, chicken hawk, cottaging, cruising, trade, drag, sisters, Lilly Law, slap, vegetarian and cod.'

'OK, I know most of those. But what's chicken and chicken hawk?'

'A chicken is a young queer and a chicken hawk is an older man who likes chickens.'

'Trade is gay prostitutes, but what's sisters, vegetarian and cod?'

'Trade doesn't always mean prostitutes. If someone is looking for trade, they are looking for business that may or may not involve cash or a bed for the night. Sisters are a couple of queens living together. A vegetarian is someone who won't suck a man off and cod refers to someone who is vile, although more often they're described as naff, which used to mean 'Not available for fucking.' Learn that lot and ask if you hear anything you don't understand – after all, you're supposed to be new to the scene. Any questions?'

'Not about the lingo, but I have been thinking. Aren't you taking a risk? I mean, you don't seem to hide the fact that you're a homosexual. Has no one ever tried to blackmail you?'

'It's a strange thing. I've come across a lot of right bastards who are queer. They'd steal the pennies off their dead mother's eyes, but I've never heard of a queer trying to blackmail another. It's just not done. If you tried it and word got out, you'd never get another shag in this country. I suppose it's a sort of group loyalty. We're all boys in the same band and you don't sacrifice a band member to the coppers or the great British public— ever.'

'But in this case you are willing to sacrifice a band member—'

'True. But you have to be a human before you can be queer and this murdering bastard is sub-human.' Mark took a sip of his drink before he said, 'You may know next to nothing about the queer world, but all I know about the police is what I've read in scripts. So, how do we go about this investigation?'

'I assume that homosexuals—'

'We call ourselves queers, so use that.'

'I assume that like most people, queers are creatures of habit and like to go to the same club or pub on a specific night. Is that right?'

'There's some truth in it, but you do get a lot of strangers in every bar who are just cruising. Maybe visiting or away from the wife or girlfriend for the weekend.'

'All right then. We visit the venues on the night or day the killer struck and spend a couple of hours in each. So it's the Manhattan Club this Friday, followed by the Toreador on Saturday and the pub in Stratford on Sunday afternoon.'

'Sounds good,' said Mark. 'Give me your address and I'll pick you up at eight thirty on Friday.'

Collins jotted down his address and telephone number. As he handed the details to Mark, he said, 'Lastly, you need to get my undercover story right, so write this down. I'm a Senior Claims Investigator at Knightsbridge Insurance. I usually work out of the London office, but I'm in Birmingham on secondment helping out on a big fraud investigation. My boss is Archie Moore and if anyone does phone Knightsbridge Insurance and asks to speak to Mr Moore, they'll be put through to a friend of mine at the Yard's Fraud Squad. Got that?'

'Yep, but there is one more thing I need to ask. Is the rest of your wardrobe as conservative as what you're wearing?'

'What's wrong with what I'm wearing?'

'Nothing, but it screams straight. I've got a lovely plum coloured velvet jacket and a matching shirt and cravat. We're about the same size – they should fit you a treat. Hang on and I'll get them.'

Moments later, Mark returned with a large paper bag with Rackhams printed on both sides. 'You'll look fantabulosa in this,' said Mark, in a very passable impersonation of Richard.

Collins took the bag and gave a quick curtsey.

Cavendish laughed, stepped forward and, with a sharp click of his heels, bowed. 'You're a natural, Detective Constable

Collins. Keep this up and you'll be a fully paid-up member of the band before you know it.'

Not in a month of Sundays, thought Collins, but remained quiet.

Handsworth 17.00hrs

Back at the station, Collins decided to check the internal post. It was a long shot, but there was a chance that the autopsy reports from Peter had arrived. WPC Marie Bolding, who would be on the Boundary Café stakeout, was sorting the last internal delivery of the day. 'Anything for me, Marie?'

'Yeah, I've just put a wodge of papers in your pigeon-hole. Do you mind if I ask you a question, Sarge?' Michael shook his head. 'Are you expecting trouble tomorrow night?'

'Not really. And even if there is, you'll be in an unmarked car with your "boyfriend" and by the time you get to the trucks it should all be over. Why? Are you concerned?'

'No, Sarge. More like I'm fed up being wrapped in cotton wool. It seems WPCs are only useful when it comes to looking after women, children and old men, but when something cracks off, we're put on a shelf out of harm's way. I joined up to be a copper, not a nursemaid.'

'Fair enough. I'll see if I can move you a bit closer to the action,' said Collins, picking up the reports.

Two minutes later, Collins stuck his head around the CID door. 'I'm going to push off, Sir, if that's OK. I want to go over the plans for tomorrow night one more time and have a read of the autopsy reports on the murders in Stratford and Wolverhampton.'

'How's that going?'

'Just starting, Sir. I'm going to visit each venue over the weekend with Mark Cavendish as my guide.'

'The TV guy?'

'Yes. He and his friends think it's one man.'

'And you?'

'I'm not sure yet.'

'Well, keep me in the loop. By the way, I've spoken to West and the CID in Wolverhampton and Stratford – they don't mind you having an unofficial mooch around, but if you find anything they want to know. West thinks you're wasting your time.'

'Fair enough, Boss. I'll do that.'

Birmingham, 18.00hrs

As he'd expected, Clark found the Toreador virtually empty when he walked into the lounge bar. A young man with blond curls, too much eyeliner and a very tight pair of slacks was polishing a wine glass half-heartedly. He saw Clark's uniform and steeled himself for the worst. Last time he spoke to a police officer, he'd spent a night in the cells and pissed blood for a week. No charges had been brought against him.

Clark flashed his warrant card and asked, 'Is Mr Everett about?'

'I think he's in the office. Would you like me to get him?'

Clark noticed that the man's hands were shaking. 'In a bit,' Clark said and smiled. 'Maybe yow can help me.'

'I'll try.'

'What's yowr name?'

'Tony Warren.'

'Well, Tony, were yow working Saturday 20 April?'

'You mean, the night Joe was killed?'

Clark nodded.

'Yes, I was here. It was a shame what happened. Joe was nice, real friendly, and no bother to anybody.'

'Did yow see him that night?'

'It was me who served him and the other guy. The killer. Makes me shiver to think about it. It does. I told all this to Sergeant Kaye and his Inspector.'

'I know,' lied Clark. 'I'm just doing some follow-up interviews. People sometimes remember things a few days later, after the shock has worn off. So tell me, what did yow see and hear?'

'It was about nine when the man came in. He was by himself. I think he had a half of mild. Then he did a quick reconnoitre of the place.'

'Reconnoitre?'

'That's what I call it,' said the young man, as he put the glass down and began to wrap the towel around his hand. 'I saw it in a film once where this spy comes into a bar and does a quick recce of the place and then sits watching the doors. Waiting. It was really good. I think Dirk Bogarde was in it.'

'Do yow get many spies in here?' asked Clark and smiled.

'No, but then how would I know?' and this time he responded to Clark's smile and visibly relaxed. 'We get a lot of one-timers in here. People just passing through. I divide them into the watchers and trackers. The watchers sit in a seat where they can be seen and wait for someone to approach them. Often they're a bit young and shy. The trackers are older, more confident. They come in, do a recce, and if they spot someone they like they'll make the first move.'

'And this guy was a tracker?'

'Definitely. He ignored one or two people who gave him the eye, but was all over Joe as soon as he walked in. Wasted no time at all asking him if he wanted a drink.'

'So he were confident then?'

'Oh yes. Definitely knew what he wanted.'

'What about the one's he dain't want. The ones he ignored. What were the differences between them and Joe?'

'That's a good question. The other copper didn't ask me that. Let me think. He wasn't at all interested in the queens. The two guys who tried to catch his eye were both about thirty. Good-looking, smartly dressed, thickset but not very tall. I mean, you couldn't describe them as tall, dark and handsome. More average height, dark and handsome. Is that any good?'

'Oh yeah, that's bostin. But just to be clear, yow'd describe Joe as tall dark and handsome?'

'Oh yes. Tall, dark, handsome and slim with a lovely bum.'

'Yow seem to remember this tracker very clearly. Was there something about him that caught yowr attention?'

'Sorry, love. Nothing extra special like a scar or a tattoo. I just noticed him because I fancied the arse off him. He was blond and had on a lovely dark blue, two-piece suit, with an open-neck white shirt. The shirt really set his tan off. I mean, a tan at this time of year! And it wasn't out of a bottle, I can tell you. He also had this gorgeous pair of American sunglasses. You know, the type the pilots wear.'

'Do yow remember anything he said to Joe?'

'It was pretty busy.'

'Yow didn't hear him introduce himself?'

The barman bowed his head, trying to remember what he'd seen and heard nearly two weeks earlier.

'Was it Joe who spoke first or the man?'

'No. Definitely the man. He asked Joe if he wanted a drink, or if he could buy him a drink. Something like that. I think the man then introduced himself because I can remember Joe saying something like, "My name's Joseph but my friends call me Joe."'

'But yow dain't hear the man's name?'

'Not that I can remember.'

'Listen, yow've been a big help. Was there anyone else about who might have noticed the man?'

'Simon and Mr Everett were in. But Simon spent a lot of the night in the cellar trying to sort out a problem with the beer lines and Mr Everett was having his weekly free shag from Gordon, our current resident tom, in his office between eight- thirty and nine-thirty. Regular as clockwork, that man.'

'Gordon?'

Tony leant forward and, in a conspiratorial whisper, said, 'Mr Everett doesn't like prozzies working in the pub. Male or female. Attracts police attention, he says, and that frightens off customers, but he knows that some customers require the services of a professional at times. You know, a bit like the fourth emergency service. "Which service do you require, sir? Police, fire, ambulance or wank?"'

Clark smiled at the image.

'Anyhows, he allows Wilkee to run his pair of pit ponies from the pub and charges him £25 a week for the pleasure. He also allows one nice young man who's on the game to work free from the pub in return for—'

'A bit of rumpy pumpy and Gordon is his current squeeze?'

'Got it in one, officer.'

'Yow weren't here when the first lad was killed?'

'No, but I've got the number of one of the barmen who was. He's a friend of mine. It was him who tipped me the wink that he was leaving and that there would be a job going. Here, I'll write it down for you. Tell him I sent you.'

'Just one last thing. Yow mentioned Wilkee. Would that be Wilkee Burns?'

'That's him. You know him?'

'Oh yes. Me and Wilkee go back a long way.'

Clark shook hands with Tony and headed towards the stairs behind the bar for a meeting with Mr Everett.

Ten minutes later, Clark was back in the bar. Mr Everett had confirmed he'd been in his office from just before 8.30 until about 9.40 on Saturday 20th April. According to him, he'd been trying to reconcile the pub's bank statement with the cash book. Unfortunately, he'd made three incorrect entries, which he had to find and correct before he was able to agree the balance.

Clark commiserated with him and expressed his admiration at Mr Everett's patience and stamina to keep looking for his cock-up when a lesser men would have given up after one try.

Everett also confirmed that he'd been ill and away from work when the first murder had been committed. He was happy to provide the names and contact details of the two barmen who had been at work that night, but assured Clark the police already had them on file.

Back in the bar, a few office workers were stopping by for a quick drink before heading home. He waved at Tony and was almost out the door when the young man rushed after him and grabbed him by the arm. 'It was Ron or John. That's what he called himself. I'm sure it was. Is that any use to you?'

'Yow bet it is, lad, but yow sure about it?'

'Absolutely. I couldn't hear it clearly, but I'd swear on a stack of Bibles that he said Ron or John.'

Handsworth, 18.00 hrs

Agnes was in the lounge watching the BBC 6 o'clock news when Sheba came trotting in from the kitchen. Her normally folded over ears were standing upright – a sure sign that her master was nearly home. Barking once, she took up position eight feet from the front door and sat down, her jet-black tail bouncing off the wooden floor.

As Collins opened the door, 28 pounds of Staffordshire Bull Terrier launched itself at him. The first time she'd done this five years earlier, she'd managed to catch Collins in the chest with her front legs and his groin with her back legs. He'd been propelled out of the front door only to find himself lying on the path in agony with Sheba licking his face. Now, he had his reactions down to a fine art and caught the dog in his arms before she could actually hit him. Unfortunately, he hadn't found a way to stop her slobbering all over him.

When she heard the usual kerfuffle, Agnes emerged from the lounge. She barely gave Collins time to place Sheba on the floor before she flung her arms around this neck, kissed him on the lips and said, 'I've booked a table at The Golden Dragon for 7.30. We're going to celebrate your promotion.'

'But I need to—'

'But me no buts. We're going. I didn't get all dressed up to sit at home. Now, go and have a shower and change.'

Still holding her hand, Collins stepped back and admired the view, 'You most certainly have got dressed up. Do you think there's any chance that I might undress you later?'

'We'll see. It depends how badly behaved you are.'

Forty minutes later, Collins walked into the lounge to find Agnes reading the autopsy reports of all four victims. Sheba curled up at her feet.

'Not pleasant reading,' he said.

'No, they're not,' she replied, with that distant look in her eyes that told Collins she was trying to decipher the message that lay between and beneath the words she was reading.

'Are we still going?' he asked.

Looking up, Agnes smiled and said, 'Of course we are, but I want you to tell me all about the investigation over dinner.'

Collins smiled to himself. When he had brought the files home, he'd known Agnes would be unable to resist looking at them – and that once she had, she'd want to be involved in the investigation. Over the years, Agnes had helped him analyse data and information from several cases. Initially, Hicks had objected to a civilian looking at police files, but Agnes' unofficial contribution to so many cases was too valuable to ignore. Hicks now consoled himself with the knowledge that she still enjoyed Most Secret clearance from MI5, and turned a blind eye to it.

Even at the age of forty-nine, Agnes drew admiring glances from the male customers of The Golden Dragon and envy from the women present as she walked confidently through the restaurant. Her knee-length, black, silk and cotton dress, with an embroidered red dragon on the right shoulder showed off her slim five foot nine frame to perfection and the matching white pearl necklace and earrings made a striking contrast to her short auburn hair and emerald green eyes. As always at such moments, Collins found it hard to believe that this beautiful, elegant, intelligent woman had chosen to love him.

Handsworth, 23.00hrs

When they returned home, Agnes' plans to review the autopsy reports and Collins' hopes of ending the evening on a more romantic note were destroyed when the phone rang.

Agnes picked it up, but before she could say anything, a familiar voice said, 'Agnes, this is Mary, sorry to call so late, but I have another customer for you.'

Agnes was used to such calls at all times of the day and night, and if Mary was calling then it had to be important. 'No need to apologise. What's the problem?'

'One of Toby Drew's girls has been badly beaten. She won't tell me who did it. She's really scared of something or someone.'

'When did it happen?'

'Last night. She'd been holed up alone for 20 hours before another of the girls called round. Anyhows, Paige brought her to my house. She thought it would be safer.'

'OK, I'll be there in about thirty minutes.' Hanging up, Agnes turned to Collins and grimaced. 'Sorry, Michael. That was Mary. I have to go out.'

'Serious?'

'It sounds like it. A girl's been badly beaten but won't say who did it.'

'Probably her pimp.'

Agnes nodded in agreement, 'I won't be long.'

'I'll wait up for you.' Collins didn't bother to offer to drive Agnes because he knew she would want to meet the woman alone, without any men present. Only when she'd won the woman's trust would she suggest that they come and stay with her until they were well again. Not all wanted to come. Many of the women had children and although they were welcome to bring them, problems with schools and other family members often made it difficult.

At the moment, there was only one guest in the house. However, Collins knew how quickly that figure could swell, especially in the hot sweaty summer months when drink and high temperatures led to frayed tempers, sexual frustration and violence. As Collins climbed the stairs to ready the yellow guest room, he heard Agnes drive away.

It was nearly 2am when Agnes returned with Margaret Lewis. She was eighteen, nineteen tops, five foot two, and maybe eight stone. Collins couldn't tell if she was pretty or not, or what colour her eyes were. There was too much bruising and swelling for such judgements. All he was sure of was that her sandy blonde hair was still streaked with blood.

By way of introductions, Agnes said, 'Margaret, this is Michael. He's here to help protect you. So you've no need to worry about Drew and his thugs.'

She squinted through her swollen eyes at Collins and nodded. 'Can I have that bath now please and go to bed?'

'Of course you can. Would you like Michael to carry you up the stairs?'

For a moment she hesitated, then nodded.

As gently as he could, Collins slipped his left arm around the girl's back and under her armpit, and his right arm behind her knees. Bending, he picked her up and moved slowly up the stairs with Agnes following behind. At the bathroom door, he set her down and stepped back, smiled and winked at her. A flicker of a tiny smile started to appear, but was squashed by the pain of swollen lips. Still, it was enough for Collins. Given a bit of time, Margaret would be OK. She still had some spirit in her.

Placing her right palm on Collins' chest, Agnes said, 'You should go to bed. I'll be in shortly,' and kissed him on the lips.

When Agnes finally did make it to bed, it was nearly 4.30 and Collins was fast asleep. Quietly, Agnes undressed and slid in beside him. Her last thought before she fell into a deep sleep was, *Well that was some night of celebration.*

Thursday 2nd May 1968, 11.00hrs

Handsworth

Michael slept in on Thursday morning. He had no idea when he would finish that night. It would all depend on what time the hijackers made their move. The kitchen was empty and he hummed under his breath as he prepared a bowl of porridge. Taking the boiling pan from the stove, he sprinkled a handful of currants into the bubbling mix before he put it back on the cooker. While he waited, he made a pot of tea and flicked through The Times.

He was pleased to see that Albion had continued their good run by beating West Ham 3-0, with Astle scoring another hat trick. That was seven goals in five days for the King. Maybe Clark was right and this was Albion's year. He sighed at the thought of the pass-by-pass description of the match that Clark would force him to endure later in the day. Still, it could be worse, he thought. If they'd lost, I'd have to put up with him moaning non-stop for the next week.

He was on his fourth spoonful of porridge when Agnes came in, kissed him on the top of the head and sat down opposite. She was carrying the murder files that Katie had given him, along with a sheaf of handwritten notes and a magnifying glass.

Collins raised his head and looked at her. She was dressed for work in a grey skirt, white blouse with mother-of-pearl buttons and a black cardigan. She wore no make-up, yet Collins was still struck by how vibrant she looked. 'I see you've been busy, Sherlock. Find anything?'

'I can't be certain but I think so.'

Collin eyes sparkled and he leant forward, 'Tell me about it.'

'I think it's one man you're looking for, but I need you to ring around for me and check something.'

'Go on,' said Collins, his porridge forgotten.

Agnes laid two photos on the table. The first was of Daniel Stokes, the other of Joseph. Both men were lying on the autopsy table, naked, their arms resting a few inches away from their sides. 'Notice anything?'

Collins picked up each photo in turn and studied it carefully. Both men had suffered a sustained and prolonged attack, but Collins could see nothing to make him think that one man was responsible for both killings. 'I can't see anything—'

'Here use this,' said Agnes and pushed her ancient magnifying glass across the table.

Collins picked up the photo of Joseph and examined the picture again. After perhaps ten seconds, he raised his head and smiled. 'Well, I'll be damned.'

'Quite possibly, but tell me what you see?'

'The skin on his wrist is lighter than the rest of his hand, from wearing a watch.'

'And?'

'There was no watch in Joseph's list of belongings.' Collins picked up the picture of Daniel and looked for the circle of pale skin. There it was again. 'I take it there was no watch listed in his belongings either?'

'You would be right.'

'What about Alan Green and Perter Marshal?'

'There's no indication they wore a watch. But can you check if any other personal items were taken?'

'Will do.'

Agnes stood up and crossed behind Collins. Bending down, she kissed him on the side of the neck. A tremor ran through his body but before he could reach for her, Agnes straightened. 'Right, I'm off to Bull Street. I won't see you before tonight, so take care of yourself and tell Clarkee not to take any risks. Not with the baby on its way.'

As Collins was washing up, Sarah, whose husband liked to use her as a punch bag, entered the kitchen. She was five foot five, thin with mousey blonde hair and a friendly nature. One of life's optimists, she always looked for what was best in people – even the bastard of a husband she'd been married to for two years. In that time, she'd had to stay with Agnes seven times. The latest beating had been the worst, but after her eight-day stay, the latest batch of bruises were fading fast.

'Morning, Michael. Was that Agnes who just left?'

'Yeah. Did you want her?'

'It can wait. I just wanted to tell her that I'd be off tomorrow.'

'Going back to hubby?'

'No. Agnes finally convinced me that he ain't never going to change. Me dad's picking me up, I'm going home.'

'Good for you. Does your hubby know?'

'Oh yeah. When I asked to come home, me dad wanted to know what was up. I told him what's been going on for the past two years, and he and a couple of his mates went round and had a word with Bill. He'll be in hospital for at least a week.'

'Well, good for your dad and his mates. Tell him I'll buy him and his friends a pint anytime.'

Handsworth, 15.00hrs

As soon as he arrived at the Station, Collins picked up the police files that had arrived from Stratford and Wolverhampton, located the contact details for the victim's next of kin and jotted them down. Finally, he looked for any reference to a close male friend and did the same.

Twenty-five minutes later, he had confirmed that Alan Green, the second victim, didn't have a wristwatch but always wore a pocket watch and fob that his grandfather had left him. The watch had been mass-produced by Smith and Sons of London in 1913 and his grandfather had carried it with him throughout the First World War. It had not been returned to the family.

Peter Marshall's mother confirmed that her son did not have a watch as he didn't want to be a slave to time. However, she did ask if Collins had managed to find her son's signet ring with the initials PM engraved on it.

A quick call to Patrick confirmed that Daniel had owned a self-winding Tissot watch with a day/date facility and made of stainless steel. Engraved on the reverse was *To Daniel, with love on your 21st. Mom.*

Finally, he phoned Tom Laurence, who confirmed he'd given Joe a gold plated Omega Seamaster watch with a crosshairs dial and date function for his 21st birthday after Joe had seen it on a trip to the Jewellery Quarter.

Collins sat back in his chair, fingers laced behind his head. Not for the first time, he marvelled at Agnes' eye for detail. Whatever you got up to at that place in Bletchley, Mrs Winters, they trained you well, he thought. As soon as Agnes had mentioned Joseph's missing watch, Collins had known that she was onto something. The killer, and Collins was now certain that it was just one man, collected souvenirs from his victims. *He likes to relive what he's done. Probably wanks off thinking about it*, Collins thought.

Unfortunately, while he and Agnes might feel that the evidence was compelling, it wasn't conclusive, and Collins knew that until such time as it was there was no chance that a joint investigation would be launched. Too many police officers had gone on record saying that there was no connection between the killings. No one would acknowledge that they'd cocked it up unless there was conclusive proof.

Collins wondered what, if anything, Clark had uncovered at the Toreador the previous day, but he'd have to wait until he got back from the hospital. Ruth had an appointment and as far as Clark was concerned, everything else took second place to the needs and welfare of Ruth and her babbie. Collins found it strangely moving to see how his friend, the man of action, was so protective of his wife and their unborn child.

I've earned a cuppa, he thought and, slipping his jacket on, he headed for the canteen. On the short walk, he exchanged greetings with four people. None of them stopped to chat or even smile. They looked serious and tension showed in their eyes and in one instance, he could see the damp patches under a man's arms.

Collins had always found it strange that people should get tense in such situations, when his own feelings were more akin to excitement and anticipation – a bit like how he used to feel before an important hurling match back home. The planning and preparation had been done. The opposition's strengths and weaknesses had been identified and now he was going out confident that he'd be on the winning side. Besides, they had Clark in their team. What could go wrong? Sure, there was more chance of getting hurt in a game of hurly than from a bunch of amateur robbers.

Alice had just finished washing up after the lunchtime rush and was enjoying a quiet cigarette and a cuppa in the deserted canteen, when Collins walked in. 'If yous looking for grub, yous missed it. There's only some curled-up sandwiches left.'

'I'm just after a cuppa and a Kit Kat.'

'Well yous in luck. I just made one,' said Alice, pointing at the teapot resting on the counter.

Collins poured his own tea, picked up a Kit Kat and left a shilling on the counter before joining Alice for a chat. Running his thumb down the silver paper, he opened his Kit Kat and offered the woman a finger of chocolate.

'No thanks, love. I have to look after me figure or else me hubby complains that I'm losing me sex appeal.' Collins smiled at Alice's self-deprecation. At 5' 1", she weighed at least 13 stone and had a figure like a Doric column. 'Anyway, what's up? Got something on tonight, have you?'

'Now, why do you think we'd have something on?'

'Maybe because everyone is a bit quieter than usual or it could be because there's a queue for the lavs.'

'You should be a detective, Alice. You miss nothing.'

'Only me waistline, love. Only me waistline. But listen, you take care out there and look after me chicks or you'll have me to answer to. I don't want any of 'em hurt.'

'I'll try me best.'

'And look after yourself, too.'

Collins was certain that time had actually slowed down as the afternoon dragged on and tension rose among those on the job tonight – which was just about everyone on the afternoon shift. How any shift that ran from 14.00 to 22.00 hrs could be called an afternoon shift had always puzzled him. In all likelihood, nothing would happen until after the night shift had come on duty, but the men had to be in position well before then if they were to avoid attracting attention. This meant that the show belonged to those on afternoons.

He had tried to fill his time writing up reports, catching up on mail and memos, and doing some much-needed filing, but it was a half-hearted effort. He was thinking about sharpening every pencil in his drawers when Clark stuck his head around the door and said, 'I could murder a cuppa.' Collins left his pencils for another day and headed once more to the canteen, which was now nearly full with most of the afternoon shift enjoying a full fry-up before the action started. Collins made a mental note not to use the toilets on this side of the nick for the rest of the shift.

Collins waited until he and Clark both had a mug of tea and a couple of rounds of toast in front of them, before asking, 'Did you get anything from the staff at the Toreador?'

'Well, I met a very nice boy named Tony. He really likes

arses. He seems to remember them better than faces. Yow'd get on really well with him.'

'Please tell me he remembered the killer's arse?'

'Oh yes.' Clark spent the next ten minutes outlining what he'd learnt from the barman.

'So what you're saying is the killer likes young men who are tall, dark, handsome and slim. Not much for an afternoon's work,' said Collins, disappointed.

'Oh, I don't know. I got the bastard's name as well.'

'You what?'

'Using me innate Black Country charm and deep understanding of the homosexual mind, I discovered that the killer called himself either Ron or John. Tony couldn't be sure with all the noise.'

'You wind-up merchant. What else did you find out?'

'I've got the names and contacts of the barmen who were working when Daniel Stokes was picked up. And as a bonus prize, I got Wilkee Burns. He was in the joint the night Joe was picked up, along with a couple of his lady friends.'

'That little shite.'

'The same – but he's a hard-working shite, always on the lookout for the—'

'Next potential punter.'

'Yow got it in one. He'll have given everyone in the joint the once-over. Better than having a copper as a witness.'

'You should also talk to Rita and Marilyn. It's a pound to a penny they were the toms with him. They may have seen something.'

'Ain't wi going together?'

'Na. Last time I saw him, I sort of broke his nose. Best if you handle it alone.'

'You broke his nose and dain't tell me?'

'It was an accident.'

'I bet it were. Anyway, that's no excuse, yow coming and that's it. I need protection.'

'From Wilkee?'

'Na from Rita and Marilyn. Them's a right pair of vicious bitches. Yow know they once auditioned for Hammer Pictures but they were turned down. Too frightening.'

'OK, we'll do it Saturday. There'll be too much on tomorrow.'

'Fair enough. How did yow break Wilkee's nose?'

Collins ignored the question and said, 'You know what we should do on Saturday as well? Go and see the two barmen who were working when Daniel was killed.'

'OK, but I want to know how yow broke the snidey little git's nose.'

'Don't you want to hear about the watches?'

'What watches?'

Handsworth/West Bromwich Border, 22.40hrs

Clark left the Woodman pub ten minutes after closing time. As he stepped into the soft rain, he pulled his cap down and turned his collar up. At 5 foot 5 inches and wearing two jumpers and a donkey jacket, he was the best replacement that Collins could find for the short, fat, balding, sixty-year-old truck driver who had been given an unexpected night off.

Collins watched from inside the darkened Boundary Café as Clark stumbled slightly, recovered and walked on as if he wasn't entirely sure where the ground was. He should be on the stage, thought Collins.

Clark reached out to steady himself against the blue brick wall that housed the turnstiles for entry to the Brummie Road End at the Hawthorns. Slowly, he pushed himself away from the wet, cold bricks and meandered across the pavement.

Collins kept half an eye on Clark as he checked once more that everyone was in position. Earlier that night, Clark had reversed the truck to within 8 feet of the low brick wall that separated the Café's dirt and cinder car park from its neighbour, the Bradford Bakery. As he jumped down from the cab, he'd banged once on the side of the trailer to alert the two police officers inside that he was leaving.

Twenty yards away, on the other side of the wall, Hicks sat in an unmarked police car with PC Dave Harris in the bakery's car park. The bakery's night shift had come on at 10pm and the police car was just one of nearly a hundred parked there for the night. The bakery's bright lights illuminated Clark's truck and the smell of baking bread drifted across the wall, making the waiting police long for a fresh cup of tea and a piece of toast. Or better still, one of the bakery's doughnuts, which were freely dispensed to any beat bobby by Joey, a huge good-natured Jamaican, whose sole job at the bakery was to inject each doughnut with jam.

Clark was halfway across the road when a Land Rover with a raised and reinforced bumper had to brake hard to avoid hitting him. The driver sounded his horn and Clark responded with a two-fingered salute. Ten yards further on, the Land Rover turned into the car park and drove towards the side of the café furthest from the bakery. Once there, PC Robert Hughes and WPC Marie Bolding did a U-turn and pointed the car's nose towards the main road. Anyone seeing the vehicle would assume that the occupants were enjoying an intimate moment or two.

With the pieces now in place, Collins knew that all he could do was wait.

They arrived sooner than Collins had expected. At a little after 11.30, two Ford Anglias turned onto the car park. Both did a slow circuit of the ground before drawing up side by side, no more than six feet from Clark's front bumper. If he tried to escape now, he'd have to drive over both cars.

'They're here,' said Collins into his radio. 'No one jumps the gun. Wait for my signal.' As he spoke, a worm of doubt started to borrow into his mind, Why have they got two cars for just four people?

He got his answer when two men jumped out from each car, leaving the two drivers behind. Three of the men were carrying pickaxe handles, the preferred weapon for most armed robbers. Collins couldn't make out what the fourth was holding, maybe a crowbar or something of similar size. Just then, a misaligned headlight from the main road briefly illuminated the four men. Collins felt a cold hand grab his guts and squeeze.

'The fourth guy is carrying,' he said, calmly, into his radio, 'looks like a sawn-off.' His mind was now working overtime. DCI Hicks was the senior officer on-site but he was in no position to see the shooter, so it was Collins' decision. Should he throw the light switch and have everyone jump the gang now or let it play out? If I give the go-ahead, that lunatic could start shooting and we'll have a bloodbath, he thought. No, safer to let Clark handle him.

'Are you going to let Clarkee deal with it?' asked Andrews.

Collins nodded and pressed send on his radio, 'Everyone waits until Clarkee disarms the sod and I give the go.'

A small, grim smile appeared on Andrews' face. This was going to be interesting.

Two men took up position each side of Clark's cab. Shotgun smacked the driver's side-window with the barrel of his gun. A bleary-eyed Clark looked up from his makeshift cot behind the seats, saw the shotgun and immediately raised his hands.

'Open up, old man, and nowt will happen to yow.'

Clark stumbled into the driver's seat and fumbled for the door handle.

'Hurry up, yow bleeding cretin, or I'll blow yow and the fucking window.'

'Don't. Please don't,' shouted Clark and opened the door.

Shotgun reached into the cab, grabbed Clark by the jumper

and pulled him out. Clark landed hard on the uneven ground and a loud groan escaped his lips.

'Gimme the keys,' demanded Shotgun.

Swaying unsteadily Clark climbed slowly to his feet. Finding the keys, he held them out to Shotgun, a look of defeat and shame on his face.

Shotgun's right index finger was still on the trigger, with the barrel of the gun resting against his leg. As he reached for the keys with his left hand, Clark dropped them, grabbed the man's hand and twisted the wrist and arm hard to the left. Shotgun's head and body were immediately pushed downwards. His left arm was now straight, elbow locked. In one fluid motion, Clark brought his forearm down on the exposed joint. The crack of breaking bone sounded like the fracture of ice in the cold blackness of a winter night. Shotgun howled in agony. His screams grew even shriller when he saw a jagged slice of bone sticking through the sleeve of his jacket.

Still twisting, Clark forced Shotgun onto his back on the ground. Despite the pain, the youth tried to raise the barrel of his gun and fire. Clark saw it coming and stamped down on the trigger guard, breaking one finger and crushing two others. Less than four seconds had elapsed since he had dropped the keys.

Clark heard the lads from the back of the van jump out and, from the corner of his eye, he saw Collins and Andrews heading in his direction. Looking at Clark and what he'd done to Shotgun, the hijacker in front of him dropped the pickaxe handle and started to run towards the Anglias. Collins cut him off. Out of desperation, the man swung a wild, slow right hook. Collins blocked with his right forearm and pushed the blow over his head. It left the man's stomach and chest wide open. Collins raised his knee to waist high and snapped out a straight front kick into the man's solar plexus. Over the years he'd practised the kick thousands of times under Clark's watchful eye and it gave him enormous satisfaction when the ball of his foot connected perfectly with its target and lifted the man a couple of inches off the floor. Air left the man's lungs in one loud gush. Unable to breathe and unable to cry out, he dropped to his knees and fell forward onto his shoulder.

Looking up, Collins saw the Land Rover swing out from the shadows and head for the parked Anglias. Neither driver saw Hughes coming before he rammed into the passenger door of the first Anglia and pushed it into the side of the second car. The first driver was trapped, but the second jumped from his damaged car and started to run towards the far end of the car park. His aim was to reach the trucks and try and get into the backyard of Webley and Scott's, the gun manufacturers. If he made it into their grounds, it would be easy to escape onto Park Lane and then lose himself in the Handsworth cemetery that edged much of the lane.

Before he'd covered five yards, WPC Bolding was out of the Land Rover and chasing after him. Within seconds, she had closed the gap and, to the amazement of her watching colleagues, launched herself headfirst at the man. Her shoulder hit him behind his knees as her arms encircled his legs in a perfect rugby tackle. He went sprawling in the dirt. Twisting onto his back, he tried to free his legs and kicked out. Still holding his legs with her left arm, Bolding freed her right arm and slammed her clenched fist, hammer-like, into the man's groin. She heard a loud 'Oh!' from her colleagues as she scrambled up the man's body. Sitting astride his waist, she punched him in the mouth and all the fight left him. By the time Collins and Andrews had arrived, Marie was sitting on the man's chest examining her grazed knees and, worse, her torn tights and ripped skirt.

'Sod it,' she said, 'I only put these on today. That's another 2/11 down the drain.'

Holding out his hand, Collins pulled Marie to her feet. 'Remind me to take you along to the next punch-up I'm in.'

Marie blushed with a mixture of pride and embarrassment

at the comment. She wasn't used to such praise from male colleagues.

Seconds later, they were joined by Clark and Fletcher.

'Did we get them all?' asked Collins.

'Yep, all six of them,' said Fletcher.

'Including Keating?' asked Collins.

'He weren't with them,' said Clark.

'He wasn't?'

'No,' said Clark, as an unspoken message passed between the two men.

Collins took a deep breath. *Now wasn't the time to say anything about Keating, but what the hell's was he playing at?* he thought. *First he gets the numbers wrong, then he forgets to warn us about the gun and finally his brother doesn't make the job. I need to have a chat with Mr Richard bloody Keating.*

Fletcher and Clark pulled Marie's catch to his feet and they headed back to the café. Hicks had called for the Black Maria parked on Oxhill Road and an ambulance. Shotgun was still moaning in agony and swearing revenge on the little cunt that broke his arm. While they waited, someone suggested they get the kettle on. Marie started to move towards the kitchen when Clark shouted out, 'Hang on a sec, killer. I'll give yow a hand.' It was the second time that night that Marie had blushed with pleasure. For the first time since she'd joined the station, she felt like one of the lads.

While they waited for the police van, Hicks called Collins over. 'Why did you go ahead with the op when you saw the gun?'

'In a word, Clark. I knew he could handle that toe-rag, gun or no gun. If I'd scrambled everyone, the eejit could have started shooting.'

'Good call,' said Hicks.

Collins nodded, a flicker of a smile on his lips. Turning, both men watched for the arrival of the Black Maria and the ambulances. Collins suddenly felt exhausted and spent. Every bone, muscle and sinew in his body was suddenly demanding sleep, as the adrenalin he'd been running on all day finally ran out. He decided that it was bed for him. The Custody Sergeant had enough to charge the moronic idiots with armed robbery and they could cool their heels in a cell or hospital ward overnight. Statements could wait until tomorrow.

Friday 3rd May 1968, 10.00hrs

Handsworth

A refreshed Collins walked into the CID room, looking forward to the day ahead. To avoid disturbing Agnes, he'd slept in his old room. She had already left for a meeting at Friends House, Euston, when he finally rolled out of bed at 8.10. He'd have to wait until tonight before he could tell her about the watches and the killer's name.

He'd barely had time to take his mac off when Marie limped into the room, her left knee heavily bandaged. 'That'll teach you to go diving around in car parks,' he said.

'It's the bloody bandage that's the problem, not me knee. The ambulance man insisted on taking me to A&E. I think he fancied me. I had to get a taxi home.'

'Well, I don't want you out of pocket. Put a petty cash chitty in for your skirt, tights and taxi fare. The Inspector will sign it.'

'Thanks, Sarge.'

'Anyway, what do you want? I was just about to grab Clark and interview our would-be robbers.'

'A couple of messages. West Brom nick called. Their Desk Sergeant needs to talk to you. Sounded urgent. And Sergeant O'Driscoll asked if you'd get over to The Soho Chippy this morning. Seems that Mr Vassiliou had his shop vandalised again, but O'Driscoll thinks there might be more to it than that.'

'OK. Is Clarkee in?'

Marie nodded.

'See if he fancies a walk before we get stuck into the Great Train Robbers.'

Collins dialled the number for the West Bromwich Station

from memory. The phone was answered on the third ring. 'Sergeant Andrews.'

'Hi, John. It's Collins. You left a message for me.'

'Yeah, thanks for calling back. I enjoyed last night. Clark were at his best.'

'True, but Marie was the star of the show.'

'She had the energy, but Clark had the experience. Just remind me not to try it on with her next Christmas. Anyways, to more serious matters. We found yowr name and number in a woman's pocket.'

Collins felt a cold chill spread through his entire body and was already blaming himself before he asked, 'How did she do it?'

'She took a load of pills, then hung herself. She may even have been standing on the chair when she passed out. We'll never know. It looks like she was beaten up pretty badly a few days ago.'

'She was,' Collins quickly outlined how he had first met Jean Rogers and his subsequent visit to the hospital.

'Christ,' said Andrews. 'She must have been in one hell of a state. Poor cow. She didn't mention anything about suicide to yow?'

'No, not directly. She said she knew what she had to do. She had to get away from it all. Her exact words are in the statement I took. I should have known what she meant. How could I have missed it?'

'Yow can't blame yourself, Mickey. Yowm not a mind reader.'

'Look, I've got a few things on me plate this morning. I'll get my report copied and I'll bring it up late this afternoon, OK?'

'Fair enough.'

He'd only been at his desk for ten minutes and already Collins could feel the day turning on him. He should have spoken to the doctors about Jean. Checked if she'd seen a shrink or at least called her the day she got out. 'Sod it,' he exclaimed and slapped his hand on the desk.

'Sod what?' asked Clark from the door, picking an imaginary piece of lint off his immaculate uniform. This would be the last time he'd wear it before his transfer to CID on Monday.

'Me and my stupidity.'

'That old chestnut. What have yow cocked up this time?'

'I'll tell you on the way to the chippy.'

Clark listened without interrupting as the two men walked along Thornhill Road. Turning onto Soho Road, Collins stopped for breath and Clark jumped in. 'Yow know, Mickey, yow have the most overdeveloped conscience of any person I know. It doesn't matter how small a part yow have in something, if it goes wrong yow blame yourself. I've seen it in other left-handers. I reckon that church of yours must inoculate yow with guilt when yam about five. That way they can keep yow under their thumb for life.'

Collins tried to interrupt, but Clark ignored him. 'Yow got nowt to reproach yourself over. The hospital should have picked up that she were suicidal and if the professionals missed it, how the bloody hell were yow supposed to see it?'

'But I spoke to her.'

'Fair enough, but you dain't know her. It's OK for yow to feel bad about it, but it weren't yowr fault. It were her choice. She could have called yow and she dain't. Her choice. Her responsibility. Now, come on. Let's see what the local rockers have been up to this time.'

Soho Road, Handsworth 10.30hrs

The Soho Chippy occupied a prime spot on the main road. It was the last in a small row of shops that ran from Minerva Street to Cleopatra Road. Situated near the Palladium Cinema, the technical college, the fire station and Thornhill Road nick, it had a ready-made supply of customers from midday to around 2.30pm and again from 5pm until 11pm.

Mr Andreas Vassiliou and his formidable wife, Mercedes,

had arrived in Birmingham in 1946, bought a rundown chippy from an old couple and had quickly established a reputation for good chips, fresh fish and large portions. Until recently, the only contact they'd with the police was when the odd customer, who'd had one too many, got in a fight over a girl or some geezer tried to jump the queue. However, recently they'd had a couple of run-ins with a gang of rockers.

With the shop shut up, Collins and Clark walked down the side entry and knocked on the side door. After a short wait, a large woman with black hair and arms that could strangle a pig opened the door. Turning, she shouted, 'Andreas, it's your worthless policemen friends.' Turning back, she said, 'Come in, misters policemen, and wipe yours feet two times.'

Collins and Clark followed orders and wiped their feet on both the mat outside and inside the door. The back room was where the chips, fish and other food was prepared for deep fat frying and it was spotless. Every surface was gleaming; every piece of chrome sparkling. Mrs Vassiliou was wearing a white coat that would have made a great advert for Omo.

The same could not be said for her husband. He appeared from the rear stairs unshaven, wearing a rumpled pair of trousers, a less-than-clean shirt and a jumper with egg stains on the front. He was also sporting a cut and swollen lip, and a bad gash and bruise to his left temple. He moved like a man who was hurting all over.

'Bad night, Andreas? asked Collins.

'Yes, my friend. A bad night, as you say. I just got up.' The big man walked on unsteady legs to the only chair in the room and sat down with a thud.

'Yow look like you been in the wars. Have yow had the doc take a look at that bruise on yowr noggin?'

'He's a brave big man,' said Mrs Vassiliou. 'He won't go to the hospital. I tell him next time they come, they kill him. Serve him right.'

'Who's going to kill you Andreas, the rockers?' asked Collins.

Andreas remained silent. 'Tell him,' shouted Mrs Vassiliou. 'For the love of the Blessed Virgin, tell him.' Tears appeared in the woman's eyes and when she next spoke, her voice was pleading and full of fear. 'Please, Andreas, tell him.'

Andreas hauled himself out of his chair and put a giant arm around his wife's shoulders. She suddenly looked small in comparison to this lumbering giant of a man. 'All right, I tell them.'

'Everything?' she asked.

'Everything. Make us some coffee, Mitera.' Looking towards Collins, he said, 'Come, we talk upstairs.'

The living room that Andreas led Collins and Clark into was as spotless as the room they had just left. The room was furnished for comfort, with a large settee, two comfortable armchairs, and rugs and mats covering much of the expensive carpet. A large picture of Athens by night hung over the fireplace.

Andreas eased himself into the armchair. Collins watched and guessed that whoever had worked him over had probably cracked a couple of ribs. Once settled, the big man's story came out in such a rush that Clark had trouble keeping up with it for his notes. Andreas didn't even slow down when his wife placed a tray of coffee on the dining table and handed around plates, which she then filled with two types of homemade cake.

When he finally stopped, Clark said, 'Right, just so's I get this right. Yowr saying that about ten weeks ago a couple of rockers came in and caused a bit of bother pushing customers about and smashing your jar of pickled eggs and the front panel of your counter?'

'Yes.'

'Then yow had a phone call from someone saying that unless you paid them a ton a month, yow'd be seeing the rockers again and this time yow'd get hurt. But yow told them to go fuck themselves.'

'That's right. I no pay.'

'Then the rockers came back and pushed yow about, but yow still said no.

Andreas nodded his big, black-haired head slowly.

'Then last night you say that three men in dark suits came. They locked the front door, took you in the back room and—'

'That's right,' said Mrs Vassiliou.

'Can you describe them?' asked Collins.

'They were big, maybe twenty-nine or eight. Smart suits. Dark suits, like them Kray Brothers,' said Mrs Vassiliou.

'Any distinguishing features, like a scar or tattoo?'

'No,' said Andreas.

'The skinny man, he had a bad limp,' said Mrs Vassiliou.

Collins saw a smile of recognition cross Clark's face, but a limp wasn't enough to go on. 'How tall was this man?' Collins asked.

'He was two or three inches taller than you.'

'So about six foot two?'

'About, but he not big like the other men. They were big men,' said Mrs Vassiliou and held her arms out in a circle to show what she meant. 'He skinny, like Clint Eastwood.'

'Now, this is important. Which was his bad leg?'

Mrs Vassiliou sat thinking. Before she could reply, her husband said, 'Right leg.'

'You're sure?'

'I'm sure. He kick me with his left foot when I on the floor. Bastard.'

Once outside, both men looked at each other and nodded. 'It has to be your mate, Johnny Sheppard,' said Collins.

'As sure as me auntie is missing a pair of brass balls.'

'You told me she had a pair of brass balls,' said Collins.

'She has. They're usually hanging over her bed. She gives them back to me uncle once a month.'

'What does he use them for?'

'Nowt I want to think about,' said Clark.

'More importantly, we need to find where Mr Sheppard hangs his balls these days and who he works for. I know just the colleen to ask. But first, how's about a chat with Bert to see if he's had any problems.'

Bert Mitchell's Greengrocery Shop was the other side of the lights, just 300 yards from the chippy. Bert was one of the most trusted shopkeepers on the Soho Road – trusted by his customers and his peers. If other shopkeepers were being pressured to pay protection, he'd know about it.

Bert was outside his shop, sorting the fruit and veg in their boxes, throwing out the rotten and damaged.

'How they hanging, Bert?' Clark asked.

Without looking up, he said, 'At my age, shrivelled up. I suppose you pair of reprobates want a cuppa?'

'Never say no to a cuppa,' said Collins.

Inside and waiting for the kettle to boil, Bert asked, 'So what can I do for you? Is this about Andreas?'

'Got it in one,' said Clark.

'Well, all I can say is that there's been no trouble this side of Minerva Street, but there's been a bit of bother near the New Inns.'

'Where?' asked Collins.

'There's a small row of shops, about seven, just opposite where the old Albion Cinema used to be. Three of the owners have been leaned on to cough up a monthly payment.'

'Why just three?' asked Collins.

'They dain't bother the English owners. Just the foreigners.'

'Now, that is interesting,' said Clark. 'Any mention that one of the heavies has a limp?'

'Yeah, some bastard broke Mr Singh's nose and cheek with a silver-handled walking stick. After that, the other two paid up – or so I hear.'

Bert handed the men their mugs of tea and pushed a bag of sugar and a packet of biscuits towards them. After taking a couple of Fig Rolls Clark threw the packet to Collins. 'Now, to much more important things. Clarkee, have yow got any spare tickets for the Final?'

'Na. I just have the one I got courtesy of the vouchers they gave out at the reserve game.'

Turning to Collins, Bert said, 'He's a right jammy git. Goes to one reserve game all year and it's the one where they hand out three vouchers, one each for the quarters, semi and the Final.'

'Yow got one from that reserve game as well. What's the problem?'

'John is off to the States on the first of June, and I'd like one last day out with 'em before he goes.'

'Still determined to join the American Army?' said Clark.

'He ain't changed his mind since he were six years old. I blame John Wayne.'

'He does know that as a regular he'll be first in and last out of Vietnam?' said Clark.

'Yeah, but what can I do? He's 21 and immortal.'

'I'll drop by and see him before he goes.'

'Thanks, Clarkee. Tell him the truth. He may believe you. He never took any notice of me.'

Walking back to the station, Collins said, 'Bert seems worried.'

'So he should be. A jungle war is the worst type of war for a white man to fight. We ain't built for it. I don't take me hat off to anyone in the military, with two exceptions: the Gurkhas and Wingate's Chindits. The Chindits fought behind enemy lines in the Burmese jungle. They had to contend with snakes, leeches, ants and disease, not to mention the fucking Japanese Army who really did believe that it were better to die than surrender.'

'What are you going to tell John?'

'As much as he'll listen to, which probably won't be much.'

Handsworth, 12.30hrs

Back at the station, Collins called Katie McGuire and explained what he wanted.

'An address will cost you a box of Cadbury Milk Tray.'

'Done.'

'I haven't finished me demands yet.'

'Go on.'

'Delivered by you, dressed as the Cadbury Milk Tray Man.'

'All right, I'm sure I've got a black polo neck somewhere. When can you let me have it?'

'If only I could. If only you would. I'll call you later with the addresses.'

Collins hung up with a smile on his face, just as DCI Hicks came in. He'd been at court all morning listening to the judge's summing up of one of his robbery cases.

'How did it go, Boss?'

'OK, I think. The jury's out. My guess is they'll reach a verdict this afternoon.'

'Giving them a nice restful weekend with nothing to worry about.'

'Thus has it always been with juries. What have you been up to?'

'I'm just about to pick up Clark and brace the hijackers. Do you want to be in on it?'

'No, I've got bloody paperwork to clear and, like the jurors,

I want to finish it off before the weekend. Call me if you need me.'

Collins found Clark in the Desk Sergeant's cubbyhole, reading the charge sheets against the hijackers.

'Ready?' asked Collins.

'As always.'

'Who do you want to start with?'

'Francis Mahoney. He's most likely the ringleader.'

'I agree.'

Francis Mahoney was built like a Gaelic Football player from Cork. A large round head sat on a thick neck, joined to a rotund chest, while his arms and legs testified to plenty of hard work in his father's building company. Either red hair or freckles covered every exposed inch of his skin. He glared sullenly at Collins and Clark with piggy, little eyes as they sat down.

'I got fuck all to say to yow two. I want me solicitor.'

'Fair enough. If you don't want to cooperate and halve your sentence, I'm sure one of your moronic mates will. I mean, we're looking at long stretches all round here. The gun changes everything,' said Collins.

'Yeah, it will be twenty years before yow feel a woman's hand on yowr dick again.'

'But you're entitled to say nothing,' said Collins. 'In fact, I admire you for it. Shows a bit of integrity.'

Collins stood up and had his hand on the door handle before Mahoney said, 'Wait. What do yow want to know?'

Collins returned to his chair. Ignoring Mahoney, he asked Clark 'Is this the guy Marie punched in the balls?'

'Yeah, that's him.'

Mahoney's face turned into a speckled crimson orb as he

blushed with humiliation. 'Do you reckon we can trust a bloke who gets taken down by a girl?'

'Yeah,' said Clark. 'If I think he's telling porkies, I'll get Marie to come in and punch him in the nuts again.'

'Good idea.' Then, turning to Mahoney, Collins asked, 'Who planned the job?'

'I did.'

'Where did you get the idea from?'

'Just some guy in a pub.'

'You mean some guy in a pub just gave you the info for a valuable hijack for nothing?'

'He was pissed. I thought he was talking bollicks. You know, coming the big I am. But when I checked it out, I could see it were on the level.'

'What were this guy's name?' asked Clark.

'Just some guy.'

'What were his name?' asked Clark and, rising, he positioned himself behind Mahoney's chair. 'I won't ask yow again.' Clark swiftly slapped the back of the man's head.

'I only heard his first name. He called himself Marty.'

'What did he look like? asked Collins.

'He were over six foot and skinny. Had fair hair and he were pale-looking.'

'Nice touch about the pale skin. Are wi supposed to believe he just came out of the clink?'

'It's the truth.'

'Do yow believe a word he's saying, Constable Clark?'

'Na, I don't think this bastard would know the truth if it bit him on the arse.' This time, the accompanying slap was harder.

'It was Tony Keating who came to you with the job, wasn't it?'

'No I've never met the bloke. On me mother's grave.'

'Yowr mother's still alive and living in Bromsgrove according to our records,' said Clark and cuffed him again.

'OK, we'll leave that for a while. When did Tony Keating drop out of the job?'

'I told you he were never in it.'

'The idiot with the shotgun. When did he come on board? Was it after Keating dropped out?"

'Lenny was in from the start. I dain't know he was going loaded until he turned up with the sawn off. Honest to God.'

'Why didn't you take the gun off him?'

'Cos he's a nutter and he was on sommut when he turned up. I weren't going to get shot over a sawn off.'

Collins remained silent as he thought about what he'd heard. Certainly Lenny's behaviour last night had been anything but rational. He decided to change tack. 'Had you always planned it as a six-man job?'

'Yeah. The guy in the pub said it were at least a four-man job, plus a driver. But I dain't like the idea of five blokes in one car. More chance of being pulled over by you lot.'

'And which of you was going to drive the rig away?'

'Bill. He works at the Shell tanker depot. He drives rigs all the time.'

'Why didn't you use some of your father's men?'

'My dad's legit, that's why.'

'Of course he is. Was it a chance to show your old man what you could do?'

'No. He's going to go apeshit when he finds out.'

The interrogation lasted another 40 minutes. Mahoney was happy to shop his mates and outline how he'd planned the job, but he refused to say which fence he'd planned to use or change his story about a pale-skinned man in the pub called Marty being the source of the tip-off.

The remaining four interviews were shorter and no new information was revealed. As first-timers, the four men were only too happy to cooperate with the police. Their statements supported Mahoney's story about a man in the pub and Lenny turning up unexpectedly with the shotgun on the night.

Over a cuppa in the canteen, Collins asked, 'What do you think?'

'I think them's telling the truth, even Mahoney. They're all shitting themselves 'cos that Lenny character came tooled up. They know what that means in prison time.'

'I agree. In which case, what was the cock-and-bull story that Keating fed me all about?'

'Maybe Tony Keating heard about the job and wanted in on it, but before he got involved he went to his older brother, who told him not to be a prat. Like all kid brothers he needed to save face, so he strung big brother along and made out he was going to do the job.'

'Possible, but it doesn't feel right.'

'That's because yam going on a date tonight with a man yow hardly know and yowr nervous. Now, remember: don't give it to him on the first date. Make him wait for it – otherwise he'll think you're a scrubber.'

'He'll be waiting 'til hell freezes over and then some if he expects anything from me.'

'Yow never know. The music, the lights, the romance.'

Collins gave Clark a two-fingered salute and headed out.

Handsworth, 16.00hrs

Sarah had packed the few belongings she had arrived with and now stood in the hall, saying her goodbyes to Agnes as her father waited patiently in the car.

'You've been a life-saver, Agnes. I'll never forget what you've done for me, or ever be able to repay you.'

'I'm glad you're going home. You'll be safe there and in a little while, you can start to rebuild your life. Don't let one vicious so-and-so put you off looking for a good man. If you want to thank me for what I've done, try and help some other poor woman who's been battered.'

'I will.' Sarah hugged Agnes, picked up her small bag of belongings and started to open the door, then closed it again. Lowering her voice, she said, 'I don't know if this will help or not, but I was talking to Margaret yesterday and I think she's in serious trouble. I know she's on the game, but it wasn't an ordinary punter that beat her up. She was cagey about what happened exactly, but I think it was someone important who likes that sort of thing. Worst thing was her bosses were there and let him do it and she's terrified that next time he might go all the way.'

'Thank you for telling me. I'll do some digging and see what I can find out.'

West Bromwich Police Station, 17.30hrs

Collins parked in the car park at the rear of the police station and went in the back door. Although in separate police forces, there had always been a lot of cross-border cooperation between the Handsworth and West Brom stations and more than a little rivalry. West Brom still resented the fact that Clarkee, one of their own sons born and bred, had ended up working for the sodding Brummies. Not many police forces could boast a VC holder on their payroll. But as Clark had explained many times, he'd applied to both forces on the same day. It was just that Birmingham was the first to bite his hand off.

Collins found Sergeant Andrews in a small CID office, next to the snooker room on the first floor, writing up some reports. 'Mickey, good of yow to come.'

'No trouble. Here's the copy of the files I promised. They should cover everything you need. If there's anything that's not clear, call me.' Clark slumped into an old captain's chair that was in need of varnishing.

'I will, but it seems pretty straightforward from what we found and yow said on the phone. There's just one thing that don't sit right – she was pregnant. Not many pregnant woman top themselves.'

'The baby wasn't her husband's. It belonged to lover boy.'

'She told yow that?'

'Yes. It's all in the report.'

'Well, that explains it. I've been waiting for the doc's full report. Poor little mite, dead before it's born. How's it going with yowr hijackers?'

'Bunch of idiots. Amateurs. Only one of them has got any form – Francis Mahoney.'

'Bloody hell. Was he in on it? I must be getting old or else he's changed in the last three years. I dain't recognise him. That's really going to hurt his old man.'

'How so?'

'Haven't yow heard. The old bastard's got cancer. Terminal, they say. He's been training Frankie boy up to take over from him. Now, the Prince will be inside when the King snuffs it.'

'So who'll inherit?'

'Difficult to say. Edward Mahoney's always been a suspicious sod. If anyone even looked like they might threaten him, he'd cut them off at the knees. On one occasion, literally – or so the legend goes.'

'No lieutenants to take over?'

'Na. His recruitment policy was simple but effective. Employ big, vicious bastards, who were just bright enough to follow orders to the letter.'

'So someone might move in on his turf when he goes?'

'It's a good bet.'

'Who?'

'Maybe the Johnson Gang from Dudley way or the Emmerson Family from Walsall.'

'No one from Birmingham?'

'I suppose it's possible. Toby Drew picked up Smethwick when old man Smith had his accident.'

At the mention of Drew, Collins sat upright. 'Accident?'

'Yeah. Smith was killed in a hit-and-run.'

'Are you sure it was an accident?'

'Certain. We caught the guy who did it. No record, just a drunk driver. He topped himself while in custody. Why?'

Collins felt an unease in his stomach, an irritation that wouldn't go away. 'What was the driver's name?'

'I can't remember. I can look it up for yow before yow go.'

'Thanks. Has Drew picked up any other patches in the Black Country recently?'

'None that I know of. You think he's up to sommut?'

'I'm not sure. Maybe.'

Fifteen minutes later, Collins left with the name of the drunk driver safely tucked away in his notebook. Phillip Mabbit had lived with his wife and two children near the Regal Cinema at the top of Soho Road. I'd better give Clarkee a call and bring him up to date thought Collins as he drove away.

Handsworth, 20.00hrs

Collins entered the lounge, feeling very self-conscious. Thank God, Clark couldn't see him. He'd never hear the last of it from the small man. He was wearing black slip-on shoes, black slacks, a mauve shirt and Mark's plum-coloured crushed velvet jacket with silver buttons and a matching cravat. He looked like an escapee from The Kinks.

Agnes stood up and couldn't stop herself from giggling like a young girl. 'Well, I have to say you look the part.'

'And what part is that?'

'Why, the handsome young man desperately trying to decide if he likes boys better than girls.'

'We both know which I prefer.'

'Ah, but do we? Who's to say? Maybe tonight, across a crowded dance floor, you'll see the face that you've been searching for all your life.'

'Unless there's a lesbian in the joint that likes men, that's not going to happen.'

'Oh, so you'd toss me aside if you found a nice-looking lesbian?' Agnes teased.

Before Collins could reply, the doorbell rang and he went to answer it. Moments later, he returned with Cavendish, who was dressed very conservatively in a three-piece, dark grey mohair suit, white shirt and burgundy tie.

After the introductions were made, Collins asked, 'How is it that I'm done up like a bloody peacock and you look like a well-dressed businessman?'

'That's because I'm a well-known queer while you have to convince people that you might be a queer.'

'That sounds very logical to me,' said Agnes, patting Collins on the chest. 'Now, do stop complaining and put on your happy face. You're supposed to be enjoying yourself. Just don't enjoy yourself too much.'

Mark eased the Triumph TR5 onto Hamstead Road and made for the A34. The quickest route would be down the A34 to Walsall and then pick up the Wolverhampton Road. Cavendish was a confident driver and didn't feel the need to accelerate away from traffic lights in a blur of blue exhaust fumes, unlike the idiot in an old MG who was intent on proving his virility to the young woman sitting beside him.

Cavendish smiled and said, 'There's always one.'

Collins nodded in agreement. He could sense that Cavendish had something on his mind, but said nothing.

They had covered nearly six miles before Cavendish asked, 'Just between you and me, what does your gut tell you? Are we looking for one man or several?'

'If you'd asked me that on Tuesday, I would have said it was 80% certain we were looking for more than one killer. Now, I think it's 90% certain we're looking for one man.'

Cavendish glanced across at his passenger, 'You've found something?'

Collins remained silent. The first rule of police work was to tell no outsider anything about a case.

'OK, I understand,' said Cavendish. 'Loose talk costs lives and all that, but for what it's worth, I'm convinced more than ever that it's just one bastard and that he's one of us.'

'A homosexual. Why do you say that?'

'He's been able to pass himself off convincingly to four young men and get them to go with him somewhere deserted for sex. A straight guy couldn't do that. He wouldn't risk going into a pub or club or talking to someone. He'd wait outside. When he spotted a victim, he'd follow and jump them when he got the chance.'

'Let's assume for the moment that I agree with you. Why is he attacking other queers?'

'For the same fucked-up reasons that men kill women. For the thrill of it. For revenge. Because he hates himself. For some mad, fucked-up version of sex.'

Collins decided to play devil's advocate. 'I don't think it's for sex. There's been no sign of sexual abuse on the bodies, if you exclude the systematic beating of the entire body including the genitals, and there's been no sign of semen at any of the scenes of crime.'

'What if the beating is the sex? I knew a guy once who liked to be humiliated by lads off the street, but he was married and terrified of catching something. So he'd strip off and they'd tie his hands behind his back and then insult and belittle him, threatening to piss on him and shag him – all the usual stuff. After about 20 minutes, they'd untie his hands and he'd only have to touch himself to go off like a Roman candle.'

'A bit of a risk being tied up by a stranger?'

'You're right. Eventually, one of them kicked the hell out of him and he ended up in hospital.'

'How did he manage to explain it away?'

'He couldn't. They caught the 17-year-old who did it, but the jury accepted his plea of self-defence and he walked free. My friend lost his wife, kids and job. About a year later, he took an overdose.'

'I'm sorry.'

'So was I, but I don't suppose we'll ever see the day when queers are seen as ordinary people who happen to like other men.'

'No, I don't suppose we will.'

The Manhattan Club, Wolverhampton 21.20Hrs

The Manhattan Club was on the outskirts of Wolverhampton, surrounded by a high wall and factories. It had probably been a working men's club or a company's social club in the past, but now it was just another rundown, nondescript building in the industrial centre of Wolverhampton. There wasn't even a sign outside advertising its existence. Nor was there much noise coming from behind the steel shuttered windows.

Cavendish knocked on the door and a grille was briefly pulled back, then shut. Collins heard the mortice lock click and a bolt being drawn back. As the door opened, he was hit by a blast of hot air and noise from a dark cavernous dance floor, which was illuminated by spotlights, glitter balls and a few underpowered fluorescent tubes dotted around the walls.

The dance floor was maybe 45 foot by 30 and around it was a tiled area with tables. A well-stocked bar ran the width of the room and three barmen were busy filling orders. A stage that could have taken a six-piece band sat at the top end of the dance floor and a DJ was playing I'm a Believer at maximum volume. A self-appointed backing group of four queens stood in front of the stage and sang a revised version of the chorus.

The noise was incredible. With no way to escape, it seemed to echo around the room and set up a vibration in Collins' stomach. He couldn't see how the hell he would be able to talk to anyone in here. As if reading his mind, Mark leaned over and shouted in his ear, 'Don't worry, there's a quiet room to the side of the stage where people go for a chat and to cool down. I'll get you a drink. Orange all right?'

Collins nodded and followed Cavendish. Leaning on the bar, Collins was able to survey the crowd as his eyes adjusted to the dark. There were very few women in the room. Maybe eight or nine. In this light, they could just as easily be men in drag, he thought. The majority of those dancing were between eighteen and thirty. There were also a number of older men sitting around the edges of the dance floor. Most of these seemed to have a younger friend.

Many of the younger men looked as if they had stepped out of a Carnaby Street boutique, while their older companions looked like customers of Austin Reed or Rackhams – stylish without being flamboyant. With some embarrassment, Collins realised that, although a little old, he fitted into the boutique group.

Cavendish handed him his drink and nodded towards the quiet room. The room was an oasis of peace after the noise of the disco. *The place must be well soundproofed*, thought Collins.

About twenty men were present and all heads turned as Mark walked in. Everyone seemed to know him and he responded to their greetings with a hug, a kiss on the cheek or a wave like the star he was. 'Come on, I'll introduce you to Raymond. He owns the place. I spoke to him earlier and he said he'd spread the word that we're looking for information.'

Raymond reminded Collins of Sidney Greenstreet in Casablanca. All that was missing was a fez and a fly swat. At over 20 stone, he filled the two-seater settee that was lodged in the far corner of the room. A variety of cushions were arranged around him to support his bulk. He didn't stand up when he shook Collins' hand.

'So, you're Mark's friend. He told me about you.' His deep bass voice boomed around the room while his clear blue eyes seemed to look right through Collins and his pathetic disguise. 'It's fortunate that you're here. God alone knows we need some help to catch this madman.'

'I hope I can help,' said Collins.

'I'm sure you will.' Raymond beckoned a tall skinny youth over and asked him to tell the DJ to cut the music and make the agreed announcement. 'Now, we wait and hope,' said Raymond.

Over the next 40 minutes, five men dropped by. From the way they looked at Cavendish, Collins quickly concluded that they were far more interested in meeting Mark than helping to solve Alan's murder. After that, things slowed down.

Thirty minutes crept by and Collins was ready to call it a night when a young, skinny man, wearing a low-slung pair of blue hipsters, a bright yellow shirt and a touch of foundation, edged into the room. His chestnut brown hair was parted in the middle and hung down to his shoulders, framing a face that Michelangelo would have loved to immortalise. He looked uncertainly around the room, saw Mark and walked over.

'Hello, my name's Martin, but my friends call me Marnie,' he said and gave a nervous little laugh. 'I don't want to waste your time but I think I may have seen, or at least heard, something that might help.'

Immediately, Collins' hopes were raised. In his experience, the people who had to force themselves to come forward, who doubted the value of their information, were often the most valuable witnesses. 'Why don't you sit down and tell us about it?' he said, indicating the spare chair opposite himself and Mark. 'Would you like a drink?'

'No, I'm fine thanks.' Looking at Collins, he continued. 'I was in the club the night Alan was killed.'

'You knew Alan?

'No, I only found out his name afterwards. Anyway, that night I was by myself and I saw this guy. He was the wrong side of thirty, but not old enough to be a chicken hawk, and a bit flabby around the waist. For some reason I fancied him. I tried to catch his eye, but he didn't react. So I went over to the bar and stood about four foot from him, just to let him know I was interested. He just walked away, glass in hand, looking at the dancers. It was obvious I wasn't his type.'

Mark was about to interrupt and ask a question, but Collins caught his eye and shook his head. The message was clear: Let him tell his story his way.

'Anyway, I got fixed up with someone else – a bit older than my usual, but nice – and then I saw the guy move in on Alan, who'd just come in. They were standing at the bar. I don't know why, but I wanted to see what this bloke had that I didn't. Maybe he had a perfect arse or something. So I said to the fella I was dancing with that I was going to get a bag of crisps. While I was waiting to be served, I earwigged on the conversation. They were talking about music. And every time Alan said he liked a group, the older guy would say he liked them too. Typical pick-up line, I know, but he seemed to know what he was talking about. Anyway, I was just leaving when Alan said, "What did you say your name was?" and he said "Mark".'

Collins leant forward. 'What did you say the guy was wearing?'

Martin paused, 'I think it was a grey or black suit, but he definitely had a blue shirt. I remember 'cause blue is my favourite colour.'

'And you're sure that he called himself Mark?'

'Certain.'

'Why didn't you tell the police this at the time?'

'I was living at home then. It would kill me mom to know about me, and my old man would go loopy. I've got me own place now and, besides, you're not the coppers. Has any of this been useful?'

'It's been really useful. Would you mind jotting down your name and address on this?' said Collins, as he pushed a piece of paper and a Bic pen across the table. 'It's just in case I need to contact you again.'

Collins and Mark waited a further forty minutes but no one else dropped by. Bidding goodnight and thanks to Raymond, the two men returned to the disco. The opening chords of Elvis's Jailhouse Rock greeted them and this time the queens' chorus didn't need to change any of the words.

Suddenly, Cavendish grabbed Collins' hand and pulled him onto the dance floor. 'Come on, it's a pity to waste the music. Let's have one dance before we go?'

For an instant, Collins resisted and then he remembered what Mark had said about blending in. With a laugh, he followed his "date" onto the dance floor and the two men enjoyed two and a half minutes of rock 'n' roll perfection.

As they left the disco, a casually dressed man wearing an Omega Seamaster Cosmic watch with crosshairs and date function followed them out the door.

On the journey home, both men were quiet. Collins was replaying in his mind what Martin had said. He had no doubt that the young man could provide a detailed description of the murderer – maybe even help build up an identikit picture or sketch – but if the man was in disguise, how useful would that be? No, it was the name that was significant. He was now certain that he was after one man.

Mark wasn't thinking about Martin or the case. He was thinking about how Collins' hand had felt in his.

Lost in thought, neither man saw the dark blue Rover 2000 that followed them back to Birmingham.

Handsworth, 23.30hrs

Agnes was still up when Collins let himself in. As always, Sheba greeted him with her usual enthusiasm and, as a reward, Collins led her into the kitchen and gave her a slice of corned beef.

'You spoil that dog,' said Agnes from the doorway.

'I know,' Collins replied, as he put the kettle on.

'Did you learn anything?'

Collins nodded. 'It's one man. I'm sure of it.'

'Tell me.'

'Clarkee says that the guy who killed Joe was called either Ron or John.'

'You told me.'

'Well, we have a witness who heard the killer of the second victim call himself Mark.'

'My goodness. That, plus the watches, really does point towards one killer.'

'Exactly.' Collins put a spoonful of sugar in his tea and stirred the brew. 'But now it's time for bed.' Holding his tea mug in his left hand, he slipped his right around Agnes' waist as they headed for the stairs.

As they ascended the stairs, Agnes said, 'Remind me to tell you about Sarah's conversation with Margaret tomorrow.'

Saturday 4th May 1968, 10.15hrs

Handsworth

Collins rang the doorbell and was confronted by a very large version of Ruth. 'Ruth, me darlin', what's happened to you? You look like you've eaten Clarkee.'

'Why, Sergeant Collins, you do know how to make a girl feel attractive.'

'You know I always think you look beautiful. In fact, to-day you look twice as beautiful as normal. Are you carrying twins? Is that it?'

'Time will tell,' Ruth said and kissed Collins on the cheek. 'His lordship is upstairs. He'll be down in a tick.'

Ruth led the way into the lounge, slumped into an armchair and put her feet on a leather footstool. 'My ankles are agony,' she said, by way of explanation.

'But you're all right, aren't you?'

Ruth saw the concern in Collins' face and smiled, 'I'm fine. Some women barely put a pound on during pregnancy. Others, like me, blow up to be the Michelin Man's sister. How's Agnes?'

'Grand, she sends her love.'

'Who's sending love to my wife and do I need to worry about it?' asked Clark, who was trying to tie a Windsor knot in a knitted tie without success. Giving up, he settled for a single knot and asked, 'So, who wi going to see first?'

'I thought we'd start with Wilkee, then his vampires. See if they saw anything the night Joe was murdered. Then, I'd like to talk to Mrs Mabbit. I've got a feeling that Drew is up to something big that might involve my good friend Mr Richard Keating. So we'll end with him.'

'Yow're leaving Drew until yow have something more concrete?'

'Yeah.'

'Sounds reasonable, but remember yow have another hot date with Mark tonight. Yow don't want to be late for that and yow'll need time to get yowr face on.'

'You can hit him if you want to, Michael,' said Agnes.

'I would, except last time I tried he nearly killed me.'

Hockley, 11.15hrs.

Wilkee owned a three-storey house at the end of Soho Road that overlooked the Hockley flyover and provided a panoramic view of Birmingham, which was just 2 miles away. He lived on the top floor and rented out the first and second floors. He was content to confine himself to the upper floor, but enjoyed the regular visits he made to every flat in the house when the tenants were out. He particularly enjoyed his inspections of those flats occupied by female tenants. He seldom left a trace of his visit, but when he did he always washed, dried and replaced the knickers in the correct drawer before he left.

Collins was about to press the bell when two young women came out. 'Who are you after?' the taller of the women demanded.

'We're here to see Mr Wilkee.'

'More fucking perverts, I suppose?' said the shorter woman.

'Yes madam, but wem a better class of perverts. Wem police perverts,' said Clark as he pushed past the two women with Collins, trying desperately not to laugh, following closely behind.

Clark banged on Wilkee's door with the palm of his hand. He continued doing so for a good 90 seconds, stopping every now and then to listen for any sound of life. Finally, a sleepy, irritated voice asked, 'Who the fuck's that?'

'Hello, Wilkee, it's your old mates, Detective Constable Clark and Detective Sergeant Collins. Now, open up before I put me foot through your door.'

'OK, OK. Hold your high horses.'

The door opened to reveal an overweight, five foot eight man in his mid-fifties, with grey hair and a closely cropped salt-and-pepper beard. His four front teeth were still in a glass by the bed, which explained why his face seemed to have collapsed in on itself. He pulled his grease-stained dressing gown around himself, but it was too small to cover his belly, which, over the last two years, had decided to go a-wandering. The result was that his Y fronts and string vest were on display to all and sundry. *Not a pretty sight*, thought Collins, as he stepped into the flat.

'You keep that fucking maniac away from me, you hear, Clarkee. Last time he came in here, he broke my fucking nose.'

'Yow should have reported it to the police, Wilkee. In fact, as I'm here, why don't yow tell me all about it?'

'We don't have time for the full story, do we, Wilkee?' said Collins, his eyes full of unspoken threat.

Wilkee seemed to get the message. He ignored Clark's question and instead asked, 'What do you want?'

'Yow were in the Toreador Saturday two weeks ago?' said Clark, wandering over to Wilkee's collection of erotica, which he laughingly called an art collection.

'When the queer was killed?'

Clark nodded, as he rummaged in a bowl of matchbooks picked up in various clubs throughout England and Europe.

'You know I were, otherwise you wouldn't be here.'

'Did yow see anything?' Clark asked, selecting a match book from The Black Kitty Club in Amsterdam, which showed a well-endowed young lady and a close friend, and tucked it into his breast pocket.

'Na, the bloke you're interested in was served at the other end of the counter from where I was. He certainly wasn't interested in the girls. Looked fit, though. You know, as if he worked out a bit.'

'Nothing else?'

'Na, not in the bar.'

Clark exchanged looks with Collins. 'Are you saying you saw sommut outside the bar?'

'Maybe.'

'OK. We'll bite,' said Collins. 'What do you want?'

'My girls are up for soliciting in two weeks. They could go down for a month or three and—'

'And yow'd lose their money.'

'And their company, Mr Clark.'

'Yeah, Rita and Marilyn have real winning personalities.'

Wilkee ignored the sarcasm. 'Have we got a deal?'

'If it's useful and if it checks out, we'll put a word in,' said Collins.

'Good enough. Rita had taken a client around the back. You know, the alley where the Temple Gym is. I was looking out for her, making sure nothing happened, when I saw the bloke leave with the young kid.'

Wilkee was drawing his story out for all it was worth and Collins was starting to feel irritated. 'For feck's sake, get to the point.'

'It was dark all right, but I saw the car they got in. It was a Rover 2000.'

'Did you get the reg number?' asked Collins, the familiar thrill of the hunt starting to come to life.

'Na, it were too dark.'

'What colour were the car?' asked Clark.

'Blue or black, summut like that.'

'Anything else?' asked Collins.

'Sorry.'

'OK, we'll be off. Yow take care now and stay away from the sixteen-year-olds, or I'll ask Sergeant Collins here to call on yow again.'

'Can I tell the girls you'll drop the wink?'

'Yeah, but how much wi ask for will depend on what yowr info throws up.'

Hockley, 12.10hrs

Outside, Collins turned his collar up to the rain and both men made a dash for the Mini parked by the side of the road.

'What did you make of that?' Collins asked, once they were in the car.

'Without some corroborating evidence, it's bloody worthless. The little sod would happily tell us a load of bollocks if it kept his girls out of the clink and on their backs earning him money.'

'Well, on this occasion, m'lud, I think I must concur with my colleague's expert opinion,' said Collins.

'Which barrister were that supposed to be? It dain't sound like anyone I know.'

'That's my Sir Reginald I. Standforalot. He's me generic barrister.'

'I don't think Mike Yarwood has anything to worry about.'

Wilkee's vampires lived in a recently built block of council flats in Hockey that overlooked the Lucas Great King Street plant. Around each newly built tower block was a rolling sea of grass, where just a few years ago there had been some of the worst slums in Birmingham. The tower blocks had been the death knell for overcrowded, rat-infested, dirty, back-to-back houses with one outside toilet shared between four families.

Each tower block was clean, modern and space-efficient, with lifts that could whisk you to the fifteenth floor in a matter of seconds, according to the city planners. The architects' dream for the twenty-first century had been built by Birmingham City Council in the twentieth. And now every family in Newtown was beseeching the council for a flat in the clouds.

The vampires, Rita and Marilyn, occupied a ground-floor apartment. They were expecting Collins and Clark. Rita answered the door on the first ring with her well-rehearsed greeting. 'It's that Irish cunt, Collins, and his dwarf mate, Clark,' she shouted over her shoulder.

'And it's grand to see you, too, Rita. Can we come in?' Without waiting for a response, both men brushed past her and headed for the dining room. Marilyn was sitting on the floor in a white terry towel bathrobe, drying her hair. Without her inch-thick make-up and her hair hanging in damp tendrils, she looked the spit of Medusa. A desiccated left breast that was on show did nothing to improve the image. How the hell does she ever gets a bloke to pay her for a shag? thought Collins. They must be really bloody desperate or really, really pissed.

'Don't you fuckers never knock, before barging in on a lady?'

'Always,' said Clark, 'but while yow'd pass the physical, yow'd fail the decorum test.'

'Piss off,' said Marilyn.

From the doorway, Rita said, 'Wilkee called. He told us that you were going to put in a good word for us with the prosecution, on account of the info he gave you. Is that true?'

'It is, if the information he gave us turns out to be worth anything,' said Collins.

'Typical of that lying bastard. He told us it were all sorted,' said Marilyn.

'It could be if yow saw the guy who killed the young lad,' said Clark.

'Yeah, we saw him all right,' said Marilyn, 'but that won't do you much good. He was in disguise. Had a wig on.'

'Mind you,' said Rita, 'a lot of them do that. No one loves a bald queer,' she sneered, displaying an upper set of teeth that were yellow with age and a mismatched set of perfectly white false teeth below.

'How do you know it was a wig?' asked Collins.

'It was blond. Good quality, but I could see brown hair sticking out behind his ear.'

'That's the trouble with a wig,' said Rita. 'You really need someone to help you fit it or you can miss bits.'

'Well, I'm not sure that knowing he was wearing a wig is that useful.'

'He was also wearing make-up,' said Marilyn.

'Him and half the queens in the pub,' said Clark.

Marilyn smiled sweetly, or she thought she did. What she actually did was remind Clark of one of corpses with broken fingernails discovered by Vincent Price in Premature Burial.

'You're right. A lot of them do wear make-up, but he was the only one whose make-up didn't have a fragrance. It dain't smell.'

'What do you mean didn't smell?' asked Collins.

'It wasn't perfumed. It was stage make-up.'

'Yow must have got bloody close to him to be able to not smell his perfume,' said Clark.

'I was. How else would I have been able to half-inch this?' said Marilyn, taking a pocket watch made by Smith and Sons circa 1913 from the pocket of her robe. 'I've polished the watch case, but you might find prints on the chain or face – if you're lucky.'

'Is that enough for you to speak to the prosecution?' asked Rita, knowing full well it was.

New Inns, Handsworth 13.30hrs

Soho Road was busy with shoppers. Middle-aged women struggled with two or three bags of shopping, while their husbands enjoyed a pint in the Grove pub. Younger mothers had brought the kids to give them a hand. It probably cost them a Beano or packet of Spangles, but it was worth it as it meant they didn't have to struggle home with four or five bags of shopping. One or two old dears had a shopping trolley, a deadly instrument in the hands of those who regularly proclaimed, 'I've lived through two world wars and I've got me rights', as though it gave them permission to mow down any other shopper that crossed their path.

Mabbit's house was on Crockett's Road, less than half a mile from the Hawthorns. At the Regal Cinema, Collins pulled into the empty car park. The kids' Saturday morning show was over and the first showing of In the Heat of the Night with Sidney Poitier, Collins' favourite actor, was not on until 2.30. Collins had seen the film twice already but made a mental note of the film times, just in case he could catch it again.

Both men got out of the Mini and went in search of the late Mr Mabbit's house. They found it with a freshly erected For Sale sign in the small front garden. Clark rang the bell and, moments later, a woman in her mid-thirties appeared, a tea towel in her hands. In the background, Collins could hear two children arguing.

'Yes?' the woman demanded.

'Mrs Mabbit?'

'Who wants to know?'

'I'm Detective Sergeant Collins and this is my colleague, Detective Constable Clark. Can we come in please?' Both men held up their warrant cards.

For a moment, the woman looked as if she was about to say no, but then she relented and stood back. 'You'd best come in, I suppose.'

She led the men into the small room at the end of the hall. The room was clean and the few sticks of furniture in it were well used. But other than a 17-inch, black-and-white television in the corner, there were no pictures, ornaments or clocks in the room. All gone to the pawn shop, thought Collins.

Mrs Mabbit had just made a pot of tea and it was now brewing on the table. Steam was curling from the sprout. She saw Clark look at the pot and asked, 'Would you like a cup of tea? It's fresh made.'

'That would be bostin, thanks.'

Mrs Mabbit disappeared into the kitchen and returned with two clean mugs. 'I suppose this is about the money. I always knew it was too good to be true. It was our one chance.' Her shoulders suddenly slumped and, banging the mugs down onto the table, she began to sob quietly.

Whatever reaction Collins had expected to their visit, this wasn't it. He took a clean handkerchief from his pocket and handed it to the young widow. Clark looked at him as if to ask, What the hell's going on? Collins' silent response was equally clear, Stay quiet. Say nothing.

When the sobs eventually stopped, Mrs Mabbit looked more like forty-five than the thirty-six recorded in her file. She was beaten. She was tired. What was the point? Maybe Phillip had been right when he'd wrapped the sheet around his neck.

'You were saying about the money, Mrs Mabbit?'

'Call me Liz. Everyone calls me Mrs Mabbit since Phil died. It makes me feel so old.'

'OK, Liz it is.'

'I didn't say anything about it at the inquest. Phil said I shouldn't tell anyone or else the tax man would be after it – or you lot. It was when he was on remand that he told me he was due some money from the bookies. That surprised me because they'd been after him for what he owed for months. But he said he'd sorted it out and that the last bet he'd put on had come up. An accumulator worth nearly 1,000 to 1, he said.

'Well, I'd heard it all before. The big win that would solve all our problems. That would change our lives. So I thought nothing of it. But a few days before he died, this tall, pasty-faced bloke drew up outside and said he had Phil's winnings. I reckoned it would be just a few quid, but when I counted it came to £5,000 exactly. I couldn't believe it and I couldn't wait to tell Phil. I went to Winson Green the next day. He was really happy. He said it was for me and the kids, and that

I should move and make a fresh start 'cos his brief had told him he was going down for at least four years.

'I said I'd wait, but he said that me and the kids would be better off without him. I told him not to be daft. It was that night he hung himself. It was as if he was waiting for the money to be delivered.'

'Yow said he'd sorted out the money he owed the bookies. Do yow know how he did that?'

'No and I didn't ask. If I had to guess, I'd say he nobbled a horse or two for them.'

'How would he be able to do that?' asked Clark.

'He sold animal feed and I know he sold to some trainers. They used to give him the odd tips. They were the only times he ever won anything.'

'And yow think he may have used his contacts to slow down a few favourites?'

Liz nodded.

'Do you know who your husband's bookie was?' asked Collins.

'He had loads. Arthur Lamb, Michael Grant, Skip Monroe and Steve Woodhead were just some of them. But I think it was it was Harry Trylford he owed money to.'

The Betting and Gaming Act of 1961 had legalised betting shops and slot machines in pubs from May 1961. Arthur Lamb owned a shop on Soho Road and was rumoured to be standing for the Council in the next election. No one had a bad word to say about him. The other three had also decided to go mainly legit, meaning they did a bit of stuff off the books, but nothing to worry the police.

Harry Trylford was a different beast, though. He had a reputation as a right royal bastard. The police had been after him for years. With one exception, every time they got close to locking him up, a witness would withdraw their statement or a new witness would come forward claiming that Harry had been in church when some poor sod was being beaten senseless.

Trylford had decided to stay as an illegal bookie for business reasons. It meant he had lower overheads and could offer slightly better odds and no tax deduction on winnings. The trouble was, if you owed him money you could very easily end up with a broken leg or worse. If Mabbit had owed Trylford money, then both Collins and Clark knew he must have been in serious trouble.

'Did your husband ever talk about the accident?' asked Collins.

'All the time. He felt terrible about it. He couldn't forgive himself. He kept saying if he could go back he'd do things differently, but what could he do differently? Mr Smith just stepped in front of the car. He was killed outright, the inquest said. Even if he'd stopped and tried to help, the poor man would have died. But there was no talking to him.'

'Were this the first accident he'd been involved in?' asked Clark.

'Except for the usual bumper scrapes. The prosecution said he drove away because he was drunk, but Phil hardly ever drank. Gambling was his weakness, not drink.'

'And you're convinced that he did kill himself?' asked Collins.

'Yes. My Phil knew he'd never last four years in jail. Well, I suppose you want the money. I'll go and get it.'

'That won't be necessary at this stage. If the winnings are unconnected to the accident, then it's legally yours,' said Collins, standing up. As he opened the door, he collided with a young girl of about fourteen and her younger brother, who was chasing her with a wet sponge. They stopped abruptly when they saw him. Collins stood aside and they went and stood by their mother. They'd seen enough police to recognise their visitors.

'I'll see you out.'

'That won't be necessary. I just need a quick word in private with Constable Clark.' Both men moved to the end of the hall. 'What do you think?'

'I know what yam thinking, you soft-centred bugger. Yow can't promise her anything. Wi don't know the full significance of the five grand.'

'I know.'

'As long as yow do. I'll wait outside.'

As the front door closed behind Clark, Collins called out, 'Liz, could I have a quick word in private before I go?'

Mrs Mabbit joined Collins in the hall and closed the dining room door.

'I've been thinking,' said Collins. 'The £5,000 may be part of a criminal conspiracy. If it is, you're going to lose it, but it's very unlikely that any court would force you to repay it if you'd spent it, in good faith, on say a new house for you and your kids. Also, you shouldn't be so quick to tell the next copper you meet how you got the money.'

For the second time in twenty minutes, tears welled up in Mrs Mabbit's eyes and, standing on tiptoe, she kissed Collins' cheek. 'Thank you.'

Clark didn't ask Collins what he'd said. The less he knew, the better. Instead, he asked, 'What do yow make of it?'

'It seems obvious. His debt was written off for killing Smith.'

'Agreed. And when he were caught, he was given a choice to either top his self and five grand went to the widow—'

'Because that way there would be no suspicious circumstances. But if he refused—'

'He'd meet with a nasty accident in prison and his bosses would take their chances with a police investigation.'

'And the widow would go penniless. How do yow think the message were delivered?'

'Same as you. His solicitor and the promise of at least four years in prison.'

'What can I say? When yowm right, yam right. Yow picked up on the pasty-faced bloke, dain't you?'

'Yeah.'

'So where next?'

'We're right by Mr Singh, so let's have a quick word with him before dropping in on Keating.'

'Fair enough.'

Mr Singh's shop was small, less than 600 square foot, but he still managed to stock a wide range of curtains, table clothes, lino and carpet mats ranging in size from six feet by four, up to twelve feet by nine, along with hall runners up to twelve feet. How it all fitted into the shop was a mystery to which only he knew the answer. The smell of wool pervaded the small shop, and the white flock from the net curtains covered the floor like a light dusting of snow.

Hearing the doorbell jingle, Mr Singh waddled out of his little office at the back of the shop. The bruising was still visible where he'd been hit by the walking stick.

'Mr Clark, Mr Collins, what brings you to my shop? Maybe Mrs Clark wants a new carpet for her new baby's bedroom, or perhaps curtains? I do them at a special price for my friends.'

'My God, can't a fella's wife have a baby without everyone knowing about it?'

'Ah, but everyone knows Mr Clark, and everyone wishes you and your wife well.'

'Well, thank yow for that,' said Clark. 'It's much appreciated, but wem here to see if wi can help yow. We heard that some guys took a few liberties with yow. Care to tell us about it?'

'It's nothing. Trouble I don't want.'

'Being beaten up isn't nothing. You're not the only

shopkeeper whose been tapped up for protection. We think we know who's responsible, and with your help, we can put him away,' said Collins.

'You can put away the man who beat me, but not the man behind him or the one behind him. It's no good. I tell you, I get beaten and still I have to pay. The only difference will be that my money will be collected by a different man.'

'We're interested in getting all the men,' said Collins.

'And I hope you do, but help you I can't. I have three daughters and wife to look after.'

'OK, Mr Singh, we understand. Just nod if the man who hit yow was about 30, 6 foot 1 tall or thereabouts and had a gammy right leg?'

Mr Singh nodded. 'Please don't tell anyone I told you.'

'Yow don't need to worry, Mr Singh. We heard nowt from yow. We'll be in touch.'

Soho Road, Handsworth 14.40hrs

Once outside, the two men headed for Keating's showrooms. Both understood Mr Singh's predicament. Andreas had no daughters living at home to worry about.

'How do yow want to handle Keating?' Clark asked.

'There's three things I want to know. One, how come so much of his information about the hijack was wrong? Two, did he realise he was grassing up Francis Mahoney when he spoke to me? Three, what, if any, relationship does he have with Toby Drew?'

'Yow don't think that's a bit too ambitious for one interview?'

'Na, you're leading it. He's my snout but I want you to put the frighteners on him. Let's shake his tree a bit and see what falls out.'

Clark looked at his friend. If Keating had been playing Collins along he was about to regret it. 'Fair enough.'

Keating's car showroom was only a short walk from Singh's shop. The day had turned fresh, clear and sunny. The soot had been washed out of the sky by the early morning showers and the colours of nature and man seemed fresh and vibrant. As if answering a primeval call, young girls and women had dug out their summer dresses for the first time that year. The only difference between them was that the women had wisely decided to wear a cardigan to guard against the chill breeze that rustled the leaves.

Keating owned a Ford dealership, but the 200 plus used cars on the lot represented just about every possible make sold in Britain. All were under five years old and none of them had been clocked. Among the used Austins, Fords and Vauxhalls, there was a fair smattering of Rovers, Jaguars and even two Jensen Interceptors built just down the road in West Bromwich. *He has ideas to sell luxury cars and not deal with the plebs*, Collins thought, as he opened the showroom door.

The main showroom was reserved exclusively for new Fords. Before the door had closed, a keen young man in a blue mohair suit leapt from behind the latest Ford Escort model and greeted them with a grossly over-the-top, 150-watt smile, 'Good morning, gentlemen. How can I help you this fine day?'

'Yow can tell Mr Keating that Detective Constable Clark and Detective Sergeant Collins want to see him right now, on official police business.' Clark spoke loud enough for two customers at the other end of the showroom to look in his direction.

The smile disappeared from the man's face, 'Of course,'

he said and hurried away towards a door marked Private. Moments later, he reappeared with Richard Keating, who somehow managed to look simultaneously annoyed, baffled and yet pleased to see the police.

Keating's office was bright and airy, furnished entirely in the latest Swedish offerings. His pine desk looked more like a table than the traditional pedestal desk, and the steel and wood chairs dotted around the room had been chosen more for their looks than comfort. Away from the desk was a coffee table, edged by two small blue Ercol settees that matched the chairs. There was also a large red ball chair, with cream interior, suspended from the ceiling. It was the first time Collins had seen one in an actual room.

'Mr Collins, I know why you're here but did you have to announce yourself in such a dramatic fashion? You scared the customers, for God's sake.'

'Well, it dain't scare them half as much as the sight of a sawn off shotgun did me. It very nearly cured me constipation, I can tell yow,' said Clark.

Ignoring Clark, Keating continued, 'Look, Mr Collins, Michael, I'm really sorry about what happened. I only heard the full story from that dopey brother of mine on Friday.'

Collins remained silent and walked to the suspended chair and climbed in. 'I always wanted to try one of these ever since I saw Diana Rigg sitting in one in The Avengers,' he said. 'Did you get one of those round telly's to go with it?'

'No, Mr Collins—'

Collins rotated the chair to face away from Keating.

'Yowr information could've got me killed, so I'd like yow to tell me how you fucked up so badly,' said Clark.

For the first time, Keating turned his attention to Clark. 'It seems my pleading with Junior worked. After we'd spoken, he went back to Mahoney and said he was out.'

'So why dain't you update Mickey?'

'Because Tony was still pissed with me. He didn't want to

admit that I was right. He didn't tell me he'd dropped out until Friday. You know how younger brothers can be?'

'Na, I don't. I'm an only child. Good job really, 'cos I don't play nice with others. What about the gun?'

'Tony says there was never any mention of a gun. He says Lenny is a right tosser who likes to act the gangster. He didn't have a gun when they were planning the caper. Like everyone else, he was going with a pickaxe handle.'

'And the numbers. Six is two more than the four yow mentioned to Mickey. If we'd known it were six, we'd have had at least three more coppers on the job.'

'That was just an honest mistake. What Tony had meant was that there were four guys to grab the truck. He didn't count the drivers as part of the crew. Honest, it was just a misunderstanding. You've got to believe me, Mr Collins, I feel terrible feeding you this crap. It won't happen again. You have my word.'

Clark walked behind Keating and rested his hands on the younger man's shoulders. 'That's the trouble, Mr Keating. There's been, what yow call, a breakdown in trust. Both Mickey and me are having trouble believing a single fucking word yow say.' With that, Clark's fingers dug into the soft skin at the bottom of Keating's neck, just above the clavicle. The effect was immediate. Keating gave a muffled cry and tried to squirm away from the pressure, but Clark held him tight and pressed harder. After 20 seconds, Clark released his hold and slapped the back of Keating's head. The force of the blow knocked his head forward and he half rose, half turned as if to retaliate, but quickly regained his composure and sat down.

'Now, think careful before yow answer the next question. Did anyone ask yow to pass duff info to me, mate?'

'No! For God's sake, I'm not stupid enough to set a copper up.'

'Well, I'm not sure wi can take that claim on face value. What do yow think, Mickey?'

Collins remained silent.

'I think yow've really upset him, yow know. He's gone all quiet. I hate it when he goes all moody. Hell to live with. Yowr going to be in his bad books for a really long time. So, final question for now, did you know that Edward Mahoney is dying of cancer?'

'Get on. That old bastard. I'd not heard a whisper. Honest.'

'Yow know something, Mr Keating, yow use the word honest far too often for an honest man.'

Collins stood up from the ball chair and walked over to the desk, where he stood flicking the corners of a sheaf of correspondence that was addressed to Keating Cars. Without looking up, he said, 'Just one more question, Richard, where were you last Monday night?'

Keating thought for a moment. Collins wasn't sure if the delay was because he couldn't remember or because he was trying to work out what, if anything, Collins knew about his whereabouts. After a few seconds he settled on telling the truth. 'I was at the wresting in the Digbeth Civic Hall. I ran into Toby Drew and his mad fuck of a brother. We had a few beers and a laugh.'

'I'm surprised, given your aversion to prison, that you'd risk being seen with dangerous characters like the Drews.'

'I was hoping I might learn something you could use, Mr Collins.'

'And did you learn anything useful?'

'Na.'

'No, I didn't think so. OK. That will be all for now,' said Collins.

Outside, Clarke suggested they grab a cuppa. The two men wandered across the road to Stan's Café and each ordered a tea and two rounds of toast. Sitting in the window seats in comfortable silence, Clark munched his way through a round of toast before saying, 'Yow reckon he was lying then?'

'Don't you?'

'Oh, he were lying all right, but I ain't sure what about.

Yow do realise that if Trylford arranged Smith's death and Keating shopped Mahoney junior to benefit Drew, then wi got a problem. If word gets out that the Drews are trying to take over Brum, we'll have a full-scale gang war on our hands.'

'True. But what worries me the most is we don't know who's behind it all. It might be the Drews or it could be someone else pulling the strings.'

'Yam right. It could be anyone of a dozen bastards.'

Handsworth, 17.00hrs

Agnes had prepared spaghetti bolognaise for dinner and had invited Margaret to join her and Collins. Margaret's face was still stiff and sore, but the pasta required limited chewing. In the three days she'd been in the house, Margaret had kept to herself, slipping into the kitchen to prepare a snack only when she was unlikely to run into anyone else. All her conversations with Agnes and Collins had consisted of the usual greetings and pleasantries. The only real conversation she appeared to have had was with Sarah and Agnes wanted to know what had been said.

As Collins cleared away the dinner plates and Agnes ladled ice cream into three dessert dishes, she asked, 'Have you thought about what you're going to do when you leave here?'

'A bit. I think I should go home.'

'And where is home?' asked Collins.

'Sheffield. A place called Hallam.'

'Well, if you need any money to get home or even a lift, I'd be happy to help,' said Agnes.

'Thanks. A lift would be great, but I don't want to go just yet, if that's OK. I don't want me mam and dad to see me like this. They don't know what I've been up to.'

'You can stay as long as you like,' said Agnes.

'Thanks. I were thinking I'd go next Saturday. Is that all right?'

'Yes, that's fine. You told Mary it was a customer who beat

you up. Why did you go to Mary for help instead of the Drews? Was he an important customer?'

Margaret remained silent, biting her lower lip and thinking whether she should say anything.

'You don't have to tell us anything, but if you do we may be able to use it to warn others,' said Agnes. 'For example, if you could tell us what your attacker looked like, Mary would spread the word among the girls and warn them to be on the lookout for him.'

Margaret looked at the melting ice cream in her dish and a tear appeared in her right eye and slowly ran down her cheek. She didn't try to wipe it away. As it dripped off her chin, she made her mind up. 'It weren't a punter. It were one of Toby's mates. They had a private party. There were three other girls there and Toby's stuck-up girlfriend.'

'And the men?' asked Collins.

'Well, there were both Drew brothers, O'Connell and Blanco who look after the girls and two guys I've never seen before. One was from Brum. The other was a Londoner. Everyone seemed scared of him, even Toby. It was like he was in charge.

'Well, the fun started at about 10 in Toby's flat and everyone was well into the booze by midnight. The girls and me were flitting between the men and all of them had fucked at least one of us, except Toby, who was too busy screwing his girlfriend to get involved. Then, the London guy came over and grabbed me. He wasn't that big, but he was really strong and you could tell from his eyes that he didn't give a fuck about anyone.

'He asked "Have you ever been arse fucked?" and I said no. And he said, "Well, it's about time you were." Then, he bent me over the back of the settee, pulled my knickers down and started to push his cock in. Dry! The pain was awful. I thought he were going to split me open. I started to struggle and he hit me. Well, that were it, I panicked. Somehow I managed to turn around and I went to knee him in the balls. Only I didn't connect right and he went for me.'

'Did no one try to stop him?' asked Agnes.

'Na. Toby and his mates thought it were a right laugh and the girls were too afraid to get involved.'

'What about Toby's girlfriend? Didn't she help?' asked Collins.

'No, she just stood up and walked out of the room. It went on for ages. He was punching, kicking and slapping me. A couple of times, he smashed my head against the back of the settee. Anytime I fell down, one of the men would pick me up and throw me back to the ape. I passed out a few times, but I don't think he even stopped then. The last thing I remember was lying face down on the floor, with him shoving his cock up me. When I came round, I was in the car with O'Connell and Blanco. '

'Did they say anything?' asked Collins.

'Just to keep me mouth shut unless I wanted more of the same. Told me to say I got beaten up by a punter if anyone asked.'

'But you don't know his name?'

'No, but like I said, he had a London accent. But I think he might have come from Ireland.'

'Why?'

'It was the way he said certain words. Like arse was arrce and film was fillum. He sounded a bit like an Irish lad I went out with before I came to Brum.'

'What about the other man, what did he look like?'

'Just ordinary-looking. Dark hair. About six foot, well dressed and he smelt nice.'

'And the woman?'

'Me mate, Paige, told me that she's Toby's secretary. '

'You know there's enough evidence here for me to go and interview the Drews. Do you want me to do that?'

'God no, they'd kill me. I just want to go home and forget all about it.'

Although he wanted to pursue the case it was clear to Collins that Margaret would never give evidence against the Drew brothers, and even with her testimony it would be very difficult to get a conviction, therefore he settled for a non-committal 'Fair enough.' But he promised himself to take a good look at the Drews when he had the chance.

Toreador, Birmingham 21.00hrs

It was ten past nine when Collins and Cavendish entered the Toreador Pub. No one paid them much attention except for Wilkee, who saw Collins and immediately turned his back on the policeman.

Unlike the Manhattan Club, there was no problem in being heard and Collins asked, 'Can I get you a drink?'

'You could, but protocol demands that I do the buying. Orange juice?'

Collins nodded his head and wondered if Mark buying the drinks meant that he was the "male" in their relationship. He was still thinking about it when a man in his late thirties touched his elbow. 'I'm Alan,' he said. 'I'm a friend of Mark's. He phoned me earlier and said you'd be in, but he didn't say he had such a beautiful new friend.'

Collins felt his face redden. No one had ever described him as beautiful before and he found it extraordinarily embarrassing. 'Thank you. I'm Michael, pleased to meet you.'

Alan's grip was firm but sweaty, and Collins had to resist the temptation to wipe his hand once it had been released.

Mark returned from the bar carrying a half pint of mild for himself and an orange and lemonade for Collins. 'I see you two have met,' he said, shaking Alan's hand. Collins noted that there was no great warmth in either man's smile.

'Yes,' said Alan, 'I was just telling him he's far too good for you.'

'I've been telling him the same thing since we met, but what can I say, the man's infatuated with me. But enough about my charms. Were you able to put the word out after I called on Thursday?'

'The notice was a bit short. You may get a few people dropping in, but I've only got one firm customer for you. He's over here.'

Alan led Mark and Collins to a quiet corner that overlooked Temple Row. A man in his late twenties was nursing a pint of bitter. He stood up as they approached and Collins was struck by his overwhelming size. He was at least six foot five and 15 stone, but there wasn't a spare ounce of fat on him. His forearms rippled with muscles and his chest strained against the tennis shirt he was wearing. Even when he sat down, he towered over the other three men.

'Before we start, I need to make it clear that Terry is only speaking to you on the understanding that his name will never be divulged to the police and that this will be the first and only meeting he will ever have with you.'

'Why such stringent conditions?' asked Collins.

'Terry is unwilling to say anything until you have agreed to his conditions.'

'It's all right, Alan,' said Terry. 'They have a right to know. I'm eighteen months into my police training. If the force find out I'm queer, I'll be out on my ear.'

'Do we have a deal, gentlemen?'

'Yes,' said Collins.

'OK. Tell them what you saw,' said Alan.

'I was at the Manhattan Club the night Alan Green was murdered. I'm pretty sure I spoke to the killer, but it was clear I wasn't his type. He couldn't wait to end the conversation and get away from me. Anyway, I think I can describe him pretty clearly, if that's any help.'

Collins' heart sank. Terry was risking his job by coming forward with information they already had.

'Let's leave his appearance for a minute,' said Collins. 'Was there anything else that you picked up on?'

'He had a posh voice. Very middle-class. But it sounded stilted, as if he'd learnt to speak that way.'

'Elocution lessons?' asked Mark.

'Maybe, but it sounded a bit hammy. Like all those actors in the 1950s films. It sounded like he was putting it on.'

'Anything else?'

'He had two scars on his left wrist. They were about an inch apart and ran up his arm for about five inches.'

For the next 20 minutes, Collins took down Terry's detailed description of the murderer. It added nothing substantial to what he already knew, but the information about the killer's voice and the presence of two scars on his wrist could prove to be very useful.

When he finished, Terry stood up and said, 'I think I'll mingle.'

Thirty-five minutes later, Collins saw Terry mingle out of the front door with a very pretty young man in hipsters and a billowing white silk shirt with mother of pearl buttons. Alan followed Collins' gaze. Leaning across, he said, 'I do hope that lad has been broken in. Rumour is that Terry has a twelve-inch cock with a girth to match.'

'God, if that's true he must pass out from lack of blood to the brain every time he has a hard-on,' said Mark.

The men remained chatting and drinking for the next hour, but no one, other than the odd fan looking for an autograph, or something more from Mark, approached the table.

Calling it a night, Collins drove the short distance to Mark's flat and came to a stop on the drive. 'Sorry it was such an unproductive tonight,' said Mark. 'I was sure we'd get a better turnout.'

'Don't apologise. The info about his accent supports your theory that the guy may be connected to show business and the scars are evidence that he's made at least one serious attempt to commit suicide. They might help us identify him.'

'But he cut up his arm. Doesn't that sound more like an

accident than a suicide attempt? I mean, don't most people cut across their arm?'

'That's true, but they don't know what they're doing. It takes time to bleed out from a horizontal cut and it's fairly easy for a doctor to staunch the blood from a cut across the veins. Very few doctors ever get the chance to treat someone who's cut their veins longitudinally. The poor sods bleed out long before any help can reach them.'

'You sound as if you've had experience?'

'First year as a copper, I found an old tramp sitting in a garden of remembrance. He'd cut both wrists longitudinally and somehow he'd even managed to rip the veins out of his left arm. Up to that point, it was the worst thing I'd seen on the job.'

'But worse was to come?'

'Oh yeah.'

The man sitting in his car beneath a flowering cherry tree did not follow Collins as he drove away. Instead, he waited ten minutes, then got out and crossed the busy Hagley Road. A courtesy light automatically came on as he entered the enclosed porch and illuminated the names of tenants. He ran his finger down the list, stopped at Mark Cavendish's name and quickly wrote the number on the back of an envelope. He had so much to remember these days that it was easy to forget important details. With one final check of the number, he stepped out of the light and headed for his car. He felt comforted by the darkness, relieved to be out of the light.

Sunday 5th May 1968, 12.15hrs

Handsworth

Collins arrived home from Mass at St Francis' to find Agnes in the lounge reading the Sunday papers. He kissed her on the neck and asked if she wanted a coffee.

'Please,' she said.

As he left the room, he heard her say, 'Liar.' Then, while making the coffee, two more cries of annoyance broke the silence, 'Never' and 'No, you didn't.' When he returned, he found she'd thrown the newspaper on the floor.

'What's got your dander up?'

'People claiming credit for the work done by others in the war.'

'Anyone in particular?'

Agnes picked the paper up and showed Collins a picture of a very well-known British actor, who had made a name for himself in horror films. 'Him,' she said.

'He's been claiming to be a war hero?'

'That's just it. He's very clever. He never makes any claims. He just suggests he was involved in certain incidents, then charmingly says, "But if I tell you the details, I'll have to kill you." Liar.'

'And you know this because?'

'I knew the agents involved in some of his stories and many of them didn't come back. Now he's using what they did to enhance his reputation. Disgusting.'

Agnes took a deep breath and exhaled, letting the anger flow out. 'I had such a good Meeting this morning. No one offered ministry and the silence was particularly profound. Besides which, Jamie phoned. He's coming home from university on Thursday for the weekend.'

'That's grand,' said Collins, trying to sound enthusiastic. 'It'll be good to see him.'

Agnes read his feelings. 'Don't worry. We haven't looked after him for the past five years to lose him to some homosexual-hating murderer. I'll keep him busy and away from the fleshpots.'

Their conversation was interrupted by the distinctive sound of Cavendish's TR5 parking behind Agnes' Rover. Collins stood up.

'Don't eat too much. Remember, we've got Ruth and Clark coming for dinner,' said Agnes.

Collins kissed her on the lips, slipped on a tailored blue blazer and went outside.

After greeting Cavendish, he said, 'We'll take my car.'

Collins put the Mini in gear and headed for the A34 and Stratford. Once past Shirley, the traffic and people seemed to melt away and the men found themselves in the beautiful Warwickshire countryside on a warm spring day. The roadside daffodils and few early tulips swayed in the sunlight, and Collins felt his spirits rise as he witnessed the English countryside coming to life once again.

The variety of trees they passed was stunning; ash, silver birch, a solitary crab apple, towering elms, majestic oaks and toxic yews – ancient provider of the deadly English longbow. Each tree was at a different stage of unfurling its leaves, and displayed a hundred different shades of green to be seen and marvelled at.

Cavendish sat beside Collins, with his head stuck in a Samuel French play, book-learning his lines – one of the less glamorous jobs that every actor has to perform.

'Do you mind if I ask you a personal question?' asked Collins.

'I've been waiting for this,' said Mark, with a smile, and closed the script.

'Waiting for what?'

'You want to know when I first realised I was a homosexual? Everyone I've ever met has asked me that question.'

'So what's the answer?'

Mark smiled. 'When I went to senior school.'

'You went to public school?'

'God, no. I'm queer by choice!'

Collins smiled at the response.

'I'm from up north, lad. Solid working-class. Me family's from Sheffield on Dad's side and Barnsley on me Mam's. I were first in family to go to grammar school,' said Mark, using the South Yorkshire accent he always employed when he made a visit home.

'So what happened to convince you?'

'In junior school I'd never been one to play football with the boys. I preferred playing with the girls and all my close friends were girls. So it wasn't surprising that the lads saw me as a sissy. But they never bullied me or anything. I was just Mark. The odd lad who didn't like football.

'At grammar school, it was different. I was good at English; loved poetry, music and drama; and wrote little plays and short stories in my spare time. That was enough for some of the older boys to call me names and stick my head down the loo. They started calling me a poof and a queer long before I understood what the words meant. That went on for most of the first year. I begged my father to let me change schools, but he said, "Son, yowr different from most lads and because of that people will treat yow different yowr whole life. So you best get used to it and learn how to deal with it.'"

'So what did you do?'

'Nothing. What could I do? Then, one day, a new boy came to the school, Gerald Niven. He was in the year above and a head taller. He was built like the proverbial shithouse and played rugby for the school's first 15 when he was only 14. He terrified most of the opposition, who were three or four years older than him. Utterly fearless – but the funny thing was that off the field, he was very quiet and shy. He hardly spoke to anyone and never threw his weight about.

'One day, the lads grabbed me and dragged me into the toilets for my weekly humiliation. Gerry saw them and followed. They'd just pinned my arms up my back when Gerry grabbed the ringleader, dropped the nut on him and broke his nose. There was blood everywhere and the boy was crying and shouting hysterically. He'd never seen so much of his own blood before and it scared him witless. Of course, his friends backed off immediately.

'Without a word, Gerry put his hand on my shoulder and sort of steered me out of the toilet. After that, he used to wait for me every day on the High Street and walk me to school, and in the evening he'd wait by the school gates and walk me back. He became my guardian angel and no one ever bullied me again. Funny thing was, he never spoke to me or hung out with me in school.'

'So he was your first love?'

'It was a bit more complex than that. One evening, on our way home, he put his hand on my shoulder, just like he had in the toilets, and walked me to the back of some disused shops. He didn't say anything. He just looked me in the eyes and opened his flies. It was the sexiest thing I'd ever seen and I was only too happy to slip my hand inside his pants, pull out his cock and wank him off. Funny thing was he didn't touch me or kiss me. Not once. Of course, when I got home I rushed to the toilet. I'd barely touched myself before I had the most powerful orgasm in my life. Nothing has ever equalled it. That was the moment I knew I was queer.'

'And from that your love affair developed.' It was a statement, not a question and Collins was surprised by the response it brought from Mark.

'It never developed. We continued walking to and from school together and then maybe once or twice a week we'd disappear up an ally and I'd wank him off. In the three years he was at the school, he never kissed me or made any attempt to grab my cock or do anything other than allow me to wank him off. We never talked about what we did. It was as if it didn't happen.'

'What about when he left school?'

'By then, I was a big name in the school. I'd appeared at the Lyceum Theatre in a couple of professional productions, been on the radio several times and was the director, star and sometime writer of most of the plays the school put on. I was everyone's pet queer.'

'What about Gerry?'

'I never saw him again. I heard that he started to train as a Chartered Accountant in Sheffield, but something happened and he disappeared. Some say he skipped the country just ahead of the police and joined the French Foreign Legion. Of course, the Legion bit may be a load of old twaddle. I still think about him regularly. We never forget our first love, do we? No matter how strange the circumstances are.'

Collins remained silent, but he remembered something Clark's father had once said to him, "There's nowt so queer as folk, lad".

Stratford-upon-Avon, 13.30hrs

The crowd from The Other Queen's Head had spilt out onto the pavement. The mixture of men and women leaning against the pub's ancient wall formed a gregarious but non-threatening mob of about twenty happy people. As soon as Mark was spotted by friends from the theatre, he was enveloped by a mass of bodies.

Collins found himself standing alone on the periphery. 'I'll get some drinks,' he shouted and started to work his way into the pub. *Bloody heaven for a pickpocket,* he thought as he tried to reach the bar. He'd almost made it when Marie Bolding walked in from the beer garden. With her was an older woman, well dressed and with an air of authority about her. Marie's face drained of blood when she saw him. She said something to the older woman and pushed her way back into the garden. Collins quickly followed.

Marie had her back to him when Collins enveloped her in a hug, nuzzled her neck and whispered, 'It's all right, Marie. Introduce me as a friend.'

Before he could say more, the older woman appeared at their side and said, 'Marie, won't you introduce me to your friend?'

Still shaken, Marie tried to recover some composure. 'Of course, Sylvia, this is Michael. He's the brother of one of my oldest friends. I had no idea.'

'No idea that I'm queer.'

'Well, yes.'

'In truth, the jury is still out. You might say I'm on a voyage of discovery. I'm here with a friend. Mark Cavendish.'

'You're the insurance investigator looking into the murder of those poor young men,' said Sylvia.

'That's right.'

'Well, I'm glad that someone is doing something at last. When Mark phoned the theatre last week, news about what he was doing spread like a particularly bad case of the clap. Unfortunately, from the gossip I've been hearing, no one has any new information.'

'That's a shame. We've picked up some useful stuff in the last couple of days, but we need more.'

'I hope I'm wrong, but now, if you'll excuse us, Marie and I have a dinner appointment.'

Marie stepped forward and kissed Collins on the cheek. 'You won't tell father, will you?' she asked, her eyes pleading.

'There's not a snowball's chance in hell that he'll hear anything from me. Don't worry,' said Collins, returning her kiss.

As they walked away, Sylvia briefly stopped to say hello to Mark who was emerging from the bar with a drink in each hand. 'I see you've met Sylvia,' he said, handing Collins his drink. 'She cast me in my first ever TV show. You know the old stories of female casting directors being tough bitches?

Well, Sylvia really is the hardest cow I've ever come across, but scrupulously fair. I've never known her give a role to anyone other than the best actor, which is more than I can say for most male casting directors. And for that, we all love her.'

Michael took his drink and sipped it. 'Sorry, I set out to get the drinks, but got side-tracked. Sylvia said that she doesn't think we'll learn anything new.'

'I got the same message from the theatre lot. Seems that anyone who saw or heard anything spoke to the police at the time.'

'Sounds like there's a better understanding between the police and homosexuals in Stratford than in Brum or Wolverhampton. Why's that, do you think?'

'Two reasons. Firstly, there are more homosexuals in Stratford than you find in most towns outside London. Secondly, and much more importantly, a lot of the queers here have influential friends. They know where the royal, rich and important have buried their skeletons. You remember the scandal about five years ago, with those young girls who were murdered? That happened right here.'

Collins response was non-committal, 'Vaguely.'

'Well, that was just the tip of the iceberg. You'd be amazed to see up-close what our betters get up to with the lower classes.'

No I wouldn't, thought Collins.

In terms of collecting new information about the murders, the afternoon proved to be a complete waste of time. But Collins received a crash course in queer society as he sat in on several conversations that ranged from the growing student protests in France to a discussion on which famous Hollywood hunk enjoyed throwing house parties for his friends dressed in a tutu. Listening to some of the stories,

Collins began to wonder if there were any heterosexual actors left in Hollywood.

As they neared Birmingham, Mark asked, 'What's the story about the woman you were talking to? Is she a policewoman?'

Collins thought for a moment before responding. Was he breaking his promise to Marie if he said yes? He decided that he could answer truthfully.

'Yes, we work at the same station. She saw me and was terrified I'd report her.'

'Did it not occur to her that if you were there, you might also be queer?'

'She knew I was doing some undercover work. She just didn't expect to see me.'

'Will you report her?'

'Why should I? Who she wants to screw is up to her. Besides, she's a bloody good copper. Proved it the other night when she took down a pickaxe-wielding young thug with a lovely rugby tackle and then punched him in the nuts to make sure he stayed down.'

'I'm glad you feel that way. No one should lose their job just because they prefer to share their bed with someone of the same sex.'

Back in Birmingham, Collins dropped Mark off outside his building and drove away, looking forward to his dinner with Agnes, Ruth and Clark. As he parked up, he saw that Mark had left his script on the back seat. *I'd better give him a call*, he thought.

Edgbaston, 18.00hrs

Mark climbed the stairs slowly. He felt tired and a little dispirited. They'd learnt nothing new about the killer. Either he's a bloody criminal mastermind or damn lucky.

Still, a nice warm bath, a drink and a sandwich and I'll be ready to learn my lines. It was only then he realised he'd left the manuscript in Collins' car. *Damn and blast. I'll phone him and pick it up tomorrow*, he thought as he reached the top of the stairs.

He was still thinking about the mislaid script when he opened the door. It was then that something smashed into the side of his head. A huge black spotlight engulfed him and he found himself falling into a deep pit at his feet. In the instant before all conscious thought was extinguished, he wondered if this was the end.

Handsworth, 18.15hrs

Ruth and Clark had already arrived and Agnes was just about to serve dinner when Collins opened the front door.

Shouting a quick 'Hello', he dropped the script by the phone and ran upstairs to have a quick wash and brush up. On his return, even before he'd sat down, Clark asked, 'How's the boyfriend? Did yow pair have a lovely day reciting Shakespeare's sonnets to each other?'

'It was a working arrangement, my good man. Besides, a gentlemen never speaks about such things,' said Collins, in a strangled upper-class accent.

'Well, did yow at least learn anything new?' asked Clark.

'Not a thing, but it was a nice drive in the country.'

Agnes passed the vegetables to Ruth. 'Let's leave discussion of the case until after dinner,' she said and conversation quickly turned to Ruth and the fast approaching birth of Baby Clark.

It was only when he and Clark were clearing away the dishes that Collins spotted the script lying by the phone. Leaving the plates on the draining board, he went to phone Mark.

Edgbaston, 19.05hrs

Mark woke slowly. His hands and ankles were tied to one of the dining room chairs. The room was in semi-darkness. The heavy curtains shut. Just one lamp burnt in the room and sitting in front of it was a man holding a Smith and Wesson .45 Army regulation revolver. The gun looked huge in his hand.

'You're awake at last, Mr Cavendish. I was afraid I'd hit you too hard. I must admit, I don't know my own strength at times.'

'What happened?' Mark asked, his mind barely functioning, his throat as dry as the sand inside an egg timer.

'You've been unconscious for nearly an hour. I was going to wake you, then I thought no. It's only fair to let you enjoy one last languid sleep before I send you to the special hell reserved for you and all your kind.'

'What the fuck?'

The man leapt from his chair and backhanded Mark across the face. 'Do not add foul and filthy language to the list of your heinous and abominable crimes.'

Mark was now sufficiently awake to understand what was going on. 'You followed me from the Queen's?'

'No, I followed you from The Manhattan on Friday night, and your friend, Sergeant Collins, from the Toreador last night. You see, I was onto you from the very start of your pathetic little charade.'

'And now you're going to torture and kill me.'

'Oh no. You are not going to be given the chance to repent. The young men I killed had been led astray by men just like you, with your easy charm, money and fame. I showed them the error of their ways and once they accepted they had sinned and repented, I sent them to God in a state of grace. They are now sleeping in the bosom of the all merciful Lord.'

'But I get no chance to repent?'

'No. You and your kind, who prey on young and impressionable boys, are beyond redemption. You have already been judged in the eyes of the Lord and I'm here to deliver his sentence.'

The phone rang and interrupted the killer's diatribe. Both

men turned to look at the phone. It rang out seven times. When it stopped, the silence was more deafening than an express train.

Without warning, the killer stood up and fired. Mark felt a punch in his side and a gush of warm blood. Looking down, he could see dark, almost black blood, flowing from his right side. There was surprisingly little pain. *Probably the shock,* Mark thought, as he realised he was about to die. *Well, let's make it a decent final curtain.*

'You're dying, Mr Cavendish. I'm a very good shot and I've just lacerated your liver. You have ten, fifteen minutes at most before you bleed out. Do you have a valediction you'd like to make?' he asked, grinning.

Mark raised his head and looked at his killer, 'Yes. Fuck you and all your kind. You cunt.'

The man's face quickly turned from red to blue. Rage burnt in every cell in his body. How dare this piece of filth defy him? Didn't he realise who he was speaking to? Spittle formed at the edges of his mouth. He was unable to speak. His hand shook with rage as he raised the gun again. The last thought Mark had before a .45 bullet smashed a hole as big as a man's fist in the back of his skull was: *Gerry.*

Without checking for signs of life, the killer put the gun in his pocket and left. He took care to close the door gently behind him and check that it was locked. The rage had gone. He felt at peace. The ecstasy he had known when the sodomite died was all the proof he needed that the Lord was pleased with him and his work. Only when he reached the Hagley Road did he take off his driving gloves.

Monday 6th May 1963, 08.30hrs

Edgbaston

Dark clouds scurried across the sky and rain lashed down as Collins parked in the driveway outside Mark's flat. Making a dash for the shelter of the small porch, Collins shook the rain from his hair and pressed the buzzer for Flat 24. He did this twice before he decided Mark was out.

Turning, he bumped into an elderly gentlemen who had a copy of The Telegraph tucked under his arm. 'Filthy day,' the man said and took his umbrella down.

'Tis that,' agreed Collins.

'Who were you after?' the man inquired.

'Mark Cavendish.'

'Ah, my next door neighbour. Lovely man. If it's a delivery, I can take a letter or parcel in for him.'

'That's very kind of you,' said Collins. Taking the script from his pocket, he continued, 'He left this in my car yesterday. He needs it to learn his lines.'

'I think he must have a second copy, as I heard him practising last night.' The man looked at the playbook. A Mew's Murder. 'Well, that explains the shouting and sound effects last night.'

'Sound effects?'

'Yes, the gunshots.'

The blood drained from Collins' face. 'Open the door. Now!' he shouted. As soon as the door buzzed, he pushed through it, 'Stay here. Don't move.'

Collins took the stairs three at a time, but he already knew he was too late. He knew what he would find.

Approaching Flat 24, he hugged the wall and knocked twice on the door. The sound that greeted him was unmistakeable. The flat was devoid of life. Stepping into the corridor, he kicked the lock twice with the ball of his foot. Nothing. Turning his back to the door, he raised his knee to waist high, then, leaning slightly forward, kicked backwards. He caught the lock with his heel and the door sprang open.

Clark had been the first person Collins called and he was the first to arrive, quickly followed by Chief Inspector Hicks and Inspector West, plus the entire CID shift from Steelhouse Lane. This was their patch and it would be their case.

West was his usual blustering self, with a half-smoked Senior Service cigarette stuck in the side of his mouth. His belt was on the last notch and his beer belly hung over the leather like a threatening ledge of snow about to fall from a mountain slope. Standing over Collins, he said, 'So what were you doing here so early? Or did you spend the night?'

Collins looked at him with disdain. A good man was dead and West was making bad jokes. 'I was with him yesterday. He left his script in my car and I was returning it.'

'You were with him yesterday? What was all that about?'

'Mark was helping me with the investigation into the murders of the four young homosexuals. Now, he's dead because of it.'

'What the fuck do you mean?'

'Isn't it obvious? We were getting close to the killer of those lads, so he went after Mark.'

'Bollocks. I told you before, the murders of those four poofters are unrelated. As for this, I think it's pretty obvious what happened. He picked up some bloke, tried it on and the guy killed him. I've seen it before.'

Hicks could see that Collins was about to lose his temper. Gently taking West's arm, he manoeuvred him away from

Collins. 'If your theory is correct, where did this bloke get the gun from or did he just happen to have it on him?'

'It probably belonged to that nancy boy on the floor. When he tried it on, the young lad – and it probably was a young lad or some bloke down on his luck – lashed out. That's when Romeo there grabbed his gun and started waving it about for protection.'

'And the lad or bloke grabbed it and shot Mark Cavendish twice?'

'That's how I see it.'

It was too much for Collins. Pushing Hicks aside, he eye-balled West. 'How the fuck did you ever pass the Sergeant's exam, let alone the Inspector's? You must have shit for brains.'

'Watch it, sunshine, or I'll have you up on a charge before your bog-trotting feet can touch the floor, you jumped-up Irish cunt.'

'Well, at least cunts are useful. I'm having trouble working out what you're good for.'

'I'll tell you, lad. I'm good at taking thieves, murderers, sex attackers and filthy shit-stabbing queers off the street. If it were up to me, I'd give the guys who killed those four queers a medal each and two to the bloke who did this. Can you imagine how many kiddies he's been able to fuck just because he's a TV star?'

Clark saw Collins move slightly back. It was a sure sign he was going to start swinging. Clark swiftly moved between the two men and grabbed Collins' arm. 'Sorry about that, Sir, but I reckon he's suffering from a bit of delayed shock. I'll take him out for a bit of air.'

'That sounds like a good idea. And remember, laddie, we can do without poofter-loving coppers in this force. My Sergeant will see you later for your statement.'

Collins tried to turn back, but Clark's firm hold of his arm and precautionary wrist lock prevented him from taking the Inspector apart.

After they'd gone, Hicks approached West, 'You know,

Inspector, Collins might be wrong about there being only one killer, but he was right about one thing. You are a complete and utter arsehole.'

Before West could reply, Hicks marched out of the room.

Handsworth, 11.30hrs

Back at the station, Collins slipped the pocket watch that the vampires had given him into an evidence bag, sealed it and dropped it into the Fingerprints pigeon hole. With a bit of luck, he'd have an answer by tomorrow.

Still seething, he headed for the canteen, where Clark deposited a steaming cup of tea and a bacon sandwich in front of him. Clark sat down opposite and picked up his own sausage, egg and bacon sandwich. Collins looked at the sandwich accusingly. 'What yow looking at? Thanks to yow, I missed me breakfast.'

'I'll never understand how you stay the same scrawny runt I met five years ago.'

'What can I say? I'm just one of nature's natural athletes. Sound in limb and wind, that's me. But what about yow? Have yow calmed down now?'

'Just about.'

'Good, 'cos what just happened is what yow wanted.'

'Eh?'

'If Inspector "Prick" West had agreed with yow, then our investigation of the lads' deaths would be closed down and a cross-border task force set up. This way, wi can continue looking into the killings. West can't stop us. If he did, he'd have to admit yow were right.'

For the first time that morning, Collins smiled. 'You know for a Baggies fan, you can be surprisingly cute at times.'

'Cute?'

Collins sighed. 'Didn't they teach you English at school? "Cute" is Irish for "smart".'

Clark looked at him disdainfully, then burst out laughing.

'What's so fecking funny?'

Clark was still laughing when Katie appeared in the doorway. Dropping her file on the table, she slumped into the chair beside Clark. 'What's so funny?' she asked.

'I've no idea. This moron has no idea what "cute" means.'

'Ah sure, that's because he's English.'

'Hang on a minute, don't yow pick his side. I saved him from bopping your gaffer this morning.'

'Ah Christ, Clarkee, why did you do that? The lecherous slob deserves a good bopping.'

Laughing, Collins got up. 'What would you like, Katie?' Standing on tiptoe, he surveyed the remaining cakes on the counter. 'They've got a couple of éclairs and some ring doughnuts left.'

Clark looked at Katie, then both of them looked at Collins and dissolved into yet louder laughter.

'Suit yourself. I'll get you a tea and an éclair.'

For some reason, this only added to the now uncontrollable laughter and the tears streaming down Clark's cheeks.

By the time Collins returned to the table, some sense of order had been restored. 'So, tell me what you've got on Sheppard and Drew.'

Opening the file, Katie extracted two sheets of notes. 'As you know, Sheppard used to work for Eddie Bishop, but when he was taken down he went to work for the Drews. How this happened isn't clear, but it looks like Sheppard convinced most of Bishop's boys to follow him. For this, the Drews made him a sort of lieutenant.'

'Sheppard is a deputy to the Drews?' Collins asked, astonished. 'He's got the brains of a retarded stick insect.'

'No, not deputy. He's sort of in charge of the heavies, keeps the boys in line. I don't think the Drews have a deputy. Toby is the brains and Reggie scares the bejesus out of everyone. There's another couple of guys: a Scot called Connelly and a coloured guy, Blanco. They're small fry. Basically just a couple of pimps.'

'Other than taking over Bishop's team, have the Drews picked up any other firms?' asked Clark.

'Well, when Smith was killed in the road accident, the Smethwick lads went to him. Seems they liked how he'd treated Bishop's old boys. I think they approached him, not the other way around.'

'Anything fishy about Smith's death?' Clark asked.

'Not that I've got on file. Why?'

Collins told Katie about his meetings with Sergeant Andrews and Mrs Mabbit, and his suspicions that the hit-and-run may not have been an accident.

'It's possible, I suppose,' said Katie, 'but it doesn't sound very likely. I mean, it's a bit elaborate, don't you think? Toby is bright enough, but I don't think he's a criminal mastermind.'

'Sometimes being underestimated is yowr greatest asset,' said Clark.

'True enough. Anyway, I have to be going. There's a summary of the information I have on both the Drews and Sheppard, including where you can find them. Anything else you need, give me a shout. I'm available any time.'

'Don't yow start that again,' said Clark.

As Katie stood up to leave, Collins asked, 'Do you have anything that ties either Richard Keating or Harry Trylford to the Drews?'

Kathie looked surprised. 'You know more about Keating than I do and I've got nothing that links Drew to Trylford, but I'll take a look. Why are you asking?'

'A girl that works for Drew got badly beaten at a private party. The description she gave of one guests could fit Keating. The guy who beat her up had a London accent, but might be Irish.'

'I'll look into it and get back to you.'

As both men and most of the other males in the canteen watched Katie leave, Clark asked, 'What now?'

'Let's pay Sheppard a visit.'

Perry Barr, Birmingham 13.00hrs

Katie's address for Sheppard was in Perry Barr, not far from the IMI Kynock works. The site stretched from the main A34 down to the island at Witton, just shy of Villa Park, and employed thousands of workers in such diverse firms as Opella Bathroom Fittings, Amal Carburettors, Eley Munitions manufacturer, Lightning Zip Fasteners and IMI Titanium, the country's leading supplier of titanium to the aircraft industry. ICI, the holding company for them all, had effectively built a microcosm of the multifarious industries that operated in Birmingham and explained the city's reputation as the workshop of the world and the city of a thousand trades.

Sheppard lived in a road of smart interwar houses. Most were three-bedroom semis, though there was a good smattering of larger and grander four- and five-bedroom detached houses. A strange place for a thug to live. *I bet his neighbours think he's a lovely man,* thought Collins.

Clark parked the unmarked police car on the drive behind a bright blue Lotus Elan. 'Business must be good,' he said, as he locked the car.

Nodding at the still drawn bedroom and downstairs curtains, Collins said, 'Well, at least we know he's home.'

'Na, don't be like that. Yow know the poor lad works nights.'

It took three minutes of constant ringing and pounding before both men heard the sound of bare feet stumbling down the stairs. The door opened about six inches and a head appeared. Bleary-eyed, unshaven and smelling of beer, Sheppard was instantly awake when he saw who it was.

'What the fuck do you want?'

'Now is that any way to greet an old friend?' said Clark. 'Ain't you going to ask us in?'

'I'm not dressed.'

'Yow ain't got anything we ain't already seen,' said Clark and pushed on the door.

Sheppard stumbled backwards. For once, he was telling the

truth. He was naked except for a vest and pair of Y fronts with an array of stains on the front, the origins of which Collins didn't want to speculate on. A scar on his right leg ran from above his knee to the top of his shin, but the compound fracture that Clark's side kick had caused five years earlier had left more than a scar. The knee's functionality was seriously compromised and allowed for very little movement. The result was a pronounced limp and the silver-topped walking stick that rested beside the door.

'You can't come in here without a warrant. So fuck off.'

'I could have sworn I heard Mr Sheppard say, "Come in". What about yow, Sergeant Collins?'

'Oh, I definitely heard him invite us in.'

'Bastards,' said Sheppard. Taking his cane, he hobbled into the kitchen, which was surprisingly clean with all mod cons, including an expensive Kenwood food mixer and a pine kitchen set with two matching Welsh dressers.

'Yow taken up cooking?'

'Me bird likes this sort of stuff,' Sheppard replied and lit the gas under the kettle with a shaking hand. 'Anyway, what the fuck do you want? Come to bust me other leg, have you?'

'Na, that's all in the past. I'm a reformed character. I seldom cripple anyone these days. Ain't that right, Sergeant?'

'That's true. I don't think I've seen him cripple anyone in at least—' Collins paused for effect, 'six weeks.'

'Look, ask your questions, then take your Morecombe and Wise act and piss off.'

'Shall I start, Sergeant?'

'Please do, Constable Clark. I'll just sit here and have a good laugh at Mr Sheppard's feeble attempts to sound as if he's telling the truth.'

'Wi hear yow're working for the Drew brothers these days. How did yow get the job?'

'I don't work for no one. Me bird runs a couple of hairdressers and I help in the business.'

'Using your financial acumen, I suppose?' said Collins.

'What?' Sheppard looked confused. 'I just pick up and deliver things and keep the shops stocked, that sort of thing.'

'But yow don't do anything for the Drew brothers, is that it?' asked Collins.

'I told you. I don't know the Drew brothers. I spent over two months in hospital, thanks to you bastards, and by the time I came out, Bishop was gone. So, I went straight. These days, I walk a straight line.'

'Not with that fucking leg, yow don't,' said Clark, and grabbed Sheppard by the balls and squeezed. 'Stop fucking us about. We know that last Thursday yow and a couple of the Drews' heavies visited Andreas' chip shop and gave him a good kicking because he wouldn't cough up a ton a month for protection.'

Through gritted teeth, Sheppard gasped, 'Not me.'

Clark squeezed harder, 'I don't believe yow, yow scumbag.'

'It's the fucking truth,' croaked Sheppard.

'I'm starting to think I might have to break his other knee. What do yow think, Sergeant?'

'It might get to that, but for the time being why don't you give Mr Sheppard his balls back and wash your hands?'

Clark released Sheppard, who sank onto one of the pine chairs. At the sink, Clark washed his hands as thoroughly as a brain surgeon about to operate.

Collins suppressed a smile. 'Let me tell you what we know. When you got out of hospital, you helped the Drews take over what was left of Bishop's empire. For that, they put you in charge of the heavies. Last Thursday, you went to the Soho Road Chippie and gave our good friend, Andreas, a right royal kicking.'

'You got to believe me, Mr Collins. I'm straight. I know about the Drews, everyone in Brum does, but I ain't connected.'

Clark's right leg flashed out and stopped a half inch away from the man's damaged knee. An involuntary scream escaped from Sheppard.

Collins held up his hand. 'Let's leave that for a minute. How's Richard Keating linked to the Drews?'

'Yow mean the car bloke on Soho Road? How would I know? I don't know either of them. Besides, word on the street is that Keating is a snout, so why would he be in bed with the Drews?'

'That's what wi want to know,' said Clark.

'Now, last question. Did the Drews organise Ray Smith's accident in order to take over his patch?'

'How the fuck would I know? I keep telling you, I ain't connected to the Drews.'

Stepping forward, Clark slapped the back of Sheppard's head. 'Yowm a lying little toad. Now, when wim gone, get on the phone and tell yowr boss we're on our way to see him.'

Settled in the car, Collins asked, 'What do you think?'

'He's lying about working for the Drews and about duffing up Andreas. He also knows that wi know he's lying.'

'And Keating?'

'Yow took him by surprise. Even so, he tried to protect Keating by telling us what wi already know. Yowr feeling about Keating was right. He's dirty. As for Smith's accident, he probably suspects something, but I don't think he were in on it.'

'Nor me. He's too low on the totem pole.'

'Yow know, I'm beginning to think yow watch too many westerns.'

'What makes you say that, stranger? Now, how's about we mosey on down to them Drews boys.'

Digbeth, Birmingham 14.30hrs

The Drews had not chosen a particularly salubrious location for their office. The whole of Digbeth was given over to wholesalers of manufactured goods and foodstuffs.

Work began early and, among the multitude of legal transactions, there were plenty of dodgy deals done and stolen
goods fenced.

In the summer, the smell of diesel fumes from the Midland
Red Coach Station hung over the area, the blue and purple
haze of the fumes shimmering in the sunlight and catching
in the throat. All this was overlaid by a year-round stench of
semi-rotting food from the Wholesale Food Market and the
stalls in the Bullring Market.

The Drews' offices were located behind the Digbeth Civic
Hall. This meant that they were equidistant from the
Birmingham Dogs Home (Est. 1892) and the oldest pub in
Birmingham. The Old Crown had been built in 1368 and
had been quenching thirsts for 600 years, but no one seemed
interested in celebrating its 600th birthday.

The offices for Drew Bros. Importers and Exporters was
a four-storey affair, if you counted the basement. The basement was used to store heavy items and a ramp connected
it to the goods in and out bays on the ground floor, where
the lighter merchandise was stored. The second floor was for
offices and the third was reserved for the Drews, who lived
and worked on the premises. Each side of the building was a
bomb peck, courtesy of the Luftwaffe circa 1941. The land
had been flattened and was now used for car parking during
the day. However, the chances of parking on top of an unexploded bomb remained fairly high.

Collins and Clark waved their warrant cards at the uni-
formed commissionaire at the bottom of the stairs and headed up to the third floor. Before they reached the first floor
the old man had grabbed the phone and called the bosses'
secretary. She was waiting for them when they reached the
top of the stairs.

'Good day, gentlemen. You are from the police. Can I help
you?' Miss Lisa Larsson was under thirty with a Scandinavian
accent, blue eyes, long blonde hair and glistening white teeth.
The long legs on display, thanks to a very short green mini

skirt, showed the sculptured legs of a runner. This woman was seriously beautiful and knew it. Clark, too busy looking at the vision in front of him, slipped and missed the last step.

Collins caught him under the arm and said, 'Sorry about that. My friend's been celebrating the birth of his seventh child. I'm sure you understand. Too much vodka, not enough self-control.'

'Of course,' she said, doubtfully.

Showing his warrant card, Collins said, 'We'd like to speak to Mr Toby Drew and his brother, please.'

'May I ask what this is about?'

'Yow may,' said Clark, 'but it don't mean yow'll get an answer.'

'I see,' said the woman, staring at Clark as if he was something unpleasant she'd picked up on her expensive shoes. 'This way, please.' She led them into her office. It had been furnished in the same Scandinavian style that adorned Keating's office. The only thing missing was the red ball chair.

Walking to the door behind her desk, the woman knocked and, without waiting for an answer, opened the door. 'Two police officers to see you, Mr Drew,' she said and, standing aside, ushered Collins and Clark into a much larger office.

The room was furnished in the same style as one of the more exclusive gentlemen's clubs in London – the sort of establishment where a flunky ironed the newspapers before arranging them symmetrically on an oak table that had stood against the same wall for 200 years. The only difference was that instead of a range of portraits adorning the walls, the Drews had chosen World War Two battle scenes, depicting the war in the air, on land and at sea.

Toby and Reggie had identical desks, which sat side by side near the window. In front of the desks were four straight-backed chairs, guaranteed to be uncomfortable and make anyone sitting in them feel self-conscious. Both desks had a leather inlay surface, two empty baskets marked in and out, and a pristine ink blotter. There wasn't a single piece of paper in sight. An oak conference table with eight chairs sat in the middle of the room. The only concession to modernity was a steel drinks trolley near the bay window.

Standing up, Toby Drew crossed the room with his hand extended, 'Good day, gentlemen. What can I do for you?' Toby had recently turned 40. At one time he'd fancied himself as a boxer, but four defeats in six bouts had changed his mind. Even so, he still moved like a fighter and beneath the inch or two of fat he had recently put on, it was obvious he still worked out regularly. Collins took Drews' hand – it was small in his, but the grip was strong. Clark ignored the offered handshake. He and Drew had met before.

'We would like to talk to you about one of your employees, Johnny Sheppard. It seems that on your behalf, he was sent to intimidate Mr Andreas Vassiliou and to demand from him the sum of £100 per month,' said Collins.

'It's very unlikely that I employ anyone of that ilk in my organisation, but please sit down and I'll ask Miss Larsson to check. My brother will keep you entertained while I'm gone.'

Collins and Clark sat at the conference table, where they were soon joined by Reggie Drew who glared at them, saying nothing. He was about the same size as his older brother, maybe an inch taller at 5 foot 9. He had the same sandy brown hair, light brown eyes, thick eyebrows and small mouth, but the similarities ended there. Collins knew this man was dangerous. It was in the way he held himself, and the taut stomach muscles and biceps that strained at his suit sleeves. Most of all it was in the hate and anger that lay behind his eyes. Hate for everyone, perhaps even himself.

Toby returned, smiling. 'Sorry to keep you, but Lisa couldn't find anyone by the name of Johnny Sheppard on our payroll.'

'No, I didn't think there would be,' said Collins.

'Do yow know a guy named Keating?' asked Clark.

'Yes, Reggie and I do. He owns a garage doesn't he? We've run across each other once or twice. In fact, I saw him recently at the wrestling in Digbeth. Mick McManus beat some lad from up north. Good show, even if it was fixed.'

'Did yow ever hear of a guy called Phillip Mabbit?'

'No. Why do you ask?'

'Cos he's the guy yow hired to kill Ray Smith so yow could take over his patch.'

'Really, Constable Clark. I know we had a run-in a few years ago, but it really does sound as if you've been reading one too many detective stories.'

'That's supposing you can read,' said Reggie.

'I can read all right. I'm particularly good at reading psycho bastards like yow. I can also predict the future. Before this is over, I'm going to stamp yow into the ground, then piss on yow to see if yow'll grow.'

Reggie's face went pale and he started to stand up, but his brother held his wrist and pulled him down. 'Please, Sergeant, can't you restrain your Constable? There is no need to be so crude.'

'I agree, but he scares the shite out of me so I tend to let him do pretty much what he likes. So, let's get this straight. You've not taken over Smith's patch?'

'Of course not. You seem to think I'm some sort of gang-land lord. I'm a business man. I've never even been arrested, let alone found guilty of any crime.'

'Well, there's always a first time,' said Collins, rising. 'We'll speak again.'

As he rose, Clark asked, 'What about a bookie by the name of Trylford, ever work with him?'

For the first time, Toby Drews' calm deserted him. Momentarily, doubt flickered in his eyes, but it quickly disappeared. 'I know of Mr Trylford. Over the years, I've had to give one or two employees an advance on their wages to pay off gambling debts. He's not a man you should owe money to.'

'That's about the first true thing yow said since we came in this office,' said Clark and winked at Reggie.

As they closed the door, both men heard Reggie say, 'Fucking queers. The pair of them.'

As they walked back to the car, both men smiled. 'That dain't go too badly, did it?'

'No, pretty good considering.'

'Yow do know that if we keep the pressure on Reggie, he'll do sommut stupid.'

'That's what I'm counting on.'

'So yow want him to come after yow?'

'Na. I want him to go after you – and the way he was looking at you, he will.'

'Thanks for that.'

On his way home, Collins made a small detour and dropped in at St Francis' Church. He lit a candle and spent 10 minutes praying for Mark Cavendish. Somehow, he doubted that Mark would spend an eternity in hell. It was more likely that they'd meet up again in purgatory, a few years down the line.

Agnes was at home and he told her of the day's events as they laid the table for dinner. She hadn't really known Mark, but was upset at the pointless death of a talented man. However, when the conversation turned to the Drews, her attention level went up several notches. These were the men who'd sold Margaret on the street and when she'd tried to defend herself, they'd beaten her.

As they sat down to dinner, Agnes felt vaguely unsettled. Something Collins had said was playing hide-and-seek in her subconscious. Something important, but she couldn't think what it was. Never mind, she thought. Forget about it and it will come to me.

Tuesday 7th May 1968, 10.00hrs

Handsworth

Collins arrived at work just after 10. He parked up and went through the back door to check if the fingerprint results had come in. They had, but there were no matches on file and several were those of produced by leather gloves. *We'll have to get the bastard some other way*, Collins thought. *Shame.* Stopping off at the canteen, he picked up two teas and a coffee for Hicks.

The Inspector was leaning back in his chair, blowing stinking, blue and grey smoke rings. Clark was reading a report of a possible assault on Albert Road and looked bored. Both men looked up as Collins entered, bearing gifts.

'Feeling better today, Sergeant?'

'Yes, Sir. Sorry about that. Unprofessional.'

'Maybe, but also human. Finding someone you know with their head blown off is never a nice experience. It brings death closer to home.'

'That it does, Sir.' Collins' phone rang and he picked it up, listened for a few moments and said, 'I'll be right down.'

'What was that?' asked Clark.

'Marie on the front desk. Seems I've got "a couple of bloody big blokes" asking for me.'

'What do they want?' asked Clark.

'Wouldn't say. Fancy backing me up?'

'Sure.'

Clark and Collins exchanged glances when they saw the men. The description of the men as "bloody big" hardly did them justice. Gigantic was more like it. They were both over six foot four, broad-shouldered, with well-muscled chests, slim waists and powerful thighs that even their expensively tailored black suits couldn't hide. They looked like a particularly fearsome pair of funeral directors.

With a nod to Marie, Collins left the glass cubicle that housed the Duty Sergeant's desk and the station's telephone exchange. 'Good morning, gentlemen. I'm Detective Sergeant Collins and this is Detective Constable Clark. I understand you want to talk to me.'

The larger of the two men stepped forward and said, 'Good of you to see us, Sergeant Collins. My name's Gerald Niven. My card.' The card was expensively embossed and read, "Gerald Niven, Founder and Chairman of Elite Forces Security Services. London and Paris."

Looking up, Collins handed the card to Clark and said, 'I assume you had special training before starting your business?'

Niven smiled, sadly. 'Mark told you the story?'

'Yes.'

'He must have trusted you.'

'Are you here about his death?'

'Yes. Can I buy you and your colleague a cup of coffee and discuss what happened?'

'No, but I'll buy you one,' said Collins and lifted the counter flap.

Seated at the back of the only decent coffee shop in Handsworth, Collins, Clark and Niven stirred their drinks. The wonderful smell of coffee and freshly baked pulla infused every part of the shop. The Finnish owner sat behind the counter, reading the paper. Claude, Gerry's personal bodyguard, stood six feet from the table, making sure they weren't interrupted.

After the initial pleasantries were exhausted, Gerry placed

his elbows on the table and said, 'Can you tell me what happened?'

'Most of it, but not all.'

'I understand.'

Collins outlined the events that had occurred from the first time he'd met Mark to when he'd found his body on Monday morning. He did not reveal what he'd learned about the killer and Gerry didn't ask.

Gerry sat back, tears glistening in his eyes. 'Just shake your head if I'm wrong,' he said. 'You're after one killer. He probably spotted you and Mark at either the Manhattan or the Toreador and then followed Mark home. On Sunday, he watched until Mark had left, then broke into his flat and waited for him to return. Is that about it?'

'You should be a detective,' said Collins.

'I want to help.'

'I appreciate that, but you're a civilian.'

'This man is dangerous. A killer. I'm used to dealing with such men.'

'I've had a bit of experience with that meself,' said Clark. 'So far, I'm ahead.'

For the first time, Niven looked closely at Clark. Maybe it was the eyes or maybe it was at some subconscious level, but he recognised a fellow warrior and, bowing his head, said, 'I apologise, Detective Clark. I meant no offence, but if I can provide you with any support in terms of personnel or equipment that you might need, let me know. No questions asked.'

'I'll bear that in mind. One thing you could do is offer a reward for information on the man who killed Mark.'

'That will drive West round the bend,' said Clark.

'Well, that would be a bonus.'

'You want me to annoy the killer. Try to get a reaction out of him. Maybe even provoke him into coming after me. Is that it?'

'Yes. If he does take the bait, I think you've got the skills to survive.'

'You can take that to the bank. How much should I offer – five or ten grand?'

'Make it ten. That will really piss the bastard off.'

'Done.'

'OK. Clarkee and me have a bit of business to take care of, but tell me where you're staying and I'll drop by later. There's some stuff that Mark said that I think he'd like you to hear.'

On the way back to the station, Clark said, 'I hope yow know what the hell yowm doing.'

'So do I. The only thing I'm sure of is that if the killer does go after Gerry, there'll be no need for a trial.'

'That's for sure.'

Handsworth, 17.00hrs

Agnes picked up the phone on the third ring. It took her a few seconds to recognise the voice, which sounded muffled and in pain. 'Mary? Is that you, Mary?'

A slurred 'Yes' confirmed it was.

'Are you hurt?'

'Yes.'

'Are you at home?'

Again, a pain-filled, 'Yes.'

'I'll be right over.'

Hanging up, Agnes redialled. When she got through to the switchboard at Thornhill Road, she asked to speak to Sergeant Collins.

Edgbaston, Birmingham 17.35hrs

Agnes had already arrived by the time Collins drew up outside a well-maintained, two-storey house near Cannon Hill Park and the Warwickshire County Cricket

Club. He jumped from the car and sprinted up the short path. His hand was raised to knock when Agnes opened the door.

'Is she all right?'

'It's bad, but she'll be OK.'

Collins followed Agnes into the kitchen, where she was had been working to patch up her friend. He'd seen a lot of beatings in the last five years, but this one had been carried out by professionals. Mary's left eye was entirely closed. There was a cut on her right cheek where she had been backhanded and a ring had torn the flesh. Her right eye and lips were swollen. A wound on the back of her head was seeping blood. The finger marks around her throat suggested that someone had grabbed her with one hand and slammed her head against the wall or floor. Her breathing was shallow, a sure sign of damage to her chest and stomach.

'Any idea who did this?' asked Collins.

'I don't know their names,' Mary mumbled.

'One of them didn't have a gammy leg, did he?'

'No. I've seen them around. A pale guy and a black.'

'What did they want?'

'They wanted to know where Margaret was.'

'Did you tell them?' asked Agnes.

Mary shook her head and grimaced at the pain, 'No, but what I don't understand is that everyone on the game knows if you get beaten up, you go to either Agnes or the nuns. Any of the girls could have told them. Why did they have to beat me up?'

'God damn it,' Collins cried. 'Where's your phone?'

'In the hall.'

'What's wrong, Michael?' asked Agnes, following him out.

He quickly dialled the CID direct line. The moment the phone was picked up, he said, 'Clarkee.'

'Yes.'

'Get over to Agnes' house. I think Drew may be trying to grab Margaret. I'll be there as soon as I can.' Turning, he kissed Agnes on the cheek. 'Look after Mary. I'll call when I know what's going on.'

'Be careful.'

Handsworth, 17.55hrs

Collins arrived fifteen minutes after Clark, whose car was in the drive. He let himself in and immediately heard Sheba scratching and barking at the kitchen door. Entering the kitchen, he found Clakee sitting at the table, watching as Sheba tried to gnaw her way through the bottom of the kitchen door. The hole was already big enough to put your fist through, but Clark had no intention of putting his hand anywhere near Sheba's mouth. She was one pissed-off doggy. Agnes had put her in the garden when she left and Sheba had not been able to protect her house and the people in it.

Collins opened the back door. At the sight of her master, Sheba's tail started to wag and she brushed against his legs. No jumping. She knew something was wrong. Bending down, he patted his dog's head and calmed her down before removing three large splinters that were protruding from her snout. Only then did Collins ask, 'Well?'

'The girl's gone. There are signs of a bit of a struggle on the stairs where she made a run for it. Whoever took her picked the lock. She must have heard sommut and come down the stairs. Sheba was in the garden when I came. She couldn't get in, but judging by the state of the kitchen door, she tried bloody hard. What's happened to Mary?'

'Badly beaten. Very painful. Lots of bruises. Probably needs her ribs X-rayed. Agnes will look after her.'

'So what do yow reckon is going on? Why did they grab the girl now?'

'It has to be something we said yesterday that scared them. Before that, Margaret had been here a week and they'd done nothing.'

'OK then. What were it wi said that set them off?'

'They batted off Keating and Mabbit.'

'They dain't seemed worried about Smith either.'

'No, the only bit of a reaction we got was when we mentioned Trylford,' said Collins.

'That did surprise them, dain't it. Mind, he recovered quick.'

'True, but let's assume they were worried we knew about Trylford. Why would that cause them to grab Margaret?'

'If Trylford is thick with the Drews, maybe he gets to play rough with the girls. Perk of the job, like.'

'And maybe Margaret could link him to the Drews.'

'Or he were the one that beat her up.'

'It's possible.'

After a pause, Clark asked the question that was on both their minds. 'Do yow think they'll kill her?'

'Pound to a penny they do. Probably done it already.'

'OK, who do we see first? The Drews?'

'No. Let's pay a visit to Mr Trylford.'

Longdon, Staffordshire 19.00hrs

Trylford owned a rambling 17th-century farmhouse in Longdon, between Lichfield and Rugeley. Built halfway up a gently rolling hill, it provided spectacular views over the Staffordshire countryside and, in the distance, the spires of St. Mary's Church and Lichfield Cathedral. The grandeur of the land was breath-taking and Collins wished he could take his shoes and socks off and go for a walk in the damp grass of the meadow below.

Collins' reverie was cut short by Clark banging on the heavy oak door. A woman in her mid-fifties opened up. With dyed blonde hair, lots of make-up and a figure that had given up the good fight about 10 years ago, she was now the epitome of mutton dressed as lamb. Her skirt was too short and her blouse too tight, but her eyes were cheerful and seemed to say, "I know what you're thinking and I don't give a damn".

'Yes? What do you want?' she asked in a London accent.

'We'd like to talk to Mr Trylford, please,' said Collins, flashing his warrant card.

'Best come in then. What's the old git been up to now?'

'Nothing wi can pin on him,' said Clark and she laughed.

Pointing in the direction of a door at the end of the hall, she said, 'He's in his office.' Then, she shouted, 'Harry, you got two coppers to see you,' and returned to the living room.

Collins knocked and went in. Harry Trylford was sitting behind a small desk reading the *Sporting Life*. Folding the paper in two, he laid it down and glared at Clark. 'What are you doing here, short arse?' he asked.

'Is that any way to talk to an old friend, Harry? What's it been, six, seven years?'

'Not fucking long enough. Who's your wanker mate?'

'I'm Detective Sergeant Collins.'

'Shit. They've promoted a young bog-dwelling bastard over you, Clark. You must be really be thick.'

'Yeah, I am, but I'm the only one who ever put yow away. What does that make yow?'

'Mr Trylford, much as I like listening to the banter between you pair and your views on my lineage and brain power, I have a few questions to ask. I suggest you shut the feck up. The sooner you answer my questions, the sooner we'll be gone.'

'OK, away you go.'

'Do you know a prostitute by the name of Margaret Lewis?'

'No.'

'Are you sure? Blonde hair, about five foot tall, aged 19, last seen wearing multiple cuts, bruises and abrasions. Her attacker had a London accent, medium height and strongly built. Sounds a bit like you, wouldn't you say?'

'I told you. I don't know any tom by the name of Margaret.'

'So you do know some prozzies then?' said Clark.

'I didn't say that.'

'She worked for the Drew brothers. Do you know them?'

'Of course I do. Everyone knows about Toby and his mad fucker of a brother.'

'What about Phillip Mabbit?'

– 161 –

'Yeah. He was a punter of mine. The type bookies love. He could bet on the time the tide went out and he'd still lose.'

'Wi were told he owed yow a lot of money and then suddenly he didn't.'

'Yeah, that's right. He paid it off.'

'By bumping Ray Smith off for you? Is that how he cleared his debt?' asked Collins.

'And why the fuck would I want Smith dead?'

'So yowr mates, the Drews, could take over Smith's Smethwick patch.'

'Fuck me. Are you two mental? I've never been in business with the Drews. As for knocking off Ray Smith, we were mates for Christ's sake. Ask anyone. Besides, I've never done anyone.'

'So how did Mabbit pay off his debt?' asked Clark.

Trylford sat and scratched his chin. He knew Clark from old. He knew he was a persistent little fucker and the Irish bastard seemed to be cut from the same cloth. If he didn't answer their questions, they'd be back, and having coppers calling on you day and night was bad for business.

Placing his elbows on the desk, Trylford rested his chin on the back of his hands and asked, 'If I tell you, will you piss off and leave me alone?'

'Depends on what yow have to say,' said Clark.

'OK. Mabbit didn't pay it off. Out of the blue, I got a call from some geezer. He said he'd heard I was holding a note on Mabbit and he'd buy it off me for twelve bob on the pound.'

'That sounds generous. Did you ask him why he wanted it?'

'No, I just bit his hand off.'

'How much did Mabbit owe you?' asked Collins.

'Close to three grand.'

'And there's nowt yow can tell us about this mystery buyer?' asked Clark.

'Only that he had a London accent with a bit of Irish mixed in. That's all I know and all I've got to say.'

'One last question,' said Collins. 'Who picked up the note and delivered the money?'

Trylford sat back in his chair and smiled. 'You got me on that one. It was one of the Drew boys. He had a wog with him.'

As they closed the front door behind them, Collins and Clark heard Mrs Trylford scream, 'Which fucking toms have you been shagging now, you cunt?' This was followed by the unmistakable sound of pottery hitting the wall. Both men were still smiling when they reached the car.

'What do you think?' asked Collins.

'I don't know.? He sounded legit, but mark my words: Harry Trylford is a slippery, dangerous bastard.'

'Agreed, but is he a killer? We could ask Sheppard if he knows anything about Trylford and Mabbit when we chat to him about Margaret. What do you think?'

'Good idea. I just hope he's got his pants on this time. I'm still washing me hands in disinfectant.'

Handsworth, 20.45hrs

Sheppard wasn't at home, which didn't seem to upset his very attractive girlfriend. 'You'll find him at the snooker hall on Soho Road. Do me a favour, arrest the slob. I've been trying to get rid of him for the past four months.'

'So runs the path of true love,' said Clark, as the men returned to the car.

'You know, Clarkee, that's what I like most about you. You have the heart of a poet.'

'Yow know that's very perceptive. I've been telling people for years that I could've been a poet. Of course, me best work was done when I were young and idealistic. I'm particularly proud of:

Roses are red.

Violets are blue.

Tell me the truth or

— I'll kick the shit out of you.'

'I can't understand why they don't believe you.'

The Soho Road Snooker Hall was nothing like the typical dive described in most crime novels. It wasn't run by gangsters. No liquor was served and any betting that went on was low-key and small-scale. Rarely were the police called to it and when they were, it was usually a punch-up between friends, which seldom resulted in any charges being made.

'Evening, Neville,' said Clarkee. 'Wi looking for Johnny Sheppard. Is he in?'

'Hello, boys. Yeah, he's on table sixteen. No rough stuff in the hall, please, Clarkee. It might give some of the other idiots ideas.'

'Don't yow worry, Neville. We'll take him outside.'

Sheppard was lining up an easy pot on the pink when Clark nudged his elbow. He miscued and the white disappeared into the middle pocket. 'What the fuck!' said Sheppard, but stopped himself from launching into an abuse-filled tirade when he saw Clark. With an audience of three mates watching, he decided to play it tough. 'What do you bastards want now?'

Collins draped his arm over the man's shoulder. 'We'd like to have a quiet word with you, Mr Sheppard. Shall we go outside?'

'Fuck that. I'm staying here, where I got witnesses.'

'Yow see, Mickey, I told yow a nice polite approach wouldn't work with this scumbag.' Taking hold of one of Sheppard's finger, which was curled around the cue, Clark bent it backwards. Sheppard's face dissolved into pain and he dropped the cue. 'Shall we go?' asked Clark.

Still holding Sheppard's finger, Clark headed for the rear exit, followed by Collins. The yard was a mess of broken chairs, benches, empty pop bottles and the wooden crates that equipment had been delivered in. Collins pulled a 3' x 3' crate across the concrete and pushed it against the door.

'Don't want to be disturbed, do we, Johnny?'

Sheppard looked scared. He knew what Clark was capable

of; less than a hundred yards from where they were standing, the bastard had crippled him with one kick. He felt his bowels loosen and fought hard to stop disgracing himself. 'Look, I'll tell you whatever you want to know.'

'That's good of you,' said Collins. 'Where's Margaret Lewis?'

'Margaret Lewis? Never heard of her.'

Clark pulled the finger back another inch. A groan escaped Sheppard's lips. 'She's one of the Drews' girls and she's gone missing. Now, where is she or do I have to rip yowr finger off?'

'I know nothing about that side of the business. You want a guy called Connolly. Cockney bastard. He keeps the girls in line.'

'A Cockney you say. What's he look like?' asked Collins.

'About 35, six foot tall, thin but not skinny. Tough bastard. Never goes in the sun because he burns bright red.'

'He's pale-skinned?'

'Yeah.'

'These guys normally work in pairs. Has he got a mate?' asked Clark.

'Yeah, a wog by the name of Blanco. I think he's French. About the same size as Connolly, but a couple of stone heavier.'

'What's he look like?

'How the fuck would I know? They all look the same to me.'

'Where would we find them?'

'They hang out at The Tug Boat Café during the day. At night, they could be anywhere. One of them watches the street and bar girls. The other acts as driver for the top line slags. Delivers them to customers.'

'OK, let's leave that for now. You ever hear of a gambler called Mabbit doing a job for Toby.'

'What type of job?'

'Any type of job,' said Clark and bent Sheppard's finger a little further back.

'Fucking hell, stop. I ain't never heard of a guy called Mabbit.'

Collins nodded and Clark relaxed his hold on Sheppard's finger. 'OK. What about a bookie by the name of Harry Trylford?'

'Everyone knows Harry.'

'Ever seen him with the Drews?'

'Na, never.'

'OK. We'll check it out. If yow been lying, we'll be back.'

'I ain't.'

'So, where do yow want it?' asked Clark.

'In the face. It will show up better, but not by you.'

Collins didn't like punching a defenceless man, even such a poor specimen as Sheppard, but it was necessary. The bruises were his insurance policy. It was proof to his mates and the Drews that he'd said nothing.

Collins made it quick and delivered a straight right jab to the eye and a left hook to the cheek. Both blows would blossom nicely by the time Sheppard reported the encounter to the Drews.

Birmingham, 21.20hrs

Back on the street, Clark said, 'It ain't worth going after Connolly or his mate tonight. We've no idea where to find them. Besides, like yow said, if they took the girl to kill her, they'll have done it by now.'

'I agree. We'll brace them tomorrow. I'll drop you off at home, then I need to see Gerry.'

'Nowt serious between you two, I hope?'

Collins responded with a non-committal, 'Bollocks,' before asking, 'How's Ruth?'

'Close. Real close. I reckon babbie will arrive before the Final.'

The Alhambra Hotel was the premier hotel in Birmingham, just 100 yards from the newly refurbished New Street Station, it was situated on the Queensway close to both the Hippodrome and Alexandra theatres. This meant that it was a popular stopping-off point for rich businessmen and performers from stage, screen and TV, although not many stage actors could afford the nightly rates for even the smallest room.

Collins knocked on the door of the Empire Suite and was greeted by Claude, who opened the door and said, 'Come, please' and beckoned him in.

Gerry stood up as Collins entered and waved him over to the outsized L-shaped settee, which looked small in the huge suite. Claude switched off the 26-inch Philips colour TV and went to stand guard in the corridor.

'Can I get you a drink?'

'No, I'm fine, thanks. Have you announced the reward?'

'Yeah. The *Birmingham Post* will run it in the morning and the *Mail* tomorrow night. I'm also trying to get on *Midlands Today*.'

'Good. Just so we're clear. You realise I want the bastard to go after you.'

'Not half as much as I do. I tried very hard to wind him up in the newspaper reports. I described him as "a perverted homosexual who enjoys killing young men".'

'I just wanted you to be sure that you understood your role as the tethered goat.'

'Your warning is duly noted. Now, you said that Mark had said something that you thought I should hear?'

'When Mark spoke about you, it was obvious you were his first love and that he'd never forgotten you. In fact, I'm pretty sure he still loved you.' Tears appeared in Gerry's eyes and he wiped them away with the back of his hand. 'He couldn't understand why you never contacted him after you left school.'

Gerry tried to stop the sobbing that caused his shoulders to heave and the air in his throat to feel like the scorching desert wind of Morocco. When he regained control, he said, 'When I left school, I promised myself that I'd never mess around with another man again. I really didn't want to be a queer, but I couldn't get Mark out of my mind. I missed him so much. I'd lie awake thinking about him and promising myself that I'd call him the next day, but every day I resisted the temptation. I did that for nearly nineteen months. Then, I gave in and wrote to him. I asked if we could meet. He didn't reply. I was broken-hearted. I assumed he was angry with me or he'd found someone else. So I did what a lot of other stupid little schoolboys did in the fifties when they were disappointed in love. I ran away and joined the Legion. And now you tell me that I spent five bloody years in the Legion because of a misplaced letter.'

Looking around the room, Collins said, 'It looks like you learned a thing or two in the Legion.'

'You're right. It suited me. I liked the physical side of it and I found that I had a flair for languages, provided they were taught in the right way.'

'And when you came out?'

'I set up the business with a couple of sergeants I knew. Our first case was protecting an industrialist. We stopped an attempted kidnap, killed two of the gang and captured the other two. Within twenty-four hours, we had more clients than we could handle in a year. Inquiries came from all over the place, but mainly France and Italy. Within a week, the firm went from three employees to twenty-two.'

'All ex-Legionnaires, I assume.'

'Yep. I didn't have to do any interviews. Everyone we signed up we'd worked with and we took no one below the rank of sergeant. We've expanded since then and now I've got the odd Royal Marine. I made enquiries about your mate, Clark. Tell him if he ever wants a job, I have one for him at about six times the pay he currently gets.'

'Will do. What I don't understand is why you didn't contact

Mark after you left the Legion? I mean, you could have just dropped in on him backstage.'

'I didn't want to intrude on the life he'd built. Then, on Monday, an English client mentioned his murder. After a few inquiries I knew I had to come. I never gave him anything in life. All I did was take. Now, maybe, in death, I can give him justice – or if not that, vengeance. Just like the old days.'

'I think you gave him a lot more than you realise. You gave him love, even if you were unable to express it, and in return he loved you.'

It was too much for Gerry and tears filled his eyes again. Collins placed a hand on his shoulder and said, 'I'd like to arrange a meeting between you and Mark's friends. I think it would be good for you and for them. They can tell you a lot more about him than I can and I'm sure they would want to meet you.'

Wednesday 8th May 1968, 08.15hrs

Digbeth, Birmingham.

Sheppard waited nervously outside the Drews' office. Inside, he could hear the muted tones of Toby Drew and Richard Keating, and the occasional loud, angry interruptions from Reggie. After twenty minutes, he was called in.

Toby and Keating were sitting at the conference table and Reggie was prowling the office like an unfed tiger at Dudley Zoo. 'Tell me everything that happened and leave nothing out,' said Toby.

Sheppard described the events of the previous night, but embellished the ending. 'I was sure that fucking bastard Clark was going to kill me. I thought "What can I tell 'em that they already know or could easy find out?" So I told them that Connolly and Blanco looked after the girls – that was all. I mean, any of the toms could tell 'em that.'

'And you said nothing about this guy, Mabbit?' asked Toby.

'How could I? I've never heard of him.'

'What about Trylford? Did they mention him?'

'Yeah. I said everyone knew Harry, but I'd never seen him with you, Mr Drew.'

'Did they ask about me?'

'Not a word, Mr Keating.'

Toby looked at Keating and Reggie. Both of them nodded. 'OK, you can go. Here's a pony for keeping your mouth shut,' said Toby, handing Sheppard two tenners.

After the door had closed, Keating said, 'We may have to do something about that long streak of piss.'

'I agree. He'd shop the lot of us if his neck were on the line,' said Reggie.

'Well, I think we can leave that for a bit. It seems Clark and Collins are working on conjecture and guesswork at the moment, but if they link Mabbit to us or London, we'll have to do something.'

'Such as?' asked Keating.

'What do you think?'

'You'd better talk to the boss about that before you do anything.'

'Do you think I'm fucking stupid? snapped Toby, annoyed that Keating thought he was mad enough to move against a couple of coppers without clearing it with the boss. 'Of course I'll talk to London before making a move. Bloody hell. Talk about stating the bleeding obvious.' Toby ran his hands through his hair. 'Of all the fucking times for the plod to start nosing about, just as we're making a move on old man Mahoney.'

It was the first time in a long while that Keating had seen Toby lose his temper. He's feeling the pressure, he thought. Maybe there's an opportunity here for me. However, one look at Reggie was enough to remind him to be cautious.

Handsworth, 09.00hrs

Collins poured hot milk on his Shredded Wheat and then covered them with three spoonfuls of sugar.

'Michael, you're worse than a child. Three spoonfuls, really?'

'You can never have too much sugar. It's good for you.'

'I'm not so sure about that.' Sitting down at the table, Agnes made a steeple out of her fingers, and looking over them, said, 'I was thinking about something you said last night.'

'Remind me, I said a lot.'

'You said that Trylford and Connolly were cockneys. Margaret also said that the man who raped her had a London accent. Have you considered that there might be a link to one or more of the London gangs? In the past, whenever a London gang tried to set up shop in Birmingham, they received a visit from the Welcome Wagon, which wasn't adverse to using violence to persuade them to return home. What if they changed their strategy and instead of trying to

set up in Birmingham, they've decided to build a partnership with a single gang in Birmingham with the aim of taking
over the city and surrounding areas. Like Fifth Columnists. I
know it's fanciful, but I'd like to call a friend in London.'

'Last time you were in contact with your friends in
London, we were up to our armpits in MI5 and assassins
from Bulgaria, remember?'

'Well, Sybil isn't a spy. She works at Scotland Yard.'

'All right then,' said Collins his fears partially assuaged.
'Your instincts are usually right. If you think it's worth it,
give her a call. Now, I need to be off.'

'Call me if you hear anything about Margaret.'

Birmingham, 09.20hrs

When the killer picked up The Birmingham Post, he
immediately saw the headline, which read, "Reward
Offered for Capture of Actor's Killer". As he scanned the story, his anger rose, but he pushed it down and locked it away
in his gut and used it to produce more bile. Did they think
he was so stupid that he would react in anger to their lies
and make a mistake? If so, they had underestimated him. I'm
better than all of them and I always will be because God is on
my side. God will guide and protect me, for my work finds
favour in his eyes.

'It's Collins who's behind this,' he muttered to himself.
'Well, first I'll kill his friend, then that whore of a landlady
and then him, but I'll wait. I'll wait until his defences are
down. I'll wait until after the next trip.'

But as he walked back to his flat, an idea started to take
shape – another inspiration from God. They'll expect me
to go after Collins or this queer-loving Niven. They won't
expect me to save another lost soul. That would be a nice
going-away present to leave the bastards.

Handsworth, 10.00hrs

A tired looking Clark was just getting out of his car as
Collins drove into the police yard.

'How's Ruth?'

'Two false alarms last night. On the second, we was half-way down the stairs before she said, "It's passed." After that, I couldn't get back to sleep. Sleeping with a pregnant woman is noisier than with a billet full of commandos.'

'Yeah, but the cause is your fault.'

'I bloody hope so.'

'Besides, it's good training for what's to come.'

Suddenly, the control window opened and, leaning out, Marie shouted, 'Sergeant, a body has been found on the tracks. Young, white female.'

'Where?'

'By the bridge on Holly Road. Looks like she jumped or was dumped over the parapet.'

Clark and Collins exchanged glances. Both men were thinking the same thing. Collins felt his stomach turn over. Even if it wasn't Margaret, he hated train deaths. No matter how many he attended, they never adequately prepared you for the unique horrors of the next collision.

'We're on our way. Phone the British Transport Police and get uniform and forensics down there.' If it was Margaret, he'd have to declare it as a suspicious death and take over control of the investigation from the Transport Police.

'Will do.'

As he and Clark headed back to his Mini, the only thought in Collins' mind was, I hope she was unconscious before they threw her over.

It took less than a minute to drive to the park's Holly Road entrance. Clark picked up his wellingtons off the back seat and Collins removed his from the boot. Neither man spoke. Locking the car, they headed for the iron railing that separated the park from the railway embankment.

Later, the police would remove a stretch of railings to improve access, but for now both men clambered over. They
slowly edged their way sideways down the steep embankment, slick as ice thanks to the regular rain showers of previous days. They reached the tracks and walked the few yards
back towards the bridge. Almost immediately, Clark saw
Margaret's severed head. Battered, bruised and bloody, but
still recognisable, it had been flung clear of the track and lay
twenty feet up the embankment.

Clambering back up to the head, both men saw immediately that it was surprisingly intact. The train wheel had severed the neck cleanly. 'Her neck must have been lying across
track,' said Clark.

Collins nodded in agreement. 'What do you make of this?'
he asked, pointing to a hexagonal indentation on the top of
the head.

'Could be a hammer, but might be a bolt she landed on.'

'If it was a bolt, she must have dived off the bridge headfirst.'

'Yowr right, but yow know as well as me that strange things
happen to a body when it's been hit by a train and this one's
been hit by more than one.'

'I know. Do we have enough to call this a suspicious death?'

'More than enough. Do yow want me to go up top and
stop the world and his wife from traipsing all over our crime
scene?'

'Please. Send scene of crimes down when they arrive. Keep
the rest up top until I say otherwise.'

As Clark trudged up the embankment, Collins returned
to the trackside. Body parts lay everywhere. A complete leg,
part of a hand, a section of the torso, small unrecognisable
bits of connected blood, flesh and bone, and even smaller slivers of flesh and bone and small lumps of red mince-
meat. Collins saw an almost complete hand, with a cheap
"gold ring" and even cheaper stone, still on the third finger.
He picked it up and it collapsed in his hand. Most of the
flesh, bone and gristle had been expelled from the hand by

the force of the train. What he was holding was little more than a bloody glove. He felt his stomach lurch, but fought his revulsion down and placed the hand as gently as he could by the side of the track.

Scenes of Crime were now appearing on the embankment and by the trackside. He spoke to the lead officer and showed him where the head was. 'I'm pretty certain that the poor kid was knocked unconscious and then dumped on the tracks. I want to know if the bastards threw her from the bridge or rolled her down the hill. Photograph everything. I'm heading back to the station to brief DCI Hicks. He'll want to see things for himself, so move nothing until he gives the go-ahead.'

Collins climbed up the embankment and eased himself through the gap in the railings that forensics had made.

'Are yow all right, Mickey?' asked Clark.

'Yeah, I'm fine. I just find train deaths really hard.'

'I suppose I'm lucky. I saw worse in the war, but it ain't nice. Yow do realise that the bastards who did this were bloody clever.'

'I know. It's going to be near impossible to prove that she was thrown in front of the train unless we find an eyewitness, and the damage caused by the trains will mask any other injuries she had.'

'If they tipped her off the bridge, we might get lucky and find a witness.'

'It's worth checking out. My guess is they came in after dark. Threw her over the railings, rolled her down the embankment then laid her on the track.'

'Laid her on the line?'

'That's my guess. The sick fuck who did it arranged her body so that the first train through would decapitate her. Probably thought it was funny. Of course, I can't prove it – just as I can't prove it was Connolly and Blanco that did it.'

'All true, but since when couldn't wi defend ourselves

against a vicious and unprovoked attack by a couple of heavies?'

For the first time since he'd arrived on the scene, Collins smiled in anticipation.

Handsworth, 10.15hrs

Agnes phoned New Scotland Yard and asked to be put through to Miss Sybil Harker in the Intelligence Unit. Agnes had worked with Sybil at Bletchley. Unlike so many there who had the ability to analyse the detail, Sybil had a rare talent for seeing the interconnection between disparate pieces of information – the overview position. This enabled her to see and recognise the interrelationship between individuals, groups and even the distribution of goods and supplies. It was if she was able to construct a 3D map of complex relationships and fill in the blanks with extraordinarily accurate guesswork.

'Sybil Harker. Who's calling?'

'Hello, Sybil. It's Agnes.'

'Agnes, how lovely to hear from you.' The formerly brusque tone had been replaced with a warmth and joy that would have surprised many of her subordinates if they'd been within earshot.

'I'm fine, but I feel a little guilty. I'm after a favour.'

'You know I'll do anything I can to help my favourite linguist. What are you after?'

'My friend, Detective Sergeant Collins, is looking at the activities of a gang in Birmingham. They seem to be consolidating power, taking over rival gangs when the opportunity presents itself. A couple of people he's looking at have Cockney connections and I was wondering if someone in London might be orchestrating the entire campaign.'

'That would be one way to infiltrate Birmingham. Your unofficial Welcome Wagon has been very effective in dealing with undesirable visitors from London over the years. My all-time favourite story has to be how Eddie Hazard was suspended naked by his ankles from the fourth floor window of The Grand Hotel while a Superintendent read him a selection of Burns' best poetry. From what I hear, it wasn't even Burns Night! Anyway, what names have you got?'

'A bookie called Harry Trylford and his wife, and a thug named Connolly.'

'Martin Connolly?'

'I'm sorry. I don't have a first name.'

'Is one of the other names Blanco?'

'Yes. How did you know?'

'Martin Connolly and Blanco go back years. Established thugs. Then, about four years ago, they disappeared from London. I've not heard of them since. I'd assumed that they were both helping to hold up one of the new London flyovers, but if they're alive, then they could be working for Harry Gregson.'

'Gregson?'

'The number two gang boss in London. He and his vicious cousin, Patrick O'Neil, are well capable of organising a takeover of Birmingham from afar. What other names do you have?'

'Toby and Reggie Drew, and Richard Keating.'

'OK. Leave it with me and I'll call you back later today.'

Birmingham, 14.00hrs

Back at the station, Collins and Clark briefed Hicks and outlined their suspicions. They agreed they had no hard evidence that Margaret Lewis had been abducted or murdered. Any defence barrister in the land would have been able to argue that given her work, the trauma of being raped, her lack of money, and being alone and desperate, it was reasonable to conclude she'd committed suicide.

Their only hope was that the hexagonal-shaped injury to the head had been inflicted prior to death. Hicks agreed to call the ever-charming Mr McEwan, Chief Pathologist, and ask him to closely examine the injury to the head. The good doctor's personality had not mellowed since his appointment over time and he was now universally despised by fellow pathologists, police and fire officers, and every mortuary assistant who had ever worked with him. However, he had one redeeming grace: he was good at his job.

While Collins and Clark wrote up their reports, Hicks visited the scene of death.

It was nearly 3pm before Collins and Clark were able to head off to Broad Street and the notorious Tug Boat Café. Everyone in Birmingham knew it was owned by a gangster, but no one could name him. Everyone also knew that it was a hangout for burglars, fences, hard men, hold-up artists, thieves, pimps and robbers, yet there was never any trouble. It was also a fact that the plates of egg, chips and peas served by a monosyllabic greaser with long hair, multiple tattoos and a less-than-clean apron were cheap and very tasty. This meant that the students from the nearby college filled it to the rafters every lunchtime and early evening, regardless of its reputation.

Connolly and Blanco were sitting at a Formica-covered steel table at the back of the café, next to the door marked "Private". Neither looked up as Collins and Clark approached.

'Mr Connolly?'

'Who's asking?'

'I am,' said Clark and, without warning, he hit Connolly in the side of the face with a roundhouse kick. Connolly flew backwards off his chair and landed in a crumpled heap in the corner, dazed and semi-conscious.

Blanco tried to stand up, but Collins hit him with a right hook that accelerated as it travelled downwards. It hit Blanco an inch to the left of his jaw and was hard enough to ensure that he landed on top of his friend.

Clark tipped the table over on the men. Its metal edge pinned their tangled legs to the floor. Collins ensured they stayed there by leaning on the top edge.

'We just wanted to introduce ourselves, gents. My friend here is Detective Constable Clark and I'm Detective Sergeant Collins and when we have the evidence that you abducted and murdered Margaret Lewis, we're going to come back and put your arses behind bars for life.'

'And lads, when we do, I really do hope yow resist arrest,' said Clark.

Turning, Collins and Clark walked out. No one looked at them. No one moved. No one stopped them.

Handsworth, 15.20hrs

Collins was glad to get home. He shut the door, caught Sheba in full flight and slipped into the rocking chair in the lounge. He felt a lot older than his 28 years. If he'd been a drinking man, now would be the time to knock back a double scotch. However, he wasn't, so, after taking his shoes off, he stumbled into the kitchen and put the kettle on.

Two hours later, Agnes found him curled up on the settee, asleep. She gently closed the door and let him sleep. It was only when he finally woke up at 9pm that he told her of Margaret's death.

'You'll get them,' she said, sadly, patting Collins on the knee. 'You'll get them.'

Thursday 9th May 1968, 09.55hrs

Handsworth

It was nearly 10am when Sybil called.

'Agnes, I'm so sorry I didn't call last night. I was in the file room until well past nine, and back there again this morning. I've found a photo that might be of interest, but I don't want to send it through normal channels. Could I meet you later this afternoon in Birmingham?'

'Of course. There's a Lyon's Coffee House at the top of New Street, the Town Hall end.'

'Sounds just like old times. I'll see you there at four.'

Handsworth, 14.30hrs

Collins and Clark had spent most of the day checking the documentation for the hijackers' trial. It was tedious work but essential. No copper wanted to see a villain walk free because of an error in the paperwork. They were just about to break for a mid-afternoon cuppa, when Sergeant Ridley stuck his head around the door and said, 'You ain't going to believe who I've got at the desk asking to see you two urgently.'

'Unless it's Sophia Loren, I don't care. I'm off for a cuppa,' said Collins.

'Close, but no goldfish. It's Upright Freddie and he says it's vital that he speaks to either you or Clark.'

'What's it about?'

'Wouldn't say. He'll only speak to one of the dynamic duo – his words, not mine.'

'OK. Put him in Interview Room 1.'

Five minutes later, Collins and Clark joined Freddie in the Interview Room. He'd filled out since his unfortunate encounter with a rusty nail. He now cut something of an imposing figure. His bearing was confident and he sought eye contact rather than trying to avoid it. Of course, the starched dog collar and spotless suit helped as well.

Collins placed one of the cups he was carrying in front of Freddie. 'Strong tea with three sugars. Just as you like it.'

Clark took up his usual spot standing by the door, sipping his cuppa.

'Thank you, Mr Collins, you remembered.'

'It's difficult to forget yow, Freddie. Anyways, what's you here for. You haven't been shagging the entire Dagenham Girls Pipe Band, have yow?'

'Mr Clark, you know that since I found Jesus I've been faithful only unto him. Why can't you accept that it was through you and Mr Collins' intervention that I saw the light and was saved?'

''Cos in my book, once a wanker always a wanker. That's why.'

'I pray that one day the Lord may show you that I've truly changed. Until then, I have some information that I think will go some way to repaying you for what you have done for me.'

'Information?' What sort of information?' asked Collins.

'As you know, there are many lost souls out there seeking a path to the Lord. Every Wednesday night, I hold an open meeting at my church. Anyone can attend and ask questions or put forward their own ideas about God and the Bible. Last night, I had a new visitor. He was very quiet during most of the meeting. Happy to doodle away on a bit of paper. But when Anthony gave thanks to the Lord for saving him from a vile teacher who sorely used him for pleasure, the newcomer became interested. He asked me what the Bible said about homosexuality. I told him that it was an abomination in the eyes of God.

'That pleased him and he asked, "Do you agree with me that homosexuals should be put to death?" Well, I thought we were entering dangerous ground and so I prevaricated. This seemed to enrage him and he started quoting Leviticus at me. I'm sure you know the chapter and verse, Sergeant Collins.'

'Please remind me,' said Collins.

'Lev 20:13, "If a man has intercourse with a man as with a woman both commit an abomination. They must be put to death; their blood on their own heads."'

'Oh, that old one,' said Clark. 'I have a framed copy of it over me bed at home.'

'Laugh as you will, Mr Clark, but when I tried to show him that Christ's mercy was available to all – even those cast down into Satan's pit of filth and debauchery – he became very agitated. He said if I were a true Christian, I would seek out and destroy all sodomites. I tried again to suggest that the Lord's forgiveness was open to all, but he became more and more angry. Finally, he stormed off, shouting that we were no better than apologists for those that wished to infect the young with the most deadly disease known to man. "A disease," he said, "that kills both the flesh and the immortal soul unless sinners repent and die for their sins."'

With this final statement, Collins exchanged a glance with Clark, who pushed himself away from the wall and sat down at the side of the table between Collins and Freddie.

Trying to be a casual as he could, Collins said, 'That's very interesting, but the guy hasn't killed anyone, has he?'

'Not that I know of.'

'So what's it got to do with me and Clark?'

'This,' said Freddie. He took out a folded sheet of foolscap paper and laid it on the table.

'Fuck me,' said Clark.

Using the end of his biro, Collins drew the paper closer. The page was covered with the usual meaningless scribbles, doodles, triangles and cartoon monsters with fangs, talons and pitchforks except for the middle of the page, where there were four tombstones. Written on each was a single name: Daniel, Alan, Peter and Joseph. Each drawing had been struck through with a large X. Lower down the page, there were four further tombstones. These were named Cavendish, Clark, The Woman, Collins and Niven. Only the name of Cavendish had been struck through. On the bottom line, four more names had been written and embellished with scrolls and flowers: Paul, Timothy, James and Peter.

'I tell you what, Freddie, me and Clarkee are going to have a chat and check something out. While we're at it, we'll get you another cuppa and a bacon sandwich.'

'That's very kind, but I need to be going. It's Bible class tonight.'

'Sorry, Freddie, but yow'll be missing the class tonight and if I were yow I'd take that sarnie. It could be a long night.'

Freddie looked from Clark's face to Collins'. It was clear he'd be going nowhere. 'Can I have butter on my bacon butty, please, and call my assistant?'

'Course yow can,' said Clark.

In the corridor, Clark asked, 'Are yow thinking what I am?'
'Pound to a penny, I am. It's a record of who he's done and who he's going to do.'

'How come he's got me before yow? I ain't even been to the dives of debauchery that yow have.'

'What can I say? He wants to make me suffer by killing Agnes and you before me.'

'Do you think he'd believe me if I told him I can't stand yow and all your Papist ways?'

'I doubt it. OK, I tell you what, you grab us all a bacon butty and fresh teas, and I'll phone Agnes and tell her to give Ruth a call.'

Fifteen minutes later, Collins and Clark returned to the Interview Room. Clark had even managed to pinch an unopened pack of Fig Rolls for their honoured guest.

Freddie had been doing some thinking. 'Has this man killed someone already?'

Placing a fresh brew in front of Freddie, Collins said, 'We're not sure, but we're interested in what you've got.'

'I suppose you want to know what he looked like?'

'That would be a bostin start,' said Clark.

'He was in his late twenties or early thirties. A little shorter than you, Mr Collins. Just an inch or so, but bulkier. He looked fit. There was no fat on him. For some reason, I thought he might be in the army.'

'OK, that's good,' said Collins. 'What about his facial features, hair colour, eyes, any scars – that sort of thing?'

'I didn't see any scars, but he had brown hair.'

'Dark brown or light brown?'

'Just brown. I think his eyes were a sort of blue and he combed his hair the wrong way.'

'The wrong way?'

'The parting was on the left and he let the fringe hang down over his right eye. He had a slim nose, but it was turned up a bit and made him look stuck-up.' A bit like Kenneth Williams in the Carry On films.'

'That's very good. What else?' asked Collins.

'His mouth was small and pouty.'

'Would you recognise him if you saw him again?'

'Definitely.'

'OK. While it's still fresh in your mind, I'm going to get an officer to bring in his identikit and see what the pair of you can produce. He'll be in in a jiffy.'

'OK, but what about his car? Don't you want to know about that?'

'Wi was just coming to that,' lied Clark. 'You see, I'm the mechanical one in this team, since my Sergeant here never saw a car before he came to England.'

Collins, hands in his lap, and shielded from Freddie's view, gave Clark a two-fingered salute.

'What can yow tell us about his car?'

'It was a dark blue Rover 2000.'

'What about its registration number?'

'No idea.'

'So basically yow know next to nothing about the man's car?'

'That's right.' Clark sighed heavily and Collins dropped his biro on the table. Freddie seemed to be enjoying himself. He was trying to hide a small smile that was just starting to form at the corners of his of his mouth. 'But I bet Robbie Moore does.'

Leaning across the table, Collins asked, 'Who the feck is Robbie Moore?'

'A little lad who lives two doors down from my church. He collects car numbers. Mad about them he is. He records the make, model and colour of every car he sees, and the date and time he saw it. He likes it when the church has a meeting because we get visitors from other parts of the Midlands.'

'And he was there last night?'

'Never misses.'

'What's his address?'

'Antrobus Road. A blue door about two or three houses down from the church.'

'Right, you make yourself comfortable. Ring the red bell by

the door if you need anything. The Identikit Officer will be with you in a tick,' said Collins.

In the corridor, Collins said, 'I'll brief the Boss and find Ridley. Can you and Marie go and see this Robbie Moore?'

'Why do I need Marie?'

'So you don't scare the poor kid.'

'Me! I'm loveable, I am. Eccentric, but loveable. Like Walter Brennan in Rio Bravo, but with me own teeth and without the gammy leg.'

'Yeah, I can see the resemblance. Now, push off.'

New Inns, Handsworth 16.00hrs

Marie rang the bell and a man in his early thirties wearing a mechanic's overall answered. Before either Marie or Clark could say anything, the man turned and bellowed, 'What the fuck have you been up to now, Robbie? Get down these stairs. Now!'

Turning back to the police officers, he said, 'You'd better come in. Go in the front room.' Standing at the bottom of the stairs, he shouted, 'Robbie, I won't call you again.'

The front room was the repository for everything broken in the house, and there was a pervading smell of damp, caused by a large spreading patch under the front window. Robbie came down the stairs slowly, head down. He couldn't think what was up. He hadn't done anything since pinching the birthday cake from the bakery on Soho Road last January and pretended it was his. Even his mates hadn't been fooled. The outline of the iced message, which he'd so carefully removed, was still clear: "To Jill, Happy 7th Birthday". Maybe someone had complained about him taking down their car number.

Grabbing him by the arm and shaking him, his father said, 'What you been up to this time?'

'The lad's done nothing wrong,' said Clark.

'So why are you here?'

'We think he can help us.'

'Help you, how?'

'Just some information,' said Marie. 'Would you mind, Mr Moore, if Constable Clark and I cadged a cuppa? We've been on our feet all afternoon.'

'Na. The kitchen's this way.'

At the door, Marie turned and winked at Robbie. His face broke into a grin.

Clark moved a record player with no arm off a broken stool and, after testing the stability of the seat, sat down. 'OK, Robbie, Mr Bartholomew, the vicar down the road says yow like to collect car numbers. Is that right?'

'Yeah, but I never touch the cars. Scout's honour.'

Clark doubted if the underfed nine-year-old in front of him had ever been to a Scout meeting. The one-shilling subs per week were too high. 'I know yow don't, but last night there was a meeting at the church. Did yow go there and record the numbers as usual?'

'Yeah. There was a red Jag there. Is that the one you're after? A getaway car?'

'No, not that one. It's a dark blue Rover 2000 I'm interested in.'

'Yeah, there was one. Good nick and all.'

'And did yow take down its number?'

'Of course I did – otherwise how would I prove I'd seen it? It was a Walsall number from June, July or August 1965. It were EDH 686C.'

'Yow memorised the number?' asked Clark, astonished.

'I know the number and description of every car I've ever listed,' said Robbie, proudly.

'Could I see the book yow recorded the numbers in?'

'Sure.'

Robbie returned with his book just as Marie came into

the room with two mugs of tea, followed by Robbie's father. 'Well, has the little twerp been able to help you?'

Clark ignored the comment and instead took the scruffy sixpenny pocket book, in which Robbie had recorded the registration numbers. 'It's on the last page, third one from the top,' he said, helpfully.

'I think the policeman can find it without your help.'

Clark saw Robbie flinch and the smile of excitement leave his face. The recorded details matched exactly what Robbie had said. 'Can I borrow yowr book, Robbie? I'll bring it back.'

'Well—' he said, doubtfully.

'Of course yow can borrow it. It's worth nowt,' said Mr Moore.

'I wasn't speaking to yow, sir. This book contains vital information in a very serious ongoing criminal investigation. The information that yowr son has collected may even save lives. So, I ask the owner of the book again, can I borrow yowr book, Robbie?'

'OK, but you got to promise to bring it back.'

'I promise. Tell yow what, Robbie, what's your favourite car of all time?'

'That's easy. James Bond's Aston Martin DB6. Billy Dodds has the Corgi model with ejector seat, machine gun and all the works. It's great.'

'Well, I'll pay yow one Corgi DB6 model to borrow yowr book. How about that?'

The lad's face lit up with total joy. He was about to get everything he lusted after, but he still had some demands. 'Can I have the gold version, please?'

'Sure.'

At the front door, Clark leaned into Mr Moore and whispered in his ear. The man's face clouded over, then drained of colour. Marie couldn't hear what was said except the last word that Clark uttered before he stepped back, 'Understand?'

'Yes,' came the whispered reply.

Jumping in the car, Clark looked at his watch and said, 'Stop at the first phone box yow see.' The nearest was opposite the New Inns where the old Albion Cinema, now demolished, had once stood. Directory enquires gave him the number of the Walsall Licensing Office and as he dialled, he prayed he wasn't too late. After six rings, the phone was picked up. However, before Clark could start to speak, it was replaced again, cutting the connection. Clark looked at his watch and swore.

Back in the car, he told Marie what had happened. 'Some pen-pushing sod hung up on me without speaking. A minute to closing time and he dain't want to get stuck with an enquiry that might mean working five minutes over his allotted time. Bastard.' He slammed the door panel with the side of his fist.

'What are you going to do?'

'Be there in the morning when the bloody office opens.'

Birmingham, 16.25hrs

As Sybil emerged from the bowels of New Street Station and onto the main concourse, Agnes smiled. Sybil hadn't changed much since they had first met twenty-five years earlier. She was still a stone or two overweight, and her blue eyes still danced with life and a hint of mischief. Her hair was full and curly, as it always had been, but the added grey made her look even more like Harpo Marx.

They exchanged a hug and pleasantries, before making their way through the partially built shopping centre that was being constructed on top of the newly renovated station, then walked arm in arm the short distance to the Lyons Coffee House. Both ordered tea and toasted teacakes, before climbing the stairs to the near-deserted first floor. The room looked as if it hadn't been painted since the war. At one time, the room had boasted magnolia walls and a white ceiling, but now everything, except the numerous damp patches, was a dirty yellow thanks to years of cigarette smoke.

'Shall we take a window seat?' asked Sybil.

'Why not? We can watch the world go by.'

'Just like old times. Anyway, tell me about your policeman. The grapevine tells me that you two are an item.'

'Yes. We've been together for about five years now.'

'Hasn't he popped the question yet?'

'Repeatedly.'

'And you've said no. Why, for goodness sake?'

'I'm 22 years older than him. When he's 38, I'll be 60. I don't want him to wake up one morning and find he's tied to a dried-up, old hag.'

Sybil's eyes seemed to change. The sparkle was gone, replaced by an icy stare that was able to see past subterfuge and any amount of disassembling. 'That may be part of it, but it's not all. Come on, out with it. What's the real reason?'

Agnes paused before answering. She wasn't a woman who bared her soul very often, but she knew she could trust her old friend. 'I'm worried. Michael is an Irish Catholic. He always will be. It's who he is and part of that is wanting a family – a family that I can never give him.'

'Have you told him that?'

'Yes.'

'And what was his reply?'

'That he loves me and that we can always adopt.'

'But you're not convinced?'

'I know he loves me now, but what if he meets a woman his own age who can give him all the babies I think he craves? I don't want to hold him back if he ever gets that chance. '

'And if that happened, you're worried he might leave you?'

'That's the problem. He'd never leave. He's too loyal. He'd stay with me however he felt.'

'My God, you're the first woman I've ever met who turned down a marriage proposal because she loved a man who is too loyal to leave her.'

Agnes smiled and said, 'Let's change the subject. What

have you found that put you on the train to deepest, darkest Birmingham?'

'Not yet,' said Sybil. 'Do you remember what it was like in the war? What we were like? We lived for today because there was no guarantee that there would be a tomorrow. It was exciting and we felt alive. For many of us, it was the best years of our lives. Well, you need to remember those times because you are behaving as if you have a lifetime in front of you. That is plain stupid. You're 49; you could be dead this time next year from any one of a thousand illnesses or walk under a bus on the way home.

'Then, there is your friend, Sergeant Collins. I know all about him. I know what he did in 1963 and some of his exploits since then, like jumping out of a burning hotel. He and his pal, Constable Clark attract danger like a magnet attracts iron filings. They could both be dead by next week, let alone next year. Don't you see that you can't live your life in the future or allow what might happen to determine what you do today? You have to grab what makes you happy today and hang on for dear life. You, above all people, should know that.'

'Finished?' asked Agnes.

'Yes, provided you promise to think about what I've just said.'

'Very well, I promise, but now can you tell me what you've found out?'

'It's not much, but I think it's important,' Sybil said, as she opened her briefcase and extracted a slim file marked "Confidential" in red. Leaving the thin file unopened, she handed it to Agnes and said, 'In London, Harry Gregson, gangland boss, was second only to the Krays in reach and importance. Since the Krays' arrest yesterday, he's now number one and all the signs are that he's making a move on the twins' empire.

'Now, there are only about four people in England who know what I'm about to tell you. That's why I caught the train. This information goes no further than you and your friend. It cannot become common knowledge in police circles, because if it does it will get back to the Krays and their friends, and people will die. So, absolute discretion is essential.'

'I understand.'

'Mr Gregson provided the Met with information that helped us nab the Krays. Your Mr Keating has also provided information to your friend, Sergeant Collins, which in some cases has weakened competitors of the Drew brothers.'

'But we still haven't proved definitively that there is a connection between Keating and the Drew brothers, and we certainly have no evidence that the Drews are working with Gregson,' said Agnes.

'Which brings me to this,' said Sybil, as she withdrew an 8 x 10 black-and-white photo from the folder and laid it on the table. The picture had been taken in what looked like a nightclub and the quality wasn't particularly good, but it was easy to make out the faces of the three men facing the camera. Pointing, Sybil said, 'The one with grey hair is Gregson. The one on the right is Connolly and beside him is Toby Drew.'

Agnes picked up the picture and examined it carefully. 'Any idea who the two men and the woman with their backs to the camera are?'

'The man on the left, with his back to the camera, is Nigel Worthington. He's Gregson's accountant. We've not identified the other man or woman yet.'

'When was the photograph taken?'

'The snap was taken on the May 4th, just four days before the Krays were arrested. From all accounts, the boys were enjoying something of a celebration. When I asked for the Gregson file yesterday, one of the clerks had just returned it to the stacks with this photo in it.'

'So, a strong prima facie case that the Drews are involved with Gregson.'

'I would say so.'

'What about the bookmaker, Trylford and his wife?'

'I've got nothing on file for either of them, except a conviction for illegal gambling in 1960 for Harry Trylford in Birmingham.'

'So, there's still a chance that Trylford is involved, but has been very careful to keep a low profile – or, equally, it could be another bookie entirely?'

'That's about the size of it.'

Handsworth, 18.30hrs

When Collins arrived home, he was greeted first by Sheba and very quickly afterwards by Jamie, who enveloped him in a heartfelt hug. Holding the young man at arm's length, Collins said, 'Let me look at you, Jamie. My God, I don't know what they're feeding you at that university, but you look good on it.'

Gone was the small, skinny fourteen-year-old that Collins and Clark had first met five years earlier sleeping rough behind Bert Mitchell's shop. In his place was a five foot nine man, who had filled out and now looked like a middleweight boxer. Also gone was his Birmingham accent and poor diction. The lad with a love of literature had found a home, first with Agnes and now at Cambridge.

'You don't look too bad yourself, Michael.'

Agnes stood in the lounge doorway and smiled. 'Dinner will be ready in half an hour. Why don't you boys take a walk around the garden before then? I'm sure Sheba wouldn't mind a bit of attention.'

Sitting near the apple trees, the men took turns throwing a much-chewed tennis ball for Sheba to chase.

'So, how's it going this year?' asked Collins.

'After last year, it's a lot easier. I know Agnes called in a few favours to get me in, which I'm really grateful for, but, my God, did I have a lot of catching up to do.'

'Don't run yourself down. It's a bad habit that us working-class ne'er do wells suffer from. Yeah, she pulled a few strings, but mainly she asked the admission team to look past where you were at the time and instead look at your obvious potential. They took you on because they could see how good you could be.'

'If you say so.'

'I do and if you disagree, I'll ask Clark to recite to you the full unabridged history of West Bromwich Albion.'

'No, please, no. Anything but that.'

'Anyway, are you working on anything at the moment?'

'Not really. I'm doing a few sketches for the Footlights, but I don't have the time to tackle anything bigger. I might try and write a novella over the summer. What about you? What are you up to?'

Collins told him of the two investigations that he and Clark were working on. He spent most time on the murder case as a none-too-subtle way of warning Jamie of the dangers of wandering into Birmingham in search of a boyfriend or a one-night stand while he was home.

Jamie knew what he was doing and when Collins had finished talking, he said, 'Tell Agnes not to worry about me. I've got a steady boyfriend at college. He's a historian. His speciality is Anglo-Irish history. You'd like him.'

'As long as he blames the British for everything, I'm sure I will,' said Collins and laughed.

Dinner finished and washing up done, Jamie disappeared into his room to finish reading *Farewell, My Lovely*, by Raymond Chandler. It wasn't on any of his reading lists, but he'd only recently discovered the joy and genius of Chandler's work and was in the process of reading all of his books for the second time.

Alone, Agnes briefed Collins on what Sybil had said and ended by showing him the photo of Drew, Connolly and Gregson. Collins examined the picture closely and, after a couple of minutes, asked, 'Have you got your magnifying glass handy?'

'For you, anything,' said Agnes. Getting up, she went to her study and returned moments later with the Victorian magnifying glass that her father and grandfather had used to examine their butterfly collections.

Years earlier, Agnes had shown Collins how aerial and other photographs had been studied in minute detail by placing them under a grid drawn onto a piece of clear Perspex. Although he didn't have any grid to help, Collins checked each square inch intently.

Agnes' curiosity finally got the better of her, 'What is it?'

'I don't know, but there's something here I'm missing. I just can't see it.'

'Why don't you forget about it for now? Watch some television and sleep on it.'

'Why not indeed.'

At 4am, Collins awoke and was immediately wide awake. There would be no more sleep for him that night. He had his answer, but he hoped he was wrong. He needed to speak to Clark and Sybil.

Friday 10th May 1968, 08.00hrs

Walsall

Collins picked Clark up at 8am sharp and set off for Walsall. On the way, he briefed him about what Sybil had told Agnes.

'Well,' said Clark, 'the pieces are beginning to make some sense. What wi really need to do is prove a business connection between Gregson, the Drews and Keating, and find out if they were involved in the death of Ray Smith.'

'There's more,' said Collins. 'Have a look at the folder on the back seat.'

Clark twisted around and reached for the pocket folder. From it, he withdrew the photo of Drew and Gregson with and a single sheet of paper containing a few lines of Collins' familiar handwriting.

Clark read the notes and then looked at the photo closely. Finally, he said, 'It's a possibility, but, God, I hope yowr wrong. What are yow going to do next?'

'I'll call Sybil when we get back to the station. It will take her until at least Monday to check it out. So, I think we can put the Drews and their friends on the back burner until we've caught this bastard. We're closing in on him and I don't want to be distracted.'

'Fine with me.'

Collins and Clark were waiting outside the Walsall Motor Licensing Office when it opened. By 9.05am, they were in the manager's office.

Fred Henshaw listened attentively to what they had to say about the urgency of their request. When Collins had finished, he said, 'I have some friends who are concerned about the murder of some young men over the last year. Is this registration number connected to that case?'

'I'm not in a position to say at this stage. However, I'm absolutely certain that your friends will welcome the arrest of the man we're seeking,' replied Collins.

'I understand. I'll get my clerk to find it for you. If the number you've given me is correct and our typist has recorded the details correctly, and the card has been filed properly and not lost, you should have your answer within five minutes. However, if there has been a mistake in any of those procedures, you could be waiting a long time.'

'Strewth, yow make it sound like a miracle that any registration number is ever traced.'

'I'm sorry, Constable Clark, that's not my intention, but humans make mistakes. Unless you can suggest a way to mechanise the whole process, there will always be errors.'

'My colleague didn't mean to be critical. It's just that he, too, has friends who want us to catch this killer.'

'Oh, I see,' said Henshaw, looking with new interest at Clark. 'In that case, why don't you wait here? If we haven't got anything for you by ten, you can head back to your office. I'll ensure that every possible combination of the number is checked and I'll phone you every hour on the hour with a progress report.'

'That would be bostin, Mr Henshaw,' said Clark. 'We'll grab a cuppa at the café across the street and be back at 10.'

Collins and Clark sought out the comforts of the Saddler's Café and nursed their tea and toast while they waited for results.

'Yow know, back with Henshaw, did yow imply to him that I was a poofter?'

'Yes! I think I did.'

'Cheeky bastard.'

'Maybe, but it got his cooperation.'

Nothing had been found by 10am and it was two disappointed men who drove back to Handsworth.

Handsworth, 13.00hrs

On returning to the station, Collins called Sybil Harker. She seemed genuinely pleased to hear from him and said, 'I'm so pleased to speak to you finally. Agnes has told me all about you.'

'Not everything, I hope.'

'Enough to know that your frontal assault on her is gaining ground. Keep going. Don't give up. My feeling is that she's very near to capitulation. And I, for one, hopes she does surrender to you. She deserves some happiness.'

Collins felt his face redden with excruciating embarrassment. How the hell did the woman know so much about his relationship with Agnes? His first reaction was to tell Sybil Harker to keep her nose out of his personal affairs, but just as he felt the heat radiating from his face, he was conscious of a second stronger emotion. A wellspring of joyous hope was stirring inside him.

Afraid that he might show emotion in front of Clark, he quickly changed the subject. 'What I'm calling about is the photo you gave Agnes. Could you do me a favour?'

'I will, if I can.'

'I need some more information about the people in the photo.'

'Fire away. What is it you want to know?'

As Collins outlined what he wanted, Clark looked at the picture again. With a shake of his head, he put it back in the folder.

Collins and Clark found it difficult to concentrate on any work while they waited for Henshaw's call, but 11am, 12pm and 1pm came and went without any good news. 'Let's grab some lunch,' said Collins.

The canteen was crowded. Men from the afternoon shifts were grabbing a bite before going on duty and the office staff were just finishing up their lunches. The smoke and noise made the place look and sound like a lively working men's club, which, in many ways, it was.

Both men had the special of the day, fish, chips and mushy peas. Alice filled their plates and added a bit to Collins.

'How come he gets more chips than me?' complained Clark.

'Cos he's bigger than you and needs it. Besides, I don't fancy you.'

'Oh Alice, Alice, where did it all go wrong for us?'

'I think it were when yow first said hello and that dewdrop on yowr nose fell in yowr porridge.'

'I tell yow, Mickey, there's nowt like a woman scorned.'

Alice dropped an extra ladleful of chips on Clark's plate and said, 'For Pete's sake, shut up and stop blocking the line.'

'Yes, my gorgeous one.'

Sergeant Ridley and Marie were just leaving and the men slid into their still warm chairs. They were halfway through their meal when Katie appeared in the doorway. More than one copper watched as she ordered a tea and bun and walked over to Collins.

'Hiya, can I rest me aching feet with you?'

Mouth full, Collins indicated the empty chair next to him with his fork.

'How's the case going?'

'Which one?' asked Clark.

'The queer fellas.'

'Keep it quiet from that prat of a boss of yowrs, but wi may have something later this afternoon.'

'That's grand. And the other one?'

'We've put that on the back burner until we clear up the killings,' said Collins.

'So nothing new on it?'

'We've confirmed that Connolly's not Scottish, he's a cock-ney - and he used to work for a gangster called Gregson in London. You should update your records,' said Collins.

'Thanks, I will. Some of the stuff I get is shite.'

'Well, this is accurate. We might also be able to link Keating to Drew and Gregson.'

'Yeah, we have a photo that shows the back of someone's head, who could be Keating sitting at the same table as Gregson, Drew and Connolly - but it ain't very clear. Best of all, though, we might have a lead on the bastard that raped Margaret Lewis, but keep it under yowr hat for now. The fewer people who know, the better.'

'I will, but you'll have to tell me all about it when it's over.'

'We will,' said Collins. 'Anyway, what are you doing here?'

'Came to see your Super again. This time, he wanted some background stuff on a couple of city architects.'

'I wonder what it's all about,' said Clark.

'My guess would be corruption, but you didn't hear that from me. Anyway, and much more importantly, Mr Collins, you still haven't delivered me box of Milk Tray. When's it going to arrive?'

'The first day I have free. I promise.'

'I wouldn't be adverse to a night delivery.'

Before Collins could respond, Marie appeared at the door and shouted, 'Sergeant Collins, phone call.'

Collins looked at his watch and immediately jumped to his feet. Clark was only slightly slower. As both men waved and called a 'tara,' Katie said, sotto voce, 'If only he jumped like that when I call.'

Collins need not have rushed. There was still no news. He was starting to lose heart.

Ruth phoned at 2.50pm and managed to give Clark a fright, but all she wanted to do was remind him that mom and dad were coming for dinner and to bring some peas home with him. At 4.54pm, the phone rang again and Clark grabbed it quicker than an alcoholic who's been dry for a week grabs a bottle of vodka.

It was Henshaw. As Clark listened, his face lit up, 'Give us a bit of paper, Mickey,' he demanded and quickly scribbled down an address. After reading the address back, he said, 'Mr Henshaw, that's bostin. Thanks very much.'

Replacing the phone, he said, 'We've got it.'

Walsall, 17.00hrs

As they jumped in the car, Collins asked, 'Why did it take so long?'

'Seems that someone transposed the numbers and then filed it out of order. It's a bloody miracle they found it at all.'

The address they had been given was for the registered owner of the car, a Mrs Nora Yates, who lived in Walsall near the Arboretum's main entrance on Lichfield Road.

Collins drove past the house slowly. A dark blue Rover 2000 was in the driveway. His heart missed a beat and he felt the adrenalin flood through his veins. He continued driving to the island at the bottom of the hill and used it to make a U-turn. Parking fifty yards away from the house, he cut the engine. 'How do you want to handle this?' he asked.

'Wi know he's seen yow, so best if I go to the door.'

'He might be armed.'

'Unlikely, he don't know that we have his car number or address. Besides, if he's carrying a gun, it'll be in his pocket or behind his back and I'll put money on meself to floor him before he can get to it.'

'Okay. I'll hang back.'

Collins drove the fifty yards to the house and parked in front of the drive. Whatever happened, the Rover 2000 was going nowhere. Clark walked briskly up the drive and rang the bell. Collins wound down the passenger window to hear the conversation and undid his seat belt and opened the driver's door a couple of inches, ready to jump out if needed.

A light came on in the hall and a small, grey-haired woman

in her late sixties, wearing slippers and a cardigan, opened the door.

She took one look at Clark and said, 'Oh, hello. You must be one of Norman's friends. I'm sorry, you've just missed him. He left a few minutes ago. He said he was going to his flat first and then to the pub for a farewell drink with his friends in Birmingham.'

Whatever Clark had expected, this was not it. Instinct told him not to frighten the woman. There was a fragility about her that told Clark she needed to be treated gently. He knew that he'd get more from her if he kept her sweet.

'Oh, that's a pity,' he said. 'Yow see, I'm not actually one of Norman's friends. I'm Detective Constable Clark and that gentleman in the car' he said pointing, 'is Detective Sergeant Collins. We need to speak to Norman urgently.'

'Oh! He's not in any trouble, is he?'

'No. No, nothing like that. He popped into the station the other day to report seeing a suspicious character near some shops and last night one of the shops was robbed.'

'That sounds just like my Norman. Always looking out for other people. You'd best come in and I'll give you his address.' Clark gave Collins the thumbs up and followed Mrs Yates inside. Over her shoulder she said, 'He doesn't have a phone in his flat. Says it's not worth it as he's away so much. Just a sec and I'll jot down his address.'

'That's very kind of yow, Mrs Yates. Yow say he's away a lot. What does he do for a living?'

'Oh, he's got a really glamorous job. He works as the entertainment officer for a cruise line. His next voyage starts tomorrow night at six from Southampton.'

'And where's he going?'

'Around the world, would you believe it? But he never forgets me. Always sends me a card from every port he visits. I have them all upstairs. They fill two shoe boxes. And the Christmas before last, he bought me that lovely Rover. Of course, I don't use it much, but Norman drives it when he's home. Would you and your Sergeant like a cup of tea before you go?'

'No thanks. Wi need to catch Norman before he goes out. Yow don't have a picture of him handy, do yow? Just in case we have to follow him to the pub.'

'Why, yes. You can borrow the one on the mantelpiece.'

Back in the car, Clark said, 'Do yow have Gerry's number on yow?'

'Yes, in me notebook.'

'Phone him. Tell him to get to the Toreador as quick as he can. I think the bastard is going to try for one more kill before he goes on his bloody holidays.'

Collins put the car in gear and drove to the top of the hill, where there were two red phone boxes. Skidding to a halt, he jumped out and, pulled his notebook from his breast pocket and wrenched open the door of the nearest box. The phone line was hanging down with no handset in sight. He was luckier with the next box and called the Alhambra Hotel.

Two minutes later, he was back in the car and Clark was briefing him on everything Mrs Yates had said. He finished by saying, 'We need to go to his flat first.'

Collins nodded in agreement and, once on the Chester Road, floored the accelerator.

Edgbaston, 18.20hrs

The address said Reservoir Road, Edgbaston, but the house sat on the corner of Hagley Road and Reservoir Road, less than 600 yards from where Mark had been murdered. The three-storey Edwardian house had been converted into flats, but still retained much of its architectural elegance. Collins checked the list of tenants. Norman Yates had the attic flat. Stepping back from the door, Collins looked up but could see no lights on the third floor.

Returning to the door, he found Clark picking the lock. After no more than twenty seconds, the door sprang open.

'Easy peasy,' said Clark.

Inside, the hall and landing were in darkness. Collins switched on both lights before moving quietly up the stairs. Yates' flat was the only one on the third floor. The only other door on the landing led to an iron fire escape.

Clark placed his ear against the door and listened intently. After ten seconds, he stepped back and shook his head. Taking out the selection of metal probes that he had been trained to use so effectively by a supposedly retired burglar during the war, he quickly opened the door. Feeling for the light switch, he flicked it on.

The flat consisted of three rooms: a dining area and kitchen unit combined, a single bedroom and a bathroom. The room was neat, clean and tidy. There wasn't a book or cup out of place. A black-and-white TV, a Roberts radio and a stereo record player rested on the sideboard. A two-seater settee was positioned opposite the TV and set between the two was a small laminated coffee table. The only other furniture in the room was an old rocking chair. Both sides of the chimney breast had been converted into storage areas. Shelves had been fitted on the left and housed a selection of Penguin Classics; several books on the Bible, mainly written by American evangelists; and an LP collection of popular classical music. On the right, the space had been converted into a lockable cupboard. There were no paintings on the walls and, except for a picture of his mother, taken when she was about forty, there were no photographs or pictures on display.

Collins opened the bedroom door. It resembled a monk's cell, with just a single bed, a chest of drawers and a small wardrobe. Above the bed was a wooden cross, but without the figure of Christ. Well, at least he's not a Catholic, thought Collins. A quick check of all three items of furniture revealed nothing unusual.

'Mickey, come here. I think I've got sommut.'

Returning to the dining room, Collins saw that Clark had opened the doors to the wooden closet. 'What the feck is that?' he asked, looking inside.

'That, my mate, is a made-to-measure security cabinet with combination lock.'

'Can you open it?'

'Course I can, but it'll take a bit of trial and error. Find me a tube that I can use as an earpiece.'

While Clark examined the safe and spun the combination a few times, Collins disappeared into the bathroom and kitchen, before returning with a glass tumbler and a cardboard tube from a toilet roll.

'Couldn't yow do any better than that?'

'No, and if you think you can, be my guest.'

'It were never like this in the war.'

Twelve minutes later, the lock tumblers clicked into place and, with a bow, Clark pulled the doors open. 'She were a bit of a beast, but I got her in the end.'

'Let's have a look at what we've got.'

The safe contained a collection of male sadomasochistic books and magazines, photo albums, rolls of 8mm film, postcards from around the world, diaries and a box containing about twenty items of men's jewellery, including watches, gold chains and two religious medals.

Clark opened one of the photo albums marked "New York 1966, Gene". Each page contained a single Polaroid photo together with a few lines of handwritten text. Clark didn't need to flick through all the pages to realise that what he had in his hands was the record of a young man's murder. Silently, he handed the book to Collins and started counting the number of albums.

When he'd finished, Collins asked, 'How many?'

'Twenty-three. The bastard has a body in every bloody port. '

'Come on. Lock it up. We have to get over to the Toreador. I just hope to God the fecker shows up.'

The Toreador, Birmingham 19.20hrs

When Collins and Clark entered the Toreador. Gerry was standing near the bar and gave the briefest of head shakes to indicate he'd seen nothing suspicious.

Collins ordered a shandy and went to sit near the door. His position ensured that he couldn't be seen by anyone entering the pub until they were inside, and even then they would have to look directly left to spot him.

Meanwhile Clark meandered around the room as if looking for a friend. Finding nothing he bought half a bitter and sat down in the middle of the "queens' domain".

Nearly two hours passed. Nothing. Collins watched two single males enter the pub in quick succession, but neither looked, even vaguely, like Yates. A third looked more promising and Collins was about to intercept him when the man smiled broadly and waved at a group of friends chatting at the end of the bar. He was still watching the man when a fourth entered.

The man stopped momentarily and looked to the right. As his head swivelled to the left, he met Collins' eyes. For the merest instant, recognition flared in Yates' eyes. Collins saw the look, but before he could react, Yates turned and ran. At the top of his voice, Collins shouted, 'Clarkee, he's running,' and crashed through the swing doors after him.

Clark heard the shout as he climbed the stairs from the toilets. He immediately started running, knocking over a table of drinks – around which four queens were talking – and nearly flattening a middle-aged man in a black jacket and salt and pepper striped trousers, who looked as if he had just escaped from a Masons' meeting. Clark and Gerry reached the swing doors simultaneously and barrelled into the street. They saw Collins disappear around the corner onto New Street and set off in pursuit.

Collins could see Yates twenty yards ahead. I've got you now, he thought and increased his pace.

Looking up, Collins realised that he was gaining on Yates. Collins knew that Yates' only hope was to reach New Street Station and try and shake him off in the partially constructed Palisades shopping development. But he needed more time. Collins saw him fumble inside his windcheater. A quick look confirmed to Collins that he was less than twenty yards behind. Then to his surprise Yates sprinted in front of a car, crossed the road and hunkered down behind a parked van. Collins dodged a Ford Zephyr and was halfway across the road when Yates stood up, holding the revolver with both hands.

Collins threw himself down, but before Yates could fire, two shots rang out from behind. It was Gerry. He was twenty yards away. His hands, resting on top of a grey Daimler, held a German police Luger. The first bullet had smashed the windscreen of the van and the second had hit the roof, just inches from Yates, who ran, crouching, towards the pedestrian ramp that led to New Street Station. Pedestrians were screaming and running for cover behind parked cars and hiding in shop doorways.

Jumping to his feet, Collins followed the killer. A quick look behind confirmed that Gerry was following, gun in hand. Clark, who had never stopped running, was already across the road and heading up the ramp.

During the day, the ramp was crammed with people either going to or coming from the trains, but now it was nearly deserted. The few people who had been on the ramp were now huddled in Woolworths' doorway. Others had taken cover in the Danish Centre Restaurant, where a quick-thinking member of staff had shoved the metal leg of a chair through the door handles to keep the gunman out.

As he ran, Collins heard Clark shout, 'Police. Clear the area. Armed gunman at large. Clear the area.' Reaching the top, Collins was confronted by a huge building site. A wire fence with wooden slates marked the outline of a path that travellers could follow to and from the escalators, leading down to the station's concourse. The rest was, to the un-trained eye, a haphazard array of house bricks, breeze blocks, scaffolding, concrete bags, plaster boards, wooden beams, planks and building dust. Numerous walls for the planned shopping units had been erected. The space for their doors, empty. The result was that much of the area looked like a particularly untidy maze.

'Mickey, get down, yow prat!' cried Clark. As if to empha-sise the point, a bullet pinged off a length of scaffolding two yards in front of Collins. Keeping low, Collins ran to the pil-lar behind which Clark was sheltering.

'Where is he?' asked Collins.

'Not sure, but I think he's trying to work his way towards the escalators. Where's Gerry?'

'Don't know. He was behind me.'

'Okay, yow work yowr way around to the right and make a bit of noise to distract him. Don't get yowrself shot. I'll go left and try to get behind him.'

'What then?'

'I'll shoot the fucker. Yow dain't think I came unprepared did yow?'

Collins moved quickly left. While he made every attempt to maintain cover, he was happy to sound like an elephant stampeding through the bush. After thirty yards, he turned sharp left. Yates still hadn't fired in his direction. He heard the scraping of board on the concrete floor and a loud bang as it was dropped. What's the bastard up to now? he thought and moved towards the sound. After less than twenty yards, he saw Yates hiding behind a low wall, his entire attention focused on Clark.

Collins whispered a prayer and picked up a yard-long piece of 2x2 timber. Watching where he placed his feet, he silent-ly edged forward. Fifteen yards away, ten, eight. There was a loud crack as the thin plywood beneath his feet snapped.

Flailing wildly, he tried to push off from the floor before it disappeared entirely from beneath him. As he started to fall, the end of an iron rod raked his leg and instinctively he made a grab for it.

Looking around, Yates grinned. There was no sign of Collins. Got you, you queer-loving bastard. Then he was on his feet and running hard towards the escalators.

Clark had seen Collins disappear into the bear trap that Yates had set and, ignoring the killer, raced towards his friend, dreading what he might find. Looking down, he saw Collins hanging on with both hands to a steel rod that extended from a reinforced concrete post. Twenty feet below him was the ceiling of the station concourse. Hit that, and Collins would go straight through to the concrete floor below.

'What the fuck yow doing down there?' asked Clark.

'What does it look like? I'm hanging on for me fecking life. Now, get me out!'

Suddenly, the bar tore through part of the concrete it was embedded in and a ten-foot crack appeared in the pillar. The bar's angle dropped by several degrees, and Collins found himself scrambling to keep his left hand from slipping off the bar. Then the bar moved again and he was suspended by just his right hand as his left hand slipped off.

Clark dived on the floor and shouted, 'Give me yowr hand.'

Collins tried, but he couldn't reach Clark's outstretched arm. He tried to swing in an arc, but as he did so he felt his fingers slip on the bar. Seeing that he'd never reach Collins, Clark ripped his leather belt off and made it into a noose. Wrapping the end once around his hand, he edged forward on his belly and dangled the noose just above Collins' left hand.

Clark's stomach and chest were now suspended in mid-air. Collins grabbed the belt and slipped the noose around his wrist. 'OK, Mickey, now comes the hard part. Grab the belt with yowr other hand.'

'For Christ's sake, I'll pull you down.'

'No, yow fucking won't. Now, grab it with both hands, for fuck's sake, before I get a hernia.'

'Let me go, Clarkee, or I'll pull you down.'

'Fuck that. If yow go, I go. Now, grab the sodding belt or I'll come down there and thump yow.'

As Collins let go of the bar and made a grab for the belt, two shots rang out in rapid succession. Clark ignored them. He was now supporting Collins' entire eleven and a half stone and his only anchorage was his stomach and leg muscles. Slowly, he edged backwards and pulled Collins up. He felt the belt stretch and was conscious for the first time of the sweat covering his entire body. The pain in his hand, where the looped belt was cutting into the soft tissue, was bad, but nothing compared to the cramp in his legs and lower stomach, which were the only things preventing both him and Collins crashing through the station's ceiling. However, it was his shoulders that were screaming in absolute agony. He could almost feel individual muscle fibres stretch and snap as he pulled his friend up.

Collins' hands were almost level with the floor when Yates reappeared. He was still clutching his revolver in his right hand, but his left was clamped over his stomach where a large red stain was spreading across his shirt. Blood dripped from his fingers onto the dusty concrete floor at his feet. He saw Clark and Collins' head and raised the gun. Grinning, he held the gun with both hands, ignoring the thick black blood that was spurting from his stomach, and took careful aim.

Clark made one last effort to pull Collins' arms through the hole and onto the floor before Yates fired. He was too late. The sound of a shot echoed around the empty space. Instinctively, Clark tensed in readiness for the pain and shock, but there was none. Looking up, he saw Yates crumple onto his knees. He'd been shot through the back of the neck. The bullet had destroyed his larynx, part of his trachea and much of the surrounding cartilage. On exit, it left a hole the size of a small tangerine, from which blood was now pumping uncontrollably. In the remaining four seconds of life, Yates' eyes registered surprise, anger, fear, and finally terror as the blackness of death enveloped him. Pitching forward onto the floor face first, he twitched once and lay still.

A moment later, Gerry ran across and ignoring Clark grabbed Collins under the arms, and pulled him up. Collins and Clark lay crumpled on the floor, breathing hard and sucking in huge lungfuls of air, while Gerry went and checked on Yates.

As they waited for West and his men to arrive, Clark said, 'There's only one thing I don't understand.'

'What's that?'

'How did yow break Wilkee's nose?'

'You're not going to give up, are you?

'No.'

'Okay. I went to question him about an underage girl, who'd been picked up for soliciting. Well, he went to get dressed and I wandered about that weird art collection of his. He had this two-foot purple and yellow tube thing. It was really strange. I picked it up to get a better look. It was made of porcelain and obviously expensive. When I heard him return, I spun around to ask him what it was and that's how I managed to break his nose with a two-foot dildo. I've never been sure which upset him more, the broken dildo or the broken nose.'

The image of Wilkee being laid low by a two-foot prick was too much for Clark, who started to laugh and found he couldn't stop. After several seconds trying to keep a straight face, Collins joined in. All the tension of the last two hours had been exorcised by the thought of Wilkee getting his nose broken by the representation of the very thing that kept him in business. That was irony, on a grand scale.

By the time West and his team arrived ten minutes later, both men had regained their composure and were sitting on a low brick wall, keeping watch on the body. Yates' gun still lay where it had fallen, but Clark was holding Gerry's German police Luger. Miraculously, it was now covered in two sets of prints. Yates' own, overlaid by Clark's – even the shells were covered in Yates' prints. There was no sign of Gerry.

'That's the man who killed Mark Cavendish. The gun he used is next to him. He's also the bastard who killed the four homosexual men, along with an unknown number of other men and boys around the world. You'll find all the evidence you need in his flat. Here's the address,' said Collins, handing West the slip of paper that Mrs Yates had given Clark earlier. 'Now, I'm going home. I'll be at Steelhouse Lane tomorrow morning to give a full statement.' Before West could say anything, Collins walked away.

Clark handed the Luger to West and said, 'Bloody lucky he dropped that or else we would be dead meat. I'll see yow tomorrow, Sir. Like me mate, I'm too overwrought to give a statement right now.' As he turned away, Clark couldn't resist a smile. 'Mickey,' he shouted, 'wait up for me.'

As they walked down the ramp, Collins asked, 'Did you give West the combination for the cupboard?'

'Na. He can open it his self.'

'Good man.'

Saturday 11th May 1968, 08.00hrs

Handsworth

Collins was the last to arrive at the hastily convened meeting between Hicks, Clark and himself. He was surprised to see that Clark was wearing his uniform. The two rows of campaign ribbons on his chest and the award of the Victoria Cross for valour in the face of the enemy testified to the eventful war he'd had in the Commandos. He might be a plainclothes detective, but this was his battledress. A sure indication he was not going to take any prisoners in their meeting with Inspector West. Any concerns that Collins had about the meeting quickly dissolved and a small smile crept onto his lips.

A hot cup of tea was waiting for Collins. 'Morning,' he said. 'Sorry I'm a bit late. I've been running around Hill Top like an eejit trying to catch Sheba.'

'Yow could do with a bit of exercise. Yow're getting to be a fat git.'

Collins responded with a two-fingered salute.

'OK, lads, I know you can look after yourselves, but I think you pair may need an independent witness if things get rough. So, I've decided to come with you. I'm also concerned that, left to your own devices, one of you may bop West if I'm not there.'

'I'd never do that, Boss – least not in front of witnesses. I'd wait for a dark and stormy night,' said Clark, 'then I'd thump him.'

'I'll pretend I didn't hear that. Anyway, tell me what you're going to say to West.'

Collins outlined everything that had happened from the time Upright Freddie had come to the station the previous Friday up to the death of Yates. There were only two inaccuracies in the statement. Firstly, that Clark had found the Luger on New Street near the Moss Brothers' shop. Secondly, that it was he who had shot and killed Yates as he had approached an unarmed Collins. No mention whatever was made of Gerry Niven.

When he'd finished, Hicks said, 'You know, lads, you two make a cracking pair of liars.'

'Us, Boss? Never,' said Clark.

'Don't insult my intelligence. You had help and it's my bet that it came from this Gerry Niven character you saw last Tuesday. I've been looking into him. I don't know what his connection is with all this and I don't want to know. Two shots, one in the chest and one in the back of the neck doesn't exactly support your story the way you tell it. However, it does indicate someone with training, like an ex-Legionnaire who now runs a security firm.'

Clark was about to respond, when Hicks held his hand up. 'Stick to your story, Clark, but remember you shot him first near the escalator. That will account for the trail of blood. And you finished him off when you saw he was about to shoot Collins as he climbed out of the hole. OK?'

'Yes, Sir.'

'Come on then, let's get going.'

Birmingham, 09.30hrs

West and his team were waiting for the men in one of the station's meeting rooms. An eight by three conference table covered by a green baize cloth dominated the room. Already lined up on one side were Inspector West, his two Sergeants and an Assistant Chief Constable. Katie McGuire sat at the top of the table, ready to take notes. Collins, Clark and Hicks sat down opposite the assembly. Once seated, Hicks lit up a Gauloise and added its distinctive aroma to the cloud of smoke already hovering above the table.

Wasting no time on pleasantries, or asking how Collins and

Clark were after their ordeal, West said, 'Okay, let's hear your story from the first moment you got involved in the case to the death of Yates. Leave nothing out. After that, we'll take your formal statements.'

Taking turns, Clark and Collins described the events that had taken place since Tom Laurence had first visited Clark up to Yates death. They included a full description of the angry exchange between West and Collins the day Mark's body had been found. Again, the only thing they left out was any reference to Gerry Niven. When they had finished, West immediately went for the jugular.

'I've got witnesses who say there was a fourth man. They describe him as well over six foot tall and they say that it was him who fired the two shots at Yates on New Street.'

'How many witnesses have yow got?' asked Clark.

'What does that matter? I've got witnesses.'

'I repeat my question, how many witnesses have yow got?'

Conscious of the ACC beside him, West decided not to bluster. 'One,' he muttered.

'I'm surprised yow got one. After I picked up the Luger, I were running down the road, screaming "Armed gunman! Take cover!" which is exactly what everyone were doing. There were no heroes on that road sticking their heads up, I can tell yow. Most were behind cars or stuck in doorways, or running away from the station ramp in blind panic. Yow can't rely on any eyewitness in that situation,' said Clark.

'If you'd picked Yates' gun up, why were you screaming about an armed gunman? How did you know he had a second gun before he fired for the first time?' asked West.

Clark's response was as quick as a Mohammed Ali left jab. 'I knew he'd killed Cavendish with a .45. I couldn't take the chance that he dain't have that gun on him.'

'Quite right,' mumbled the ACC, loud enough to ensure that everyone at the table heard him.

'When you found out from Mrs Yates where her son lived, why didn't you call for support? Come to that, after visiting his flat and discovering his hoard of filth, why didn't you call for support?'

'Because we dain't know if he would strike again and if he did, we dain't know when or where. When we went to the Toreador, we was just playing a hunch.'

'Bollocks. You pair of glory hunters wanted him for yourself. Maybe you'd already decided you were going to kill him. Revenge for Mark Cavendish, was that it?'

'Inspector West,' said Hicks, 'I don't think it's appropriate to use that tone with my officers. After all, it's they who risked their lives and, in doing so, caught a man who is responsible for at least 23 murders – five of which you said were unconnected. It sounds to me like you're trying to cast doubt on the veracity of my officers' story, just to deflect criticism from your own shortcomings as an investigator.'

Both inspectors glared at each other and, for a moment, Collins thought that Hicks was about to thump West. Quickly, Collins said, 'Sir, given our previous disagreements, I didn't want to take the chance of involving you in something that was based on a hunch. We went to his flat to interview him. No more than that. Then, when we found his stash of filth, our only thought was to get to the Toreador as quickly as possible, just in case he did strike again. We were lucky. That's all.'

West saw that he was being offered a chance to back down without losing too much face and nodded. The bastards had him and he knew it.

After a short pause, the ACC spoke, 'Unless you have any further clarification questions, Inspector, I suggest you move on to taking Detective Sergeant Collins' and Detective Constable Clark's formal statements. Having done that, and reflected on the bravery of both men in tackling an armed killer without support and initially without a weapon, you might come to the same conclusion as I have – that both men should be recommend for the Queen's Police Medal for gallantry.'

'An excellent idea, Sir,' said Hicks, with a broad smile.

Birmingham, 13.40hrs

Their statements completed, Collins and Clark found Hicks waiting for them by the front door. 'Come on, I'll buy you a drink. You've earned it.'

Crossing the road, they entered The Turks Head, a favoured watering hole for barristers from the nearby courts during the week, but almost empty on a Saturday afternoon.

While Hicks went to get the drinks, Clark slipped outside to the call box on the corner. His first call was to Tom Laurence. His second, to Gerry Niven. As he returned to his seat in the bar, Collins asked, 'All set?'

'Yeah. Tomorrow, around 7.30.'

'What's all set?' asked Hicks, depositing three drinks on the table.

'We're just trying to arrange a get-together with some friends,' said Collins.

'I thought this morning went well,' said Hicks. 'I didn't expect the ACC to suggest Queen's Medals all round, but you earned them – even if you did have a bit of assistance.'

'Sir, I take exception to yow questioning the veracity of our statements,' said Clark with a straight face and all three laughed.

'Anyway, with all the excitement about Yates, I've not asked you about Drew and Co. for a few days. What's happening there?'

'Well, as of last Thursday, we put it on the back burner to deal with Yates. We'll pick it up again on Monday. We may have a new lead, but I'm trying to confirm it with a Mrs Harker at the Met,' said Collins.

'Sybil Harker?'

'Yes, Sir.'

'Bloody hell, is she still there? Don't ever call her Mrs to her face, mind. She's definitely a Miss. Unmarried, lives with a very attractive actress half her age. They've been together for years. How did you know about her? No, don't tell me. She's a friend of Agnes, isn't she?'

'Yes, Sir.'

'Knew it. Probably served together in Intelligence. Bloody bright woman, I'll tell you. Every copper in the Met bows to her knowledge of the London Underworld. Memory like two elephants and an ability to connect the dots even when they're invisible. What did you call her for?'

'We've got a photo of Drew and Connelly in a London nightclub with Harry Gregson. There's another man in the picture with his back to the camera, who Sybil is trying to identify.'

'Well, keep me informed.'

'Will do.'

Hicks dropped Collins and Clark off at the station and headed home to Aldridge.

Over a cup of tea in the nearly deserted canteen, Clark said, 'Still playing your cards close to your chest?'

'Yep, until we're sure what's going on.'

'Fair enough. So what next?'

'We wait to see what Sybil has found. Then, we start to shake a few trees and see what falls out.'

'Fucking hell. I thought I was aggressive once I got the bit between me teeth. Yowm as bad as Sheba. Yow've already set God knows how many hares running. Have some patience. They'll come after us soon enough.'

Collins smiled and said nothing.

'Listen, yow Cheshire fucking cat, I'm getting too old for this shit.'

'I don't believe you.'

'Me neither.'

Both men smiled.

Handsworth, 17.00hrs

The events of the week had left Collins feeling on edge. Too much had happened, and too much still might happen for him to relax. Agnes had seen the signs and when he returned home, he found her holding two theatre tickets. 'We're going to the Rep tonight. They're doing a Peter Shaffer double bill: *White Liars* and *Black Comedy.*'

'I'm not great company at the moment. Why not take Jamie?'

'Because it was Jamie who recommended the plays and bought the tickets. Apparently, it's a sell-out.'

'What's it about?'

'You'll find out soon enough.'

Reluctantly, Collins traipsed upstairs to get ready.

Handsworth, 23.30hrs

Collins wasn't impressed with *White Liars*. He found it boring. However, *Black Comedy*, a farce played out in a basement flat where the lights have gone out, had him holding his stomach in pain with laughter. By the end of the play, he felt relaxed for the first time in days. The adrenalin that had been coursing through his body for much of the week had drained away.

When he finally lay down in bed, he was asleep before Agnes had time to undress. She looked at him, with a serious expression on her face. She'd made her mind up – almost.

Sunday 12th May 1968, 10.15hrs

Handsworth

Following the best night's sleep he'd had for weeks, Collins slept in. When he finally rolled out of bed, he realised he'd have to catch the 11.45am Mass at St Francis'. Checking the weather, he was pleased to see that the sun was shining and a gentle wind was rustling through the trees. A good day for Shanks' pony, he thought as he set off on the 20-minute walk to the church. Every now and then, a smile came to his lips as he remembered another moment from *Black Comedy*.

He was surprised to find that Agnes was still at her Quaker Meeting when he returned home at 1 o'clock. Fasting before communion, and Father Emery's sermon on the loaves and the fishes, had given him an appetite. With no Agnes to stop him, he decided to forego his usual breakfast of porridge and raisins and have a fry-up. Sheba approved of his decision, as it meant she was assured of getting at least half a sausage and the bacon rinds from Collins' plate.

Collins was just washing up when Agnes opened the front door.

'You're late from Meeting.'

'Yes. I stopped to chat with some people afterwards and one thing led to another.'

'For a silent sect, you Quakers do a lot of talking.'

'It's our way of making up for all that silence. Anyway, from the smell in here, you obviously decided to celebrate your recent success with a fry-up.'

'Old habits die hard.'

'Well, why don't we take Sheba out and you can walk off your old habits?'

The sun was warm on Collins' face as he and Agnes reached the summit of Hill Top. Sheba was down the hill playing with a black-and-white Collie. Ahead, they could see a young boy running as fast as he could to get his kite off the ground. Suddenly, a gust of wind caught the diamond-shaped cloth and the kite fluttered into the air. His father beamed with delight and clapped his son's achievement.

'Where was it that the man committed suicide?'

Collins pointed to the clump of trees about 30 feet above them and 40 yards to the left.

'I don't suppose that either he or his wife ever imagined that their marriage would end the way it did.'

'No, probably not,' said Collins and sat down on the perimeter wall of the old ack-ack gun emplacement.

Agnes joined him and ran her hand over the rough steel and stone reinforced concrete that had been used to build the guns' fortifications. The surface beneath her fingers reminded her of the machine gun posts that had protected Bletchley during the war and the bomb shelters that had been built for the precious staff that worked there. Neither had been required. Amazingly, the Germans never directly bombed the park, probably because they didn't know it existed.

With her hands resting on the concrete behind her, Agnes leant back, closed her eyes and lifted her face to the sun. For a few second, she disappeared into the past as memories flashed through her mind. Each image lasted only a fraction of a second, but its significance fully recognised and understood.

Collins looked on and his heart missed a beat. He tried not to breathe, to remain perfectly still. He didn't want to break the moment. The woman he loved was beside him and she was beautiful and always would be.

When Agnes finally spoke, eyes still closed, her voice was soft and sure. 'A good friend recently reminded me that the reason why so many of us remember the War with affection is that it was when we were most alive. A time when we lived each day as if it would be our last and never worried about what would happen tomorrow.

'Well, I've been living in the future too much. I'm terrified that one day you will leave me because you'll find a woman who can give you children. But worse than that, I'm haunted by the thought that if I marry you and you met such a woman you would never leave me because of the vows you made. We'd go on living together, but over time you would grow to resent me and our love would die and I don't think I could bear that.

'On Friday, you could have been killed. Every day you leave for work, you could be killed. I don't want to live in the past or the future anymore. So, I've made a decision. Will you, Michael Collins, marry this woman with all her faults and idiosyncrasies?'

Ruth opened the door, took one look at the smiles that were plastered all over the couple's faces and asked, 'Yes?'

'Yes,' said Agnes.

'Clive, they've done it. They're getting married,' she shouted with joy.

Clark appeared from the kitchen. 'It's about bloody time yow pair stopped messing about. Come in. Come in.'

Clark wrapped his arms around Agnes and gave her a bear hug, while Ruth embraced Collins and kissed him on the cheek.

'I've got a bottle of champagne around here somewhere for just this occasion. Give me a tick and I'll find it.'

'So how did he pop the question?' asked Ruth, when they were all seated in the lounge, a drink in hand.

Agnes looked slightly embarrassed. 'He did it many times and in many ways, but it was me who proposed to him today.'

At that, Ruth's eyes filled with tears.

'Pay no attention,' said Clark. 'She's been like that for the past month. I blame the babbie.'

As she blew her nose in a hankie, Ruth kicked Clark in the ankle. Recovered, she asked, 'Have you set the wedding date?'

'No, but it will be some time this year.'

'The sooner, the better,' said Collins. 'I don't want her changing her mind.'

'Well, now that you pair will no longer be living in sin, Ruth and me were wondering if you'd be godparents to the great bump, whenever he or she is born?'

'We'd love to!' said Agnes.

'While we're doling out jobs, I was thinking that I need a best man, but I don't know anyone who fits that description. So, I was wondering if you'd be interested, Clarkee?'

By the time Agnes and Collins left, at 5.30 the bottle of champagne had been consumed, mostly by Clark. For that reason, it was agreed that Collins would pick Gerry up and then return for him. There would be another celebration at Tom Laurence's house tonight, but Collins knew it would be very different to the one he'd just enjoyed.

Sutton Coldfield, 19.45hrs

Collins realised that trying to fit a six foot five ex-Legionnaire and Clark into his beloved Mini would require a shoehorn, which was why he picked Gerry up in Agnes' new Rover. He'd not seen Gerry since Friday night and was surprised by the change in his appearance. The dark rings under his eyes, which had given him a slightly haunted, sinister look, had now disappeared and the tension in his body had drained away. He was at peace with himself. He'd fulfilled the promise he'd made to Mark.

Slipping into the passenger seat, Gerry reached backwards and deposited a bottle of champagne on the rear seat. 'I thought we should toast Mark's life with something special.'

'Good idea,' said Collins, dreading the thought of having to drink a second glass of champagne in one day. *More bloody bubbles up me nose*, he thought.

Gerry was interested in what had happened since Friday night and Collins gave him the highlights of the meeting with West on Saturday.

'He sounds like a right wanker,' said Gerry.

'That's a very astute summation of the man,' said Collins, smiling.

'But they have no idea I was involved?'

'I think everyone suspects, maybe even knows, that a fourth man was involved. But they can't prove it and, if truth be known, I don't think they care. With Yates dead, there will be no trial and West won't face any embarrassing questions about how he handled the case.'

'I find it incredible that he killed 23 men over the years and no one picked it up.'

'He was clever. He killed people all round the world and over many years. It was always going to be hard to find any links. What gives me the willies is that I'm certain he killed a lot more than 23. Those are just the cases where he kept a photographic record. If he only killed one person in every port he visited, his tally could be nearer a hundred,' said Collins, drawing up outside Clark's house.

Thirty-five minutes later, the three men were standing in Tom Laurence's lounge with Patrick, Richard, James and Peter.

'You must be Gerry,' said Richard, shaking hands. He seemed reluctant to let go of the hand he was holding or to break eye contact.

'Unhand the poor man,' said James, 'and stop trying to seduce him before he even gets a chance to sit down.'

'Pay no attention to the old queen. She's just jealous because I saw you first.'

Gerry laughed and sat down, the ice broken.

'How much can you tell us about what happened on Friday?' asked Tom.

Collins looked at Clark and jerked his head sideways. Tom had approached Clark for help and it was only right that he explain what had happened. His summary of events was succinct and accurate. He stuck to the official line and explained how Yates had dropped the German police Luger, which he'd picked up and used to kill Yates. Only when he'd finished did he add, 'That lads, is the official position and it's the one every one of yow will tell your mates. Right?'

There was a murmur of agreement around the room. 'The real truth is that without Gerry over there, Mickey and I would probably be dead. It were him that got the bastard. Now, if that gets out, Gerry could be in deep trouble and I wouldn't like that and neither would Mickey.'

It was Tom who spoke first. 'You don't have to worry about that. We're not going to do anything that might cause Gerry a problem. Are we, boys?' A chorus of 'No' and 'Never' rang around the room.

'OK then,' said Tom, 'let's drink Gerry's champagne, remember our friends and give thanks that the bastard responsible for their deaths is, at this moment, burning in hell's deepest pit.'

The celebratory wake was in full swing when Collins and Clark left an hour later. Following an offer from Patrick to drive him back to the Alhambra, Gerry had remained behind. Richard was crestfallen.

Monday 13th May 1968, 09.10hrs

Handsworth

The whole station was talking about the events of Friday night. There were three strands of thought about what had actually happened. A few accepted the official version, more thought that there was a fourth man, but most just assumed that Clark had gone tooled up. After all, everyone knew he had his own extensive collection of firearms, although no one had ever seen it.

At 9.30, Clark and Collins got a call from the Chief Constable, in which he said he would be supporting Inspector West's recommendation that both men be nominated for the Queen's Police Medal.

Hanging up, Clark said, 'I bet West got a twisted hernia writing that memo.'

'Serves the tosspot right,' said Collins.

'Yow know, after 5 years, I reckon yowr starting to pick up the lingo. That's quick for a bog-dweller.'

'That's rich from a Yam Yam, who no one outside West Brom and north Birmingham can understand.'

The men's bickering was interrupted when Marie stuck her head around the door, 'Got a minute, lads?'

'For yow always,' said Clark.

'I've got Gloria outside. Says she has important information about Margaret Lewis's death. Want to see her?'

'Show me favourite prostitute in,' said Clark. Collins and Marie exchanged looks and burst out laughing. Marie was still giggling when she returned to the front desk and lifted the counter lid for Gloria.

Gloria looked just the same as when Collins had first met her five years earlier. The only difference was that she didn't have a black eye and extensive bruising to the face. Bustling into the office on four-inch high heels, wearing her trade-mark short skirt and fishnet stockings, she looked as if she'd been out in the sun.

'Hello yous. How's me favourite pair of coppers? Heard you caught a big one on Friday?'

'Yeah, it were a nice collar,' said Clark. 'What can we do for yow?'

'I've been down in Great Yarmouth for a couple of weeks with me brother. Lovely place, but you can't understand a word the locals say. Anyway, it were only on Friday when I got back that I heard about Margaret. She were only a kid. Dain't never hurt no one. Poor cow. Anyhows, I ran into Betty Grable—'

'Betty Grable?'

'Yeah, yous know Betty. About 50, jet-black hair, skinny, long nose. Looks like a vulture who ain't eaten for a while. Works Lozells Road. Well, her daughter, lovely-looking girl, works for Toby Drew and she was at the party where Margaret got beat.'

Both men leaned forward on their chairs. 'Go on,' said Collins.

'Well, she were at a different party a while back where the guy who beat Margaret was. She heard Toby Drew call him "O'Neil". I thought yow should know, just in case you could do sommut. After all, it were him that caused the poor cow to top herself.'

'That's cracking information, Gloria. I tell you what, let's yow and me grab a cuppa and a bun, and I'll take yowr for-mal statement,' said Clark. 'Then I'll need the contact details for Betty Grable and her daughter. OK?'

'Yeah.'

'Smashing.' Clark held the door open for Gloria and, after

she had passed, he turned and gave a thumbs up sign to Collins.

L eft alone, Collins tried to get on with the mountain of paperwork that had resulted from the Yates case, but his heart wasn't in it. The ringing of the phone was a welcome distraction. He picked it up and before he'd finished saying his name, Sybil Harker cut him short. 'I hear congratulations are required.'

Confused for a moment, he said, 'Did Agnes tell you?'

'Tell me what?'

Realising that he'd made a mistake and that she was talking about the Yates case, which had made the national press, he said, 'Nothing.'

'Don't lie to me, Sergeant Collins. You haven't got the experience or the skill to get away with it. Have you and Agnes decided to tie the knot? Is that it?'

Trapped, Collins gave in and admitted that he and Agnes were indeed going to be married. Sybil was overjoyed, but Collins asked her to say nothing when Agnes phoned her later in the day with the news.

'You can count on my discretion, Michael,' she said. 'I'm a much better liar than you!'

Michael laughed. He was looking forward to meeting Sybil. 'Anyway, what information do you have for me?'

'You were right. The man on the left is Keating. We blew up the photo and you can see the scar going into his hairline. We also found a picture from two years ago where he's standing near a table at which Drew and Gregson are sitting.'

'That's great. It's going to be a pleasure to put him away, the devious git. Just one more thing before you go. What can you tell me about Gregson's cousin Patrick O'Neil?' Collins thought he heard Sybil mutter something under her breath.

It was a couple of seconds before she responded. When she spoke, it was to warn Collins 'He's a psychopathic bastard. I'm very aware of Constable Clark's considerable fighting talents. His reputation is well known in the Met. I imagine that in your partnership he deals with the more vicious thugs, while you have his back. Is that it?'

'Yes. That's how we've operated from day one.'

'Very wise. Very understandable. However, if Constable Clark ever finds himself fighting O'Neil, he must be careful. O'Neil is not just any ordinary thug. Clark can't afford to underestimate him. He's not that big, but he's muscular and solid. He was trained by the SAS and saw action in Aden. They threw him out in '62 for nearly killing a young lad who had objected to him chatting his girlfriend up. He's a vicious bully, fearless and won't back down. If Clark gets in a fight with him, he'll either have to kill him or break both his legs and arms before he'll give up. My suggestion would be to shoot the bastard on sight.'

Collins could hear the repressed anger and hatred in Sybil's voice. 'It sounds as if you've had personal experience of him.'

'Not personal as such. About four years ago, a WPC went undercover. She disappeared. When she turned up six days later, she'd was dead and had been tortured and raped multiple times.'

'What was she working on?'

'She was trying to collect evidence against Gregson's prostitution and blackmail rackets. She was talking to the street girls. We were never able to prove anything, but the viciousness of the attack had all the hallmarks of O'Neil. He's also suspected of the torture and murder of at least two rival gang members.

'As I told you previously he and Gregson are cousins. The families go back to before the war, but they've always been seen as two separate gangs who only came together when one of them is under threat. If he's working with Gregson, then either they've merged or they came together to bring the Krays down.'

'So he's the muscle and Gregson is the brains?'

'No,' said Sybil, her voice strident, underlining what she was about to say. 'You must not think like that. He's actually very bright. His army records show that his IQ is in the third percentile nationally. Underestimate him and he'll kill you.'

'I see.'

'I should have realised when Agnes first called me. The idea to undermine gangs in Birmingham by damaging their operations and removing their leadership structure is just the sort of plan O'Neil would come up with. He and Gregson must have decided to join forces in order to take control of both London and Birmingham. I'll call you this afternoon. By then, I'll have pulled together a file on O'Neil and checked out the other thing you asked me about. But please, warn Clark about O'Neil. Warn him.'

When Clark returned with Gloria's signed statement and contact details for Betty Grable, Collins briefed him on his conversation with Sybil. He didn't seem too perturbed about the possibility of going up against a dangerous psychopath.

'Yow know the trouble with these SAS geezers,' he said. 'They all have something missing in their noggin. They ain't like the rest of us. Most of them genuinely have no fear. That's their weakness and that's how I'll beat O'Neil if we do run into each other. Just remember, if our paths do cross, keep out of the way and run like hell if he kills me.'

'Who's going to kill you?' asked Katie McGuire, from the doorway.

'The Mrs, if I miss the birth.'

'It's close now.'

'That it is, but what brings yow to the station twice inside a week?'

'Just picking up some stats from Sergeant Ridley, plus I didn't get the chance to say well done on Saturday. It was a great collar.'

'We're still getting calls about it,' said Clark. 'Mind yow, the most interesting call we got today was confirmation that Keating, Drew and Gregson know each other, and that Gregson's cousin, someone called O'Neil, may have been responsible for Margret Lewis's death.'

'You going to pick him up?'

'Not yet. The case has more holes in than a colander. We need more time to plug the gaps,' said Collins, 'before we make it official.'

'Well, good luck. By the way, I still haven't forgotten my Milk Tray.'

'Ain't you heard that, as of yesterday, he's spoken for?'

'Is that true, Michael?' she asked, her voice a mixture of surprise and disappointment.

'Afraid so, my love.'

'Congratulations you sod. Do I at least get a consolation kiss?'

'Of course you do,' said Collins, standing up and leaning in to kiss Katie on the lips.

Katie wasn't going to miss her one and only opportunity. Stepping forward, she wrapped her arms around Collins and planted a long wet kiss on his lips while her arms threatened to break his ribs. Finished, she stepped back.

'That's what you've been missing, gorgeous,' she said, with a smile, before adding, 'I hope you and Agnes will be really happy.'

Birmingham, 16.30hrs

Toby Drew picked up the phone. Placing his hand over the mouthpiece, he mouthed to Reggie, 'It's Gregson.'

Reggie observed the one-sided conversation with mounting impatience. What the bleeding hell were they talking about?

As soon as Toby hung up, he asked, 'Well?'

'Gregson's heard from his snitch in the Met. They know about O'Neil and have a photo showing Keating, Gregson and me together.'

'Shit and double shit,' shouted Reggie and slammed his hand down on the desk, making the phone jump and spilling a half-empty cup of coffee. 'What we going to do?'

'Nothing. Gregson is sending O'Neil down to sort it out.'

'When?'

'Tomorrow.'

For the first time that day, Reggie smiled. He was still smiling when he pressed the intercom button and told Miss Larsson to come in and wipe up the coffee he'd spilt.

Tuesday 14th May 1968, 11.00hrs

Handsworth

Clark picked the phone up on the second ring. It was Marie.

'Clarkee, we've got uniform requesting attendance of CID at 28B Leyton Road.'

'What's it about?'

'There was a fight between neighbours and blows exchanged. One man is dead.'

'Tell 'em I'm on me way and get scenes of crime out for me. Ta.' Clark hung up and asked, 'Mickey, do yow fancy a bit of fresh air?'

'What's happened?'

'Open-and-shut case, by the sound of it. Neighbourhood dispute ending in a death.'

'Okay, but you can do the work on this one.'

Leyton Road ran parallel with Holly Road, with the back gardens overlooking each other. For a change, the sun was warm and the sky almost cloudless as Collins and Clark drew up outside 28B.

A small crowd had gathered outside the house, where the body of the householder lay covered on the pavement, protected by Probationary Constable Alex Fletcher. Standing by the door was Constable Dave Harris. Bending down, Clark lifted the blanket, briefly examined the deceased and noticed the pool of blood surrounding his head. He looked up at Collins and both men nodded.

The man's body lay on the pavement, but his head had hit the 3-inch step that led to his small front garden. He was in his seventies, unshaven, unkempt and although over six foot, he looked skinny and frail. He wore a less-than-white shirt with no collar, and a matching pair of grey stripped trousers and a waistcoat with a watch chain. Clark dropped the blanket and turned to Dave Harris. 'What happened?'

'The deceased is Mr Arthur Hay. I've known him years. A nice old bugger. His wife died about a year ago. He's gone to rack and ruin since. I'm not sure he even knew how to boil an egg. Anyway, Mr Joe Ward, who lives at number 46, got home from his night shift at about ten this morning. Soon after, he came round to see Hay and started banging on the door. When the old man answered, he immediately started shouting at him and pushing him.

'The neighbours heard the kerfuffle and came out. Mostly women. They tried to restrain Ward, but his blood was up. They managed to get him on the pavement, but by then Mr Hay had lost his temper. He followed Ward onto the pavement and said something like, "You're mad." That's when Ward swung at him. The old man went down and banged his head on the step. Shame. I liked the poor bugger. He and his misses used to give me and me mates sweets when we were kids.'

'What's the row all about?' asked Clark.

'Ward says the old man felt his daughter up.'

'How old is the daughter?' asked Collins.

'Susan's 13.'

'Where's Ward?' asked Clark.

'Inside,' said Harris.

Ward was sitting in the front room, the door guarded by PC John Woodhead. He nodded a silent greeting as Collins and Clark entered the room. Ward was in his mid-thirties, five foot nine and powerfully built. He didn't look contrite. He looked angry and annoyed at how he was being treated, as if he was the injured party in this affair and not the old man lying dead on the pavement.

Both Collins and Clark remained standing. After a brief

introduction, Clark asked, 'Can yow tell us, Mr Ward, what yowr row with Mr Hay was about?'

'I didn't mean to kill him, but he had a good beating coming to him. No jury is going to convict me when they hear what he done.'

'OK, just tell us what it was,' said Clark.

'My little girl. He stuck his fingers up her. The filthy bastard.'

'He assaulted yowr daughter?' asked Clark.

'That's what I just said. He asked Susan and her mate, Myra Tanner, in. Said he had some chocolates for them. Then, when he got them inside, he put his hand up Susan's skirt.'

'And when did he do that?' asked Clark.

'Last night, about eight o'clock.'

'Why dain't yow see him last night? Why leave it 'til this morning?'

'I work nights. I'd left for work before she come home.'

'Did she tell her mother about the assault?' asked Collins.

'Yeah, this morning. She dain't want to go to school. Said she wasn't feeling well. When her mother asked what was wrong, she told her what happened.'

'And your wife told yow when you got in this morning.'

'Yeah.'

'What time were that?' asked Clark.

'About 10.'

'A long shift?'

'Yeah. One of the day lads had to go to the hospital, so I covered for him. Three hours' overtime.'

'And yow say that Susan's mate, Myra, saw the assault?'

'Yeah.'

'Where does she live?'

'On York Road. I don't know which number.'

'That's all right, Mr Ward. We'll ask Susan. We need to take yow down the station while we sort this out. So, yow need to go with PC Harris here and we'll be along shortly after we've spoke to yowr daughter and her mate.'

'Bloody waste of time, if you ask me. I mean, it were just an accident. The neighbours will tell you.'

'We just want to get everything straight,' said Collins. Now wasn't the time to tell Ward that he was facing charges of manslaughter.

'OK, speed it up, will you? I'm knackered.'

'Dave, can you show us where the alleged assault on Susan took place?' asked Collins.

Harris led Collins and Clark into the small living room, beyond which was the kitchen. There was a large chair diagonally opposite the kitchen door, which could be folded down into a bed. The previous night's blankets had been folded and left on it. A dining table, four chairs and matching sideboard were the only other items of furniture in the room. A Bush bakelite wireless sat in the middle of the sideboard.

'What do yow think, Dave?' asked Clark.

'It don't add up. I've known Hay for over 20 years. He and his Mrs had no kiddies of their own, so they always made a fuss of the kids on the road and bought them chocolates every Christmas. If there were any funny business going on, I'd have heard about it.'

'OK, I'll bear that in mind. Meanwhile, call for a car, get Ward down the station and ask Maria to meet us at Ward's house,' said Clark.

Mrs Ward had been crying and was still tearful as she led Clark and Collins to the living room at the back of the house. Unlike her husband, she was small, thin and nervous. She was no more than 35, but even on her best day she would look 10 years older – and this wasn't her best day.

Susan sat in an overstuffed armchair with her legs tucked under her, staring at a blank TV screen and looking fed up. At five foot four, she was tall for her age and still retained much of her puppy fat. Her face was plump and her small mouth was set in a permanent pout, which gave her a petulant look. The brown eyes that stared back at Clark contained a knowing smirk that he had seen many times in his career. It was a look that said, I ain't scared of you 'cos you can't touch me.

Clark reminded himself to give the girl a fair hearing and not to jump to conclusions, but her first words seemed to confirm his suspicions.

'What you locking me dad up for? That old bastard got what was coming to him.'

'A man's dead. Yowr dad can't expect to get away with that scot-free even if he had reasons for attacking Mr Hay. Now, why don't yow tell us what happened last night?' said Clark.

Collins remained standing at the door, observing the girl as she told her story.

'Me and Myra were playing in the street when that old fart came out and started to talk to us. After a bit, he said he had some chocolate biscuits in the house and said we could have a biscuit and a drink of pop. Well, we went in. He went in the kitchen and came out with two glasses of Tango and a couple of biscuits each. Myra finished her pop first and he told her to get some more. When she went out, he shoved his hand up me skirt.'

'Were yow sitting down when he did this?'

'I was standing up. It was him what was sitting down.'

'Where was he sitting?'

'In that big chair in the back room. He called me over. Said he had something to tell me.'

'And yow went over?'

'Yeah.'

'Were yow in front of his chair or beside it?'

'Beside it.'

'Which side? His right or left?'

She paused, her brown eyes clouding with suspicion. 'What do you want to know all this for? He did what I said.'

'Wi need it for our report,' said Clark. 'Now, which side were it?'

'It were his right.'

'Yow're sure?'

'Course I am.'

'How long did he have his hand up your skirt?'

'About 10 seconds. He pulled it out sharpish when Myra came back.'

'Why didn't you jump back when he put his hand up yowr skirt?'

Susan seemed surprised by the question and was slow to answer. 'I were scared. I dain't know what to do.'

'Did he use one hand to pull your knickers aside or did he just slip his hand under the leg elastic?'

'Just the one hand. Why you asking me all these questions? I'm telling you the truth. Ask Myra if you don't believe me.'

'And he put his finger inside yowr vagina?'

'Yeah.'

'What happened after Myra came in the room?'

'I grabbed her arm and said we was going home and I was going to tell me dad about what he'd done.'

'Before last night, had yow ever been in Mr Hay's house before?'

'Yeah. A couple of times.'

'Did he ever try to molest yow before?'

'No,' she said and paused. 'I were never alone with him before.' Clark couldn't be certain, but he thought he saw a flicker of a smile touch her eyes, as if she'd just done something clever.

'And when yow left, you came straight home afterwards?'

'Yeah, I was back in here by about eight.'

'That's right,' said Mrs Ward. 'She came home just gone eight o'clock.'

'Did yow tell yowr mom what happened?'

'No.'

'Why not?'

'I dunno. I was scared and I felt dirty.'

'But yow told her this morning?'

'Because I dain't sleep all night and I was so tired I dain't want to go to school.'

'And yow, Mrs Ward, yow told yowr husband when he came home at about 10?'

'Yes. Well, Susan told him, but I was here. I just wish to God I'd found out what Mr Hay wanted when he called round earlier in the morning.'

'Mom, that ain't important. I told you.'

'Yowr saying Mr Hay came around this morning while your hubby were at work?'

'He knows that Ray usually gets home at about quarter to eight. He came around at about ten to eight.'

'Did he say what it were about?'

'No. Just said he needed to speak to Joe.'

'Did you tell your husband this before he went over to see Mr Hay?'

'No, I didn't get a chance. As soon as Susan told him what happened, he went storming off. I tried to stop him. It were no good. He has a temper on him when he's riled.'

'Right then. Wi need to speak to Myra. What's the number of her house?'

'Seventeen, but I saw her go to school today. She won't be home.'

'Which school?'

'St Martin's, in Hockley. I go to Rookery Road.'

'If yow could just show us out, Mrs Ward, we'd be much obliged.'

At the door, Clark hesitated and put his finger to his lips as if he'd just thought of something. 'Mrs Ward, did Mr Hay come over before Susan told yow what happened or after?'

'Oh, it was before. Susan never comes down much before 8.15. She's always getting black marks for being late at school. Does it matter?'

Clark shook his head, 'No, nowt important.'

Outside Clark and Collins were joined by Marie Bolding. 'That were interesting,' said Clark.

'Yep, I was thinking the same. Why don't I wander back to the ranch and take Ward's statement while you go and see Myra? Take Maria with you. She could do with getting out more.'

'Okay, but yow do realise yowr still sounding like a bloody cowboy?'

'Better than sounding like a Yam Yam.'

'Say another word and I might have to beat the living daylights out of you.'

Digbeth, 13.00hrs

O'Neil walked into the office without knocking, with Miss Lisa Larsson trailing in his wake. He slipped his navy blue Crombie overcoat off and handed it to the secretary, with a smile that would freeze blood on a summer day.

'Hang that up for me, darling. It's worth more than you earn in a month – even with all the extra services you provide Toby with.'

At five foot eight, O'Neil wasn't particularly short, but no one ever mentioned his height to his face. The last two who had alluded to it, and his liking for tall women in high heels, had ended up in hospital. His body was compact and hard. His suit, the work of Savile Row, had been expertly cut to disguise his musculature and give him the greater freedom of movement he needed to kick or punch someone's head in when required.

His grey hair was combed straight back and a liberal amount of Brylcreem had been applied to keep every hair in its allotted place. His eyebrows, were thick, lush and black, which was in stark contrast to his pale white skin. A slim, sharp nose and a small mouth with an overhanging upper lip gave him the appearance of a small bird of prey. This look was enhanced by his near black eyes.

Toby jumped up and came around his desk, with his hand outstretched. O'Neil took it and squeezed. It was said that however hard he squeezed your hand indicated how pissed off he was with you. It was clear to Toby that he was annoyed, but hadn't yet reached mental.

Reggie and Keating also offered to shake hands, but he ignored them and sat down at the conference table. All three men joined him. He surveyed his new partners. Toby was a safe pair of hands. He was useful, but would never amount to anything more than a good lieutenant. Keating was shit scared of something and that made him a risk. At some stage in the not-so-distant future, his services would have to be dispensed with, even if not everyone agreed. As for Reggie, a small smile tugged at the corners of O'Neil's lips. He was looking forward to the day when he could take the mad fuck out. It would be interesting to watch him squeal.

'How's Harry?' asked Toby.

'Pissed that he had to ask me to take care of your little local difficulty.'

'We appreciate your help. We didn't want to use local resources to deal with Clark.'

'Clive Fucking Clark,' said O Neil. 'I've been hearing about him for the last ten years. It's time our paths crossed. Just a pity that he'll never know it was me that did for him.'

'So, what are you going to do?' asked Reggie, like an excited teenager allowed to play with the big boys for a change.

O'Neil studiously ignored the interruption and continued to look at Toby. 'I've arranged for a couple of the best independents in London to deal with the problem. They'll be here tomorrow morning. They'll do the pair in the afternoon and be back in London by nightfall. Clean, simple and quick.'

'Others have tried,' said Toby. 'Clark and Collins seem to have nine bloody lives and then some. Are you be sure it will work? I don't want a pissed-off Clark coming after me.'

O'Neil took out a small penknife and started to clean his fingernails with the blade. 'Do you know why no one's been able to get the better of these bastards?' His tone was condescending, as if he was talking to idiots. All three men knew that it was a calculated insult on O'Neil's part. A demonstration of his power. They also knew that they had to play along with him.

'No,' said Toby.

'Synergy.'

'Who the fuck's synergy?' asked Reggie.

O'Neil continued to ignore the younger brother. 'Synergy occurs when two plus two equals five. Like when Harry and me finally merged the family businesses. What we've got now is bigger and more powerful than what we jointly held when we were separate. It's the same with Clark and Collins. In a punch-up, Collins covers Clark's back. That's his job and from what I hear, he'd rather take a bullet than let his mate down. Clark has total faith in Collins. This means he can concentrate on the dangers in front of him, but he also fights harder because he wants to protect his mate. There's a similar effect on Collins. Clark's belief in him. His reliance on him makes him a better scrapper than if he were on his own. That's synergy.'

'How the fuck do you know all this?' asked Reggie.

'Because I've read a few books other than Biggles Goes to War and Lola Does New York. I also saw it a few times when I was in the army. It doesn't happen often, but when it does it's as obvious as a used johnny in a bowl of salad.'

'So you're going to tackle them one at a time. Is that it?' asked Toby.

'Precisely. Take them out separately and from a distance.

Although, we can get closer to Collins than Clark. On his tod, Collins is no great shakes.'

'I'm still worried about what will happen afterwards. The coppers will come for us, all guns blazing,' said Keating.

'Let them,' said Reggie, trying to sound like Jimmy Cagney in White Heat and failing.

O'Neil raised his eyes to the heavens and shook his head. 'No need to worry on that account. The coppers will have their killer within a couple of hours. Case closed and no blowback on you or our operations.'

'How?' asked Reggie.

'The less you know, the better.'

'I'm still worried about what they've already found out. There must be a record of it somewhere,' said Keating.

'They have very little, if any, hard evidence. All they really have is a photo that shows you and Toby having a drink with Harry, a well-known London character who owns a couple of clubs. Hell, just about every actor in London has had their photo taken with Harry. There's nothing illegal in the photo. All the rest is just supposition and circumstantial on their part.'

'So why kill them then?' asked Keating.

'Because from everything I know about this pair, once they get their teeth into you, they keep going until they've ripped the flesh off your body and chewed on the bones,' replied O'Neil.

Hockley, 13.30hrs

Clark parked on the street, locked the car and examined the grime-encrusted school. It had been built towards the end of the last century and had served the educational needs of local children for over seventy-five years. For most of that time, the majority of kids had come from an Irish background, but after the war they'd picked up a lot of Poles and, following the 1956 uprising, Hungarians.

Clark and Marie found the Headmistress' office on the first

floor. The diminutive Sister Etna looked ancient, her face a map of wrinkles and yellowing skin, though her blue eyes were as clear and sharp as mountain air in winter.

With introductions exchanged, Sister Etna asked, 'So what can I do for you?'

Clark quickly explained what had happened and asked to see Myra Tanner. Sister Etna rang a small brass bell on her desk and the school's administrator almost immediately knocked on the door and entered. 'Mrs May, please go to Class 2X and ask Miss Burn to release Myra Tanner and bring her here.'

A few minutes later, Mrs May returned with Myra. She bore no resemblance at all to Susan Ward. Barely five foot, she had wispy light brown hair, a thin face and frightened eyes that darted around the room as she came in. She looked like a terrified puppy and Clark instinctively felt sorry for her. There was no doubting who was the boss in her relationship with Susan Ward.

'Sit down, Myra. This policeman and lady are here to talk to you about what happened to your friend last night. There's nothing to worry about. You won't be in any trouble, as long as you tell the truth. Do you understand?'

Myra replied with a barely audible, 'Yes.'

'Speak up, girl.'

'Sorry. Yes.' This time, the voice had progressed to a loud whisper.

'I'm sorry to tell yow, Myra, that Mr Hay is dead.' Sister Etna's head snapped up. Clark hadn't mentioned any death. 'Susan's dad got in a fight with him this morning and the old gentlemen died. So, yow understand how important it is to tell us the truth.'

The blood had drained from Myra's face. Tears were welling up in her eyes, which she fought to hold back. Thin lines of perspiration appeared on her forehead and top lip. She wasn't far from going into shock. When she said, 'Yes,' it was no more than a croak.

Clark decided to cut to the crux of the case. 'When you were in Mr Hay's house last night, yow went to the kitchen to get another glass of pop. Is that right?'

'Yeah.'

'What did yow see when you came back?'

'The old man, Mr Hay, had his hand up Susan's skirt. He pulled it out when I came back.'

'Where was Mr Hay standing when yow came back?'

Myra hesitated, confusion reflected in her tawny eyes. Finally, she said, 'By that big chair in the corner.'

'And where was Susan?'

'In front of him.'

'With her back to the kitchen.'

'Yeah.'

'So how could yow see where his hand were?'

'What you mean?'

'If Susan were facing him, she would have had her back to the kitchen and yow wouldn't have been able to see what were going on.'

'I did see it. I did.' Her voice was loud now, betraying early signs of panic. 'I did. I tell you.'

'Susan said that Mr Hay was sitting down. Yow say he were standing up. Which one of yow is lying?' Clark's voice had risen and contained a hard edge to it.

For the first time, Myra felt real fear. Her eyes jumped between Clark, Sister Etna, and Marie Bolding, desperately seeking a friendly face. The tears that had threatened to appear since she walked into the room now started to roll down her cheeks.

Clark handed her a clean handkerchief, and she dabbed her eyes and blew her nose. 'Come on, Myra. Yowr a nice girl, but yow ain't a very good liar. Why don't yow tell me what really happened?'

Between sobs, Myra started to tell her story, her eyes never leaving the floor. It took about 10 minutes and when she looked up, she asked, 'Will I go to Borstal?

Marie put her hand around the girl's shoulders and said, 'I don't know, love, but we'll tell the judge that you were a good girl and helped us as much as you could.'

Handsworth, 19.00hrs

When Clark and Collins entered Ward's cell, he was lying on his bunk. Sitting up, he threw his legs over the side of the bed and stood up.

'Come to let me out, have you?' he said, smiling. 'About bleeding time. I told you it were just an accident.'

'Would you like to sit down, Mr Ward?' said Collins.

'Na, I'm all right.'

'Best if yow do,' said Clark.

'What's going on?' asked Ward, the first sign of doubt appearing in his face. Surely, the coppers weren't daft enough to charge him with manslaughter.

'We've just finished taking statements from yowr daughter and Myra Tanner,' said Clark. 'Mr Hay dain't invite the girls in. It was yowr daughter who knocked on his door and asked for pop. They'd been there before. He let them in. A lonely old man – it would be a bit of company for him. But after they had their Tango, Susan asked him for a fiver. He asked her why she needed five pounds and she said she wanted to buy some cigarettes and go to a Beach Boys concert at the Odeon in Birmingham.

'He refused to give her anything. That's when she told him that if he didn't give her the money, she'd say he'd interfered with her and Myra would back her story up. He still refused to give her a penny. He told her he would speak to yow first thing in the morning and tell yow what she'd threatened, only when he called at ten to eight this morning yow were still at work. I'm not sure if Susan were ever going to accuse Mr Hay of anything or not, but she panicked when she saw him and thought that attack were her best form of defence.

'She wound you up so much that when yow knocked on Mr Hay's door, yow weren't interested in listening to what he had to say. Yow killed an innocent old man, Mr Ward, and now yow're going to jail for it.'

Ward's face registered shock and horror in equal measure. In that moment, he knew that life as he knew it was over. Stunned, he asked, 'What about Susan?'

'Yowr daughter has been charged with blackmail under Section 29 of the Larceny Act 1916. Myra's been charged as an accessory. They've both been remanded in custody and will appear in the juvenile court tomorrow.'

'What about me?'

'You will be charged with manslaughter. Yow will appear at Birmingham Magistrates Court in the morning and yow'll be remanded in custody until yowr trial.'

'But I dain't mean to kill him. I only hit him once and he knocked his head on the step. It were just an accident.'

'You'll have your chance to put your side of the story in court, Mr Ward,' said Collins.

It was gone nine when Clark and Collins finally walked to their cars. Night had descended and there was a distinct chill in the air. In a single day, they had investigated the unlawful killing of a man and arrested the culprits, but neither felt like celebrating.

'Yow know, Mikey, I sometimes wonder what the world's coming to. One silly, spiteful little bitch has caused the death of a decent man, landed her old man in jail, ruined her mother's life and screwed up her mate's life for good measure. And for all this mayhem, she'll either get probation or end up being Queen Bee in whatever Borstal they send her to.'

'I know how you feel. I just wish I had an answer.'

Wednesday 15th May 1968, 07.45hrs

Handsworth

Collins had found it hard to sleep the previous night and was pleased when the clock finally showed seven. A quick shave and a shower and he was ready for breakfast. Agnes was already in the kitchen and his porridge and raisins were bubbling away nicely on the stove. He kissed the back of Agnes' neck and slipped his arms around her waist. She turned and kissed him on the mouth.

'What have you got on today?' she asked.

'Paperwork, mainly. You'd be surprised how much paper a mass murderer creates.'

'I don't think I would. Napoleon called the British a nation of shopkeepers. Well, today we seem to be a nation of bureaucrats. What we used to be able to do with one telephone call now involves numerous letters, meetings and calls. Ridiculous! It can't go on. But what about the Drews? Where are you with them?'

'We're waiting for them to react to a little provocation that Clark and I staged. If they don't, then we'll rock their tree again – starting tomorrow.' Collins saw no reason to tell Agnes about Patrick O'Neil and what Sybil had said about him.

When he got to work, Collins found the CID office empty. Bliss, he thought. Clark had disappeared to the court hearings for Ward and the girls, and had taken Marie with him. Hicks, meanwhile, was attending another training course. It was obvious even before he closed the closed the arson case a couple of years earlier that they had been preparing him for promotion to Superintendent. *I wonder if he'll be tapped up to join the Masons on this course, or if he's already one?* he thought.

With a cup of tea at his elbow, Collins resigned himself to another day of paperwork. As he started to write, he decided that if the Drews didn't make a move soon, he and Clark would need to stir the pot again. Something provocative, he thought. With a smile, he realised that a trip to London and a chat with Mr Gregson would certainly do the trick.

Digbeth, Birmingham 11.50hrs

The two men, who had just arrived from London, sat at the conference table drinking coffee. It had been a longer journey than expected due to a shunt on the M1 that had closed one northbound lane. The only other people in the room were O'Neil and Toby.

O'Neil had just finished outlining his plan and asked, 'Any questions, Mr Sands?' The older of the two men was the definition of nondescript. There was nothing unusual or memorable about Fred Sands. He was of medium height and build. His hair was neither long nor short, and his face was the type you'd forget thirty seconds after seeing it. In his ordinariness, he was almost invisible. Perfect, if you were a professional killer. He shook his head.

'How about you, Mr Clay?'

James Clay looked about 20, but was actually 32. He was slimmer than his friend, and whereas the older man was dark, he was fair with blond hair. His choice of clothing was conservative – grey slacks, white shirt and a blue blazer. The only thing flash about him was his Ray-Ban sunglasses, which he wore constantly.

'How sure are you that the suicide note will pass muster?' asked Clay.

'No problem. Mr Eden is the best forger in the business.'

'Separating them will be the problem,' said Sands.

'That's why I have people watching both of them. Once

we're sure they can't contact each other, you'll make your move.'

Handsworth, 17.45hrs

Clark had just returned from court and was still taking his coat off when Marie came into the office and dropped a telephone message on his desk. 'Came in about fifteen minutes ago from Mickey.'

Clark picked it up and immediately felt a crawling sensation slither down his spine. He'd had the same sensation many times before and it was seldom wrong. 'Hang on a sec, Marie. Did yow take the message?'

'Na. it was the new Special. He's OK, that one. Keen, with a brain.'

'Can yow send him in, love?'

'Sure. Anything wrong?'

'Don't know. Probably nowt.'

Two minutes later, the part-time, unpaid Special Constable was standing in the CID room, looking worried, wondering what he'd cocked up. The fact that he was facing Clarkee made him even more nervous. Everyone had heard stories about the small man.

'It's all right, lad, I ain't going to bite.' Indicating the telephone message, Clark said, 'Marie says that it were yow who took this message.' The young man nodded. 'Are you sure that Mickey said, "Meet me outside the Boundary Café at 6.15" and then signed off by calling himself Michael?'

'Certain, Sir, word for word.'

'I'm not a, Sir, lad, or a Sarge, I'm just Clarkee, OK?'

'Yes, Clarkee.'

'And he called himself Michael?'

'Yes.'

'Have yow met Mickey? Spoke to him?'

'I've seen him around.'

'Would you recognise his voice?'

'I've not spoken to him, but it was an Irish accent on the phone. Here, what's up?'

'Nowt, just me being suspicious. Ask Marie to pop back, would yow?'

Clark picked up the phone and rang Mickey at home. He let it ring a dozen times before hanging up. He was putting his coat back on, when Marie returned. 'Is Ridley back on the desk?'

'Yes.'

'Good. I need yow with me. Grab yowr coat and I'll meet yow in the car park. I need to pop to me locker first.'

Handsworth, 18.15hrs

Having spent the entire day indoors, Collins had enjoyed his walk with Sheba. It gave him time to think. To clear his head. To relax for a few minutes and realise that not all of life was about police work.

As evening approached, the sun grew cooler and the north-easterly wind, which had been blowing most of the day, suddenly felt cold rather than fresh against Collins' face. It was a pleasant feeling and, for a second, he closed his eyes. Three yards behind him trotted Sheba. She'd had a great time, chasing a young rabbit across the Hill Top's thick, lush grass, until her prey had found a friendly rabbit hole to take sanctuary in.

A car was parked outside the house and as Collins approached, a young, blond-haired man jumped out of the driver's seat, with an A to Z Guide of Birmingham in his left hand. 'Excuse me,' he said, coming around the back of the car. 'Can you tell me where Albert Road is?'

Collins checked his stride and started to walk towards the man. Sheba growled, her ears upright. Collins turned to tell her to be quiet. As he turned back, he saw the man pull a snub-nosed Colt Cobra from behind his back. Everything had slowed down. The man's right arm started to come up. The revolver was rising higher with each fraction of a second.

Soon, the gun would be aimed at his chest and then it would explode. There was no cover to be had. Collins knew he was already dead. He only had time for one quick prayer, *Sweet Jesus, look after Agnes.*

He felt a thump to his chest and was propelled backwards by the power of the bullet. He stumbled and fell to the ground. His head bounced off the iron railings and he felt a brief moment of euphoria as the gunman aimed again.

The last thing Collins saw before passing out was Sheba racing past him. While still four feet from the gunman, she launched herself at the hand that held the gun. Terrified by the sight of the black dog with just a single circle of white fur around her left eye, her lips pulled back in a vicious snarl, the gunman readjusted his aim and fired. The bullet grazed the side of Sheba's face, hit her collarbone, nicked the lung and exited behind her right front leg. The .38 bullet slowed her down but didn't stop her forward momentum. Her jaws closed on the man's forearm and locked on. Screaming, he punched Sheba in her injured side, forcing a spray of blood from the bullet's exit wound. Sheba clung on, fighting the pain and nausea that washed over her. Clay continued to punch her but her jaws held tight. She was rapidly slipping into unconsciousness. Her grip was slackening, her eyes glazing over. She fought the coming darkness, but finally it enveloped her. She fell to the ground and lay unmoving in the gutter.

By now, Agnes was running towards the gate, neighbours were coming out of their houses and a man was sprinting to the phone boxes on the corner to call for an ambulance and the police. Clay looked at the unmoving Collins and the blood dripping from his arm, and decided to get the hell out of Handsworth. He still had an essential part of his job to complete. Tucking the gun into his waistband, he ran to the Escort, jumped in and turned the key in the ignition. The engine caught straight away and he pulled away in a cloud of blue smoke.

Agnes reached Collins and knelt down. She was surprised at the lack of blood and ripped his jacket open, looking for the wound. There was none, except for a tiny trickle seeping from his shirt pocket. Agnes grabbed his jacket and examined the inside pocket. A .38 shell had struck Collins' police notebook, penetrating the cardboard front cover and the loose pages, before trying its best to plough through the back cover. However, only about one eighth of an inch had made it.

Agnes burst into tears of relief and cradled Collins' head in her arms, thanking her God for his deliverance from death. He moaned softly and opened his eyes. As they cleared, he recognised Agnes and smiled. He sat up slowly and propped himself against the railings. It was only when he raised his head that he saw Sheba lying in the gutter, her head resting on the pavement, blood trickling down the gutter.

He vaguely remembered her charging past him and the screams of the gunman. She'd saved him and now she lay dying. He struggled to his feet and pushed past the crowd that was beginning to form. At the edge of the pavement, he hunkered down. Sheba lay still, but he could see her chest rising and falling. She was alive. She was still fighting. Collins discarded his jacket, ripped off his shirt, bunched it up and used it to staunch the flow of blood from Sheba's chest. Picking his dog up, he handed her to Agnes.

'Get down to the PDSA. I'll call them and let them know you're coming.'

'Where are you going?'

'To find Clarkee and warn him.'

'Be careful,' said Agnes and kissed him on the cheek.

Boundary Cafe, West Bromwich 18.17hrs

Clark parked the unmarked police car as near to the Boundary Café as possible. The A45 in front of him was quiet. The commuter traffic had disappeared and business was slow in the café. 'Yow know what yow got to do. Stay in the café. Keep watch and if anything happens, call the cavalry and—'

'Under no circumstances, come out.'

Clark looked at the young woman. Other than a faint blush of excitement, she was perfectly calm. 'Good girl.'

Marie disappeared into the café and Clark surveyed the surrounding buildings from the relative safety of the car. If it was a set-up, the instruction to meet Collins outside meant that they needed him in the open. This implied either a shot from distance or a shooter leaning out of a car window. His money was on a rifle shot.

Slowly, Clark examined the familiar façade of The Hawthorns' Brummie Road End. Just beyond it, he could see the stand's corrugated roof. To his left was the Woodman pub, from which he had staggered just a few days before. Behind the pub, and towering above it, was Woodman Corner Score Board – a black wooden box on stilts, which two men entered by ladder at half-time and remained there to the end of the match. Their job was to display the half-time scores for all Division One matches and, if they had them before the ground emptied, the full-time scores as well.

Before stepping from the car, Clark withdrew the Webley Mk IV .38 snub-nose revolver from his jacket pocket and disengaged the safety. The gun's shorter barrel meant it was more practical for police use than most of the revolvers on sale, while still packing a hell of a punch. He tucked the gun into his waistband. He was ready.

As he opened the door, his last thought was, *Try not to shoot your balls off. Junior may want a brother or sister one day.*

Clark moved to the front of the café, staying within the shadow of the building at all times, and paced up and down. If there was someone out there with a rifle, he wanted to make the shot as difficult as possible and he knew that a shot at a moving target in the shadows would be difficult, even for an expert. As he walked, he kept watch for any car that might drive onto the car park.

When it came, the report from the rifle was loud and harsh. Clark felt the bullet pass through his suit's shoulder pad and strike the bricks beneath the café's window. One quick look was all he needed to plot the bullet's trajectory from brick to shoulder pad to Woodman Corner. *Fuck it*, he thought, as he sprinted towards the safety of The Hawthorns' wall, *this guy can shoot*. Every yard he covered made the angle worse for the sniper, but that didn't stop him trying. The second shot split the toe guard on Clark's shoe, while the next flung up black dirt and gravel mere inches from where he had been standing. The three second delay between each shot was enough to tell Clark that the gunman was probably using a single shot target rifle. It was ideal for shooting at stationary targets, but not so good when they are zigzagging at speed across a car park.

Clark reached the safety of the cool blue bricks that housed the Albion's turnstiles before the shooter could fire a fourth shot. He took three deep breaths to control his breathing, then moved towards the rubbish bin near the main exit gates. The smell told him that on the other side of the wall was what counted as toilets at the Albion. Ideal. The old khazi would offer him cover once he was over the wall. Stepping onto the bin, he jumped up. On the second attempt, he grabbed the top of the wall and pulling himself up, he lay flat for an instant. The area between him and the scoreboard was empty. He slid off the wall and dropped into the men's urinals.

How come coppers and spies in films never land in a shithouse? he thought. Flattening himself against the brick-work, he took a quick look out the exit. Still no sign of the shooter. Good. Satisfied, he started to run towards the score-board. Rounding the corner of the Brummie Road Stand, where it joined the Woodman Corner, he saw a pair of legs appear from the far side of the scoreboard. Stopping, he took aim and fired. The bullet hit the ladder rung below the man's foot and he quickly disappeared back into the box.

Clark had him bottled up. All he had to do now was wait a while and the lads from Handsworth and West Brom would be swarming all over the place like ants on a sticky bun. The problem was that the bastard in the box was armed and Clark didn't think he was going to surrender nicely.

Near the large rollover exit gates was a collection of rubbish sacks, waiting to be collected. Clark sprinted to the nearest one and opened it. It contained mostly newspapers, discarded programmes, sweet papers, and greaseproof paper which had been used to wrap home-made sandwiches. Great. The next contained mainly empty cardboard boxes from the tea stand. No use. The third was more paper rubbish and, praise be, a couple of small used gas canisters discarded by the hot dog seller. All that was in them was a few fumes but that would be enough. Grabbing the first and third sack, Clark ran to the back of the scoreboard where the twenty or so steeply raked steps to the terraces gave him cover, provided he didn't raise his head.

Fumbling in his jacket pocket, he found the book of matches he'd taken from Wilkee's flat. Kissing the model on the front, he said 'Wish me luck, gorgeous,' then dropped a couple of lit matches into both bags. The fire took hold almost immediately. He waited until both sacks were fully alight, then stood up. Before he'd cleared the first step, a bullet ripped through his jacket and he felt a sharp burning pain in his right bicep. Maybe he ain't such a good shot, thought Clark. The gun's pulling to his left and he ain't corrected for it.

Once beneath the box, Clark pushed one sack against the ladder and the other between the legs of the box. The shooter was now panicking and firing blindly through the floor. Clark knew that even a blind shot could kill, so wasting no time, he covered his head and face with his arms and rolled down the steps which he'd run up only moments earlier. As he rolled, he pulled his knees up. Reaching the bottom, he lay still, checking that nothing was broken. All present and correct, he thought and began to work his way back to where he would have an unimpeded view of the ladder.

Smoke was now billowing from the sacks and two loud explosions went off in quick succession as the nearly empty gas canisters exploded. I bet they sound like bloody grenades in the box, he thought. Fire was licking against the old wooden structure and scorching the floor above. Ten seconds passed. Nothing. Twenty. Nothing. In the distance, he heard the sound of police bells for the first time. That was enough for the shooter. He started out of the box. The flames were lapping around his legs and he jumped the final couple of feet to the ground.

'Hold it there,' shouted Clark and fired a warning shot, which hit the underside of the score box.

'Fuck you, cunt,' came the reply and the man raised his rifle for the final time. Clark's bullet hit him in the chest, smashed into his heart and ricocheted around his rib cage. He stumbled backwards, fell and tumbled down the terraces, before finally coming to rest against one of the red crush barriers.

Clark approached the spread-eagled body. It was obvious that Fred Sands was dead. Despite that, he followed his training and kicked the rifle away from the body. Walking over to the exit, he looked for a way to raise the shutters. I'm getting too fucking old for this, he thought, as he held his injured shoulder and noticed for the first time the blood seeping out of a hole in his shoe. I'm going to be stiffer than a groom's dick on his wedding night tomorrow.

As the shutter rose, the first person he saw was Mickey. He was standing there ready to do battle with his drawn truncheon. 'Only a fucking Irishman would come to a gun battle with a truncheon.'

'Where the feck do you think I'd find a gun at short notice? Unlike you, I don't have a personal arsenal.'

For the first time, Clark noticed the small patch of blood on Collins' chest. 'The bastards came for yow, too?'

Collins nodded. 'Me pocket book saved me, but the bastard shot Sheba.'

'Is she all right?'

Collins shook his head. 'Agnes has taken her to the vet.'

Both men could now clearly hear the sound of bells. 'Get out of here before they arrive or you'll not get to see Sheba before she – you know.'

Ashamed by the tears in his eyes, Collins turned and trotted back to his car.

Perry Barr, 18.20hrs

With his one good hand, Clay managed to stop the car fishtailing down the road. Fuck, fuck and fuck again, his mind screamed. Of all the bad luck to run into a fucking mad dog on what should have been an easy kill. Still, he'd got the bastard, that's all that mattered. One shot straight to the heart. Collins wasn't coming back from that. Even so, he would have felt happier if he'd been able to complete the double tap with a head shot.

Turning left at the Endwood Island Clay saw a piece of waste ground leading to a narrow alleyway that ran behind a row of houses. Pulling off the road, he checked that no one was watching. Satisfied that all was clear, he slipped his jacket off and took a less-than-clean handkerchief from his pocket and some insulation tape from the glove box. Rolling his shirt sleeve up, he folded the handkerchief in four and placed it over the dog bite. It barely covered all the teeth marks. Quickly, he wrapped the tape around the entire surface of the emergency bandage and finished off by tapping his shirt sleeve over the makeshift dressing. Not elegant, but effective. The flow of blood had ceased.

Injury or not, he had to finish the job. Gently, he eased his arm back into his jacket and reversed onto the road. Checking his watch, he saw that he was still within the schedule.

Clay drew up outside Sheppard's house. Slipping on a pair of white evening dress gloves he reached into the glove compartment and withdrew a Walter PPK .22 pistol and slipped it into his jacket pocket. Removing his gloves, he examined the road carefully. There was no one about. Good. He eased himself from the driver's seat, worried that the loss of blood might have made him light-headed, but he was fine. Slowly, he walked up the path and pressed the buzzer.

Sheppard opened the front door and stared at the stranger. 'What do you want?'

'Hello, Mr Sheppard. My name's Clay. I believe that Mr Drew spoke to you about me and my colleague, Mr Sands.'

Sheppard did a quick check of the road, then said, 'You'd better come in.' He led Clay into the lounge and offered him a drink.

'I'll have a bitter lemon and whiskey with ice.'

'No problem,' said Sheppard.

As Sheppard prepared the drinks, Clay slipped on the white dress gloves again and wandered around the room masking his injured arm as much as he could from Sheppard's view. Placing both drinks on the coffee table, Sheppard flopped onto the settee. 'So, at long last, the Drews are going after those bastards. About time. Look what they did to my leg,' he said, rolling his trouser up.

'Nasty,' said Clay, viewing the shattered knee from behind the settee. 'Did Clark do that to you?'

'Yeah. Took me by surprise, he did.'

'Well, don't worry about it. They'll be history by the end of the night.'

'That's music to my ears. Mr Drew said you and your mate would need a bed for the night. Is there anything else I can do for you?'

'Just one thing,' said Clay. 'You can die.'

Confusion, quickly followed by fear, crossed Sheppard's face. He tried to stand, but the soft cushions made it difficult and his gammy leg slowed him down further. Clay wasn't slow. He had more than enough time to place the small pistol against Sheppard's right temple and pull the trigger.

A plume of bone, brains, blood and cerebral fluid erupted from the left side of Sheppard's head and he crumpled sideways onto the settee.

Clay then took the handwritten note from his inside pocket and laid it on the table. Lifting Sheppard's right hand, he placed it several times on the front and back of the paper. He then repeated the process with Sheppard's left hand. Finally, he picked up the still warm cartridge shell casing and rubbed it up and down Sheppard's thumb, index finger and the back of his hand. Emptying the gun he rolled each of the remaining eight shells shell between Sheppard's fingers before replacing them. He then placed the gun in Sheppard's hand, making sure his prints were on the barrel, handle, trigger and trigger guard. Finally he repositioned Sheppard's arms and hands. The perfect suicide.

He drank both whiskeys then washed and replaced the glasses. A quick check before he left revealed that the road was still empty. *What a dead dump*, he thought as he walked to the car and smiled at his own witticism. Job done, he felt the adrenalin drain away, but as it did, the pain returned with a vengeance. *Fucking dog*, he thought as he set out for London and a visit to the doc's.

Hockley, 21.30hrs

Peter Wright was the People's Dispensary for Sick Animal's Chief Veterinarian Surgeon in Birmingham. He was regularly used by the police for emergencies involving animals of every conceivable shape and size. When Peter emerged from the treatment room looking grim, Collins prepared himself for the worst. Agnes placed her hand on his forearm and squeezed.

'I don't know how she's still alive,' the vet said. 'The bullet broke her eye socket, slashed down her jawline, broke her collarbone and travelled downwards through her chest, before exiting just inches behind her front leg. It nicked a lung on the way through, but managed to miss all the other vital organs.'

Standing, his voice thick with emotion, Collins asked, 'Is she going to be all right?'

'I don't know, Mickey. She's lost a lot of blood. If you can get her through the night, and if she doesn't die of shock, she has a chance. A very slim chance.'

Collins didn't trust himself to speak. He just nodded and bit his lip. Agnes came to his rescue and asked, 'Can we take her home, Peter?'

'Yes, that would be best. We have no facilities to look after animals overnight. Jill is just dressing Sheba's wounds. While you're waiting, I'll get some painkillers that you can give her if she wakes up.'

The "if" sliced through Collins' last reserves and his shoulders shook as he swallowed back the tears. He'd known Peter for four years and not once in that time had he got a prognosis wrong. Sheba was going to die.

Jill emerged from the treatment room carrying a wicker dog basket. An unconscious Sheba lay on her left side, her head and chest swathe in bandages. Collins took the basket and nodded his thanks, leaving Agnes to thank Peter and Jill properly and make a large donation to the work of the PDSA.

With Agnes driving, the short journey home was made in complete silence. The only sound was the laboured breathing of Sheba – each breath an attempt to cling onto life for a few seconds longer.

Three police cars were parked on the road and every light in the house seemed to be on. Agnes drew up by the garage and Collins parked behind her. Before the engine had died, Sergeant O'Driscoll opened the driver's door. Collins had never seen him so agitated.

'Where the feck have you been, Mickey?'

'I was at the vet's, didn't Clark tell you?'

'No. He was whisked off to the fecking hospital before any of us had a chance to speak to him.'

Fear flashed through Collins' body. When he'd spoken to Clark, he'd seemed perfectly fine. 'What's happened to him? Is he all right?'

'Calm down. He's fine. He's got a bit of concussion. They're keeping him in overnight as a precaution. He's also got a flesh wound to the arm and a badly bruised toe where a bullet split his shoe. Can you believe it? The bastard tried to take him out at long range with a BSA International Mark 3 match rifle.'

'Thank God he's all right.'

'Are you up to answering a few questions?'

'Can we leave it until the morning?'

O'Driscoll had put together half the story from the neighbours. He really should take Collins' statement while events were clear in his mind and also check what Agnes had seen. However, one look at Collins and the sound of Sheba's laboured breathing was all he needed to make his mind up. 'Yeah, of course. I'll leave a car and a couple of bobbies outside.'

'Thanks.'

'But I do need to ask you one question.'

'Fine.'

'Has Jonny Sheppard ever threatened to kill you?'

'Don't be bloody daft. He almost soils himself every time he sees Clark. Why?'

'His girlfriend found him dead when she came home from work. He committed suicide. He left a note saying that he had you both killed because you and Clark had made his life a living hell.'

Collins was silent for a moment. Thinking. 'Well that's all

very convenient for Drew and his mates. But take it from me, it's a load of bollicks.'

As the last police officer left the house, the hall clock chimed 11.15.

'Do you want Sheba to sleep in our room tonight?' Agnes asked.

Collins shook his head. 'No,' he whispered. 'Her home is in the kitchen. She should die there. I'll stay with her.'

Agnes gently placed her hand on Collins' chest and kissed him lightly on the lips. Turning to Sheba, she stroked the dog's hindquarters, about the only place not covered by a bandage. She knew that dogs didn't have a soul, but she said a prayer of thanks for the 28 pounds of muscle and personality that had saved the life of only the second man she had ever loved and went upstairs to bed.

Alone, Collins carried Sheba into the kitchen. Carefully, he lifted her from the basket and placed her in her own bed in the corner. Then, he went to the lounge and returned with two cushions, which he placed next to her bed, and sat down.

His father had never allowed him to have a pet goldfish, let alone a dog. He said animals were too much trouble. Maybe if his mother had lived, it would have been different. Sheba was the first pet, the first dog, he'd ever owned.

He remembered the first time he'd seen her. It was the middle of a bitterly cold night, behind Handsworth Market, and she had been howling to attract attention. Her master, Benny, the market's unofficial night watchman-cum-drunk, was lying dead in his small hut and she knew that he need-ed to be taken care of. Collins had never seen such an ugly, evil-looking dog as this bundle of muscle that ran past him into Clark's arms.

Clark had blackmailed him into keeping the dog by saying

that if she went to the dogs' home, she'd be put down after seven days. He'd never regretted for a single day taking on Miss Personality until now. His pain was immense. *She's only a bloody dog*, he told himself. *Stop behaving like a kid.* But it was no use, she was his bloody dog. She'd saved his life and he loved her.

I'm going to kill the bastard who did this, if it's the last thing I ever do, he thought. It was then that the tears came. Hot, salty and silent.

At midnight, he turned the light off and switched on the small night light over the fridge. For the next four hours, he sat beside Sheba with his hand resting lightly on her front paw, which twitched every now and then. He listened to her breathing, waiting for it to stop. He tried to stay awake. He wanted to be with her when she died, but at around four in the morning he fell into a fitful sleep.

Just as dawn came up, his eyes snapped open. A warm dry tongue was licking his fingers. Sheba looked at him with her one good eye, as if he was out of his mind sleeping on a hard floor when he had a perfectly nice bed of his own. For the second time that night, he was reduced to uncontrollable tears. Unable to hug his dog in case he hurt her, he went to the panty and found a tin of corned beef, her favourite, and cut two thick slices. Sheba managed to eat one slice, have a drink of water and then went back to sleep. She didn't need the painkiller. Staffies are born tough.

Collins was euphoric as he climbed the stars but he was still determined to kick the shit out of the bastard responsible for the attack.

Thursday 16th May 1968, 02.00hrs

Edgbaston

Toby's latest investment, a small rundown hotel just off Five Ways, Edgbaston, was ideal for the men's meeting. It didn't appear on any list of properties owned by the Drew Brothers; it had underground parking for six cars, which meant that no one saw Toby, Reggie, Keating or Connelly enter the hotel; and currently it only had one guest, who also acted as watchman. The hotel was also centrally located. This final feature was invaluable tonight of all nights. Try to leave the city, in any direction, and you ran the risk of being stopped by a police roadblock. Someone had tried to murder two of their own and suddenly there was no limit on police overtime and not a single officer complained about working late. An attack on one of them was an attack on all of them.

Reggie had been drinking steadily ever since he'd arrived four hours earlier. He'd consumed enough to convince himself that he wasn't scared of anyone. Not even Patrick O'Neil, the London ponce.

Fifteen minutes later, O'Neil entered the bar. Reggie didn't wait for him to take his coat off before demanding, 'What the fuck happened? Your guys were supposed to take out Clark and Collins, and what did we get instead? One dead shooter and one on the run.'

O'Neil dropped his coat over the back of a chair, went to the bar and poured himself a triple vodka. Only then did he speak, 'Toby, tell that fucking retard of a brother of yours that if he ever speaks to me like that again, I'll gut him where he stands.'

'I'm sorry, Pat. It's just that he's worried. It won't happen again.'

Reggie glared at his brother, but said nothing.

'Mr O'Neil, Reggie spoke out of turn, but we're all worried,' said Keating. 'The whole fucking Birmingham City Police Force is going to be after us in the morning. What are we supposed to do?'

'Nothing's changed since lunchtime. The coppers still don't have any hard evidence linking us together and they certainly don't have any evidence linking us to the attempt on the coppers' lives. I'm going to tell you a story about what really happened and you are going to remember it and tell it to everyone, including the cops. Okay?'

The four men all nodded.

'Once upon a time there was a little man called Sheppard, who wanted to be a big shot. But he was a nothing and he blamed his failure on Collins and Clark, who'd crippled him. For years, he dreamed about getting his revenge. He wanted to kill them, but knew that he didn't have the skill or training to do it. So, he hired a couple of specialists.

'However, he knew that the police would suspect him and, one way or another, they'd find a way to lock him up and throw away the key. Knowing he'd never be able to do the time he decided he'd top himself once the bastards were dead. It would be worth it to kill the cunts that had ruined his life and turned him into a limping laughingstock. When the killer called to pick up his money, he lied to Sheppard and said that both men had been killed. Sheppard paid up and topped himself a happy man.'

'Do you really think anyone will believe that cock-and-bull story?' asked Toby.

'Toby, Toby, what am I going to do with you?' said O'Neil, as if he were talking to a particularly dim schoolboy. 'As the best silk in London told me: "It doesn't need to be true, it just has to be sufficiently credible to create reasonable doubt in the jury's mind."

Trying to recapture some of his own credibility, Toby said, 'That all sounds fine, but what happens if your Mr Clay gets picked up by the police and tells a different story?'

'He won't be.'

'How can you be sure?'

'Don't worry about it. I've got it covered. Just go about your business tomorrow as normal and don't let anything slip when the coppers come calling.'

London, 10.00hrs

Clay woke up feeling groggy, with a dry, gritty mouth. It took him a few moments to realise that he was still at Dr Thorne's, lying on an old army cot in the storeroom. Gingerly, he moved his right arm and was surprised to find that there was little pain.

He might be a drunk, he thought, but Thorne still knows his stuff.

His grogginess left immediately when he heard a knock on the outside door and the sound of a familiar voice. It was Reagan, Gregson's bodyguard and personal enforcer – wherever Reagan went, Beasley wouldn't be far behind.

Silently, he crossed to the door and pressed his ear to the wood.

'Morning, Thorne. Hear you have Clay with you.'

'Yeah, he's in the back room.'

'How is he?'

'He'll survive. He's lucky the dog passed out, else it would still be attached to his bloody arm. Those Staffies are right sods when they lock on.'

Clay had heard enough. Taking his jacket from the chair, he bunched it up in his good hand and opened the door. 'I thought I'd heard voices. I didn't realise it was you, Reagan. How are things?' he asked and laid his coat down on the instrument tray, while tucking his shirt in and tightening his belt.

'Couldn't be better. Mr Gregson wants a word.'

'What about?'

'What do you think? He's not best pleased, but he blames

that prat, Toby. I think he wants you to disappear for a year or two.'

'As long as it ain't permanent.'

'Na, nothing like that.'

Clay picked up his jacket and headed for the door, 'Where's your mate, Beasley?'

'He's in the car.'

Clay was about to get in the front seat of the Jaguar MK 2 when Reagan held open the back door, then went round the car and slid in beside him. Alarm bells had been going off in his head since he'd heard the enforcer's voice. Now, they were ringing louder than ever. A back seat ride with Reagan rarely ended well for the passenger. One more warning sign and he'd have to take action.

After five minutes of driving, Clay said, 'I thought we were going to Gregson's.'

'We are. He's just bought a new place down by the river.'

Clay sat back and laughed, 'What is with him? Every time he sees an empty building, he has to buy it. Be cheaper if he collected girls.'

'You're probably right, but I wouldn't say that to his face.'

'You think I've got a death wish?' said Clay, as his left hand wrapped around the handle of the scalpel he'd taken from Thorne's instrument tray.

The car slowed as they approached a set of lights on amber. The taxi in front stopped and Beasley had to do the same. 'Shit, traffic gets worse every day.'

'That it does,' said Clay. Then, in one sweeping movement, he slashed Reagan's throat open. Before Beasley could react, Clay pulled the driver's head back to expose his neck. This time, he dug the scalpel in before wrenching it to the right. The cut was deep and fatal. Beasley had only seconds to live.

Not so Reagan. The first cut had not severed his carotid artery and while he tried to stem the flow of blood with his left hand, he was scrabbling for his gun with his right. Reversing his grip on the scalpel, Clay stabbed the enforcer in the eye, withdrew the blade and then stabbed him in the throat. His parting words to Reagan before he left the car were, 'Do you really think I'm so fucking stupid not to recognise a set-up?'

Clay had reached the corner before the lights changed. As soon as it became apparent that the Jag was going nowhere, the drivers in the queue started to sound their horns. Good luck with that, thought Clay, as he quickly walked away.

Handsworth, 14.00hrs

Clark had managed to escape from the hospital only to spend the morning with Collins answering questions and giving statements about the previous evening's events. By lunch, both had endured enough and were only too pleased to slip away to the noise, smells and organised chaos of the staff canteen.

It was the first time that they had seen each other alone since Clark had opened the gates at the Albion. Clark had been overjoyed to hear that Sheba was going to be all right and promised to bring her a nice juicy bone next time he called. When Collins asked about his concussion, he said, 'There was nowt wrong with me noggin. I just dain't fancy spending the night answering a load of stupid questions. It was bad enough this morning. Besides, it meant I got a good night's sleep for the first time in weeks. No snoring – bliss.'

'You mean, you abandoned your poor pregnant wife just to get a good night's kip.'

'I dain't abandon her. There were a cop car outside all night. If anything did happen, she'd would have been in hospital in double quick time.'

'Okay. I'll let you off for now. It will be remembered and it may well be used in the future to extract a favour.' Collins stabbed a chip with his fork and, using his knife, loaded the last piece of cottage pie to join it. Sitting back, he took a sip of tea. 'You do realise that even despite yesterday's attacks, we still don't have any hard evidence against Drew and his buddies?'

'Yeah, I know. If only they'd used Connolly and Blanco. We could've proved a link with them.'

'I'm not sure where we go from here. Any bright ideas?'

'Like my old Sergeant Major used to say, "When yow hit a brick wall, keep hitting it. Eventually a crack will appear." Mind yow, he were a right Scottish balm pot.'

'So, we go back and re-interview everyone?'

'Got any better ideas?'

'Na, but this time, let's see them one at a time and lean on them a little. They're not all heroes,' said Collins.

Unseen, Marie arrived at the men's table. 'Heroes twice in a week. Who would have believed it?'

'Not us,' said Clark.

'Were you looking for us?'

'Yeah, I've got a guy on the phone. Won't give his name, but says he needs to speak with Constable Clark urgently.'

'Okay. We'll be there in a tick.'

Back in the CID room Clark picked up the phone and said to Marie, 'Put him through, love.'

'Is that Detective Constable Clark?'

'Yes, who's this?' Clark didn't recognise the London accented voice.

'You can call me Clay. I did some work yesterday and got bitten by a dog. It had a white ring around one of its eyes.'

Clark felt the hair on the back of his neck and on his arms rise. Covering the mouthpiece with his hand, he hissed, 'Mickey.'

Looking up, Collins saw the urgency in Clark's eyes.

'That's interesting. I'm sorry yow got bit. If yow want to make a complaint against the dog owner, you should call in at the station. He's really keen to meet yow.'

'I bet he is.'

'Well, if yow don't want to make a complaint, why are yow calling?'

Collins hunkered down beside his friend and, leaning forward, Clark shared the earpiece with him.

'My employer wasn't very happy about my performance yesterday. He tried to arrange an extended holiday for me today.'

'He was probably worried yow'd talk to the wrong people if yow were picked up?'

'That's about the size of it. I know this isn't the States and you can't do a deal with me, but if I were to give you Gregson, O'Neil, Drew and his mates, I was thinking you might set me up in a safe house while they were rounded up.'

'And what would yow do once they were behind bars?'

'I'd disappear and no one in England would ever see me again.'

'Why make the deal with us and not the Met?'

'Gregson has too many friends in the Met – even Birmingham's not safe. That's why this deal is just between you, your friend and me. No one can know anything about it.'

'Okay, let's assume that Sergeant Collins and me go along with this. How does it work?'

'I'll give you an hour to talk it over with your mate. If we've got a deal, then we can talk about the details.'

Before Clark could reply, the phone went dead.

Hanging up, Clark asked, 'What do you think?'

'Basically he wants us to lock up everyone who wants him dead, provide him with accommodation for an unspecified period of time and then allow him to disappear at a time of his own choosing.'

'That's about the size of it. Not asking much is he?'

'Or it could be a trap. He might be trying to finish the job he started.'

'I don't think so,' said Clark.

'Me neither. If we assume he's legit, what would a killer have on Gregson and the Drews?' asked Collins.

'I don't know, but I'd like to find out.'

'Did the guy give a name?'

'Clay.'

'Why don't I give Sybil a call and see if she has anything on him.'

It took nearly 10 minutes to get through to Sybil and when she finally picked up the phone, she sounded as if she was having one of those days.

'Harker,' she snapped.

'Sybil, you sound busy'

'I am. Your lot have been on all morning about Sands. Even had the Commissioner call to say that I must extend every courtesy to our country cousins. Then, a double gangland murder this morning. Whatever you want to know, it will have to wait, I'm afraid.'

'I understand.' Collins hesitated, then made his mind up. 'Did Sands ever work with a bloke called Clay?'

'Clay? James Clay?'

'We weren't properly introduced. But it's my bet that Mr Clay did your gangsters, but you didn't hear it from me.'

'So Gregson tried to take him out?'

Collins remained silent, knowing that Sybil would quickly join the dots.

She didn't disappoint him and in less than six seconds, she said, 'He's come to you with some sort of deal, hasn't he?'

After a prolonged silence, Sybil continued, 'Clay is a professional. He was trained by the British Army to deal with problems with one solution. MI5 and 6 were both interested in him after he finished his eight years serving Queen and Country, but he went freelance. He has a reputation for keeping his word. He has also been known to deliver a disproportionate level of vengeance on anyone who fails to keep their word.' This time, it was Sybil who remained silent while waiting for a response that never came. Finally, she said, 'Well, I must get back to it. Please give Agnes my regards.'

'I will, indeed, Sybil and thanks for everything,' smiling Collins hung up.

'Why did yow shop Clay?'

'Because with the Met and Gregson after him he needs us more than ever. Besides the bastard shot my dog.'

Handsworth, 15.00hrs

Clay's call was on time and he wasted no time asking, 'Do we have a deal?'

'In principle.'

'What the fuck does that mean?'

'We want to know what yow have on Gregson and Drew.'

'I know where his accountant lives and where he keeps Gregson's books – both sets. He's got a nice young wife and a pretty little girl. He'd do anything to protect them—'

'No deal,' said Clark. 'Touch the kid or the wife and I'll kill yow meself.'

'What do you think I am, Mr Clark? I've never hurt anyone who wasn't a player in the game.'

'What about trying to kill my mate?'

'Sorry about that. Nothing personal, but as soon as you pair put on that uniform, you joined the game – you know that.'

'Okay, so what's yowr plan?'

'Use my reputation. I find it normally scares people shitless. They all think I'm a psycho. So, just the threat will be enough.'

'I told yow the wife and kid can't be involved.'

'Relax. They'll not be involved. They're away visiting the grandparents in Edinburgh. The accountant is all alone in his nice detached house paid for by Mr Gregson.'

'Why do yow need to involve him at all if yow already know where the books are kept? Why not just nick 'em?'

'I've got a lot of skills, Mr Clark, but safe-cracking ain't one of them.'

'After yow deliver the books to us, what then? How does yowr disappearing act go?'

'You find me a safe place to stay while you round up Gregson and his friends. When I think it's safe, I'll disappear.'

'Okay, but the deal is off if yow do any more than rough the accountant up and, like I said, I'll kill you meself if yow harm his family. They ain't part of the game.'

'Agreed. I'll get the stuff tonight and be in Birmingham early morning. Where can we meet?'

'Go to Dudley Road Hospital. We'll meet yow in the cafeteria at nine thirty. Ok?'

'Fine.'

Broxbourne, Hertfordshire 23.30hrs

Nigel Worthington was an accountant. He came from a long line of accountants. His great grandfather had been a bookkeeper, his grandfather had qualified as a Chartered Accountant and his father was on the Council of Chartered Accountants of England and Wales. It had therefore been something of a shock to the entire family, when, shortly after qualifying, Nigel was arrested for embezzling £19,000 from clients' funds. When asked what he'd spent the money on, he replied, with a smile, 'Women.'

He was sentenced to three years in prison, but was released after 21 months for good behaviour. In many ways, he'd been sorry to leave. For the first time in his life, he'd enjoyed real status – not just among the prisoners, but also the staff. They didn't look at him and see a skinny, 5 foot 9, 140-pound weakling. They saw a financial genius, who could take on the Inland Revenue and beat them at their own game. In the prison community, his ability to reduce the tax liability of just about anyone was the stuff of legend and it was rumoured that even the Warden had used his skills.

In the end, he left jail for the same reason he'd entered it. Women – or, more precisely, the lack of them. They occupied his every waking moment. Yet such dreams never interfered with his work. He was able to fantasise about a wide range of film stars, singers and athletes, while still accurately calculating a person's capital gains tax or the effect of double taxation relief on a foreign subsidiary.

When he left prison on April 6th 1961 at eight in the morning, there was no one to meet him – or so he thought. He'd walked maybe twenty yards when a yellow Lotus Elan, hood down, had drawn up beside him and a young lady leaned out. 'Mr Worthington, my name's June. Mr Harry Gregson sent me. He has a job for you.'

Nigel barely heard what the woman was saying. He was too busy devouring the sight of her long, strong legs, shown off to perfection by a pair of sheer black nylons, the tops of which were visible every time she shifted position. Her hair was thick, shoulder-length and dark. Her breasts seemed to be barely contained by her expensive yellow silk blouse. For Nigel, at that moment, she was the woman of his dreams and the answer to all his prayers.

'The only thing is,' said June, 'Mr Gregson can't see you until four this afternoon. I was wondering if there was anything you'd like to do between now and then? Maybe get a bite to eat or, if you prefer, I could cook you breakfast and you could have a nice quiet bath and wash off all that prison grime.'

By the time Nigel walked into Mr Gregson's office at 4pm, he would have been willing to accept any job that was offered. When he was told that he was to be Mr Gregson's personal accountant, a position that would pay well and come with a wide variety of fringe benefits, Nigel was certain he was dreaming and still in prison.

For nearly seven years, Nigel had enjoyed every moment and aspect of his job. He was daily pitting his knowledge of Company Law and Taxation against the best that the government could offer and so far he'd never lost. He'd done a first-class job for his only client; he'd been loyal; and he had June, a daughter and all the extra-curricular activities he wanted. Every Thursday night, he was allowed to try out the latest additions to Mr Gregson's ever-growing rota of prostitutes. It hadn't taken long for his stamina in the bedroom and rumours about the size of his manhood to exceed his reputation as a financial wizard.

When Nigel awoke at 11.30, he had no idea that his wonderful life was about to change forever. A noise was coming from downstairs. It sounded like the Beatles' Rubber Soul album.

But that's impossible? he thought, I haven't played it for weeks. It's in the cabinet. Taking the baseball bat from where it stood by the bedroom door, he edged down the stairs. There was no sound other than the music. As he reached for the light switch, someone grabbed his wrist and twisted it up his back.

'Drop it, Nigel, or I'll have to hurt you.'

Nigel recognised the voice and did what he was told. The heavy bat made no sound as it sank into the thick carpet. 'Good man. Now go over to the armchair and sit on your hands.'

Nigel was halfway across the room when the lights came on. He jumped and felt a trickle of urine run down his leg. Stop. No more.

When he sat down, Clay saw the stain and said, 'Relax, I'm not here to kill you or even do you harm. I've got a business deal for you.'

'What kind of deal?'

'One that will ensure that no harm comes to your wife or that lovely little girl of yours. A deal that will allow you to go on breathing after I've left.'

'I'm listening.'

'Mr Gregson tried to kill me this morning.'

'So I heard.'

'Don't interrupt, Nigel, or we'll be here all night. Therefore, I've decided that I need some insurance and you're going to supply the policy.'

Nigel knew what was coming next. 'You want his books?'

'I always knew you were a bright lad.'

'But he'll kill me.'

'Na, he won't. Give me the books and I'll see to it that he's arse-deep in coppers for the foreseeable future. That will give you plenty of time to disappear.'

'And if I don't co-operate?'

'I'll have to get rough with you and if that don't work you and me will go visit your wife and daughter. I've always wondered what it would be like to do a mother and daughter.'

Nigel had no illusions about his ability to withstand pain. Even when he played the submissive, he was screaming Red before the third lash from his mistress had landed. Such self-knowledge meant that he'd known from the moment he'd seen Clay that he was going to give him whatever he wanted. 'We'll need to go to the office. I'd better get dressed.'

'Good choice,' said Clay, who didn't bother to follow Worthington upstairs. He wasn't going anywhere.

At 2.15am, Clay set off for Birmingham. He decided to use the old A roads and avoid the M1. It would take longer, but there would be less chance of being stopped by the police and, besides, his meeting wasn't until 9.30am.

As Clay pulled into the Dudley Road Hospital car park, Nigel Worthington entered Lloyds Bank in Broxbourne. He withdrew £5,000 in cash from his own account and transferred the remaining balance to a numbered account in Zurich, which he had opened for just such a day as this. He followed this up by visiting four other banks, from which he transferred just over £600,000 from Mr Gregson's business accounts to the same Swiss bank account.

His business transactions completed, Worthington filled

up his Jaguar Daimler Mk 2, called his wife in Edinburgh and set off for Manchester Airport.

Friday 17th May 1968, 9.35hrs

Dudley Road Hospital, Winson Green

Collins had never liked hospitals much. To him, they were strange places; a mixture of care, compassion and ruthless discipline. The best were run like an elite military unit, with a clear chain of command leading back to the all-powerful Matron. It was she and the sisters she handpicked that kept the place running, not the doctors or the administrators. Every ward was inspected daily, every bed checked, and germs and lax attitudes hunted out and killed without mercy. If only the police were half as efficient, thought Collins as he stirred his tea.

Clark kicked him under the table as Clay entered the cafeteria. Collins turned around. For a moment, he was back on Hampstead Road looking down the barrel of .38 revolver. He had the urge to take cover under the table, but resisted the impulse. Instead, he stood up and turned to face the man who had tried to kill him.

Clay held out his hand. Collins ignored it and sat down, but Clark briefly shook hands. 'Have yow got it?'

'Yes,' said Clay, patting the briefcase he was carrying.

'Don't seem like much,' said Clark.

'It's just for starters. The main course is in the car. You'll get it when I see the safe house.'

'Fair enough,' said Clark, reaching for the briefcase. He quickly split the contents into two piles and handed the larger one to Collins, who was the faster reader. As they settled into a quick skim read, Clay went off to get his breakfast. They continued reading while Clay demolished two rounds of toast, two eggs, bacon, sausages and beans. As Clay wiped up the last of the tomato sauce with a piece of toast, Clark looked at Collins, who nodded.

'How's the accountant?' asked Clark.

'In perfect fettle,' said Clay, looking at his watch. 'By now, he's on his way to meet the family. He should be out of the country before Gregson knows what's happened.'

'In that case, we have a deal.'

'Good.'

The safe house was a bedsit that overlooked the Bristol Road. It had a bed, a chest of drawers, a 17-inch black and white telly that had a dodgy horizontal hold, a food cabinet with a dirty yellow drop-down door and dirty sides, two electric rings for cooking and an electric fire.

'Nice to see that every expense has been spared.'

'Yow wanted safe. This is as safe as it comes. The landlord is a mate of mine. He doesn't know who's staying here. He won't be back for a month and there are no other lodgers, 'cos when he gets back he's going to gut this place and do it up for sale. It's a reasonably respectable area, so the chance of running into anyone who would recognise yow is low.

'There's a shop two doors down. Yow should stock up on what yow need and if anyone asks, just tell them that yow're a mate of Harry Fellows and yowr looking after the place until he gets back from sunny Greece. If we need to contact yow, I'll call the phone in the hall. If yow need to contact me, here's me number,' said Clark, handing over a torn sheet of paper with his number on it. 'OK?'

'Yeah. It seems fine. Here take the keys. I'll be down after I've had a piss.'

'There's just one thing I want to say before we go,' said Collins. Clay's eyes came up and he spotted the intent a fraction of a second too late. Collins dropped low and delivered a downward punch into Clay's balls. The punch was a beauty and contained all the anger that Collins felt towards the killer. Clay fell to the floor and before he could curl up, Collins kicked him in the ribs. 'That's for my dog,' he said. 'You're lucky she didn't die.'

On the landing, Clark asked, 'Feeling better?'

'It was better than nothing.'

'I think it were a lot better than nothing. I'm surprised yow managed to hold it in for so long.'

Handsworth, 13.00hrs

Back at the station, Collins and Clark headed directly to the CID Office, each carrying a large cardboard box. Hicks was enjoying a quiet smoke when, without explanation, Collins locked the door, rang Marie on the front desk and said, 'No calls under any circumstances.'

Hicks watched silently as both men cleared their desk tops before pushing the desks together. When they'd finished, he asked, 'What've you got?'

'Everything we need to put away Gregson and O'Neil, plus the Drews and their mates.'

'What's the plan?'

'Simple. You need to review this stuff and decide if we've got enough to arrest the bastards,' said Collins. 'We're a bit too close to it. We need an outsider's viewpoint.'

'Then, if yowm happy, we'll contact Sybil and coordinate a pick-up time.'

'Sounds good. Let's get started.'

Manchester Airport, 13.10hrs

Worthington felt nervous waiting for the Air Lingus flight to Dublin. His eyes fixed on the row of telephone kiosks near the entrance of the departure lounge. He was debating with himself whether he could risk calling

Gregson to warn him of what was about to happen, but he was scared.

June had taken the news that their old life was over very well. She had no illusions about what her husband did for Gregson or what Gregson would do to the entire family if he got hold of them. Nor did she have any doubt that Nigel loved her and little Joanne, and that he wanted only the best for them, even if he did spend every Thursday night screwing a couple of the new girls. If he said they had to leave England, then they had to go.

Worthington stood up, the decision he'd been struggling with taken. He dug in his pocket and took out a handful of change. The call went through quicker than he'd expected and he found himself speechless when he heard Gregson's familiar voice, 'Yes, who is it?'

After a long pause, he found his voice. The whole story of the previous night split out in a cascade of words and apologies. 'I didn't take any of your money, Mr Gregson. I just took the £600,000 that was owed me. I'm really sorry, boss. I didn't want to do it, but I had to put the family first.'

'I understand, but you know that if I catch you, I'll have to make an example of you. I don't want to do that, so you'd better run like fuck. If it's any consolation, I'll make sure nothing happens to your family.'

'Thanks, Mr Gregson.'

With nothing else to say, Worthington put the phone down as the announcer called for passengers on the Air Lingus Flight to Dublin to go to Gate 13.

London, 13.15hrs

After his conversation with Worthington, Gregson made three phone calls. The first was to his solicitor, who had power of attorney. His instructions were clear and simple, 'Sell everything and transfer the proceeds to Zurich.'

His second call was to O'Neil, who was still in Birmingham.

Once more his instructions were clear and precise. He ended by saying 'I'll see you at the field in about three hours.'

His last call was to an old friend now living in Spain. 'I need a lift tonight. It's urgent. Can you manage it?'

'The weather's not good over Spain and the Bay of Biscay. It will slow me down. I won't reach you until after dark.'

'That's fine. Just get here as quick as you can. I'll see what we can do about the lights.'

Handsworth, 15.00hrs

Hicks closed a folder of papers and sat up straight. An inch of tobacco ash dropped off the forgotten cigarette he had in the side of his mouth. 'I'm satisfied that on the illegal payments to MPs, councillors and police officers alone, we have enough to hold them. When the experts get their hands on this paperwork, they'll be able to follow the money and that will throw up plenty of other stuff to do them on. Once the ball gets rolling, people will be tripping over themselves to provide evidence for the prosecution. You've done a good job, lads.'

'OK, I'll phone Sybil. When do you think we can be ready to move?' asked Collins.

'Couple of hours,' said Clark, and looked at Hicks for confirmation, who nodded once.

'Okay, five it is,' said Collins and started dialling.

'How many do we need?' asked Hicks.

'Clay was explicit. We've got coppers taking backhanders. Who they are is probably in there somewhere,' said Clark, indicating the sheaves of paper that lay scattered over the desks. 'But until wi know who wi can trust, wi should keep the team small.'

'Agreed,' said Hicks. 'So who do you want?

'Marie Bolding, Dave Harris and O'Driscoll. That gives us six,' said Clark.

'OK. Call them in and let's make sure they all have a gun.'

Digbeth, Birmingham 16.10hrs

'What's so urgent that O'Neil had to see us all today?' asked Keating.

'He wouldn't say on the phone. Just said it was important that we all be here,' said Toby.

'Everything is important or urgent when that tosser is involved,' said Reggie.

The door opened and O'Neil entered. 'Thanks for coming, lads. I'm afraid I've got some bad news, but I'll wait until Connelly and Blanco arrive. I don't want to repeat myself.'

'You can't say you've got some bad news and then not tell us anything,' said Keating, his nerves getting the better of him.

'I can do anything I fucking like, lad. Just you remember that.'

Silence descended on the group until Miss Larsson knocked on the door and stepped aside to let Connelly and Blanco in.

'Well, now that we're all here, I'll begin. We tried to take Clay out yesterday, but he escaped. He's now made a deal with the coppers. In exchange for his freedom, he's given them a copy of Mr Gregson's private accounts. There's enough information in them to put all of us away for life ten times over.'

'Fuck,' said Keating.

'How did he get the info?' asked Toby.

'Scared the shit out of the accountant.'

'Christ, I'd love to get my hands on the bastard,' said Reggie.

'Well, it's a good job you can't, because you'd be dead before you laid a finger on him,' said O'Neil.

'What are we going to do?' asked Toby.

'First, we need to destroy any documents that you have.'

'That's not a problem. I don't write anything down that ain't legit. The only thing I've got that's dodgy is a list of debtors and creditors that I keep in the safe. Burn them and there's nothing to connect us.'

Toby crossed to the safe and knelt down on one knee. He dialled the six-figure combination and pulled open the heavy door. Taking out a slim black ledger he handed it to O'Neil. 'What's the second point?' he asked.

'Harry has laid on transport for us out of the country.'

'Thank God for that,' said Toby, smiling. 'When do we go?'

'Tonight, but there's a slight problem. The plane only takes four passengers, which means we have three passengers too many.'

'So how do we decide who's going on the first trip and who's on—' Toby never finished his sentence. As planned, O'Neil took him out with a single shot between the eyes.

Reggie tried to pull out the gun he always carried in his waistband, but it went off and he shot himself in the balls. Connelly was laughing so much at the sight of Reggie screaming in agony that he missed with his first shot. His second hit Reggie's heart, dead centre.

Keating backed into the corner, his eyes filled with terror. 'No, please, please!' His pathetic cries were cut off when Blanco shot him in the throat and then finished the job with a shot to the head.

Less than three seconds had elapsed since the first shot had been fired. O'Neil pulled open the office door and grabbed Lisa Larsson by the arm as she tried to reach the outer door.

He dragged her back into the boardroom and threw her on the floor. OK, boys, off you go. I'll see you at Fradley Airfield later.'

As Connelly re-holstered his gun, he grinned at O'Neil, 'Ain't you coming with us?'

'No, I have some unfinished business with Miss Larsson.'

Connelly and Blanco started to laugh just as O'Neil dragged the terrified woman to her feet and threw her face down on the boardroom table. Holding her head with his left hand, he reached for the hem of her skirt with his right. 'I've been watching you ever since I arrived, looking down your nose at me. Thinking you were the Queen of fucking Sheba because you were fucking that little shit, Toby Drew. I've met your kind before. You think you're something special. That your piss is like wine. Well, I have news for you, love. You're just another fucking whore that I'm going to fuck and kill.'

'No, please. Don't. I'll do anything you want me to. Just don't kill me.'

'You'll take it up the arse?'

'Yes, anything. Just let me live.'

As Larsson begged for her life, O'Neil felt the familiar surge of power flood through his body. There was no feeling in the world like this. For this woman, he was the supreme arbitrator between granting her life or taking it away. It was better than sex. Better than any drug.

'It's a nice offer,' he whispered in her ear, 'but you see, I like my whores to struggle. Where's the fun if the bitch isn't writhing in agony and screaming her lungs out?'

With that, O'Neil kicked the woman's legs open and pulled her knickers down.

Digbeth, Birmingham 17.30hrs

It was raining heavily when two unmarked police cars came to a stop outside Drew's warehouse. Staff were disappearing for the week-end and the six plain-clothed police officers had to wade through the tide of humanity to reach the stairs.

'Oy, you can't go up there. We're closing,' shouted the commissionaire.

Hicks waved his badge in the man's general direction and added, 'Police,' for emphasis.

The commissionaire turned away and went to call Drew's secretary. He got no reply.

On the third floor, the secretary's office was empty and the boardroom door locked. There was no key in the lock. Hicks hammered on the oak door, but there was no response.

'Let's have a butchers, Boss. See if I can open it.' Clark moved to the door and inspected the lock. 'The key's been broken off in the lock. That can't be good news,' he said. Stepping back, he kicked the door a few inches below the lock. Nothing moved.

After six attempts Collins took over and, with his first kick, the door sprang open. He was unable to resist grinning at Clark.

'What yow grinning at? I weakened the bloody thing for yow.'

Whatever grins the police officers might have shared disappeared from their faces when they saw the carnage. Toby lay face down in the middle of the room, his blood and gray matter staining the carpet. Reggie sat slumped in his chair his dead eyes staring into eternity. Keating lay crumpled in the corner, his leg tucked under him at an impossible angle, his entire face and neck a mess of raw meat.

Worst of all was Lisa Larsson. She had been positioned by her killer very precisely. Her head, torso and thighs rested on the table, her legs dangling over the edge. Both her hands were raised above her head as if she was trying to surrender. Her skirt had been pulled up to her waist. Her legs open. A chair had been smashed across her body and one of its legs had been used to violate her.

'My God, what kind of bastard did this?' asked Marie, without expecting an answer. Crossing to the woman she laid her hand on Lisa's neck, not expecting to find a pulse. Incredibly she felt something. 'She's alive.'

A groan escaped Lisa's lips and she tried to open her eyes, but the bruising made it impossible. Marie took her hand and whispered directly into the woman's ear. 'An ambulance is on its way. Hang in there and you'll be okay. Press my hand if you understand.'

Marie felt the slightest of pressures.

'Ask her if it was O'Neil that did this?' said Hicks.

A sound, barely more than a groan, escaped Liza's shattered lips. Marie placed her ear an inch from the woman's lips. This time, the voice was clearer, 'O'Neil.'

'Ask her who else was here. Connelly? Blanco?' said Collins.

There was a long pause before Lisa had enough strength to speak again. This time, her answer was clear, 'Fradley.'

'Who the fuck is Fradley?' asked Harris.

Marie felt another pressure on her hand and leaned in again. Lisa's voice was weakening. She was slipping away. With a supreme effort, she said, 'Fradley Airfield.' Dropping back, she let out a final sigh.

Everyone knew she was dead, but it was Collins who asked, 'What did she say?'

'Fradley Airfield.'

'Does anyone know Fradley Airfield?' asked Hicks.

'Yeah,' said Clark. 'I flew out of it once or twice in the war, but it were called RAF Lichfield at the time.'

'Where the feck is it?'

'About 4 miles from Lichfield. It's been abandoned for years.'

'Could you still land a plane at it?'

'Yeah, but yow'd have to be brave or desperate to try landing or taking off in this weather.'

'Well, I think Gregson and O'Neil are desperate enough, don't you?' said Hicks, looking at the bodies in the room. 'Collins, Clark, I want you to get over there and see if you can stop them. Who do you want with you?'

Collins deferred to Clark, who said, 'We'll take Dave and Marie.'

'Typical,' said O'Driscoll, 'you leave out the Irishman, just because he's old, slow and fat.'

Even Hicks smiled at O'Driscoll's self-deprecating comment. Turning to Marie, he said, 'This could be dangerous. I won't order you to go, but if—'

Marie cut Hicks off mid-sentence, 'I want to go, Sir.'

O'Driscoll, who had been standing near the door, took a small revolver from his coat pocket and gave it to Marie. 'You look after yourself.'

'Thanks, Sarge.'

'And if you do have to shoot one of us, make sure it's Clark,' said Harris.

Clark's response was a quick two-fingered salute.

Birmingham/Lichfield 18.00hrs

The black clouds that scurried across the sky had turned evening into night. Soon, the rain would start and visibility would decrease further. Great weather if you're trying to creep up on a gang of criminals, thought Collins. Not so good if you're trying to land a small plane on an abandoned wartime airfield without lights.

Before they'd left Birmingham, the team had spent 10 minutes looking at maps of the area and listening to Clark as he outlined his plan for capturing Gregson and his friends. 'Marie, once we confirm they're in the control tower, yow need to scarper to the nearest house with a phone and call O'Driscoll. Us three will form a triangle around the building, about 50 yards out. That way we'll be able to see each other while covering all the exits. Wi do now't unless the bastards show signs of leaving or that they've spotted us.'

'What's the plan if they do spot us?' asked Marie.

'Wi try to keep them bottled up in the control tower. Last thing, if yow have to shoot, forget all the John Wayne crap about shooting to wound. Aim for the body and bring 'em down. But remember Marie, if a shooting war does start, yow can't hang around. Yow have to make that call.'

Clark took the A38 out of Birmingham through Erdington and into the Staffordshire countryside, then headed for Lichfield – one of the oldest cities in England. 'I've been thinking,' he said. 'O'Neil is ex-army. He might 'ave posted a couple of lookouts at the main entrances off Wood End Lane and Gorse Lane.

'I think we should go in by the Fradley gate. It were always the one the lads took when they had to walk back from the pub. It'll mean about a half-mile walk to the control tower, but I doubt they'll have it covered. What do yow think?'

With Harris and Marie nodding in agreement, Collins said, 'You're the boss on this one.'

Fradley Airfield, 19.00hrs

Clark followed the signs into Lichfield and drove past Lichfield City and Trent Valley Stations, through Streethay and back out into the country. When the sign for Fradley appeared, he turned left. Soon, he found himself driving up Church Lane and passing the village church of St. Stephen's. The sight of the graveyard stirred old memories. Several Australian flyers, at least one of whom Clark remembered well, were buried there. Unable to properly salute the brave men who hadn't made it home, he raised his hand to his temple and let it drop back onto the steering wheel. It was the only form of prayer he knew or believed in.

Collins saw the attempted salute. Why here? Why now? he thought, but he didn't ask the questions. There were some things Clark never spoke about and that was all right with Collins. He looked outside. The wet, miserable night had kept people indoors and they were all curled up in the warm, watching telly. Friday night, 7 o' clock, Take Your Pick is on, he thought and for some reason he felt a cold shiver run down his spine.

Collins was still trying to shake off the unease he felt when they reached Bridge Farm Lane and turned left. There had been a Bridge Farm on this site for as long as anyone could remember, but twenty-nine years earlier much of its land had been requisitioned by the Ministry of Defence and used to expand RAF Lichfield into one of the busiest and most important airfields in England. Centrally placed, it was an ideal collection and dispersal point for planes of all shapes and sizes. Now, twenty-three years after the end of the war it had returned to its original use. Green pastures lay drenched under dark skies where Lancaster bombers had once taxied, waiting for take-off, their crews trying not to think about the latest life and death battle they would have to fight over the skies of Germany. I'm glad I missed it, thought Collins. But unbidden he remembered a few lines from Henry V, learnt at school and never forgotten:

And gentlemen in England now a-bed
Shall think themselves accursed they were not here,
And hold their manhoods cheap whiles any speaks
That fought with us upon Saint Crispin's day.
The memory made him feel strangely sad.

The car passed the old red brick farmhouse with its black tiled roof, and the stables and barns that had to make do with breeze blocks and corrugated roofs. A hundred yards on, Clark pulled over and stopped.

'Okay,' he said. 'We cross this road and we're onto the airfield proper, so be on guard. And if yow see a headless pilot wandering about the airfield, don't worry. Everyone says he's a lovely bloke and helped more than one shot-up crew get home safe.'

'Bloody hell, Clarkee, did you have to tell me that?' said Marie.

Clark grinned. 'Just keeping the team's spirit up,' he said, before disappearing into the bushes that had overgrown a small grass track. Emerging from the thicket, the group found themselves on what had clearly once been a concrete path or runway, but had been broken up and ploughed over. 'Wi follow this path for about four hundred yards. After that, it opens out. Wi take a left when it does and if wem lucky, we'll be able to see the tower about five hundred yards away. Once wi turn left, no talking.'

Collins pulled the collar of his coat up and cursed himself for not bringing a cap or hat as rain trickled down the back of his neck. Within twenty-five yards, the path passed an old pill box. The squat concrete building, reinforced with steel rods and small stones, was overgrown by blackcurrant bushes and nettles, but it still looked as if it could repulse an attack from a heavily armed squad of German paratroopers.

All it needed was a couple of squaddies and a machine gun with plenty of ammunition.

A little further on, they came to the remnants of the guard huts. Demolished now, they were a jumble of broken concrete, splintered planks painted regulation green, and smashed glass.

After a hundred yards, the track gave way to a concrete roadway. On the right, deserted and dilapidated hangers sat brooding, their twenty-foot-high sliding doors, which had once been painted dark green, rusting silently. Corrugated roof panels blew in the wind where they had become detached. *I bet they lose a few more panels tonight*, thought Collins. Behind the hangers, trees that had been young when Queen Victoria ascended the throne reared up into the night, their branches slapping against the hangers' roofs as they danced to the music of the gathering storm.

Past the hangers were the ruins of wooden storerooms and workshops. Once essential to keeping planes airborne, they were now virtually unrecognisable, just a pile of smashed concrete foundations, broken planking, and yet more corrugated sheets.

As if reading everyone's thoughts, Marie said, 'You know, Hammer Horror Films should come here for their next flick. It would be perfect.'

'Yeah and they wouldn't have to pay for a headless ghost either,' said Harris.

On the left was a long row of flat-topped symmetrical mounds, each made of earth, maybe forty feet long and twelve high. The space between each mound was enough to store a plane and protect it from damage should the plane next to it be blown up by a lucky bomb or enemy strafing.

'How much further, do you reckon?' asked Collins.

'Not far to the turn,' said Clark. 'After that, wi should be able to see the old tower.'

'But if we can see them, there's a chance they'll be able to see or hear us,' said Marie.

'True, but the weather is on our side. If the wind gets up a bit more, I'd be able to drive a tank over the runway and the buggers wouldn't hear a thing.'

'Pity we don't have a tank,' said Collins.

'That's the trouble with yow Irish. Yowr too pessimistic. Wi might find one in one of them hangers.'

'Pessimism is what comes of living under British rule for eight hundred years.'

'That's down to us being superior beings, mate.'

'Superior, my arse. There's just more of you.'

'I hate to interrupt your discussion on Anglo-Irish history, but I'm getting soaked. Can we get a move on?' said Marie.

'Now there, Mickey, is a fine example of what's wrong with women. Always concerned with life's practicalities. They have no appreciation of the great historical debates of our time.'

'That's because you buggers have used us as unpaid skivvies, nursemaids and bed warmers for centuries and all we got out of it is a change of name.'

'That were a good deal if yowr maiden name was Snodbottom or Seaman.'

Marie was about to respond, when Clark stopped and held up his hand for silence. The blast shelters had given way to a large flat expanse of concrete. Straight ahead lay two hangers that looked as if they were still in use. Maybe storage. Might be worth checking out, he thought. There was a faded sign-post on the road leading right, which read Gate D Exit. The road to the left was unmarked.

Squatting down, Clark said, 'We turn here. From now on, we stay off the road.'

The rain was lashing down. Caught by the wind, it was being driven horizontally across the open spaces. Visibility was down to fifty yards, and the first roll of thunder and flash of fork lightening announced the arrival of the storm over the airfield. Almost immediately, Collins spotted the control tower. Someone had covered the ground-floor windows facing the runway with canvas, but light was escaping from the edges of the hastily erected curtains.

'Well, it looks like someone's home,' said Marie.

'Yeah, but is it Gregson and Co., or an old tramp trying to stay dry for the night?' asked Collins.

'Only one way to find out. Mickey, yow go and check out those hangers and I'll take a butcher's at the control tower. Yow two stop in that nice warm ditch over there and stay out of sight until wi get back. And don't shoot me when I does come back. If you have to shoot someone, shoot Mickey.'

Without waiting for a reply, Clark moved off.

Although there was virtually no chance of being seen or heard, Collins covered the last two hundred yards to the hangers bent over at a fast run. The first hanger's sliding doors were closed and locked, but a small wooden door at the side of the building was open. He stepped inside.

In the near total blackness, Collins could just make out a large tarpaulin-covered structure in the middle of the floor. He paused and listened. There was no movement. No sign of life. He hurried over to the structure and lifted the tarpaulin. What confronted him was the unmistakable back wheels of a Massey Ferguson tractor. Behind the tractor was something out of the 1800s. A two-wheeled steel contraption, measuring maybe fifteen feet across. It comprised of a seat resting on a frame, which held ten crescent-shaped rods. It took him a moment to realise that it was a semi-mechanised rake used to scrape up hay and that the handle next to the seat allowed the rake to be raised and lowered.

Feck me, he thought. *It's Clarkee's bloody tank.*

Replacing the canvas, he slipped out of the hanger and

closed the door quietly behind him. Quickly, he made his way to hanger two.

Clark covered the distance to the control tower at a steady trot. Stopping about fifty yards out, he drew his gun and lay down behind a clump of gorse bushes. The old mantra of look, listen, advance ran though his head. For two minutes, he lay there motionless while the sodden grass soaked through his coat, jacket and shirt, and the rain did an even better job of turning everything he wore into a sodden mess. Still nothing. No sound, no people. He moved closer. At 25 yards, he halted. He could hear the sound of music. A radio was playing. Someone was making themselves at home.

Making up his mind, he sprinted the last 25 yards and flattened himself against the tower's wall. For the first time, he could hear the sound of voices. More than one, he thought. But the noise from the radio drowned out individual voices. Need to have a look-see. The window nearest him had a few gaps in the canvas, but none were large enough to provide a decent view of the room. The next window looked more promising. Ducking low, he positioned himself alongside it. Again, he listened and then, standing on tiptoe, looked thought the largest gap.

Bingo. Clark felt a flood of satisfaction as he quickly picked out Gregson and Connelly. The other guy had to be O'Neil. Ducking down, his elation turned to concern. Where's Blanco. Is he coming? Is he on patrol? Where the fuck is he?

Clark did a recce of the ground floor perimeter. Still no sign of Blanco. He quickly retraced his steps to where he'd left Harris and Marie. 'Where's Mickey?'

'He hasn't come back yet,' said Harris.

'Are they there?' asked Marie.

'Three of 'em. Blanco's missing. Stay here and don't go

anywhere. I don't want you bumping into him in the dark. I'm going to find Mickey.'

As he stood up, a shot rang out from the direction of the hanger. Clark took off at speed.

Collins wasn't expecting to find anything in the second hanger. So, when he saw the unmistakable beam from a torch illuminate the half glass side door, he almost dropped his gun. Running to the hanger, he sneaked a quick look through the glass. At the front of the hanger, a man was methodically breaking open and searching a pile of wooden crates. His torch, resting on one of the storage shelves, cast enough light for Collins to identify Blanco.

Sinking down onto his haunches, Collins ran through his options. Although there were different variations, he quickly realised that he had two choices. If he left Blanco alone there was the chance he could stumble upon Clark and the others in the dark, or worse he might position himself behind the team when they surrounded the tower. Alternatively, if he took him out, Gregson would quickly put two and two together when he failed to return. Neither choice was attractive.

Collins' dilemma was resolved for him when a flash of lightening illuminated the hanger just as Blanco appeared around the front corner. Momentarily, both men stared at each other, astonished that they were face to face. Blanco was the first to recover. He dropped the box he was holding and sprinted for the cover provided by the overgrown shrubbery and trees, which covered the infield between runways. Collins levelled his gun and fired. Grit and concrete chips were thrown up near Blanco's feet. Now, he was zigzagging towards the bushes, where he'd soon have cover. Standing up and holding the gun with both hands, Collins fired again.

Blanco seemed to stagger and lurch forward, but kept running. Before Collins could fire again, the Frenchman disappeared into the overgrown foliage. Collins started to follow, but Clark's familiar voice stopped him, 'No, Mickey.'

Clark and Collins gave Harris and Marie a fright when they slipped soundlessly into the ditch.

'God, Mickey, I thought you'd been shot,' said Harris.

'No, it were him doing the shooting,' said Clark. 'He winged Blanco, which means a change of plan. Dave, I want yow to go with Marie. If she runs into Blanco out there, I want her to have some cover. Head for the houses behind the hangers. Whatever yow do, yow've got to make that call.'

'Mickey, yow and me are going to try and keep them bottled up until help arrives, or until we can think of sommut better. Let's go.'

Collins and Clark set off at a fast trot for the control tower. As they ran, an idea started to form in Collins' mind. They stopped thirty-five yards from the tower. The lights and radio were still on. That's a bit of luck, thought Collins. The storm must have masked the gunshots.

'Clarkee, where do you think they parked up?'

'What the fuck has that got to do with the price of bread?'

'Humour me. Please.'

'Just in case they have to leg it quick, they'll have parked the motors near the tower. Probably facing the main gate.'

'That's what I was thinking. Can you hold on here for ten minutes?'

'Of course I can. What yow going to do?'

Marie and Harris had gone twenty-five yards when Marie stopped. Looking around to ensure that Clark couldn't overhear her, she said, 'Dave, the nearest houses are across the runway. It'll take twice as long to reach those behind the hangers. We should head for the nearest houses.'

'But Clarkee said—'

'I know what Clarkee said and if I were a man, he would have told us to head for the nearest houses, Blanco or no Blanco. I don't want Clarkee or Collins to get hurt or worse because of me.'

Harris looked at Marie. He'd been in the force over twenty years and he could spot a good copper at a a hundred yards. They were the ones were willing to put themselves in danger for their mates and the public. Marie was one of them.

'OK, Annie Oakley, let's go.'

Single file, they moved through the undergrowth. To minimise noise, they avoided the small gravel tracks that crisscrossed the landscape and waded through the numerous small pools of cold water that dotted the area. The wind and rain smothered the sound of their movement, but the regular flashes of lightning, momentarily illuminated the darkness and made them feel as exposed as an earwig on a wedding cake.

The houses seemed tantalisingly close, but were in fact still three hundred yards away. Then, a single shot was fired. Marie turned around expecting to see Harris behind her, but he was lying on his side, clutching his chest, fighting a losing battle, trying to stop the blood flow.

A large black man stood twelve feet away, pointing a Luger at Marie's chest. 'Mademoiselle, you please to show me your hands.'

Marie looked at the body of Harris. He hadn't stood a chance. Shot in the back by this piece of scum in front of her.

'You go to the houses. Maybe for friends help you phone, eh?'

Marie remained silent.

'You say nothing. Brave, but I think I right. No call from you, no one comes. So you see why I must kill you, eh?' Blanco raised the Luger. 'I not shoot you in the face. You still be pretty in coffin,' he said, as if he were doing her a favour.

Marie closed her eyes and thought of her mother, father and Silvia.

When the shot came, she felt nothing. Stunned to be still standing, she opened her eyes to see Blanco clutching his stomach. Harris, his lips covered in blood, was smiling.

'Bastard,' cried Blanco, and turning, he fired off four rounds in quick succession. Harris' body jerked obscenely as each bullet ripped through his flesh.

Marie moved before Blanco had even fired his second shot. By the time he raised his gun to fire on her, she was thirty yards away, ducking and diving. His first shot hit her just above the left elbow. Immediately, she lost control over her injured arm. It flapped against her side as she ran, but she kept moving. By the time Blanco fired again, she was lost in the undergrowth. After running flat out for over a minute, she stopped and listened. Nothing. Harris may not have killed Blanco, but the shot had certainly disabled him. She was sure he wasn't following her.

Taking a deep breath, she stood still. Her left arm was awash with pain and it took all her self-control not to examine it. She'd have time for that later. Marie realised that she'd run slightly right, but that was okay. It was only a bit over a hundred yards to the fence.

Finding a gap in the rusted wire, she slipped through the hole. The pain in her arm was now setting in with a vengeance. She tried to move her fingers. Nothing. 'Bastard,' she muttered, as she realised that Blanco's shot had broken her left arm and probably damaged a few nerves as well, if the pain was anything to go by.

Before crossing the road, she checked the houses that were visible. There was one to her left that had phone lines running into the building. As she trotted down the road, her left arm hanging limp by her side, she wondered what she was going to say. While waiting for the door to be opened, she heard the sound of a small plane approaching.

An elderly gentleman, that day's edition of The Times in his hand, opened the door. He was confronted by a young, soaking wet policewoman, whose face, hands and legs were covered in cuts and scratches. A broken arm was hanging lifelessly from her sleeve, blood dripped from her fingers and her clothes torn and filthy.

Holding her warrant card aloft in her right hand, Marie said, 'Police. Sorry to disturb you, sir, but this is an emergency. I must use your phone.' She didn't wait for an invitation, but brushed past him and made two calls. One to O'Driscoll and then one to the Police Divisional Headquarters in Lichfield.

When she hung up, the old man and his wife were standing in the kitchen doorway. He was holding a first aid box and she was proffering a cup of tea. 'I thought you could use a nice cup of tea. I've put a little something in it,' said the old lady.

'I'm sorry, I don't have the time.'

When the old man spoke, his voice carried with it years of authority. 'You can drink your tea while I bandage your arm, young lady. Whatever it is you have to do, you'll be able to do it better with that arm strapped up.'

Marie sat down by the phone and accepted the hot drink. 'Please be as quick as you can.'

'I will.'

Collins found two cars parked forty yards from the tower, a Mercedes-Benz 600 four door saloon and a Jensen Interceptor. Very nice, he thought. Neither car was locked. Opening the Merc's boot, he found a six-inch screwdriver, a pint can of oil and an empty Tango bottle filled with water.

The Jensen's boot delivered two unopened bottles of whiskey and several oil-covered rags.

Overhead, he heard the unmistakable sound of a light aircraft. *Shite*, he thought. *Got to be quick. As soon as they hear the plane they'll be coming out to light the runway.*

Opening the whiskey bottles, he drenched the rags in Ireland's most valuable export and spilt the rest on the ground. Taking the screwdriver, he punctured the Jag's petrol tank about two thirds of the way down and filled the two bottles with petrol, before stuffing a rag into each one.

Leaving the Molotov cocktails on the ground, he climbed into the Merc. The leather still smelt new, despite the stench of petrol. Working quickly, he applied one of the many illegal skills that Clark had taught him. Twenty seconds later, the hot-wired car was purring like a particularly happy Cheshire cat.

The plane now sounded as if it was circling overhead. Buffeted by the winds, he could hear the note of the engine change as the pilot fought to keep the plane under control. Work quicker, his mind screamed.

Reversing, Collins lined the car up with the tower's rear wall. He knew that the chance of the tower collapsing from the impact was remote. He was relying on starting a fire.

As he put the car into first gear, he noticed there was a slight slope in the ground before him. Grand, he thought, and accelerated. Twenty yards out, he rolled clear of the car and covered his ears. There was a loud bang as the car hit the back of the control tower and dislodged a few bricks, but no explosion.

In the silence that followed the impact, Collins heard the plane descending. Lights or no lights he was coming in to land. Collins couldn't help but think, that guy's got some balls on him.

Finding his gun, Collins fired at the car's leaking petrol tank from his prone position. This time, the explosion lifted the car off the ground and flames shot fifty feet into the air.

The ground shook, doors blew out and every window in the building exploded in a shower of glass.

Grabbing the two Molotov cocktails, Collins approached the burning wreck and lit the whiskey-soaked rags. He had no idea how quickly the rags would burn and set off the petrol, so running around to the side of the building he lobbed both through the first smashed window he saw. Seconds later two further explosions shook the building, sending a ball of flame through the window.

By now, the plane was taxiing towards the tower. He's a persistent sod, thought Collins. Quickly assessing the situation, he knew what he was going to do.

Sprinting, he reached the Jensen, jumped in and proceeded to break his own record for hot-wiring a car. With his foot down, the car surged forward, its back wheels throwing up dirt stones and gravel. Rounding the tower, Collins saw the plane. Clark was lying between the tower and the plane. If the pilot had a gun, Clarkee would be in serious trouble.

Collins didn't hesitate. He changed up to third gear and accelerated forward. He could see the pilot's astonished face in his headlights as the car bore down on him.

The pilot knew that he had only one chance. He released the brake and moved forward, quickly gathering pace. He didn't know if he had enough runway in front of him to take off, but it was worth the gamble. Stay where he was and some mad Englishman in a £6,000 car was going to ram him.

Collins saw what the pilot was trying to do and swung the car right. The big wheels dug into the soft earth and sent a spray of dirt, stone and grass in Clark's direction. Straightening up, he drove onto the runway. Immediately, the car felt more secure. This time, there was no delay between depressing the accelerator and feeling the car surge forward. Within seconds, he was level with the plane. He could clearly see the pilot's face. He looked worried, but there was no sign of panic in his movements. The guy was a professional; he knew what he was doing.

Collins quickly assessed his options. Get in front of the plane and try and slow it down? No good, the runway was wide enough for the pilot to try and overtake him. Hit the tail of the plane and force it into an uncontrolled spin? Not an option. The plane could spin round 180 degrees and smash into him. No, the only thing to do was push it off the runway.

Collins veered towards the plane and the pilot moved left, leaving him dangerously close to the edge of the runway. Collins attacked again. This time, one and a quarter ton of the best engineering West Bromwich could produce smashed into the fuselage of the light aircraft and tipped it onto the outfield.

Collins reduced his speed and watched as the pilot fought to control his plane and get back onto the runway. He was good. He managed to straighten the plane up and move towards the runway, but luck wasn't with him. His front wheel hit a hole in the ground and the plane stopped with a violent lurch and tipped over, its nose and cabin resting on the runway.

Collins watched as a smallish man climbed from the cockpit. Reaching the ground, he fell to his knees before struggling to his feet. Straightening up, he glared at Collins thirty yards away. Only then did Collins see the gun by the man's side. The .38 Beretta semi-automatic was now moving. Collins hit the accelerator and aimed for the pilot and his plane.

A shot shattered the windscreen before lodging itself in the passenger seat. Bracing himself for the collision, Collins ducked just as the Interceptor hit the pilot, pinning him against the plane's fuselage. Struggling to get free, his revolver went off and struck the pool of petrol beneath the plane. Collins was about to reverse when he saw a flicker of fire curl up the fuselage and leap onto the car's bonnet. Opening the door, he rolled out, scrambled to his feet and sprinted away from the unexploded bomb behind him.

He'd covered fifty yards by the time the first explosion came. Its concussive force slammed him to the ground. The second explosion quickly followed as the Jensen blew up. Lying on the sodden earth he looked back. It was impossible to distinguish what was car and what was plane. Everything was just a burning load of twisted metal and plastic.

Rising, he headed back to Clark. As he slid to the ground beside his friend, Clark said, 'Yow know, Mickey, with a lot more training, yow could probably make a piss-poor Commando.'

The darkness around him hid Collins' broad smile. Praise, indeed, from the little man. 'Have they come out yet?'

'Not that I've seen, thanks to yowr Mr Tubbs imitation. Shall we give 'em a shout?'

'Good idea.'

Both men hunkered further down behind the small bank of earth and gorse they were relying on for cover.

'Come out with your hands up,' shouted Collins. 'If you don't, either the smoke or fire will get you. There's no escape. The local police and officers from Birmingham will soon be here.'

Initially, there was no response, but then a figure appeared at the door. 'We're coming out,' said Gregson.

'Come out one at a time. Stop in the doorway and throw out your weapons, then come out and lie face down on the ground. Hands behind your head,' shouted Collins. 'Constable Clark has a rifle and any funny business, he'll shoot you in the head,' he lied. Clark smiled and gave the thumbs up.

'Connolly's hurt. He might not make it.'

'In that case, he's going to be crispy fried before long. You can help him to the door, but after that he's on his own.'

Gregson disappeared into the burning building and reappeared with Connolly. He looked to be in a bad way. His right arm was around Gregson's shoulders and his left hung lifeless by his side. Much of his hair had been burnt off and he'd suffered burns to his hands and face. His condition drew no sympathy from Collins. 'Back off, Gregson. Let him come on alone.'

Connolly raised his one good arm in the air, and hopped and stumbled maybe six yards before he fell on his face and lay still. 'That's it,' he cried.

'Okay. You next, Gregson.'

Gregson threw his gun out and walked about fifteen yards from the tower, then stopped. Collins thought he saw him smile, just before a voice said, 'Drop your guns and stand up, Mr Policemen.'

Turning, Collins and Clark saw Blanco. He looked in a bad way. Blood was dripping from his arm where Collins had winged him, but much more serious was the belly wound. If the bleeding wasn't staunched in the next twenty minutes, he was done for. Most worrying, though, was the Luger that he held rock steady in his right hand. Both men did as they were told.

'Blanco, my man, I could kiss you,' shouted Gregson, picking up his gun and running towards Collins and Clark. Kicking their guns away, he said, 'Which one of you bastards set fire to the tower?'

'I did,' said Collins.

'It were me,' said Clark.

'Fuck me, you pair must have seen Spartacus.'

Leaning in, he sniffed Clark's clothes first, then Collins.' Stepping back, he smacked Clark in the face with the gun. The gun sight cut Clark's cheek and the barrel broke his nose. 'I admire loyalty, but I don't like people lying to me, Constable Clark.'

Clark stumbled, but didn't fall. 'Tough little bastard, aren't you? Blanco, keep an eye on this little cunt and don't get too near. As for you, Sergeant, you tried to burn me alive. I think I should return the favour. Get moving,' he said, gesturing with the gun towards the burning tower.

O'Neil passed Collins about twenty yards from the house. Except for some singed hair and a ripped jacket, the explosions and fire had barely touched him. 'Pity you won't get to see me take your mate apart. Mind you, I doubt it will be as much fun as killing that bitch secretary.'

Twenty yards from the tower, the heat started to feel uncomfortable and Gregson stopped. 'Keep going, you bastard.'

With no weapons available to him, Collins spat in Gregson's face. The gun didn't waver as the gangster took out his handkerchief. Before he could wipe away the spittle, a gunshot exploded from the undergrowth behind Blanco. The Frenchman stood frozen for an instant, most of his head blown off by the shotgun blast, then fell face first on the ground.

Gregson looked towards the sound, which was all the time Collins needed. He grabbed the hand holding the gun and twisted it anti-clockwise. Gregson dropped the gun and Collins kicked it towards the tower. Still holding his wrist, Collins kneed Gregson in the stomach. He doubled over as the knee sank into his solar plexus and broke two ribs. Releasing the wrist, Collins moved in, hitting Gregson with a series of combination punches.

Groggy, disorientated and struggling to stand upright, Gregson staggered backwards and stepped on his own gun. He looked at Collins, who said, 'Go for it and you're dead. Clarkee's got you covered.'

'Fuck Clark. Fuck you. Don't you know who I am?'

Slowly, he picked up the gun and started to straighten up. Collins expected to hear the sound of Clark's shot. Instead, he heard the dying groans of the control tower. Looking over his shoulder, Gregson saw the middle of the front wall buckle and fall inwards, while the top of the tower collapsed outwards. A shower of bricks, concrete, glass and burning wood crashed to the ground, covering both Gregson and Connelly.

Turning, Collins saw clearly, for the first time, his saviour. An old man in wellingtons and great coat was holding a double-barrelled shotgun aimed at O'Neil's belly. Alongside him was Marie, with her arm in a sling, and Clark, holding a folded handkerchief to his face.

'Yow all right, Mickey? For a sec there, I thought yow were a goner.'

'I'm fine. Did you contact Hicks and Lichfield?'

'Yes,' said Marie. 'They're on their way.'

'Where's Dave?' asked Clark.

'He didn't make it.'

'Fuck,' said Collins. Recovering his composure he asked, 'And where did this gentlemen come from?'

'Sergeant Collins, Constable Clark, this is Squadron Leader William St. John, retired. It was from his house that I phoned.'

'Sir,' said Clark, 'yow saved our bacon. After wi clear up here, I think we'd all like to buy yow a drink.' Coming to attention, he saluted the old man.

'That's very kind of you, Constable Clark, but not necessary. I've not had so much fun since D-Day.' Even as he spoke, both his eyes and the shotgun remained fixed on O'Neil. 'What's going to happen to him?' asked the Squadron Leader, gesturing towards O'Neil. There was no mistaking what he thought should happen

'Jail for life. Ain't that right, O'Neil?' said Clark.

'Maybe – or maybe you and me have it out right here, right now. What do you say, Mr Hero? Want to go for the championship? Or is it like they say, "Commandos are only good for one thing – buggering sailors"?'

Clark hesitated. He thought of his wife, his unborn child and the Cup Final he was going to attend tomorrow, along with a hundred other reasons why he should walk away. Against all of them, there was only one reason to fight O'Neil. The world would be a better place with him dead or, at least, crippled for life.

Crossing to Collins, he started to remove his coat and jacket.

O'Neil smiled and started to do the same.

'Clarkee, you don't have to do this. He's scum. He's going away forever and a day. Please—'

Clark held up his hand and whispered, 'Mickey, I'm 47. I'm starting to slow down. Another couple of years and I'll be strictly Second or even Third Division. This is me last big match. I promise.'

'Are you sure about this?'

'Fuck, no. That's what makes it worth doing.'

In silence, Collins watched as Clark took off his tie and re-tied his boots. Standing up, Clark said, 'Just one last thing, Mickey. If he kills me, shoot the bastard. Short of that, don't interfere. Do nothing. This cunt's mine.'

The two men circled each other, looking for an opening. Collins, Marie and the Major had moved closer together to watch the fight. All three of them remained silent.

O'Neil fainted with a punch and, stepping in, snapped out a front kick aimed at Clark's groin. Clark batted the kick away with his wrist and landed a straight right jab high on O'Neil's head.

Bending low, his knuckles brushing the ground like a sumo wrestler, O'Neil circled. A slight rock back on his heels warned Clark of what was coming. Keeping low, O'Neil charged. Clark sidestepped the lunge, but as Clark tried to follow up, O'Neil slammed a back kick into Clark's solar plexus. Winded, Clark was fortunate that the blow was strong enough to push him back eight feet, well out of O'Neil's reach.

Sneaky bastard, thought Clark. *He conned me, but he's cocky, overconfident. I need to lose a few more.*

Twice in quick succession, O'Neil tried to close the distance between himself and Clark. Twice, Clark moved back. On the third attempt, Clark took two steps forward. Swivelling 45 degrees to the left, his right arm shot out and the heel of his hand connected with O'Neil's nose. Clark felt the bone and gristle collapse beneath his hand. Continuing to turn left, Clark's spin gathered pace over the remaining 270 degrees.

As he came out of the spin, he launched a roundhouse kick into the side of O'Neil's face.

O'Neil backed up. This was harder than he'd expected.

Clark saw the blood running uncontrollably from O'Neil's nose and fractured cheek bone and cursed himself. A fraction lower with the punch and O'Neil would be dead, with splinters of bone from his nose embedded in his brain.

The next time O'Neil threw a punch, Clark delayed moving for a fraction of a second. The blow slid off the side of his face and he only partially blocked the follow-up kick.

Moving back, Clark took a deep lungful of air and rested his hands on his knees.

'What's wrong, old man? Lost your wind, have you?

Breathing hard, Clark said, 'Fuck you.'

O'Neil smiled. This was more like it. He just needed to get the midget on the ground and he was dead.

Clark saw the smile and moved in. He snapped a left-footed front kick at O'Neil, which missed. He hesitated slightly as he withdrew his leg. The delay allowed O'Neil to grab his foot and twist. It was what Clark had expected. With his left foot supported by O'Neil, he was free to leap in the air and deliver a perfect roundhouse kick to the side of O'Neil's face. The younger man staggered backwards. His jaw, now broken, hung down at an obscene angle.

Clark immediately followed up. He charged the stunned O'Neil and hit him hard in the chest with his shoulder. Off-balance, O'Neil stumbled backwards. Twisting and dropping his weight down, Clark stuck his hip into O'Neil's stomach and threw him onto the ground. Quickly following up, he flipped O'Neil onto his stomach and snapped a cuff over his left wrist. Before he could reach for the right hand, O'Neil pushed upwards with his hips and rolled onto his back, upsetting Clark's balance. Distracted, Clark failed to see O'Neil's hand reach for the small knife in his right sock. The blade was clear of its sheath and heading for Clark's neck when he saw it and rolled clear, but not fast enough to avoid being stabbed in the left shoulder.

Clark slipped on the wet grass and landed on his hands and knees. First up, O'Neil charged. His rugby kick to the stomach lifted Clark off the ground and broke a couple of ribs. As best he could, Clark rolled with the blow and regained his feet just as O'Neil closed in for the second time. The first downward slash from the knife ripped through Clark's shirt and the waistband of his trousers, and left a long angry welt from neck to groin. Painful, but not fatal.

Because he hadn't connected fully, O'Neil was off-balance. Trying to maintain the momentum and not give Clark an easy opening, he swung back up, the point of the blade aiming for Clark's stomach.

Clark simultaneously moved an inch backwards and punched downwards with both hands. At thigh level, his wrists crossed, forming a perfect X-block. O'Neil's lunge hit the locked wrists. Before he could withdraw, Clark wrapped his hands around the man's right wrist.

Slowly, inch by inch, O'Neil forced the knife upwards. When it reached Clark's stomach, the little man made his decision. If it worked, the fight was over, but if it didn't, he'd probably die. Still grasping O'Neil's wrist, Clark pushed him backwards. O'Neil resisted and Clark reacted by falling backwards. As he did so, he stuck his right foot into O'Neil's stomach. When he hit the ground, Clark straightened his leg and O'Neil somersaulted over his head. But if this was going to work, Clark knew that he had to hold on to the man's wrist and time the next move to perfection. As O'Neil hit the floor, Clark rolled backwards, missing the knife by an inch and landed on O'Neil's chest with both knees. The impact forced all the air out of O'Neil's lungs.

Now, Clark was on top and the blade was lying horizontally between the two men. Shifting position, Clark kneed O'Neil in the groin. More pain registered in the gangster's eyes, but it seemed to give him added strength. Clark kneed him again.

This time, the contact was perfect and Clark felt the strength go out of O'Neil's grip.

Letting go of the knife with one hand, Clark smashed his elbow into O'Neil's already shattered face. O'Neil's grip loosened and Clark delivered a short left hook and simultaneously kneed him in the stomach. Clark felt O'Neil's body go limp and knew he'd won. There was no coming back from the damage he'd inflicted. Slowly Clark staggered to his feet. Still holding the knife, he threw his head back and screamed, 'Yessss!' as the rain washed the blood from his face and hands.

Neither Collins, Marie nor the Squadron Leader in his long career had ever witnessed anything like it. It was a primordial scream of joy at being alive, of surviving, of winning and it sent a shiver down their spine.

Within half an hour, the air field was crawling with police, fire and ambulance, like ants at a summer picnic. The remnants of the fire were quickly extinguished and the bodies of Gregson and Connolly removed from the rubble. Blanco was confirmed dead and Marie explained how the quick actions of the Squadron Leader had undoubtedly saved the lives of both Constable Clark and Sergeant Collins.

O'Neil was taken away by ambulance. Every copper who saw his injuries would be describing to their mates what they had seen the next day and Clark's legend would grow further.

By 10.15pm, Marie and Clark were on their way to the Victoria Hospital in Lichfield. Collins went along for the ride. One call ahead from Hicks ensured that staff were waiting to see them on arrival.

While Marie and Clark were wheeled away to be assessed and treated, Collins phoned Agnes. She wasn't at home, so he called Ruth. The phone was answered on the first ring. It was Agnes. She sounded fraught and out of breath.

'It's me, darling.'

'Oh, thank God. Where are you?'

'Victoria Hospital in Lichfield. '

'You're not hurt, are you?'

'No, I'm here with Clark and one of our WPCs.'

'Oh God, Clark's not hurt, is he?'

'Nothing that won't mend. Look, what's this all about?'

'Ruth's given birth. It happened so quickly, there was no time to go to the hospital.'

'Is she all right? Who delivered the baby?'

'I did,' said Agnes and Collins heard the catch in her voice as she started to cry softly. Taking a deep breath, she said, 'Mother and baby are fine. The midwife is with them now. I don't think Ruth will need to go to the hospital. It was so wonderful.'

'Well, what is it?'

'It's a little baby boy. He looks just like his mother, except he has his father's eyes.'

'I need to tell Clarkee. I'll be over as soon as I can.'

It was two hours before Collins was allowed to see Clark. None of his injuries were life-threatening. His nose had been reset and his ribs, bandaged. The welt was mostly only skin-deep, but was severe enough near his groin to require eleven stitches. The stab wound to his shoulder was an inch and a half deep, but had failed to sever anything significant. He would have limited use of his arm for a while, but with the help of physiotherapy he would make a complete recovery.

Clark had refused a general anaesthetic, but the local plus the painkillers they'd given him had left him feeling happy and sleepy.

'I hear you're going to be all right.'

'Yeah. I'll be home tomorrow or Monday. Until then, I can enjoy an uninterrupted night's sleep.'

'Well, make the most of it while you still can. I've got a feeling that the little lad who's waiting to meet you at home is going to change your life.'

Clark heard the words. Then, a moment letter, he comprehended what they meant. He sank back onto his pillow, beaming.

After Collins had told him about his call to Agnes, Clark said, 'Yow know what this means don't yow, Mickey?'

'Yeah, it means you're a daddy.'

'Na. It means yow've got to take me home.'

'I can't do that.'

'Of course yow fucking can. Now, go and get a wheelchair.'

'But where are your clothes?'

'Fuck knows and besides who cares? Get that sodding wheelchair.'

Ten minutes later, Clark was eased into a Lichfield Police car, with a hospital blanket draped around his shoulders. Collins joined him in the back seat. He wasn't going to be the one left behind to explain to the doctors or, even worse, the ward sister what had happened.

Forty minutes later, Clark marched up the garden path to his front door with Collins behind him. Agnes was astonished at the sight of the new father, with his battered face, bandages and flowing hospital gown.

'What are you doing here, Clive?'

'I've come to see me babbie,' he replied and strode barefoot past Agnes and up the stairs. Collins didn't have the heart to tell him that his hospital gown had become undone and was fully open at the back.

For the next twelve hours, Clark only left Ruth's bedside to

have a pee and then at 6am to call Bert Mitchell about a Cup
Final ticket he no longer required.

Monday 20th May 1968, 08.00hrs

Handsworth

Collins rang Clark's doorbell at eight o'clock sharp. Clarkee was up and dressed and had never looked happier – which wasn't surprising. He was a new Dad. He'd kissed the TV screen when Astle had scored the winning goal in extra time in the Cup Final and, along with 250,000 others, he'd lined the streets of Handsworth and West Bromwich to welcome his heroes home on Sunday. The players, perched on the top of a single-decker Don Everall coach, took nearly two hours to travel from New Street Station to the Council House in West Bromwich.

'I know you're on sick leave, but we've got one loose end to wrap up before we can call it a day on Gregson and O'Neil. Do you want to join me?'

'Yeah. Come on in and hold the babbie while I get me jacket.'

Steelhouse Lane was as busy as usual when Collins and Clark arrived. At reception, they showed their warrant cards and asked for Inspector West. They were told he was in his office. Making their way to the second floor, they knocked on the glass door bearing his name.

'Come in,' said a voice that had smoked a lot fewer cigarettes than the Inspector.

'Hi,' said Clark, 'wem looking for the Inspector.'

'He's just popped down to the Intelligence Unit,' said a very fresh-faced Detective Constable.

'You'd best come with us,' said Collins.

Collins' tone didn't invite any disagreement and the young man stood up and slipped his jacket on.

Seconds later, they entered the Intelligence Office. West was enjoying a cuppa and chatting with Katie, who seemed pleased to have a break from compiling the latest crime statistics.

Looking up, West said, 'What do you two fuckers want?' Come to boast about your latest gunfight?'

'No, Sir,' said Collins.

'Wem here to tie up some loose ends.'

'Such as?'

'Like who's been passing information to Gregson, the Drews and Keating. Information that has allowed them to consolidate the criminal gangs in Brum and stay two steps ahead of us for years.'

'And you morons think it were me?'

'No, Sir, we don't,' said Collins. 'It was you, Katie, wasn't it?

Katie looked at Collins and gave him a stunning smile 'Ah, Mickey, you were always too clever by half. I spent the week-end debating with meself how much you knew and trying to decide whether to run or stay.'

'You!' said West, astounded that this mere chit of a girl had made a fool of him.

'Yes. Do you think that just because I've got big tits, I don't have a brain?' snapped Katie, her Dublin accent gone, replaced by the harsher sound of London/Irish. 'I've been running rings around you for the last four years. Maybe if you'd paid as much attention to what was happening on your patch as you did to my tits and arse, you'd have spotted what was happening, you fat, lecherous cunt.'

'I'd stop there if I were you,' said Collins, his voice heavy with sadness. 'Clarkee.'

Clark stepped forward. 'Katherine O'Neil, I am arresting you for conspiracy to pervert the course of justice contrary to the Common Law. You are not obliged to say anything unless you wish to do so, but anything you do say will be taken down in writing and may be given in evidence.'

'What gave me away, Michael?'

'I should have realised what you were up to earlier. It was after I told you what Margaret Lewis had said about her attacker that O'Connell and Blanco came after her, but I missed it. It was only when I saw this that I realised what was going on.' Collins removed the photo that showed Gregson, Drew and Keating facing the camera from his pocket and laid it on the table. He pointed to the woman sitting between the two men, their backs to the camera. 'That's you, Katie, sitting between Nigel Worthington and Terrance Keating. I'd recognise your hair pin anywhere, a Celtic Knot.'

'I always loved that pin, but there are plenty of pins like it. By itself, it's not enough to convict me. What else have you got?'

'An extensive file prepared by Sybil Harker, proving that you are Katherine Rosemary O'Neil, the daughter of Patrick O'Neil. Sybil lost track of you when you disappeared from London in 1962. However, once I told her that I thought you were the girl in the photo, it didn't take her long to pick apart your new identity.'

'I always did hate that lesbian bitch. I suppose that once you knew who I was, you passed me duff information and waited to see what happened.'

'Not all of the stuff was duff. Some of it were accurate. But yes, we just waited to see what would happen after yow reported back,' said Clark.

'I'm impressed, Sergeant Collins. You played me like an old fiddle. I didn't think you had it in you. Will you do me one last favour, Michael? Will you put the cuffs on me?'

Collins turned his back on her. As he walked past Clark, he said, 'You do it, Clarkee.'

Epilogue

Gerry Niven attended a special service at Upright Freddie's Church on Sunday 2nd June. He was there to present the good reverend with a cheque for £5,000 for information leading to the capture of Norman Yates. Freddie surprised the entire gathering when he announced that he intended to use the money to build a second church in Hockley.

After the service, Gerry, Collins, Clark and Agnes walked the short distance to the home of Robbie Moore. This time, Robbie's mother was at home. Gerry handed the balance of the reward to Robbie, who immediately gave it to his mother. The look of greed in Mr Moore's eyes was obvious. As soon as they left, he'd take the cheque and spend it on himself.

Clark looked at Moore and wanted to give him a good slap. Instead, he reached in his pocket, produced a small package and handed it to Robbie. The boy's eyes lit up when he found he was holding the Gold Edition of James Bond DB6 Aston Martin. What he wasn't so sure about was the letter in the parcel. Agnes took it from him and explained that Robbie was the first recipient of the Mark Cavendish Scholarship, an annual award to the child who, in the opinion of the trustees, had demonstrated exceptional mathematical ability in any field. The award was for eight years and covered fees, expenses and subsistence associated with attending Graystoke Academy, the best private school in Birmingham.

On Friday 14th June 1968, Constable Dave Harris was laid to rest. His funeral was attended by the Home Secretary, Her Majesty's Chief Inspector of Constabulary, the Chief Constable, the Lord Mayor, several city councillors and representatives from every police force in the country. For the day of the funeral, a skeleton crew, made up of police officers from adjoining divisions, manned Thornhill Road. This enabled every police officer on the station's roster to attend the funeral.

The mile-long journey from the Church of St Mary's in Handsworth to the Hansworth Cemetery was lined by the public, three-deep in places. At the graveside, Mrs Rosemary Harris and her 18-year-old daughter were comforted by family, friends and WPC Marie Bolding.

On Tuesday 18th June, Detective Sergeant Collins and Detective Constable Clark met with the Chief Constable at their request. There was no agenda for the meeting and no minutes were taken.

On Monday 1st July, it was announced that Birmingham's Chief Constable had recommended Constable Dave Harris for the Queen's Police Medal for Gallantry. Several officers expressed surprise that Clark and Collins had not also been recommended for their capture of Norman Yates. Older officers pursed their lips and said, "They like to ration 'em. No force is going to get three at once – or even two."

Later in the year, WPC Bolding, Detective Constable Clark and Detective Sergeant Collins received a letter from the Prime Minister's office, informing them that they had been awarded the MBE for Gallantry in connection with the events that took place at the Fradley Airfield on the night of Friday 17th May 1968. It later transpired that Squadron Leader William St. John had been similarly recognised.

Despite a widespread search covering London and the Home Counties, James Clay eluded capture. On Friday 21st June, Collins and Clark visited a rundown property on the Bristol Road that was awaiting renovation by its owner. The entire house was empty and none of the flats showed any signs of being inhabited during the previous three months.

Patrick O'Neil was discharged from hospital on Friday 5th July and transferred to the hospital wing at Wormwood Scrubs. Three days later, he was found hanging in the toilets. Whoever had killed him had used piano wire. His death had been slow and painful. The Krays denied all knowledge of the affair.

On Sunday August 4th baby Clark was christened. The choice of names had been kept a closely guarded secret. When Clark responded to the question of how the child should be known, he said, 'He is to be called Michael Abraham.' Collins found himself blinking away the tears for several moments.

Collins and Agnes delayed their wedding until early 1969. They wed on February 10th at 3pm, six years to the day that they had first met. Clark was best man and Ruth, maid of honour. Michael Abraham disgraced himself by crying throughout most of the service, but no one seemed to mind. There was no snow on the ground.

Sheba made a near complete recovery from her injuries. Although she was left with a limp, it didn't stop her racing around Hill Top and chasing her friend, the black and white Collie. At some unknown moment in time, their friendship tipped over into something more and on March 18th 1969, she gave birth to a litter of five pups. Four bitches and one dog who had inherited a white ring around each eye and walked with the gait of a drunken seafarer. Collins immediately christened him Sailor.

On Friday 22nd August 1969, after a trial lasting nearly six weeks, Katherine Rosemary O'Neil aka Katherine McGuire was sentenced to 22 years in prison, with a recommendation that she not be released before the full term had been served. The speed at which the jury had concluded their deliberations, a mere day and a half, surprised many observers.

Much was made of the fact that, as she was led down to start her sentence, she turned and blew a kiss in the direction of the public gallery. Opinion was divided between those who thought she had a secret lover in the gallery and those who believed she was merely being provocative. Only one man, sitting in the back row and wearing a black polo neck sweater, knew the truth.

The End

The End ?

Until A Death in Autumn: 1968

Out soon.... See the next few pages.

Dear Reader,

Thank you for buying my book and double thanks if you purchased either *A Death in Winter: 1963*, or *A Death in Summer: 1965*

If you'd like to know more about my writing please go to my blog at:

https://www.goodreads.com/author/show/491372.
Jim_McGrath

Cheers and thanks again,

Jim

From the Prologue to A Death in Autumn: 1968

Monday 2nd September, 11.30hrs.

Birmingham

Sir Charles Endbury was fifty, looked forty and had the energy of a twenty-five year old. He prided himself on being able to work harder and longer than anyone in his engineering company, but today he was finding it difficult to concentrate. He had read the Council reports twice for the meeting he was due to attend at 2pm but nothing was registering. His thoughts kept returning to the previous Saturday night.

He'd been introduced to Christina Murray by Councillor Hill at a Council reception for a Saudi prince, who was interested in investing in Birmingham. After a few drinks they had retired to her flat in Moseley where they had both enjoyed a night of energetic sex. Now he found it impossible to get her out of his mind. Such smooth skin, beautiful raven black hair, a lovely smile and the best arse and legs Sir Charles had seen in the last ten years. Wonderful.

Thank God Claire's away, he thought. *I've got the next three weeks to discover all of Christina's many charms.* He felt himself grow hard at the thought of what was in store for him. Of course he realised that when his wife returned from holiday his meeting with Christina would have to be less frequent. But he'd ensure that she had plenty of spending money and would be only too happy to have her describe in glorious detail her experiences with her other special friends. A smile of expectation spread across his lips, as Christina's other encounters would provide the perfect excuse for why she should be soundly punished.

He was still thinking of the wonderful description she had

given him of how she'd lost her virginity to an oily biker who'd bent her over his beloved BSA, when his secretary knocked and entered. 'I know you don't wish to be disturbed, Sir Charles, but this parcel has just been delivered by courier. It's marked private and urgent. So I thought I should bring it straight in.'

'Thank you, Silvia. It might be concerned with today's Council meeting. I'll look at it in a moment. Could you make me a cup of coffee please?'

'Of course.'

As Silvia left, he started to open the package. It was very securely wrapped, with almost as much Sellotape wound around it as paper. Irritated, he took the scissors from his desk and cut away the packaging. Inside was a small plastic box and a pack of photographs wrapped in a typed note. Laying the letter aside he turned over the first photo, already fearing the worst. It was a poor quality picture of Christina on her knees, eyes closed, sucking him off while he beat her with a short black leather whip. Blackmail. The little bitch, he thought. She'll not get away with this. The next nine photos showed how the evening had progressed to the point where he was shown having anal intercourse with Christina while restricting her breathing with his hands over her mouth and nose.

The last five photos showed Christina on her own. The first showed her badly bruised and beaten. In the second, she was naked, spread-eagled and tied to the four corners of the bed. The fear in her eyes was real and pitiful. A noose had been placed around her neck and pulled tight in the third shot. Christina eyes were bulging and it was obvious that she was choking and on the point of blacking out. The next showed her standing on two chairs, her legs two feet apart. The final photo showed her hanging from a hook in the ceiling, dead, with the chairs now lying on their side. Her stretched neck was a sign that she'd been hanging there for some time.

Silvia knocked on the door and as she entered Sir Charles quickly turned the pack of photos over.

'Are you all right Sir Charles? You look as if you've seen a ghost.'

Fighting to control himself Sir Charles said, 'I'm fine. You were right to bring the parcel in. It's from the Clerk's Office. Some additional information and photos about the new development we're looking at.'

Silvia placed the coffee on her boss's desk and left. With a shaking hand Sir Charles picked up the letter. It simply read, *Change your vote or else.*

Twenty minutes later Endbury left his office and walked down the road to the Queen Victoria Pub and ordered a large gin and tonic. He drank half of the colourless liquid then, with glass in hand, walked to the back of the pub and into the telephone box that had been built under the stairs. Closing the door he took out a scrap of paper on which he'd written a telephone number. With a trembling hand he picked up the receiver and started to call the man who had ordered Christina's death.